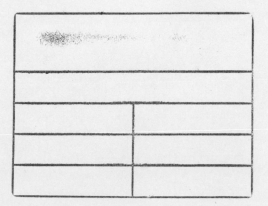

Jon Canter is the author of *Seeds of Greatness* and a scriptwriter for many of Britain's most prominent comedians. He lives in Suffolk with his wife and daughter.

A SHORT GENTLEMAN

Like his father before him, young Robert
Purcell would eventually enjoy a distinguished career as a barrister and judge.
Indeed, everything went to plan . . . until his
life fell apart. He committed a crime — and
went to prison . . . Robert's account of what
drove him to his crime finds him struggling to
come to terms with the forces that brought
him down: his wife Elizabeth; the ex-girlfriend,
Judy Page, who returned to haunt him;
Pilkington, the bully; Mike Bell, the friend
Robert was always happy to patronise. And
his father who proved not to be the man he
thought he was. Despite everything, Robert
remains heroically determined to continue
being the same magnificently pompous
man, utterly resistant to therapy, change and
the emotional demands of the opposite sex.

Books by Jon Canter
Published by The House of Ulverscroft:

SEEDS OF GREATNESS

JON CANTER

A SHORT GENTLEMAN

Complete and Unabridged

CHARNWOOD
Leicester

First published in Great Britain in 2008 by
Jonathan Cape
The Random House Group Limited
London

First Charnwood Edition
published 2008
by arrangement with
The Random House Group Limited
London

British Library CIP Data

Canter, Jon
 A short gentleman.—Large print ed.—
 Charnwood library series
 1. Upper class—Fiction 2. Fathers and sons—Fiction
 3. Married people—Fiction 4. Criminals—Fiction
 5. Great Britain—Social life and customs—Fiction
 6. Psychological fiction 7. Large type books
 I. Title
 823.9'2 [F]

 ISBN 978-1-84782-419-6

Published by
F. A. Thorpe (Publishing)
Anstey, Leicestershire

Set by Words & Graphics Ltd.
Anstey, Leicestershire
Printed and bound in Great Britain by
T. J. International Ltd., Padstow, Cornwall

This book is printed on acid-free paper

For the barristers Simon Levene, Gerard Pounder, Clive Anderson, Jane Belson and Jonny Brock

And the Aldeburgh Dawn Chorus: Helen and Janine Pole, Angela Bumby

'One is the master of what one doesn't say and the slave of what one does.'

— Francisco Paulino Hermenegildo Teódulo Franco y Bahamonde (General Franco) (1892–1975)[1]

---

[1] There'll be those who assume that if I quote General Franco, I support dictators. Oh well. That only goes to prove the truth of his remark.

'Not every crime's committed by
a criminal.'[1]

---

[1] You'll note that I've not attributed this
remark. It's not, I assure you, another of
Franco's. It was, in fact, said by me. I said it
shortly after I committed my crime.

To Elizabeth, who looked so radiant on
our Wedding Day, 21st September 1990,
St Michael's Church, Aldeburgh,[1] Suffolk

And Sir Michael Purcell (1919–2003),
my father

---

[1] Pronounced not *Awld-uh-bruh* nor *Awld-
uh-borough* but always and only: *Awld-bruh*.

Acknowledgements

Men of distinction are sent to prison to find God. That is the great tradition in our country. Common criminals leave prison with a trade. Uncommon criminals — MPs and their ilk — leave with a Bible.

On this page, then, I'm supposed to acknowledge the assistance of God. I'm due to tell you He guided me up the path from disgrace to grace. I can't, though. Can't and won't. I simply don't believe in Him. Was it, then, hypocritical of me to marry in a church? No. My father brought me up to believe in churches, not God. 'Enjoy the architecture,' he would tell me, when I was barely old enough to understand the word. (My father said little, so what he said carried considerable weight.) 'Listen to the music. See and be seen. Ignore the mumbo-jumbo.'

So, yes, I believe in church architecture, church music, church congregants who see and are seen, greet and are greeted, invite for sherry and are invited for sherry. I believe in the longevity of churches and their capacity to inspire awe. I believe in their exclusivity, their organists playing Bach, their hatfulness. (Are they not the last buildings in which women wear hats?)

I do not believe in register offices, those

bureaucratic, hatless places as awe-inspiring and ancient as that song about the candle in the wind.[1]

---

[1] Please don't assume I abhor all popular song. As light relief from the cello works of Bach, Dvořák and Bartók, my daughter Isobel enjoys Gorillaz [*sic*]. She played them to me, at my request, and was embarrassed when I pronounced them 'not without merit'. But I meant it. They were infinitely preferable, harmonically and lyrically, to the crude tomcat yowl of Oasis, to which Mike Bell treated us day and night in our villa in Andros. The effect of Oasis was the opposite of that suggested by their name. It was like finding sand in a glass of water. Mike Bell told me this was music made by 'warring working-class brothers', as if that conferred on it a value it wouldn't have, had it been made by an earl and his nephew Barnaby.

Foreword

I've never spoken publicly on any private matter, except to utter 'Guilty'. Yet I've seen 'myself' on television, heard about 'me' on radio, read in the papers about 'my' personality. I've seen the search engine references to my name multiply and rampage like worldwide weeds. Who are these 113,000 'Robert Purcells'?[1] Some are sixteenth-century bishops. Some are Canadian basketball players. They're manifestly someone else. Yet I no more recognise those 'Robert Purcells' who are (supposedly) me. They're cartoons, grotesques scratched on the wall of a cave.

My father, as a judge, prized his anonymity. I too, as a barrister, saw it as my mission to keep my name out of the papers, with the prized exception of the Law Report in *The Times*. I have not changed my view. But Elizabeth, the woman I married, the mother of my children, has urged me to speak out. She has told me to write an account of who I am and why I am who I am.

Elizabeth is not proposing I 'set the record straight' for the instruction and edification of others. She believes, in no uncertain terms — for Elizabeth, now, where I am concerned, *has* no uncertain terms — I must reveal myself for my

---

[1] Source: Google, 28th March 2006, 22.49. And again at 23.47.

own benefit. The benefit, however, cannot accrue unless I share my 'revealed' self with others. To discover myself is to uncover myself. Only by cutting myself open can I hope to heal.

'Open up or die.' Those were her exact words.[1] She implied that, if I did open up, I would, in fact, *not die*. I would walk the streets of England for eternity. 'Look!' the little children would say. 'There's the Opened-Up Man! How slowly but happily he moves! He has lived for many thousands of years, because he shares his feelings. Let us ask him how he is and spend the day hearing his answer!'

Forgive me, Elizabeth. Forgive my lapse into sarcasm. You are right, of course. I must reveal myself — to myself, to you, to the world. Everyone agrees. My daughter, my sister, my colleagues. I'm sure the cashiers in the Co-op would concur, if asked.

'Yes, love,' they'd say. 'Get it all out. It's better out than in.'

We're all open books now.

---

[1] All reported speech in this work is verbatim. I recall precisely what is said in my presence. Or, rather, I recall what matters. The retention of everything said in my presence would constitute a mental illness. Doubtless, they'd call it Purcell's disease. There'd be a documentary. I'd visit ten Tescos and repeat every word I'd heard within their walls. The producer would tell me the documentary's aim was educational, though you and I know the aim would be entertainment,

impure and simple. A sombre narrator would lend the words 'ten Tescos' a bogus gravitas. Jeremy Irons? Sir Jeremy Irons? Does he have a knighthood yet? If not, he can have mine, which I fear is no longer forthcoming.

Preface

Most books start with a fundamental disadvantage. They're written by writers. Writers are the last people one should entrust with the writing of a book. They are prone to poetic paragraphs evoking the passage of seasons. They believe that sexual acts should take longer to describe than perform. Their characteristic weaknesses make them uniquely unsuited to their chosen profession. Egocentricity, procrastination, irrationality, hysteria, self-pity, self-delusion, pretension, prolixity, alcoholism — these are handicaps in most professions. For writers, they're qualifications.

It's the egocentricity that's the worst offence. A writer experiences panic when trying to convey simple information. 'The dentist unlocked the door of her surgery and went inside.' A writer would spit on such a sentence. What can the writer write about the dentist, the lock, the door and the surgery that will draw attention to the writer's extraordinary (in his or her view) talent? The dentist is nominally the subject of the sentence; but it's the writer, lording it and larding it over the dentist, who's the subject of every sentence in the book. The dentist can't live or die without the writer — this is what the writer won't allow us to forget, when all we want is for the dentist to enter the surgery and get on with the bloody story. Is there a patient in the surgery

— with a gun? How did they get in the surgery when the door was locked?

Fear not. I'm not a writer. I'm a barrister and shall write like a barrister, dedicating myself to the ruthless pursuit of clarity. If a portico is ornate, I shall write 'ornate', not concoct a series of phrases that aspire to the condition of ornateness. Where the context demands Latin or footnotes, I shall write Latin or footnotes. Nothing superfluous, nothing fancy. *Cadit quaestio*: let that be an end to the matter. I'm not seeking, for the back of this book, those rococo puffs writers invent, as they lie in their dank (and often borrowed) beds: *richly evocative . . . hugely accomplished . . . sensitive and vibrant*. No. I'd be happy with *contains no ornate descriptions of porticos*.

I'm no longer a practising barrister, with a thriving practice in taxation and trusts. That doesn't mean I'm no longer a barrister. Sebastian Coe will always be an athlete, though no one expects him, in middle age, to run to the House of Lords.

'You are a man who has dedicated your life to the legal profession.' That is what Mr Justice Ableman said, in his preamble to sentencing. 'It is nothing short of a tragedy,' he continued, 'that a person of your distinguished provenance has destroyed years of scholarship and attainment with one egregious act.' That was not a banishment. On the contrary. It was a recognition of my continued membership of the Freemasonry of the Bar. Would Mr Justice Ableman have used the word *egregious* when addressing a fraudulent businessman, say, or a pop star embarrassed with drugs? No. He wouldn't waste *egregious* and *provenance* on them. Mr Justice Ableman was talking to one of his own.

So. I shall write like a barrister. But I shan't plead. I'm not arguing, in these pages, the case for the defence. My purpose, in opening up, is not adversarial. That is what Elizabeth has told me. I'm not here to acquit myself, retrospectively. My brief is to stand in the witness box and — with great deliberation — take off all my clothes.

Author's Note

I've been thinking further on that dentist. The one who can't enter her surgery until her creator — the writer — permits. I'm the writer of this book. But I'm also the dentist. I'm both the author of the book and its subject. I am the one who advances my story. Or not.

Here we are, on the threshold of that story, as we have been for some time. We've had Quotations. We've had Dedications. We've had Acknowledgements. We've had a Foreword. We've had a Preface. Now we're having an Author's Note.

The reader is entitled to ask: 'When will the bastard thing start? What next? 'Further Reading'?'

Forgive me. I must delay no more. There's nothing for it. I must open the door and walk in, even though as I write this I'm overwhelmed by reluctance, distaste and fear. I fear that when I open the door, I'll fall. Not on the floor, you understand. I fear that I'll fall and keep falling because there is no floor.

Author's Further Note

Criminal barristers deal in hindsight. What's done is done. No barrister's consulted *before* the crime: 'I'm considering robbing a bank. How can I ensure that — if I'm caught — I receive the minimum sentence? Would being 'high on a cocktail of drugs' work for or against me? What about 'a voice'? As I walk into the bank, should I 'hear' 'a voice'? If so, whose 'voice' should I 'hear'? My late mother's? Jesus Christ's? What about Sir David Attenborough's?'

I am not a criminal barrister. My practice was civil. Nevertheless, the point is well taken. This confession is written from the terminus, in hindsight. I have fifty years of hindsight now. Two score years and ten of hindsight — a dangerous amount indeed.

I shall start my confession with a chapter set in 1964. Let us say, for the sake of argument — a sake most precious to me — the chapter contains a reference to a Japanese man. It may be that, a year later, I learned that the man was Chinese. Nevertheless, I shall state what I thought to be the case in 1964. I shall avoid hindsight.

1
Who's Who
(1964)

When I was eight, I sneaked into my father's study, knowing he was downstairs in the drawing room with my mother, enjoying a pre-prandial sherry. This was their ritual every evening my father was at home. On the seventh chime of the grandfather clock, my mother would cry out: 'Sherry!' Not after it. On it. My mother did not waste time.

My father's study was out of bounds to my sister and me. It was where our father did his Very Important Work. What havoc, if they entered, might his children wreak? In my case, as opposed to my sister's, the answer was 'none'. I entered the study, stood at his desk and felt the might of the Law. I was in the presence of a great power. But I didn't feel oppressed. On the contrary. I felt ennobled.

As I stood there in my pyjamas, gazing at the tomes on his shelves, I must have seen for the first time those volumes which would later be my constant companions when I, like he, won a scholarship to Christ Church, Oxford, and was awarded, as he was, a first in Law: *Winfield & Jolowicz on Tort, Megarry & Wade: The Law of Real Property*. Yet it's not a legal textbook I

1

recall. The book I recall had a red spine. Its title seemed nonsensical and unfinished — why didn't it have a question mark at the end?

The book was *Who's Who 1964*. I had to stand on a chair to reach it. With both hands, I took it down from the shelf, unprepared for its mass and weight. *Who's Who 1964* cannoned painfully off my chest and onto the floor. I followed it, falling off the chair and landing on my elbow. I stopped myself from crying. I didn't want to alert my parents to my presence in this room.

But the chair, too, had fallen. Surely, the thud above their heads would alarm them. I lay there, waiting to hear them run up the stairs. But no. They remained downstairs, unmoved. I opened the book, which was mercifully unharmed. I turned its pages till I came to one that was dog-eared. There I found this: *Purcell, Michael Herbert; a Circuit Judge since 1963; b 3ʳᵈ July 1919; s of late Robert Arthur Purcell and Margaret Susan (née Hindmarsh).*

I had found my father. Before him was *Purcell, Sir John Richard, 11th Bt.* After him was *Purcell, Dame Muriel, DBE 1961.* Now I understood. The book was an alphabetical list of people. But it did not include all the people in the world. It was too small for that. It contained only *Whos*. Every person in this book was a *Who*.

The book was a register, just like the register my form teacher, Mr Fabian, took every morning at twenty to nine. The *Whos* were at a school of life. Doubtless, they had their own uniform and song. Doubtless, not everyone could attend their school. One had to be special. Hence the litany of accomplishments that followed each name. Hence the private language: *educ.*

I studied my father's entry, over and over again. Then, with difficulty, I remounted the chair and replaced the book.

I tiptoed out of the room and stood at the top of the stairs. I'd done a bad thing and got away with it. Now I wished to confess. I walked downstairs, intending to alert the authorities to my wrongdoing. The authorities, of course, were my father and mother. They dispensed justice in the house.

My six-year-old sister Freya was on the landing, with a knife and a dish.

'What are you doing?' I asked her.

'Buttering the stairs.'

I told her to stop. She ignored me. I told her what she was doing was wrong. She ignored me again. I ignored her back and, losing the courage to face the authorities, went to my bedroom.

There, I wrote this: *Purcell, Robert Timothy; b 28th March 1956; s of Michael Herbert Purcell, QC, and Valerie Mary (née Jarvis). Educ: Winchester and Christ Church, Oxford.*

That's right. At eight, I wrote an imaginary *Who's Who* entry, stating which school and Oxford college I would attend. I was not being whimsical. These were logical deductions, given my pedigree and aptitudes. It would be arrogant to call them inevitabilities. But it would also be true.

Yes, you say, but there are in life no inevitabilities. How did I know, at eight, that I wouldn't be run over, or struck by lightning, before I reached the age of a Winchester pupil or an Oxford student? There is no satisfactory answer to your question. But there's a true answer: I just knew. I was certain. My life, at that age and long afterwards, was governed by certainties. Sure enough, I passed through Winchester and Oxford with no interruption from lightning.

From then on, I wrote my *Who's Who* entry every year on my birthday. This is the last one, written on my forty-seventh birthday, in March 2003. Like all the entries, it contains an accurate record of my life to that point and a logically deduced projection of my life to come:

Purcell, Rt Hon. Sir Robert Timothy, Kt 2012; PC 2018; Rt Hon. Lord Justice Purcell; a Lord Justice of Appeal since 2012; *b* 28th March 1956; *s* of late Sir Michael Herbert Purcell and Valerie Purcell; *m* 1990 Elizabeth Rose Webb; one *d* one *s*. Educ: Winchester and Christ Church, Oxford. Called to Bar, Middle Temple 1979; a Judge of the High Court of Justice, Chancery Div 2012–18; Mem General Council of the Bar 2005–9. Publications: contrib to *Halsbury's Laws of England*; (ed jtly) *Emerson's UK Taxation & Trusts* 1989–2002. Recreations: bridge, dog-walking, classical music. Address: High Ridge, Priors Hill Road, Aldeburgh, Suffolk 1P15 5HR. Club: Athenaeum.

You can see that I have not spent my life buttering stairs.

★ ★ ★

That night, I lay awake. My elbow was hurting. Also, I was waiting for my mother to come into my room. I didn't want to fall asleep before she said goodnight. She didn't come and she didn't come. She came so late that when she said goodnight, she woke me up.

'Goodnight, Little Man. You asleep?'

'Almost,' I replied, with a tact and respect children no longer have.

'Go to sleep then, Little Man.'

'I've got something to tell you,' I said.

I confessed to entering my father's study. I felt relieved and, yes, proud. I asked her what my punishment would be. She said I should forget it. My sister had been punished for it already. She'd left a telltale muddy footprint on my father's study chair. (The footprint, of course, was mine.) She'd been smacked for it, along with her other crimes: buttering three stairs and spreading jam on two.

My mother told me to forget it, but I haven't, have I? Here I am, 'opening up' about it, over forty years later. My sister was clearly the victim of an injustice, punished for a crime she did not commit. What of me, though? I went *unpunished* for a crime I *did* commit. Was I not also a victim of injustice? Yes. I suffered shame. I suffered frustration. I was outraged by my mother's incompetence and appalled by her unconcern.

5

That is why, on the night of 29th September 2003, it was I who reported my crime. I felt a legal, moral and administrative obligation to confess my wrongdoing. Put crudely, I did not trust the police to get the right man unless the right man got himself to the police.

* * *

My report of the *Who's Who* incident suggests a boy of intellectual and moral maturity. 'Little Man', my mother's nickname for me, would tend to confirm this. In fact, I was not a miniature man so much as a miniature boy. At eight, I was the same height as my younger sister. I grew up to be three inches shorter than her.

These days, everyone has to have an *and*. Everyone who has some explaining to do has to have an *and* to explain it.

'My name's Myra and I'm an alcoholic.' 'My name's Sebastian and I was abused as a child.' These are the kinds of things you say after you commit a crime.

Very well then.

My name's Robert and I'm short.

Do you nod? Do you say: 'So *that's* why he did it — whatever the hell *it* was!'?

2

A Short Gentleman
(1968)

Some children grow up in a happy home. I grew up in two. Our London house was in Notting Hill, just off Kensington Church Street, giving me splendid access to all the museums and concert halls London has to offer. Then, most weekends and every summer, my mother, father, sister and I motored eighty-six miles north-east of London, to our Cecil Lay house, High Ridge, in Aldeburgh, on the Suffolk coast. High Ridge was high above the town, overlooking the tennis courts, twixt[1] the marshes and the sea. To call High Ridge our 'second home' gives the wrong impression. In my mind, High Ridge was as much my home as 12 Kensington Walk. You could say it was my 'first equal' home.

It was in Aldeburgh that I learned to ride a bike, sail, play tennis and swim. It was here that I saw my first stained-glass window; here that I played my first hand of bridge; here that I learned to love the music of Benjamin Britten and the ghost stories of M. R. James; here that I had my first holiday job, helping the greengrocer's man

---

[1] Yes, a winsome and 'writerly' word. But appropriate in this context.

deliver boxes of fruit and veg.

There were so many other like-minded souls from so many other good families. They too had houses in Priors Hill Road, Park Road, The Terrace or (best of all) Crag Path — which, despite its prosaic name, is the jewel of Aldeburgh. Crag Path is a seaside promenade lined with marvellous eccentric private residences, as opposed to the cheap hotels, bingo halls and souvenir shops that disfigure the seafront of most English seaside towns. Crag Path has been called a relic of the 1950s, as if that were not a compliment.

On a typical August day, in any year from the mid-sixties to the mid-seventies, I would leave High Ridge in the morning and not return till dusk, hungry as a hog for the ham and chutney and boiled potatoes and frozen peas and apple crumble that would be waiting for me on the sideboard, my ice-cream as tepid as my ham.

'What have you been up to?' my mother would ask.

And always I would give the same reply: 'Having fun!'

'Very good!' she'd say.

My partners in fun were the younger generation of these Aldeburgh house-owning families: the Holts, the Pilkingtons, the Thodays, the Moxon-Smiths, the Cattos, the Farquharsons, the Hamilton-Woods. The back doors of their houses were always open. It was true then and it is true today. Of how many places can that be said? Where in London can a back door be left unlocked, without being removed from its hinges?

After supper it was time for a bath in which to soothe my battered knees. Knees, in those days, took a most terrible battering. They were always muddy and often grazed. Then I'd stare in the mirror to see what other damage the day had brought. A bump on the head from a flying apple. An elbow bruise, acquired in some rough-and-tumble game. Or a pain in the stomach, from a punch by Pilkington, largest and most vicious of my Aldeburgh contemporaries.

Do not tell me, please, that my childhood was unhappy because Pilkington punched me. Pilkington punched Martin Thoday. Pilkington punched Stephen Catto. Pilkington punched Damian Hawes and Jeremy Hamilton-Wood. (Once, when they were standing side by side, he punched them simultaneously, with a double-fisted jab I've never seen elsewhere, not even in a film.) His punches were invisible badges of honour, forced on members of my boyhood club. Had I not been punched by Pilkington, I'd have been unhappy.

★   ★   ★

Every Christmas, on the eve of Christmas Eve, my parents invited the tradesmen of Aldeburgh to High Ridge for a drink. Year after year they came — Mr and Mrs Martin the greengrocers, Nancy and Jim our appointed newsagents, Jack the coalman, Bert the gardener, Dudley who tinkered with my father's cars, Rita who nursed

9

my maternal grandmother through her terminal years, Terry the handyman, Eric the builder, Billy who 'did' the boiler, Margaret the treasure who cleaned High Ridge for more than twenty-five years. The butcher was there, as was the baker. Had my parents patronised a candlestick-maker, he would have been there too.

My father moved from guest to guest, spending the same short time with each. Handing round the snacks, gripping the bowl as tightly as Oliver Twist, I could sense the esteem in which my father was held. My father knew how to talk to a greengrocer — not with oily charm but with benevolence. As Bert the gardener said to me, taking a fistful of crisps in his black-fingernailed hand: 'Your father's a good man, boy. Never makes me feel like a criminal.'

Indeed. My father made everyone feel they weren't criminals. Even criminals. They recognised, as did everyone else, that he sought and found in them a common humanity.

'Call me Michael,' he said, hoping his guests wouldn't call him anything. He didn't want to watch them struggling for the right form of address. Mrs Martin, who took pills 'for her nerves', called him 'Your Worship' — then, sensing she'd made a mistake, overcompensated with 'Sir Judge'.

'Give Mrs Martin a crisp!' said my father, helping an awkward moment on its way. I stepped up with the bowl. Mrs Martin looked anxiously into it and selected the only remaining crisp.

My mother, meanwhile, was in the kitchen,

where no guest ventured. My mother was the daughter of the Lord Lieutenant of Gloucestershire. It was she, not my father, who'd inherited High Ridge, built as a seaside bolt-hole by her grandparents in the late nineteenth century. But at Christmas, when my maternal grandmother — Granny P — came to stay, my mother wasn't the hostess in her own house. On the eve of Christmas Eve, she remained out of sight. Her mission was to sit with Granny P in the kitchen, keeping her away from the guests. They wouldn't have known how to respond to my grandmother's senility. They'd have been embarrassed and unhelpfully polite, unlike my mother.

I entered the kitchen to refill the crisp bowl.

'Do you know what the doctor wants to do with me now?' asked Granny P. 'He wants to send me to see a psychiatrist.'

'Do shut your cakehole, Ma,' said my mother.

'Do you know what a psychiatrist is?' asked my grandmother.

'Yes,' I said. But it didn't stop her telling me.

'A nosy Jew.'

'Bring on those crisps, Robert!' called my father, from the door.

My father was a delicate man with pronounced cheekbones and swept-back silver hair. He looked exactly as a judge should. In 2003, in Andros, Mike Bell told me my father looked 'like an actor playing a judge', as if the old man's dignity and probity had to be feigned. My father's integrity was as shiny as an apple's — therefore, it had to be skin-deep. It is a typically contemporary presumption. Bad apples are presumed to be the rule. We hear 'judge' or 'policeman' and what do we see? We see perverts, not upholders and enforcers of the law. We see the judge in — where else? — a brothel, paying a sadist to beat him up. Is he not aware that the sadist's a policeman who'd — of course! — beat him up for free?

The eve of Christmas Eve invitation said: 'Drinks. 6 to 7 p.m.' Sure enough, the guests arrived at six on the dot. By ten to seven, they'd all gone. Their main aim, in attending the party, was to leave and be seen to leave at the correct time. No one wished to overstep the mark. They could see the mark approaching on the clock on the wall and accordingly understepped it. They'd been invited for a drink and a drink was what they had. They knew their place.

It's seen as bad that such as Bert knew their place. But how bad was it to know one's place, when one's place was in a dignified Suffolk coastal town where everyone knew their place? That gave one a sense of security, continuity, rightness and order. The Queen was in Buckingham Palace. My father was in High Ridge. Bert was in the garden. Amen.

That particular night, when I was twelve, gripping the replenished crisp bowl, my sister signalled to me from the doorway of the living room to join her in the den. The den was where we children went to be ignored by adults. The den was in fact the attic, an elevated room for low behaviour.

I didn't want to leave. I had duties. I had

status. I didn't want to be ignored by adults. On the contrary, I wanted to be acknowledged. As the son of my father, I felt like a prince, one gracious enough to hand out crisps to artisans who should, by rights, be handing them out to him.

Freya grabbed me. She told me I had to come now, or I'd 'miss it'.

★　★　★

In the den were Christopher Pilkington, his henchman Stephen Catto, Catto's sister Emma, Boo Risdon, Ticky Moxon-Smith and Sam, our chocolate Labrador. Pilkington was wearing a sneer, that harbinger of trouble. I felt sick in my stomach, the one he'd so often hit. I wanted to leave but couldn't as I'd only just arrived. This was my house, my den, my younger sister. I couldn't accede my territorial advantage.

'Have you ever snogged?' he asked me. I recognised this, from my study of Latin, as a question expecting the answer 'no'. A Roman, instead of prefixing the question with a sneer, would have used the term *num*. To fill the time allotted for my answer, I essayed a silent Latin translation: '*Num ecquando snoggavisit?*' Though obviously incorrect, this formulation calmed me. I felt unique, superior, potent. Who else in that den was thinking in Latin?

'Course you haven't snogged,' said Pilkington, as I knew he would. 'I'll show you how it's done.'

He knelt down. Freya, Emma, Boo and Ticky

13

squealed with excitement.[1] I prayed that Freya wouldn't be the one to kneel in front of him. I'd be obliged to defend my sister's honour, notwithstanding she had none. The gangling, stair-buttering Freya did not think in abstractions like 'honour'. If I tried to separate Freya from Pilkington, it would be Freya that hit me first.

Pilkington leaned forward and swept Sam off his four feet.

'Snog the dog!' shouted Boo. Freya clapped loudly. Ticky covered her eyes and screamed.

'Leave our dog alone!' I said. Or did I? I have, as I've claimed, uncommon recall of the spoken word. Yet I'm not completely convinced I said 'Leave our dog alone!' A not-complete conviction is, of course, no conviction at all. I'm convinced I *thought* it. Perhaps I said it and nobody heard, leaving me uncertain if I said it at all.

There was, at this point, no need for me to interpose my body. Sam, though he lay in Pilkington's arms like a canine lover, was doing a perfectly good job of not snogging Pilkington. Whenever his (Sam's) mouth fell open, revealing his juicy pink tongue, Pilkington's mouth advanced towards it. But Sam spurned every

---

[1] Names, too, know their place. I cannot hear 'Boo', 'Ticky', 'Ping Farquharson' or 'Pidge Holt' without thinking of Aldeburgh. These names gain substance and weight when you say them thousands of times. They're no longer twee. They're inevitable.

14

advance, turning his head at the critical moment, with Garbo-like hauteur.

'I know what to do,' said Pilkington. 'Back in a couple of minutes.' He dumped Sam on the carpet. He felt nothing for that dog. Emma, Ticky, Freya and Boo fell on Sam and cuddled him. The dog was having quite a day.

Why didn't I leave? What did I hope to achieve by staying? Two minutes later, true to his word, Pilkington bounded back into the den, oozing confidence but saying nothing. Again he knelt in front of Sam. This time, instead of cradling the dog, he raised Sam onto his hind legs. Sam was only a year or so old. With Pilkington kneeling and Sam standing, the disparity in heights was negated. Boy and dog looked into each other's eyes.

The boy opened his mouth wide enough to satisfy the most officious dentist. I smelt it before I saw it: Pilkington had coated his tongue with dogfood. His eyes blazed. He willed his tongue to be bigger.

Now it was the dog who went for the snog. Sam was hungry for Pilkington's mouth. He licked Pilkington's tongue. He slurped. He salivated. Pilkington made a strange keening sound through his nose. My sister laughed and pounded the floor with her fists. Emma and Boo tried to be sick but could come up with nothing. Ticky uncovered her eyes. Her curiosity outweighed her disgust.

Downstairs, the guests were leaving. One could hear the slamming of their cheap car doors, the ignition of their small engines. Up

15

here in the den, at the scene of the crime — a phrase that will recur in these pages — I felt neither curiosity nor disgust.

I was my father's son. Amid the slurping and keening, the laughing and pounding, the retching and screaming, I found a silent space, in my head, where I could feel judicious. Judicious is distinct from judgemental. I wasn't interested in condemning Pilkington. I wanted to shine a mental light on the legal issues posed by his actions.

It was 1968. I was aware, from reading *The Times*, that homosexuality had been legalised, between consenting adults in private. Pilkington (minor) and Sam (near-puppy) were not adults. Nor was the den private. I turned to a less straightforward matter: was there consent?

Sam's consent had been procured by a trick: the coating of a tongue with Chum. Was consent obtained in this way invalid? Or did the Chum, in fact, alter the nature of the act, from sexual to culinary? Was Sam having food not sex? In any event, was a dog intellectually and morally capable of giving its consent? Sam certainly *looked* like he was consenting.

And then it was over. Sam had licked all the food off Pilkington's tongue. Sam was off now.

Pilkington got to his feet. The girls went quiet. Pilkington went quiet. I'd expected him to be triumphant — but no, he acted hurt. He behaved, perversely, as if he'd been exploited by a dog, a dog who'd got what he wanted then abandoned him. Pilkington was humiliated. Possibly, he was sexually frustrated. He'd kissed

16

a dog. Was that it? Was that all there was?

'Go on then. You snog it now.'

'No thank you,' I said.

'It's your dog. Snog it.' He turned to the girls, hoping they'd side with him. But the girls were neutral. This emboldened me.

'That doesn't make sense,' I said, which it didn't. 'Why would I snog my dog any more than I'd snog someone else's? I'd be *less* likely to snog my dog. Surely you've heard of incest.'

'Shut up!' he said. I could tell he'd never heard of incest. As he headed out of the den, he swung a punch at me, without even looking. Blood spurted from my nose.

'Why d'you do that?' asked my sister.

'What d'you do that for?' asked Ticky.

'I didn't!' said Pilkington. Then, close to tears, he shouted at me: 'I meant to hit you in the stomach! Why aren't you taller, you spazz?'

'Yeah!' said Catto, his loyal henchman. 'Grow up, you spazz!'

With that, Pilkington and Catto were gone.

★ ★ ★

I stayed in the den as long as I could. I managed to avoid my parents till it was time to brush my teeth. I put a cold flannel on my nose, umpteen times. But, evidently, Freya told them Pilkington had hit me. For Freya, it was better to report the crime than be accused of it.

My mother came into the bathroom and shut the door.

'Did you hit him back?'

17

'No.'

'Why not?'

'He's bigger than me.'

'Nonsense. You must hit back, Little Man. Hitler was short.'

'I promise,' I said.

'Good. That's more like it. There's a bit of ice cream left, if you want it.'

'No thank you. I've brushed my teeth.'

'Right. I'll have it. Goodnight then.'

'Goodnight.'

I went to bed. I switched off my bedside light. That, it seemed, was the cue for my father to enter. He wished to speak to me in the dark, in the manner of a radio. He sat on the edge of the bed and began, without any preamble.

'You're a boy of limited height. At the moment. But you've got unlimited intelligence. Don't forget that.' I felt the mattress shake. My father was trembling. 'Intelligence never stops growing. Men of violence and stupidity are always discontented. Whereas men of superior intelligence always have their thoughts to keep them happy. I'd rather you were a short gentleman than a large lout, no matter how rich or successful.'[1]

I did not reply. You do not reply to the radio, nor to a judge when he hands down your sentence. That is what I felt I had heard. A life

[1] A prophetic remark. Pilkington grew up to be Head of Alternative Asset Management at a bank whose name escapes me because it doesn't interest me.

18

sentence, if you will. It was now my duty to go off and serve it.

'Thank you,' I said. But there was more.

'Disputes must be resolved by word not deed. That's why law exists. So man can rise above his violent instincts. You'll learn all about this if you study law.'

'There's no 'if', Pater. I want to be a judge like you.'

'That's good, Robert. Good.' He sounded irritable. 'Please don't call me 'Pater'. Don't overdo it, all right?'

'Right.' I had no idea what he meant.

He paused. 'Psychiatrists aren't nosy Jews. They're professional men.'

'I'll remember that,' I said. My father, in that pause, had tuned himself to a different station. It was still my father broadcasting, but on a different theme. The volume, I noted, was louder.

'Jews and Negroes are as welcome in this house as anyone else.'

'I'm so glad,' I said. Then I asked: 'Were there any Jews here tonight?'

My question seemed to exasperate him. But I could hardly have asked if there were any Negroes. I'd have spotted them with ease.

'The point is not how many Jews were invited tonight. The point is, had there been any Jews, they'd have been as welcome to our drinks and crisps as anyone else, white, black or brown.'

I nodded. It was dark but I'm sure he *sensed* my nod.

'Goodnight then,' said my father, exactly as

my mother had done, though I'm sure there was no collusion. 'Least said, soonest mended,' he added, as if he'd already said too much. He was now, I could tell, reverting to the subject of my bloody nose and its boy perpetrator, whose name he hadn't said once.

These days, of course, we believe the opposite: most said, soonest mended. Hence this book.

★   ★   ★

I waited till I heard my mother's and father's bedroom doors shut. Then I crept downstairs to the kitchen. I found Sam in his dog basket and woke him up.

I told Sam that men of violence are always discontented, whereas men of intelligence always have their thoughts to keep them happy. He did not reply, except by licking his lips, which of course made me think of Pilkington.

★   ★   ★

On Christmas Day, 1968, as always, my mother said, 'Good-oh!' as she doused the Christmas pudding in the supermarket brandy she bought because it was cheaper and 'went further'.

I understood, as she did so, what was meant by *pudding-basin haircut*. The pudding looked like a darker version of Pilkington's brown mop. My mother struck a match and set it on fire. I watched it burn.

Many years later, on 29th September 2003, I recalled this image of Pilkington's head, studded with nuts, cherries and raisins. 29th September 2003 is the date of my crime. Please do not think of it, as my sister does, as my 'Nine Twenty-Nine', my equivalent to Nine Eleven. That is an insult not only to the dead but to the language itself. Mine was an English crime, committed in England. We don't say 'September 29'. We say '29th September'.

Call it, if you must, my 'Twenty-nine Nine'. But never call it my 'Nine Twenty-Nine'. That's not a crime but a train.

Pilkington was there, on 29th September. Tragically, my father was not.[1]

* * *

On Boxing Day morning, I played tennis with my mother, after she'd had her swim and whisky.

As I prepared to serve, she spotted Boo, Ticky and Pilkington on their bikes, riding down the path that leads to the allotments. I served but my mother made no attempt to return. Instead, she strode purposefully off the court, shouting at him: 'Excuse me!'

Pilkington was uncertain. My mother's booming voice had stopped him in his tracks. Having

---

[1] Tragically, here, means 'tragically'. I'm not using it as in: 'Tragically, Beckham's penalty ballooned over the bar.' I'm using it as in: 'Tragically, Beckham's penalty hit the post which snapped and struck the goalkeeper on the head, causing him to be substituted by a living replacement.'

21

registered the source of the boom, he was keen to get away. But any attempt to avoid my mother would have looked like an admission of guilt.

I watched, from the court, as my mother went up to him. The girls, intimidated, freewheeled down the path. They distanced themselves sufficiently to avoid involvement, yet remained within earshot.

I, thought, was too far away to hear. I watched my mother speak to Pilkington. I saw him shake his head. I knew his head-shake was a lie. It was obvious, even from distance, that a nod was the truthful answer to what my mother had asked.

My mother took two steps back and hit Pilkington on the side of the head, with her racquet, as if his ear were a ball. It was a forehand drive volley, heartily and lustily struck. Pilkington was stunned. Remarkably, he didn't move.

For my part, when I saw my mother volleying Pilkington's ear, I knew exactly what kind of man I'd be: the kind of man who'd never do a thing like that. I would wound with words, with logic, with the withdrawal or withholding of respect. I would be what my father wanted me to be: a short gentleman of superior intelligence.

3

Mike Bell
(1974)

My father had a friend called Maurice Perlstein. He'd known Maurice since childhood. My father's father, to toughen him up, had dispatched my father to a boxing club in the East End of London, which he naturally hated. Maurice, however, was kind to him, not giving him the bloody nose of which he knew Maurice was capable. A friendship was formed.

My father went to see Maurice about once a month, always on his own. Maurice was a Jewish greengrocer who lived in Whitechapel. Did these facts — the religion, the occupation, the location — explain why he went without my mother? Possibly. Certainly, the religion would account for Maurice never coming to Aldeburgh. Granny P would have asked the Jewish Maurice if he had come to lend her some money — which would have been ironic, given that she was rich and Maurice was poor.

So. My mother, my sister and I never met Maurice. But my father was always loyal to him. There was something in my father's trips to the East End — I was going to write 'something of the missionary', but my father would have disliked the religious connotation. There was something philanthropic, something benevolent. My father wished to help a man less fortunate than himself.

Mike Bell was my Maurice.

★ ★ ★

'Hi, I'm Mike, I live next door. Can you help me with my essay? You're brainier than me. I've got a bottle.'

These were the first words he spoke to me, in October 1974, when he and I were first-year law students at Christ Church, Oxford. He knocked at my door and there he was, with his copy of *Megarry & Wade: The Law of Real Property* and a bottle of Hirondelle. He was taller, better-looking and more charismatic than I — though looks and charisma, I think you'll find, are curses as much as blessings. He was, as he was literally the first to admit, less brainy than me. He was poorer, too, or he wouldn't have been carrying a bottle of a 'branded' wine that belonged in no man's cellar.

He entered with no further invitation; indeed, no invitation at all. He was unstoppable. This is what he did, without stopping: turned the light on, found two glasses, took a penknife with a corkscrew facility from his pocket, opened the bottle, poured two glasses, found a saucer to use as an ashtray, sat at my desk with his textbook, moved my papers to one side, opened his textbook, asked me about the difference between express and implied trusts and lit a cigarette.

I, meanwhile, shut the door and sat down on

my bed. He then stood up to bring me my glass of wine, which I refused. He was offended but proceeded to drink that glass as well as his own.

At no point did Mike Bell refer to the onset of midnight, or my pyjamas, or the probable congregating, on the college lawn, of badgers and other nocturnal creatures. I had a tutorial at nine in the morning, as did he. I needed sleep. But he needed help. I gave him help, clarifying the distinction between express and implied trusts with minimal fuss. I gave him my help, and continued to do so, because he was less advantaged than me.

Working-class students were rare in Oxford. Nowadays, it may be where all 'lads' study, before they join Oasis. But in 1974, working-class men and women were like blacks are, to this day, in Aldeburgh: people one is tempted to photograph.

Mike Bell came from south London. He'd attended a comprehensive school of which neither I nor anyone I knew had ever heard. His father, who ran a shoe-repair business, was Irish. His mother, who looked after him and his two brothers and sister, was Italian. He was born, he told me, as he lit his second cigarette, 'with a Guinness in one hand and an ice cream in the other'. I nodded politely. He looked disappointed. He was expecting some kind of chummy guffaw. Surely he could see I was not a guffawer.

I could not but look down on him. Yes, there was ascent in Mike Bell's immigrant trajectory. But I was born on the summit — the summit of a mountain that was English to the core, as if it were made of Gentleman's Relish. My mother, a Jarvis, grew up in a house where servants ironed one's newspaper. When Aldeburgh got its first 'happy clappy' vicar, he made the mistake of asking my mother what her family in Gloucestershire did.

'They own it,' my mother said, witheringly, embarrassing the vicar and making God look foolish for choosing him as His earthly representative, in a town so happily unclappy.

My father was a descendant of Henry Purcell, the greatest of all English composers before Benjamin Britten. On his mother's side, he was related to Prince Alfred, the second son of Queen Victoria and Prince Albert of Saxe-Coburg; hence the slightly Germanic cast of his eyebrows. When he met my mother, he was living with that most Wodehousian of creatures, an aunt with a house in Pimlico, his parents having died in the war.

When Mike Bell asked me to tell him about myself, I edited my family history to a simple: 'I'm a Wykehamist.' The confidence drained from him. He had no idea what a 'Wykehamist' was. I refused to patronise him with an explanation. That was what an education at Winchester had brought me — effortless superiority. I couldn't say that 'Wykehamist' meant 'pupil or graduate of Winchester College'. That would have been effortful.

'What branch of the law do you wish to go into?' I asked. I was keen to level our conversational playing field. I felt exactly like my father, on Christmas Eve Eve, with the coalman.

'Fuck knows,' said Mike Bell, unhelpfully. 'That's not what college is about. It's about having the best sex of your life and the best music and the best films and the best drink and the biggest drugs.'

'I trust you didn't say that at the interview,' I replied.

Mike Bell roared. My neighbour banged on the wall. Much to my embarrassment, Mike Bell banged back. Then he calmed down. He became thoughtful. He drew deeply on his cigarette. 'I think I'll use my degree to go into entertainment.' I was shocked. I had never heard of anyone 'using' a law degree, as if it were some kind of fork.

'I don't think you use the law,' I said. 'The law uses you, surely. It's a greater force than any individual. If you're an ant on the back of an elephant and the elephant moves forward, your motion is due to the elephant. But I hardly think you're 'using' it, are you?'

'Yeah, you are.'

I said nothing. I was convinced I was right. I saw no need to convince him too.

The atmosphere between us was now tense. Mike Bell poured two more glasses of wine but failed to offer me either.

'What do they call you then, Robert?' he asked, inclined to change the subject.

'They call me Robert,' I replied.

'I can't call you Robert after all you've done for me.'

I failed to see the logic of this, as I failed to see

27

the logic of so much he did and said. But he was true to his word. From then on, he went out of his way not to call me Robert. Bob, Bobby, Rob, Robbie, Roberto, Boberto, Bobbity: anything Robert-related would do.

At half past one, he said I looked tired. Since he was the one who'd made me tired, how could he sound so concerned? He suggested I go to bed. I agreed. I waited for him to leave.

'Don't wait for me to leave,' he said. 'You just get into bed.' I got into bed. 'You look much more relaxed now,' he said.

Mike Bell stood up and went towards the door. I was about to say goodnight when I saw him fail to leave. He stopped at the light switch, turned it off then sat back down again. I heard the click of a lighter and saw the tip of a cigarette, darting this way and that, like Tinkerbell.

'I'd like to be a film producer. Yeah, that's what I'd like to do. The hard thing is finding the stories. People want authenticity. You know?'

Tinkerbell dive-bombed into the saucer and was stubbed.

★ ★ ★

A week later, I was in my room at 8 p.m., writing an essay on *Donoghue* v. *Stevenson* (1932), that celebrated case in which Lord Atkin formulated what is called 'the neighbour principle'. This established that you must take reasonable care to avoid acts or omissions which you could reasonably foresee would be likely to injure your neighbour, a neighbour being a person so closely connected with and directly affected by (proximate to) your act (or omission) that you should have had them in mind when you committed the act (or omission). Compare that, in its muscularity, precision and enforceability, with the woolly: 'Love thy neighbour as thyself.'

I heard someone knock at my neighbour Mike Bell's door then wait. Having received no reply, the knocker knocked at my door instead.

She was a girl in a fawn mac, with pleated blue skirt, a blue sweater over her white shirt and a string of pearls. She asked me if I knew Mike Bell. She'd arranged to come to his room at eight but he wasn't in. I, being a civilised man, said she was welcome to wait in my room, provided she accepted I was writing an essay and could not entertain her. She seemed happy enough with this. She told me her name was Angela. I nodded, agreeing that this was the case, but did not offer my own name, fearing it would lead to supplementary remarks. I told her she should make herself a cup of tea or coffee, as long as she didn't make any noise. She declined. I offered her a chair and a copy of *The Times*. She accepted, turning the pages with commendable quiet.

After a while, though, the rhythm of her page-turning began to irritate. It was obvious she wasn't reading the pages; she was merely, after a decent interval, turning them.

I excused myself, with a nod rather than words. I left the room. It was my room and I owed no one a duty of care as to when I could leave it.

I looked down the corridor, to see if Mike Bell were, by happy chance, approaching his room. He was not. Instead, a girl was approaching. She had long dark hair, a fur jerkin and aubergine flared trousers. I shut my own door behind me, just before she knocked on Mike Bell's.

'Are you looking for Mike?' I asked, a question expecting the answer yes.

'Yes.'

'He's not in. You're welcome to wait in my room.'

'Cheers. Cool. I'm Sal.'

'I'm . . . ' I began. And stopped.

I explained she'd have to wait quietly, as I was writing an essay. She nodded. I opened my door. We entered. Sal said 'Hi' to Angela and Angela said 'Hi' to Sal. I didn't introduce them. Sal sat in the other chair, the chair by the window. She asked if I minded if she smoked. I told her I did, not wanting the noise. She looked confused. She had never thought of smoking in terms of noise: the striking of match or click of lighter, the sucking, the tap-tap of cigarette on ashtray. A smoker is, in terms of noise, on a par with a mouse. But one cannot write an essay in the same room as a mouse.

Why did I invite Sal into my room? I was testing my powers of logic. Those powers were duly found to be masterful. Sal, I reasoned, would enter the room and assume the incumbent Angela was my girlfriend, while Angela, similarly, would assume the incoming Sal was my girl-friend. This is what duly happened.

30 ^C

As I wrote my essay, I pondered Mike Bell's duty of care to me. He had evidently invited two girls to his room at the same time. He'd then omitted to show up. Could he reasonably have foreseen that this omission would injure me — in the sense of causing me to be distracted from my essay? No. I thought not. He could not have foreseen that I would invite both girls to my room.

At this point, I excused myself again. Not only was I distracted from my essay, I was fearful of the consequences of my actions. What would happen when Mike Bell returned? There would be fireworks, metaphorical but noisy. His arrival would not end my involvement. On the contrary. There would be a scene, a scene in my room.

I walked down the corridor and out of the building. I waited for Mike Bell at the entrance to the college. He arrived almost immediately, greeting me with a cheery 'What's up?'

I explained what was up. He thanked me. Then we went and had a curry.

★　★　★

Mike Bell ordered two more lagers for himself. We had known each other but a week; yet already it was established that he had two drinks for every none of mine.

'How could you do that?' Mike Bell was angry. He'd met Angela at a Wine and Cheese evening at the Oxford University Conservative Association. He'd met Sal at a Beer and Nuts at the

31

Labour Club.[1] Angela was a cheerful pudding of a girl, heartily keen to lose her virginity by Christmas, so she wouldn't have to take it home. Sal was angry, brilliant, neurotic and thin. All human female life had been present and correct, in my room. And I'd disdained it. I'd abandoned it. Who did I think I was? I ignored this question, thinking it rhetorical. It was obvious to anyone of the meanest intelligence who I thought I was. What's more, I was it.

I told him he had to choose between Sal and Angela. He told me he could do what he wanted, as could they. I explained that I was speaking politically, not romantically. He could two-time a girl but not a political party. That was vacuous and morally and intellectually weak.

'What if I don't know what I am?'

'Find out.'

'I suppose you've known since you were two.'

'Yes,' I replied, not untruthfully. 'I've inherited my politics from my father. I believe in a free market but I also believe it's the primary duty of a political party to look after the poor. The poor must be fed and clothed and housed, though preferably not next door.'

---

[1] Nowadays, of course, there's no class or food or drink distinction between our two main political parties. They're both camped in the middle of the road, trying to lure us through the wide-open flaps of their all-inclusive big tents, with the promise of the same New Zealand Chardonnay and the same Organic Red Pepper and Fairtrade Mango Crisps.

'So you're a Conservative, then.'

'No. My father's a High Court judge. He's above politics. I am too. I aim to follow in his footsteps.'

'You're so fucking sure of yourself, aren't you?'

'Thank you.'

He took another mouthful of my disgusting curry.

'You don't have to turn into your dad, you know.' He chewed and chewed upon my mutton, my mutton dressed as mutton. 'Jesus was different from God.'

What a fatuous remark. Here was a man who had a brain and chose not to use it, or, rather, he chose to underuse it. Why? It seemed to me he had no idea who he was. He was defined only by a double negative — he wanted to be someone to whom no girl would say no.

'What kind of upper-class arsehole are you? You don't hunt. You don't shoot. You don't fish. You don't bray. What are you into, apart from libraries? Boys?'

I didn't wish to discuss what I was 'into'. My virginity was no business of his.

'You're a virgin, aren't you? Boys or girls?'

It was true. I was unknown to woman and/or man, though I did not vouchsafe this to him. He persisted. 'Neither? Are you a heathosexual?'

This was a reference to our recently deposed Prime Minister, Edward Heath, who was considered to be neither heterosexual nor homosexual. I resented this intrusion into my private life. I resented the intrusion into *Heath's* private life.[1]

★　★　★

Half an hour later, as I wrote the cheque, Mike Bell insisted, expansively, that I eat both our complimentary sweets.

All the time we were in the curry house, Sal and Angela were in my room, talking to each other, as girls will. When they discovered they'd been double-booked, Sal put a note under Mike Bell's door, asserting he was a bastard whom she never wanted to see again. Angela, by contrast, was not remotely bothered.[2] She wanted an experienced man. The incident only added to his experience. She stayed by that door till he returned, whereupon she demanded he digest his curry as she craved 'a jolly good seeing-to'.

This he gave her. But it was not what he craved. The next night, he went to the inaugural meeting of the Oxford University Green Party. Its leader, Rose Wainwright, proved to be the great love of Mike Bell's first term. The night he met her, he told me, he drank two bottles of wine, in order to have more to recycle.

It did not surprise me that the Green Party girl won his heart. The Green Party had been in existence barely a year. Mike Bell was and is a

---

[1] I shall return to the subject of 'heathosexuality' at the start of my next chapter.

[2] It is notable that the left-winger (Sal) was moralistic while the right-winger (Angela) was libertarian.

slave to novelty whereas I, a born lawyer, was and am a slave to precedent.

★ ★ ★

Mike Bell was not at the scene of my crime, though he spoke to me, over the phone. It was he, in fact, who told me to do it. But it was I who did it. It is I who take responsibility. This is my book, not his.

4

I am a Heterosexual (1979)

It is inconceivable in the twenty-first century that a 'heathosexual' could be Prime Minister. The electorate believes it has a right to be in its Prime Minister's bedroom. And, while it is there, it insists on seeing some 'action'. A modern Edward Heath would not be granted the keys to Number Ten, not without a Mrs Heath to stand by him on the threshold and then, on that glorious post-election dawn, open the door to the florist. Could Mr Heath have a Mr Heath? Undoubtedly. As long as Mr Heath — the door-opening, non-Prime Minister Heath — understood that indiscretion is now the better part of valour. Boyfriend Heath, civil partner Heath, would be obliged to select and spill a few well-chosen beans. Ted's unmatching buttocks, perhaps. Ted's cries in the night. Ted's flossing obsession. There is, in all this, no 'need to know basis'. We, the electorate, simply need to know and to hell with the basis. Our man in Number Ten is not our man till we know his secrets, which we can't know, by definition, till those secrets are broken. This is what has happened in the course of my life. Things that were public are now privatised; things that were private are now publicised.[1]

Yes, I left Oxford 'unknown to woman', whereas Mike Bell was 'known' all over the shop. I, however, was awarded a first-class degree and the Hart Chambers Prize for the best paper on Company Law in the Final Honour School of Jurisprudence; he just about scraped through, with my help, which I told him I could not possibly give him during the exams. Whose 'knowledge' lasted? Whose 'knowledge' constituted better use of public money, which is to say *your* money?

It was always my intention to have two children, a boy and a girl, just as my father had done. I was, from birth, a heterosexual. But I did not pursue sex. I was not in its thrall. I controlled my feelings. What was it that drove my sister Freya, at seventeen, to get herself pregnant by a heroin addict? Why pregnant? Why an

---

[1] I must stop this. Elizabeth warned me to avoid the tendentious nostalgia that characterises the utterances of middle-aged men. I'm here to explain the forces that shaped me. That's not a licence to bang on about the passing of blue-wrapped crisp-packet salt twists or the way contemporary newsreaders say: 'Abigail's body was found just a hundred yards from her home.' Abigail? Whence derives that nauseating familiarity? A stranger has died. A stranger to the newsreader, a stranger to the viewers of the news. Yet first-name celebrity (in the manner of 'Diana') is always thrust upon the luckless victim as if — but I must stop.

addict? There were no degrees in my sister's world of feeling. It wasn't all or nothing, it was always all. Could she not merely kiss a boy who liked a glass of beer? No. There had to be needles and sex. There had to be my mother, screaming through the letter box of a basement flat in Paddington that she would bash the door down if my sister didn't open it. That she'd given up a whole day at the Aldeburgh Regatta and would not give up another.

After the abortion, my parents, in despair, sent her to live for a year in Australia with her uncle Brian, a sheep farmer, who was in truth not an uncle but a cousin of my mother's. It was the only boarding school my parents hadn't tried: a boarding school with sheep. Would that sheep could set her an example where humans had tried and failed. Would that sheep could teach her there was only advantage in passing exams, going to university, behaving in a decent fashion. Let sheep get Freya to see the virtue in acting like a sheep.

I did not keep myself celibate to make my parents proud, nor to distance myself from Freya. I was simply not interested. It had been my observation that the thickest of my contemporaries were the ones most interested in sex. By the age of sixteen, the under-O-levelled Pilkington was no longer a bully, preferring to invest his attention-seeking hulk in attracting the opposite sex. Now he wanted dogs to watch him while he snogged girls.

Was my father 'unknown to woman' when he married my mother? I never asked him and never

38

wanted to ask. He came from a time when such questions went unasked. A man could have a mistress and a wife, without the wife asking questions. A man could visit a prostitute once a week, without the wife accusing him of having 'intimacy issues', a phrase with the sound and slippery content of a sneeze. A man could have a close male friend, without that friend insisting they walk down the aisle of the Church of St Elton the John.

★ ★ ★

In 1972, when I was sixteen, I went to the Lord's Test match with my father. Australia beat England by eight wickets, with the Aussie Test debutant Bob Massie taking a remarkable sixteen wickets for one hundred and thirty-seven runs. As the players came off the pitch, my father said: 'Maurice will take you for a night in Soho when you're twenty-one!' He had to say it loudly, to be heard over the applause. I believe he'd been trying to say it all day. Now the match was over, he was running out of time.

His volume only added to the urgency. I felt I had better start preparing. For the next five years, I 'saw' this night in Soho. I 'saw' a tart laid out on a bed, like an exam paper laid out on a desk. She'd introduce herself as 'Fifi'. She'd smile. She'd call me 'darling' in Parisian cockney. Her teeth would be lipstick-stained and incorrigibly working class.

Then what? She'd tell me it was 'all right'. She'd tell me there was nothing to worry about.

Why would she tell me that unless it wasn't true? She'd get undressed. She'd tell me to 'wash'. What was I meant to wash? All of me? Parts? Where was Maurice? Was he waiting? For what? Fifi to finish with me so she could start with him?

She'd throw the eiderdown back so I could see her nakedness. I'd say, because I was an educated man: 'You look like the nude Maja by Goya.'

'Ooh, you're a saucy one!' she'd say, incorrectly assuming the word 'nude' implied 'sauce'. Nude women were not 'sauce'; if they were, the National Gallery would not admit children.

'Come on then, darlin'. Don't stand over there. You'll catch your death.'

'Goya. Seventeen forty-six to eighteen twenty-eight,' I'd reply, in the interests of delay.

She'd extend her arms, wide enough to catch a beach ball. The arms would enfold me. I'd become a man.

The night with Maurice, however, was never mentioned again. Maurice remained my father's secret.

★ ★ ★

At twenty-one, though unknown to woman, I was definitely a man. I, along with Thoday, Catto, Pilkington, Risdon and Hamilton-Wood, had the keys to the doors of our parents' Aldeburgh houses. We could occupy those houses without a parent present. We could sail the boat, dine at the yacht club, play a round at the golf club. We were a parallel generation, neither replacing our parents nor wishing to overthrow them. We wished only to do what they had done, in slightly fewer shots.

We were older, we were faster, but we were still a group. I was, irrevocably, part of that group. I was included, tolerated and sometimes admired, for my knowledge and the dryness of my wit. Though rarely sought after, I was seldom avoided.

Those, such as Pilkington, who considered me 'superior', missed the point. I *was* superior. I don't mean that I was not inferior to them in certain arenas; only that I did not belong in those arenas, which I considered inferior: the gambling arena, the car arena, the drinking and boasting about girls arena. On a Friday night in July 1979, aged twenty-three, I sat on the sea wall in Aldeburgh, at the back of the Cross Keys pub, with a pint in my hand. An hour later, I was still clutching it. It was now a half-pint in my hand. Pilkington, meanwhile, was roaring. He was telling an anecdote that had no middle. None of his anecdotes had a middle. There was a beginning, in which he drank a lot, followed by a sudden end.

On the previous Saturday, he and Catto had gone to Newmarket Races. They'd lost heavily and had consoled themselves by getting 'seriously smashed'. At six, they decided it was time to drive back to Aldeburgh. Pilkington staggered to the car park and fell into the driving seat of his Golf Convertible.

'I was so pissed I couldn't find the ignition. I was stabbing the bloody steering wheel with the key!' The End.

Martin Thoday laughed. Jeremy Hamilton-Wood laughed. I didn't, on the grounds that it wasn't funny.

'Why didn't you get so pissed that you couldn't find your car?' I asked. 'Wouldn't that have been safer for you and the car and all the other cars?' Everyone ignored me. But, weeks later, Thoday and Hamilton-Wood told me they'd wished they'd said it themselves. It was a popular remark that was simply ahead of its time.

Stephen Catto suggested we go to the late-night film at the Aldeburgh Cinema. It was a soft-core pornographic film whose name I forget.[1] I went there fully intending not to enjoy it. I'm happy to report I succeeded.

Half an hour into the film, a large man shambled into the cinema, sat in the front row and coughed. He coughed and coughed as if determined to turn himself inside out. Does one not judge a man by the company he keeps? The cougher and I were watching a soft-core porn film together, a walk away from the Red House in Aldeburgh, where Britten wrote his *War Requiem*, 'the most masterly and nobly imagined work that Britten has ever given us'.[2]

The lights came up like searchlights trained on escapees from prison. I, unlike the tramp, had a

----

[1] No I don't. I mustn't perjure myself. *Black Emmanuelle Goes East* (1976)

[2] William Mann, *The Times*, 1st April 1962.

civilisation to which I could return. I was a first-class graduate. I had the keys to a splendid house, with books and a piano and an LP of the *Requiem*. Under whose hedge would he be spending the night? I'd make damn sure it wasn't ours.

I walked a few paces behind him as we shuffled into the foyer. His hair stuck out from the crown of his head as if electrically shocked. He wore a pale brown suit, surprisingly well cut. In the foyer, he turned. He was approximately forty. His hair, which looked so copious from behind, was in fact receding. His eyes, nose and mouth were squashed into the central part of his face. He smelt overripe. One felt that if one touched him, he'd be left on one's hands. He grunted at Pilkington, then pushed the exit door, which was meant to be pulled. He pushed it again. It took him several goes to leave the cinema.

'Do you know that man?' I asked Pilkington.

'Yeah. He's got a house near my parents. Peter Something-Something. He's some kind of cousin of the Queen.'

I was shocked. My kinship with the Queen was merely that of subject. This 'tramp' was my equal, nay, my superior.

'Is he married?'

Pilkington snorted.

On 29th September 2003, I bumped into Peter Something-Something. He was the first person I met after I committed my crime. He was then about sixty-five. Over the years, I'd often seen him buying whisky and beans in the Co-op. He wore, as always, his pale brown porn-film suit. By then, it had turned a paler shade of brown. Was that on account of age? Sun? Gravy? He died shortly afterwards. His cough survived him, though. I heard it often, at night, in prison, in the throats of others, a generic male cough. I believe it has no bodily root. It's a manifestation of male despair.

★ ★ ★

Let me be clear: I was propelled into sex not by 'peer-group pressure' (men on sea walls boasting about sex) nor pornographic example (male nonentities underneath Black Emmanuelle). It was simply that I did not want to turn into Peter Something-Something. I recognised in him a likewise capacity for self-imposed isolation. It was time to have sex and find a wife, for fear of living alone with my thoughts, which were of a quality, as my father had predicted, to keep me happy without recourse to others.

I could not, as I believed my father had, find a wife without having sex. I couldn't go from 'unknown to woman' to husband. Girls, those future wives, expected sexual experience — even jolly girls, Conservative girls, girls with pearls. That is what I learned, by proxy, from Mike Bell's Angela. Nice girls did it, keenly and to a high standard.

'Sex is like riding a bike.' That's what Pilkington had told us, outside the Cross Keys, when we were fifteen and he could buy the drinks, since it was the barmaid he'd ridden.

Eight years later, outside the same pub, he told us he'd got 'totally bladdered' on the King's Road with Ticky Moxon-Smith.

'She needed cheering up,' he said, then shrugged. He picked up his packet of Rothmans from the sea wall, lit a cigarette and drew deep. I waited for The End, then realised we'd had it. The End was unspoken. The End was a shrug and a cloud of smoke.

'You going to see her again?' asked Catto.

'I dunno,' said Pilkington, staring out to sea, as if the sea contained more girls, as if there were *plenty more girls in the sea.*

Pilkington wasn't going to see her again. I could tell.

★ ★ ★

Ticky Moxon-Smith needed cheering up because she had made a mistake. A few years later, I would make one too. Allow me to discourse on hers, for it will shed light on mine.

Dick Gage, Bert the gardener's son, a former teenage tearaway, went round the world then got a job with a local catering firm. The firm catered Ticky's twenty-first. At the end of the night, when a caterer's duty is to clear up and go, Dick Gage cleared up and stayed. He 'bedded' Ticky Moxon-Smith, thereby subverting the order of things. Nor did he scuttle off with his collar up when the sun rose. On the contrary. Within a year, the caterers were back in the Moxon-Smith marquee, for the wedding of Ticky and Dick.

Geoffrey Moxon-Smith was unhappy. He did

45

what any Englishman would do — kept his unhappiness to himself. But his wife, the formidable Amanda, was determined to make the best of it. She invested heavily in Dick's debutant venture, a Mexican restaurant in Aldeburgh High Street. Amanda told everyone how excited she was. Her new son-in-law had gumption. No one had ever opened a Mexican restaurant in coastal Suffolk. It was just what a staid and fuddy-duddy place like Aldeburgh needed. But, of course, what a staid and fuddy-duddy place needs is staidness and fuddy-duddyness. After a day's sailing on the Alde, or nineteen holes at the golf course, no denizen of Aldeburgh ever said: 'Bring on the bandit food!'

Dick and Ticky would run Desperados together. Ticky, after all, had done a course in Hotel Management at Surrey University. (A restaurant, the argument went, was just a hotel without rooms.) Dick hired a chef. She was a Spanish woman he'd met on his travels. Amanda called her the 'Loony Latina'.

Two weeks before Opening Night, Amanda Moxon-Smith printed up the menu and distributed it, by hand, to everyone she knew in Aldeburgh, which was everyone in Aldeburgh, since she was a councillor, Commodore of the Yacht Club, a churchwarden and President of the Aldeburgh Society. She couldn't meet two ladies on the High Street without the three of them forming a committee. She was a force of nature, a volcanic hot spring. Geoffrey was more like a turned-off tap.

She followed up the menu with a home visit,

one week before Opening Night. Amanda arrived with a pen and pad. She'd come to take your order. You had to tell her what you wanted to eat, a week before you wanted to eat it.

Three days before Desperados was due to open — but you know it, don't you? You know The End. Dick Gage disappeared. He wasn't born to be Ticky's husband. He sent her a postcard, without an address, postmarked Seville. He was sorry. She should sell his guitar. He didn't want to see her, as that would only hurt her more. (One could sense the Loony Latina's hand on his, guiding his pen.)

Do you see? Dick Gage was Ticky's mistake. He was inappropriate. Amanda Moxon-Smith wrote him a postcard, care of his father Bert, which informed him that if he came within a hundred yards of her daughter, she'd chop off his legs and feed them to her dog, which introduces another theme to which I shall perforce return: English people place the needs of dogs above those of men.

★   ★   ★

Ticky was surprised to hear from me. She didn't, however, object to our meeting for dinner. I suggested a restaurant on the King's Road. She agreed. This was a good start. The King's Road was where she'd got bladdered with Pilkington, prior to sexual intercourse. I'd already achieved the King's Road. Now I had only to negotiate the bladdering and intercourse.

Let me, as politicians say, make one thing

47

perfectly clear: I did not wish her to compare me with Pilkington. I merely wished her to do with me what she had done with him. I was my own man.

Pilkington was not his own man. In his early twenties, he belonged to a fashionable tribe. To begin at his feet and work upwards: brown leather knee-length boots, blue jeans, a belt with an 'interesting' buckle (a Wolf's Head, a Texas Ranger), a white shirt open two buttons deep, black velvet jacket, white silk scarf, cocky mouth containing a Rothmans, unintelligent but over-confident eyes, floppy hair fielded behind his ears with a signet-ring laden right hand.

I wore brown or black brogues in leather or suede, grey trousers, a pastel blue, terracotta or white shirt and a sports jacket, all of them purchased from O. & C. Butcher, the Aldeburgh outfitters. Outfitters! Where are the outfitters now? I have never, in my life, entered a men's fashion shop. The music alone repels me. When I enter a shop, I don't want to hear music, any more than when I enter a concert hall I want the orchestra to sell me their clothes. Why would I purchase a 'fashion shirt'? Why purchase an item that proudly announces its own obsolescence? I would not buy a 'fashion hammer' to strike a 'fashion nail'. I want my hammer to endure, as my O. & C. Butcher sports jacket has endured for twenty-five years.

Pilkington was one of the tribe of *somethings in the City*. I was a barrister. I had a profession, the specifics of which people understood. No one ever said of me, he's something in the law

48

courts. What was the nature of the *something* which Pilkington did? One didn't ask, one couldn't understand, unless one were *something* too. He earned money. That's all one knew. He was too thick to do anything other than earn lots of money.

He spent his soft-earned money on cars. He'd just traded his MGB for a VW Golf Convertible. These vehicles facilitated the blowing of the wind through his floppy hair. Pilkington paid heavily to have a hairdresser flop his hair. No more than I visited fashion shops did I patronise a hairdresser. I went to the barber who barbered my father. What few pounds I paid I would have withheld had he given my hair a style.

Pilkington valued money for its own sake, as something to have and flaunt. I never valued money for money's sake. At twenty-three, in any event, I had no money to speak of. I was a barrister of just one year's call.

When Pilkington bowled up at Ticky's flat in his Golf Convertible, she heard the roar of money. I arrived at the King's Road restaurant on foot, having walked from Sloane Square station.

★   ★   ★

'Christ, you can't hear a word I say!' said Ticky, a spaghetti-thin woman as taut as she was brittle.

'Yes! It's terrible!' I replied, trying to look disappointed. This, I admit, was disingenuous. I'd chosen a restaurant with very loud music, to prevent conversation and aid eating. With good

49

service and without coffee, we'd be out of there in the hour. The meal was an overture to sex and overtures should be short.

Kieran Harris, my pupil master, had urged me to acquire charm. I demurred. Kieran, an Irishman with swept-back jet-black hair, was much given to eye contact with female jurors. He advised me, in his hand-on-shoulder way, to have 'a couple of pints' before addressing a jury. He said this would help me 'get on their level'. I could then address them as 'mates'. He told me this with the twinkle he regarded as his best feature. I thought it a sign of his compromised character. It was as if he'd applied this twinkle to his eye with a Dublin-bought trowel. He wanted to be a 'twinkling Irishman' whom jurors would take to their hearts. What if Kieran had been born a Swede? Would he have been a 'twinkling Swede'? I didn't want to twinkle. I had integrity. Ticky could not claim I was superficial. She couldn't say I was a sycophantic fellow, of skin-deep charm. Not if I had no charm. (Pilkington, I was reliably informed, had a great deal.)

'Let's get the bill! Coffee at mine!' That much I heard. Ticky drained her nth glass of wine.

★ ★ ★

Ticky was 'bladdered', as she had been with Pilkington. Of that there was no doubt. As I stood behind her, outside her front door, she lurched backwards to shine more street light on the contents of her bag, knocking me off my feet.

50

'Oh, fuck, God, I'm sorry, there it is,' said Ticky, finally seeing the glint of her front-door key. She hauled me to my feet with the strength of a girl who'd been sailing since, aged ten, she did her Beginner's Course. She staggered into the communal hall, unlocked the door to Flat B, then led me up her stairs with just one fall and a refusal, due to breathlessness. She told me to sit on the sofa. Any short man will tell you of his apprehension when given this instruction. Thankfully, my feet touched the ground. She sat next to me. I made no attempt to kiss her.

Was I curious about her? Did I wish to know how she thought? No. But, equally, I did not expect her to be curious about me.

'How many spare keys per room does a manager have?' That was the question I was planning to ask, in the knowledge she'd studied Hotel Management. Happily, she asked one of her own.

'Do you like Meat Loaf?' She was standing near her hi-fi as she said it. I therefore deduced that 'Meat Loaf' was a kind of music or, possibly, a group. Lest I be accused of resembling a judge who'd never heard of the Beatles, let me say I was positively proud of not having heard of Meat Loaf. It was my opinion, as a potential judge, that judges should be drawn from the ranks of people who hadn't heard of Meat Loaf.

'Yes,' I lied. And, to forestall more conversation, I added: 'I like my Meat Loaf loud.'

Meat Loaf turned out to be a person, with a pseudo-operatic vocal style. His songs all started in the foothills of hysteria and climaxed at its peak. But loud Meat Loaf couldn't save me. We were side by side on a sofa, with no noise from diners or waiters.

Ticky, who was a talker like her mother, talked of love. She'd been so in love with Dick Gage. Dick Gage had been so in love with her. That's what she'd thought. He'd told her how much he loved her. Why did he say that? Was it a lie? Or was it true when he said it and a lie later? Why do men tell you they love you then go off with a Spanish woman with 'big tits and a moustache'? Was that the sort of woman men really wanted? She looked at me. She wanted an answer. At that moment, I was 'men'.

'Not all men want a Spanish woman with big tits and a moustache.' This answer was true, even if there were only one man in the world who did not want a Spanish woman etc. And there was such a man. I was he.

'Oh, you can speak, can you?'

I nodded, trying not to provoke her with further speech. But she was already provoked.

'Why did you ring me up? You've shown no interest in me at all. You haven't asked me a question all night. What's the point of asking me out to dinner if you're not going to talk to me? Did you do it for a bet?'

'No.'

'Why are you here, then?' asked Ticky Moxon-Smith.

This was it.

★ ★ ★

I would defend to the death a citizen's right to be tried by a jury. But I would defend to the death my own right, as a barrister, to go nowhere near one. Kieran Harris taught me, early in my career, that my future lay in civil not criminal work. A man like me should not address a jury of his peers. What jury could be my peers? I had attended Winchester, the best school in the country. Oxford held a similar place in the university pantheon.

One could not have it both ways. Either I was a member of an elite or I was not. If the former, it was no use placing me in front of a jury. The electorate is not an elite. Those twelve men and women, chosen at random from the electoral register, are 'the people'. Have you *seen* 'the people'? It was no use expecting me, à la Kieran, to twinkle and appear like one of them — a man who 'watched the game' and 'liked a bird with big tits', with or without a moustache. I was the son of a judge. I should therefore appear in front of a judge, in civil trials *sans* jury. I understood how to speak to a judge, listen to a judge, respect a judge, assist a judge in reaching the correct decision.

So. I thought of Ticky as a judge. I would address her with respect but without ingratiation. I would give Ticky my *best point*, as I would give a judge. But one does not simply give a best point. One says one is going to give it, one gives it and, finally, one says one's given it. A best point must be made three times. It deserves to crow thrice.

I was a barrister on a sofa with a girl. I would

not pretend to be a charming seducer. I wouldn't be something I wasn't. Under pressure, I would be myself. That is what integrity *means*.

★ ★ ★

'Why are you here, then?' asked Ticky Moxon-Smith.

'I want to have sex.'

I stopped. Then I added, far too late: 'With you.' Ticky, unfortunately, spotted the pause and wasn't slow to mock it.

'You want to have sex' — she paused and she paused — 'with me. You've picked on me. Why me?' Downstairs, a door slammed. 'There you are. My neighbour's back. Why don't you ask her?'

I was in difficulty. It seemed that Ticky, not I, was the one with a best point. But any young barrister will have moments like this. I had absolute confidence in my ability to marshal my argument and win.

'I know you'll understand what I'm going to say,' I began. Now I was in command. 'I don't love you,' I continued, setting up my best point. 'I don't love you so I can't hurt you. Dick Gage loved you and he hurt you. But I don't love you. So I can't hurt you.'

'God, you're such a weird little man,' said Ticky.

Do you see? This was not a 'no'.

★ ★ ★

I took off my glasses and put them on her bedside table. My eyeballs bulged as Ticky squeezed my testicles.

'Does Christopher Pilkington know you're here?' She said his name in a curious way, as if Pilkington were a famous person she'd never met.

'No,' I replied.

'I suppose you don't know anything about foreplay,' she said.

'I know a little. But I bow to your superior knowledge.' There was respect, there was acknowledgement of Ticky's senior status. It was all I could do not to say: 'I know a little, Your Honour.'

And so it was that, sometime around 11 p.m. on Friday 20th July 1979, I had sexual intercourse. It involved Ticky in a great deal of work, which I need not detail here. Suffice to say, she'd inherited from her mother, Amanda Moxon-Smith, the ability to cajole. I was intellectually aroused — excited I'd persuaded her into bed. What happened after that was secondary. I was perfectly content to delegate everything to her.

'Fuck me!' she shouted. I found this offensive. You do not shout 'Feed me!' to a waiter. The waiter is well aware what you want and asks only for your patience.

In the morning, she said: 'You know this won't happen again.'

'I know,' I replied. This was just as I intended. I'd gone to Ticky Moxon-Smith to lose my virginity. One can't lose one's virginity twice.

'Would you mind if I got up and went to Waitrose? I want to get there before the crowds.'

'Absolutely,' I said.

'You don't have to leave. Relax. Help yourself to coffee and toast.'

In the end, it was she who made me the coffee and toast. The toast was on the cusp of burnt but I could not be seen to scrape it. The coffee was made with a volume of liquid sufficient to house a goldfish. This was all a consequence of her desire to make us both relaxed. We should have been true to our tension and parted company as soon as we could. In the event, I was obliged to remain when she left, to show her I was 'relaxed' about the toast. Once the door slammed, I poured my coffee down the sink and placed the toast in the bin, at the bottom, underneath the yogurt pots and cottage-cheese cartons, so it couldn't be seen or smelt. Then I counted to a hundred and left, which relaxed me completely. I whistled as I walked back to Sloane Square station. My mission had been accomplished. I'd passed another exam. What exam had I yet failed?

★　★　★

A fortnight later, I was in Aldeburgh for a weekend with my parents. On the Saturday morning, still whistling, I took Duncan, my parents' West Highland terrier, for a walk through the allotments then up to the river wall. There we encountered Boo Risdon and Bumper.

'Morning,' I said, with good cheer. Our

56

Duncan stopped to sniff her Bumper's bottom.

'Why didn't you tell him?' asked Boo.

'Why didn't I tell who what?'

'You ashamed of her? She's been my best friend since I was ten. *She* had to tell him. How d'you think that felt?'

'I have nothing to say,' I said. And said it.

Boo Risdon stomped off, yanking Bumper away from Duncan, as if he were one of her Bumper's turds. Of her many breaches of dog walker's etiquette — her failure to reply to my 'Morning', her failure to remark on the weather, her unsolicited intensity and 'personal' remarks — this was the most offensive. She was punishing Duncan for the crime of which she'd found me guilty. She was visiting the sins of the walker on the walked.

Of what was I guilty? I couldn't understand. Clearly, I'd failed to tell 'him' of my intercourse with Ticky. But who was 'he' and why would I tell him? Ticky had told Boo Risdon everything — that much was clear. The implication was that verbal incontinence was standard.

If I had a best friend, it was Jeremy Hamilton-Wood. What had Jeremy told me, since the age of ten, when we were not busy riding our bikes or sailing or playing tennis? Had he asked me about my private life or told me about his own? No. Was this omission harmful to our friendship? When Jeremy's mother died of cancer, when he was fifteen years old, whom did he rely upon not to ask about it, when, all around, women were demanding to know how he was and what he felt about how he was and how he was about what he felt? I said, 'Bad luck.' He thanked me. Not for saying 'bad luck' but for saying nothing more. And then I asked him if he'd like to serve first, which he knew was a form of condolence.

I walked Duncan along the river wall, towards its junction with the shingle path that leads southwards from the town to the yacht club and the Martello Tower. A VW Golf Convertible sped past on its way to the yacht club. As Duncan and I turned left at the junction and headed towards the town, our ears were pricked by the sound of a soprano engine. I turned my head to see the rear of the Golf grow larger and more menacing as it came towards us. The driver was, incredibly, reverse-speeding. Shingle spat at our ankles as Pilkington came to a stop. He yanked the handbrake as if intent on pulling it out.

'Don't ever go near Ticky again.'

Duncan barked. I merely stood there and looked at him, a task made easier by his reflective sunglasses.

★   ★   ★

Pilkington had not had sex with Ticky. His remark on the sea wall — 'She needed cheering up' — was a bluff. He'd got 'bladdered' with Ticky, yes, but nothing more. He was uncertain if he wanted Ticky or Ticky wanted him. Pilkington was inhibited. It was only after Ticky told him about our sex that Pilkington made his move.

Do you understand, as I did not? I was meant

to tell Pilkington about my intercourse with Ticky, to goad him. That was a condition of Ticky's consenting to our sex. I was meant to go from her bed to the wall outside the pub. I was meant to slap Pilkington on the shoulder and remark, in a rough-hewn sort of way: 'Guess who I had intercourse with? Ticky! Crisp?'[1]

I intended Ticky Moxon-Smith to relieve me of my virginity, without feeling, repetition or reportage. This I achieved. The relief of my virginity was the sole intended consequence of my action. I could not be held responsible for the labyrinthine consequences imposed upon my action by others. I maintained my dignity while others lost theirs: the speeding Pilkington, the offensive Boo, the manipulative Ticky.

As Duncan and I walked past Austin's Hotel, we heard a cry from the other side of the street: 'Tickyshagger!' It was Catto. Who was the undignified fool? The man who shouted 'Tickyshagger!' for all to hear? Or the 'Ticky-shagger' himself, who refused to acknowledge

---

[1] How detailed was I meant to be? Should I have told him that Ticky vomited? This was either the fruits of alcoholic intake or a kind of motion sickness. I was lying on top of her at the time, imitating the action of a man having sex. Her vomiting was not without benefit, though. We stopped. Sex stops, I'd been given to understand, when both partners achieve orgasm. Had Ticky not vomited, I believe I'd still be there, twenty-seven years later, urging her to be patient.

him, who stared straight ahead and carried on walking his parents' much-loved terrier?

★ ★ ★

A year later, Ticky and Pilkington were married. In irrational moments, of which thankfully I have few, I think of myself as somehow responsible and wonder if I should have done with Ticky what Edward Heath would have done, which is to say nothing at all.

5

My Mistake
(1983)

In *Diamond Bay Records* v. *Planet Q Records* (1983), I appeared for Diamond Bay. They had previously instructed Alan Barnes, also a member of my chambers. Barnes was tremendously able. Unfortunately, he was also forty, divorced and in search of excitement.

Alan Barnes went native. He said 'yes' to everything the record company offered. If no offer was forthcoming, he volunteered. He became an aerial hitch-hiker, inviting himself onto private jets bound for launch parties in Paris, 'video shoots' in Rio de Janeiro, stadium 'gigs' in Tokyo. He bought a white suit. He sat in recording studios and nodded his head. He became the constant companion of Jacko Holmes, the drummer of a Diamond Bay group called Madagascar Sam.

Despite the frilly shirts, the high cheekbones and candyfloss hair, Holmes was the aggressive son of a Birmingham window cleaner. He drank two bottles of brandy a day, or three if the group was flying from Heathrow to Los Angeles, thereby gaining an extra eight hours of brandy-drinking day. In a hotel room in Hollywood, Holmes punched Alan Barnes for looking at his drums 'in the wrong way', though Barnes insisted there were no drums in the room. Diamond Bay, however unjustly, sided with Jacko Holmes and fired Barnes.

By the time I was instructed, Madagascar Sam had in turn fired Jacko Holmes. They were tired of his drinking and his tantrums and the drumming to his own beat. The belligerent Holmes formed his own band, called Madagascar Sam We Are Not.

Diamond Bay sued MSWAN's record company, Planet Q, for identity theft and passing off. Counsel for Planet Q claimed that no identity could be more distinct from Madagascar Sam's than Madagascar Sam We Are Not's, whose very name defined them in contra-distinction to Madagascar Sam.

I advised Diamond Bay to hire three unemployed 'moles' to go into fifty-nine record shops in the Greater London area and ask for 'the Madagascar Sam single'. (This was in the Christmas period, when both groups had singles 'out'.) In thirteen shops, they were offered the single by Madagascar Sam We Are Not. Counsel for Planet Q argued that this was 'no more than twenty per cent' (though it is, in fact, twenty-two per cent). She also maintained that, since the record sleeve clearly stated the name of the band as Madagascar Sam We Are Not, it was a mistake any 'genuine purchaser for value' would 'easily spot' from a 'cursory glance at the sleeve', prior to handing over their money for an item they did not want.

I countered, first, that Madagascar Sam was,

on this evidence, at risk of losing twenty-two per cent of their singles sales to a devious, calculating and vengeful pirate. This was a totally unacceptable percentage. (I argued, in fact, that *any* percentage was totally unacceptable.) Second, I pointed out that the words 'We Are Not' on the sleeve of the MSWAN single were obscured by a woman's bikini-clad bottom, the blackness of the bikini obliterating the 'are' and the 'N' completely. Third, I asserted that record buyers who were partially sighted, blind, trusting or casual would not 'easily spot' the mistake from a 'cursory glance at the sleeve'. They wouldn't glance at the sleeve at all, cursorily or otherwise.

Finally, I pointed out that, just as the London Philharmonic Orchestra was known as the 'London Phil', so Madagascar Sam We Are Not was known as — wait for it! — 'Madagascar Sam'. I adduced in evidence nineteen internal memos, where they were so named, from MSWAN's *own record company*, Planet Q, who were, of course, the defendants in the case.

The judge found for Diamond Bay. I won.

★   ★   ★

In the robing room, my opponent was thoroughly vexed. Why were the three unemployed 'moles' all in wheelchairs? She accused me of 'grandstanding'. She was not amused when I asked if she meant 'grandsitting-down'.

By advising Diamond Bay to hire 'moles' both disabled and unemployed, I was not cheating.

Nothing in the rules of evidence precluded it. I was merely presenting my client the record company in the most favourable light — to a judge who might assume they were driven by forty parts drugs to sixty parts greed. No. They gave work to disabled people, one of them a woman.

At no point in the case did I refer to their disablement. I did not dab my eye with a handkerchief while they were giving evidence. I did not ask if they were tired, nor offer them glasses of water. I will grant my opponent this, though: the wheelchair ruse was a theatrical gesture, one that drew attention to itself. It was drama.

Out of court, drama was something I sought to avoid. I acquired this trait from my father. As a judge, he spent all day with murderers, rapists and fraudsters. Out of court, he never had an overdue library book. He didn't merely, in other words, not commit crimes. He did not commit infringements of any codes. He followed every footpath. He shut every gate. He eschewed altercations, confrontations, indiscretions, jealousy and lust — all the stuff of drama.

I salute him. My incident with Ticky is a perfect example. I set out to avoid drama. I had drama thrust upon me.

★ ★ ★

A grateful Diamond Bay invited me to the 1983 Record Industry Awards, which took place in mid-April at the Grosvenor House Hotel in

Mayfair. Naturally, I had no interest in going. But I felt it impolite to refuse.

The invitation said 'Black Tie', which pleased me. Dress conventions allow one to pass unnoticed in the crowd. I duly wore the black dinner jacket, black dress trousers, white dress shirt and black bow tie which my father had bought me from Moss Bros for my twenty-first birthday, in lieu of Maurice's night with Fifi.

Regrettably, though, I didn't pass unnoticed. I was the only man at my table dressed in Black Tie. I was the rule that proved the exceptions. There were bow ties, yes, but they were pink, blue or spotty. There was a red frock coat and a snakeskin jacket. Two seats away, a man with a wedding ring sported a dress.[1]

'I could do with a decent meal. We've just come back from Japan.' So said the woman on my right, with no introduction. She was large, managerial, confident and ugly. She assumed I knew and cared who she was and who 'we' were, this 'we' who'd come back from Japan. She told me 'we' were 'getting bigger' in Asia, then defensively added that 'we' weren't getting any smaller at home. She referred to Great Britain as 'the UK market', as if the entire population had fingerless gloves and a stall.

Mercifully, this woman made several visits to the lavatory, returning each time to resume her monologue where she left off, only louder. She

[1] In his defence, the dress was full-length, sky blue and chiffon, which was thoroughly appropriate for the occasion.

went there, I deduced, to take loudening drugs. Here was another convention honoured only in the breach: the use of the lavatories for lavatorial purposes. On my sole visit to the Gents, only I behaved like a Gent. Flushes were replaced by snorts. Bowls enjoyed a ceasefire. Men entered cubicles two by two, like Noah's Cocaine Arks.

I was proud to be in a minority of one, though it did not make for an entertaining evening.

'There's Simon and Roger! I gotta say hello!' said the large managerial woman, with such urgency that she surprised her chair, which fell backwards as she sprang to her feet. She waddled off, very fast, to form a big barrier between Simon and Roger and their destination.

I bent down to pick up the chair. When I stood up again, I found I was not alone. 'This is my chance to talk to you,' said Judy Page.

* * *

The table was round. Judy Page had been sitting at two o'clock from me. Earlier, during the salmon mousse, she'd stared at me. Being a gentleman, I didn't look back. I studied the label on the mineral water. She looked at me again as the waitress poured my coffee. Once more I took evasive action, studying the wording on my green-wrapped mint, to determine why Avon Radio had sponsored it. Avon Radio, it transpired, wanted me to believe I could 'make a mint' by advertising on their station. Duly embarrassed, I replaced the mint on its saucer. I looked up. Remarkably, Judy Page was still

66

staring, staring and smiling. I had never seen anyone with a smiling stare.

Now, here she was.

'I'm Judy. I've been watching you. You're the cleverest man in the room.'

'Thank you,' I said, as she sat down in the now-upright chair. 'But you haven't met all the men in the room.'

'I don't need to,' said Judy Page. The big woman returned. Judy Page didn't move. The big woman sat in Judy Page's chair.

She worked as a secretary to a music publisher. Her father was a builder and her mother worked in Boots the chemist. She'd trained as a ballerina but her career was cut short as she'd grown into 'too much of a woman'. Her mother, who'd grown up in south London, had had 'a relationship' in her late teens with a 'famous actor'. She paused to allow me to ask who it was. In gentlemanly fashion, I didn't enquire. She therefore vouchsafed the name herself: 'Michael Caine'.[1]

She asked me how I came to be at the Record Industry Awards. When I told her, she said she'd read about the case in *Music Week*. I was as clever as she'd predicted, no, *known*. She told

---

[1] When she told this to Mike Bell in Andros, she said her mother had gone out with *Sir* Michael Caine. This was untrue. Caine, when he went out with her mother, was an un-ennobled youth. Curiously, both Michael Caine and Sir Michael Caine will appear again in my story, albeit in photographs only.

me she was never wrong about people.

The first award of the night went to Simon and Roger and friends, who turned out to be in a group called Duran Duran. The man in the sky-blue dress stuck two fingers in his mouth, whistled, then stood up to applaud. Judy Page followed suit, then, sensing my discomfort, put her hand on my shoulder, leaned down and whispered: 'It's OK. You don't have to join us.' I nodded. Judy Page empowered me. She allowed me to be myself, a man indifferent to the triumph of Duran Duran. Yet she handicapped me too. I was the only person in the room not standing up. I understood, briefly but importantly, how those witnesses in their wheelchairs must have felt.

Duran Duran left the podium. Judy Page sat down. Now, since the ceremony was under way, everything she said to me was whispered. With every word, she drew my ear closer to her mouth.

'They're Princess Diana's favourite band. But I don't think you like her, do you?'

I shook my head. I felt queasy. How did she know me, to such an extent?

What seemed like a thousand awards later, the master of ceremonies said:

'And now we come to the award for the Best Award.'

No one noticed, except me. Why was I still there? Why was anyone still there? I looked at my watch.

'I have to go home now,' I said.

'Right,' said Judy Page. 'I'll come with you.

Just let me finish my drink.'

My profession and lifeblood have been the analysis of statute, contract, agreement and word. Yet I cannot explain why Judy Page said what she said. I can give an account of what happened. But I cannot account *for* it. My announcement that I was going home was a fact. How did she construe it as an invitation? Why did I walk out into the night with Judy Page's arm in mine? Why did I say 'Goodnight' to Simon and Roger as if, through my link with her, I were linked to them? One minute later, Judy Page and I were in a taxi, heading for my flat in Canonbury, London N1. Why?

With Ticky Moxon-Smith, I had a purpose. With Judy Page, I had none. The purpose was all Judy Page's. It was, I believe, twofold: to come home with me and, en route, to render herself indispensable. It was she who hailed the taxi, she who told the taxi driver my address (having ascertained it from me seconds earlier), she who talked to the taxi driver so that I could rest in peace.

'Nice night?' he bellowed, to the two prisoners in his mobile jail and, yes, she told him of the niceness of our night in all the detail he craved. When His Loudmouth asked what Duran Duran and Spandau Ballet [sic] were like, she replied: 'Haven't you had them in the back of your cab?'

'That's a good one! There's loads of them, aren't there! And the hangers-on! I couldn't fit them all in!' Thus did he helpfully explain the joke to the person who'd made it.

Then Judy Page said: 'No more talking, thank you.'

'Right you are, darling,' said the taxi driver, as silently impressed as I was. Who'd dare say such a thing? To the hailing, the giving of the address and the talking could be added the order to shut up. I thought of her, already, as the woman who saved me from doing what had to be done. Therefore, when she put her hand on my knee, I felt that a hand on my knee was a necessity, that somehow my knee was under attack or in danger of coming loose.

'I've always wanted to meet a judge. Can you introduce me?'

'Of course,' I said. 'You can meet my father. My father's a judge.'

'That's wonderful,' she said. 'I'll make sure I look nice for him.'

We stopped at the traffic lights in Theobald's Road. She took her hand away from my knee, as if, when the vehicle was stationary, my knee were perfectly safe. Then she looked down at my trousers and lowered her head. I knew at once that Judy Page had lost a contact lens, having seen my sister, from the age of sixteen, desperately scanning sofas and carpets and rugs with her fingers as if she were speed-reading Braille. I kept perfectly still, as Judy Page placed her hands on the crotch of my trousers.

'Can you see it?' I asked.

'Buttons,' she said, as if expecting a zip and, because I am a man of strong beliefs, I carried on believing she was searching for a lens, till obliged to admit no lens could have found its way onto the top of my member.

The traffic lights turned red-and-amber as Judy Page vacated her seat and knelt on the floor. They turned green as Judy Page clamped herself, orally, to said member. I had attended Winchester College, Christ Church, Oxford, *Black Emmanuelle Goes East*, the bedroom of Ticky Moxon-Smith. Nothing had prepared me for this. At twenty-seven, I didn't know the word for it, in English or even Latin — which is to say I didn't know of its existence. I was shocked. This was an act, a sexual act. Why hadn't I been asked? Whence derived Judy Page's presumption of my consent? Was she not, as it were, snogging my dog?[1]

I found it difficult to remain detached, given that my member was certainly enjoying it, even if I wasn't. I was keen to assert the primacy of mind over body. If I could be pleasured against my will, what price my will? 'To give yourself to pleasure.' There, in a nutshell, is the price pleasure pays for your soul. Nothing! If I gave myself to pleasure, I'd be giving away honour, industry, dignity and duty — my civilised self. I'd be Alan Barnes.

Mike Bell, of course, would and did argue. A 'blow job' — for that, I learned in Andros, is what it's called — a blow job was, according to

---

[1] I do not subscribe to what I call the Pornographic Fallacy. This states that a man's consent to a non-violent sexual act can be presumed, unless he's in a coma.

him, the *highest form* of civilisation. It distinguished man from animals. I conceded that, in a lifetime of watching David Attenborough, I'd never once heard him whisper 'blow job', nor seen him crouching near one. Nevertheless, the claim was absurd. What distinguished man from animals was science, law, morality, philosophy, architecture, reason, music. Had Bell never heard Bach's *Goldberg Variations*? No, said Bell, he hadn't. But he knew it couldn't compare with a blow job from Mrs Goldberg.

I looked down, in shame, which was ill-advised, as it merely afforded me an uninterrupted view of the head of Judy Page. I was struck, more than anything, by her genuflection. It suggested servitude. Yet the servitude was not as it seemed. I was the servant, she the 'master', though the physical geography told a different story.

'Was it Canonbury Park North, guv, or Canonbury Park South? Only there's two of them, aren't there? There's Canonbury Park North and there's Canonbury Park South.'

I hadn't thought of the cab driver since the blow job had begun, such was its mental grip. What did he see as he spoke to me, looking in his rear-view mirror? My head alone was visible, my Canonbury Park North. He was, mercifully, oblivious to the goings-on in the South. In order to conceal those goings-on from him, I merely had to look like man who was not in receipt of a blow job. I'd looked like such a man for more than twenty-seven years. It was simply a question of looking like myself. But I couldn't do it. I'd lost myself. I could not gain access to my own face. I looked out of the window. I pretended not to have heard.

'Did you hear me, guv? I was asking if it was Canonbury Park North or Canonbury Park South cos there's two of them,' he bored. 'There's Canonbury Park North — '

'It's Canonbury Terrace,' said Judy Page, indispensably. I thought this miraculous. I did not know that, when a woman did a blow job, she could still hear.

'Thanks luv,' said the cab driver.

My member stood proud of my fly like a glistening sentry. With what could I hide it? I wished I belonged to a former generation, in which gentlemen carried hats. Judy Page, as always — already, I say *always* — did what had to be done. She reached into the inside pocket of my dinner jacket. She removed my wallet. When the taxi stopped, she got out and paid the driver.

★   ★   ★

I barely slept, overstimulated by the presence of Judy Page, her animal warmth. At quarter to six, I got up, taking care not to wake her. She rolled over and her black hair invaded my vacated pillow.

I wrote her a note, explaining that I had to catch a train from Paddington at 06.41. I changed the ending many times. *Yours sincerely, Robert. Yours, Robert. Robert. R.* Finally, I

73

settled on a blank. I would leave her to deduce the note's author.

At 10 a.m., in the district registry in Bristol, appearing before Mr Justice Mead, I opened as follows:

'Your Honour, in this case I appear for Bristol City Council.'

'No you don't, Mr Purcell,' said Mr Justice Mead.

'You're quite right, Your Honour,' I replied. 'Thank you for correcting me. I appear for Baker-Moore Properties Ltd.' I incorporated his correction so smoothly, so fluently, that one could believe my mistake was intentional, designed to provide Mr Justice Mead with a pleasing opportunity to show he was 'on the ball'. When I thanked him, he nodded, thanking me for thanking him: if my purpose were to put the judge in a benevolent mood, I could not have succeeded better. Judy Page, the cause of my sleeplessness, had only temporarily diverted me from my path, the path up which I travelled daily, the path of cogency and forensic excellence.

★   ★   ★

When I unlocked the door of my flat, at seven that night, I heard noises from my kitchen. I had a burglar, doubtless a boy from the estate opposite my flat. I was terrified. As I stood clutching the small marble bust of my ancestor Henry Purcell, which dwelt on the table to the right of my door, I was more terrified of what I might do than what the burglar might do. A man like me, ill-versed in violence, didn't know the degree of swing needed to immobilise an intruder with a bust. I didn't even know which end to use: plinth or wig? As a law-abiding man, I was, ironically, more likely to kill him than he was to kill me. He was experienced at confrontation. He would know how to render a homeowner powerless, using minimum force, thus impressing the magistrate with his restraint. He wouldn't bludgeon me with a marble Henry. He would probably put his thumbs in his ears, waggle his fingers and go: 'Boo!'

When Judy Page came out of my kitchen, she found my brandishing of the bust 'funny'. She'd arrived an hour earlier, wanting to surprise me. She'd explained the situation to my downstairs neighbour, a doctor and Cambridge graduate whom I entrusted with a spare key to my flat.

What could I say to this intruder, who'd gained entry to my property to provide, not remove? My supper was ready. What would I have had for supper, if she'd not been waiting for me?

* * *

Later that night, I succeeded in having sex, even though my penis was thoroughly exhausted from travelling to Bristol and back in a day.

'You haven't had a lot of sex in your life, have you?'

'No more or less than I expected,' I replied.

75

Judy Page lay on the duvet and raised her legs in the air.

'What do you think?' she asked.

I replied, truthfully: 'Yes, they're very good, though I haven't seen that many pairs.'

★ ★ ★

At midday the next day, Saturday, we were buying a rug from Liberty's. She told me I ought to have a rug in my sitting room, in front of the fireplace. I'd never considered this. I simply didn't know that this was what had to be done. But she was certain and her certainty overpowered my ignorance.

'You'll get so much pleasure from this,' said the Liberty's assistant, to Judy Page and me.

'We will,' said Judy Page, doing a little shimmy, girlishly thrilled. The assistant smiled at me with an expression I hadn't seen before. It said: 'You are half of a happy couple. You are the patron of this shimmy.' I could not control what the assistant thought. Judy Page, by contrast, could.

Judy Page saw a kilim and exhaled with joy.

'God, that would look so fantastic in the attic!'

'I don't have an attic,' I replied.

'I do!' she said.

'Thank you! It's fantastic!' said Judy Page, as she put down the kilim in the attic room of her maisonette in Cricklewood.

'My pleasure,' I replied. She didn't know how long she'd live there. She felt she was destined for special things and would live in a special

76

place. But, wherever she went, she'd always take the kilim with her.

'Do you want to see me in the dress?'

'Yes,' I said, though I'd seen her in the dress in the shop, the one we went to after Liberty's and before the Conran Shop. She put on the dress. It was black with a bow at the back. At this point, a novelist or poet might describe how Judy Page looked in that dress. They'd do this to bring Judy Page 'to life'. But I'm not a novelist, nor a poet. I'm a confessor. Let me confess, then, my reluctance to bring Judy Page to life. It is not in my interests. I find it disturbing. I wish for the opposite. Not to bring her to death, for that would be illegal, but to render her obscure, opaque, inchoate and a long, long way away.

Judy Page had black hair and angular features. This makes her sound like a crow, a scary crow, as opposed to a scarecrow. She was certainly far more expensively dressed than a scarecrow.

★   ★   ★

Two weeks later, she worried about wearing her new dress for the annual drinks party in my chambers.

'Do you think it's too short?'

'Yes,' I replied.

'Why? Don't you think you can be serious and sexy? Why are Englishwomen so weird about being sexy? Why can't they be like French-women?'

I was not equipped for questions like this. My instinct was to ask her to write them down, as if reference books and time would enable me to find the answers. Judy Page, after leaving school, had been au pair in Paris to an oil executive and his wife. But the wife did not exemplify the French sexuality to which Judy Page referred. No — she herself was the exemplar. She knew, from the way the executive looked at her, that she had acquired Gallic allure from breathing the Gauloises-fumed air. By nineteen, bathetically, she was back in England, married to a builder from whom she was divorced by twenty-one. He was, she said, 'an uncouth man with a great body'. Then she added — saying what needed to be said — 'He was nothing like *you*.'

She was undereducated but, to her credit, keen to make up for lost time. I was happy to explain concepts such as 'tort' and 'common law'. I introduced her to Bach. I lent her my copy of John Rawls' *A Theory of Justice* which she told me she read on the tube, to her great satisfaction, while other girls read something called *Ms London*.

On Sunday mornings, in my living room, she'd put on Bach's Cello Suites. Unlike me, she wasn't content to listen. She said that the music spoke to her. It literally moved her. And that was why Judy Page hoovered, naked, to Bach's Cello Suites, in either the Casals or Rostropovich or Fournier versions, all of which I owned.

Did this need to be done? Absolutely. She showed me the areas Deirdre had neglected — under tables, beneath the spaghetti of wires descending from my hi-fi. Deirdre, my cleaner, who lived on the estate, came once a week in my absence. How could I be sure she came at all? I replied that the ten-pound note on the kitchen table was gone by Wednesday night. Judy Page pursed her lips. Somehow, that proved her point.

To watch her nakedly vacuuming — part princess, part Cinderella — was to witness the changes she'd wrought in my life in a matter of three weeks. The rug was new. Judy Page was new. Nudity was new.

The Bach was perforce at high volume, to overcome the hoover. Loud music and nudity were transforming my flat into some kind of audio-visual attraction. Was Judy Page not concerned that she was drawing undue attention to herself and, therefore, me?

'Let them look if they want to, if they've got nothing better to do.' The display, she implied, wasn't sexual, unless others made it so.

I took to standing at the window, on the lookout for men looking in. I couldn't admit this was my purpose, since, according to her, nothing furtive was taking place. I looked at the balconies of the council flats opposite, for Cello Suite after Cello Suite. Theo, the Cypriot who ran the mini-market round the corner, selling everything and nothing, had taken to sitting on his balcony every Sunday at eleven to read his paper, looking up between pages, which were short as his paper was a tabloid. When he looked, I waved but he never waved back, though in the shop he was always friendly, not to say fawning, which I concede I rather enjoyed. He looked through me and past me, on either side, tracing the lateral movements of

Judy Page and her Hoover.

Then, one Sunday, Theo was no longer there. When I went into the mini-market the next evening, to buy my fortnightly bottle of washing-up liquid, I heard Theo's son telling a customer that his father had died the previous week, of pneumonia.

Theo was old. He'd worked hard all his life. He'd recently endured, as we all had, a spell of bad weather. Did Theo die of sitting outside? Did he die from cold looking? Did Judy Page, frankly, kill him? No. That is far-fetched or, as we say in the law, *too remote*. She cannot be held responsible for the unforeseeable consequences of her actions, any more than I could be held responsible for the marriage of Ticky and Pilkington.

What one can say is this: she provoked the circumstances in which Theo's death was facilitated. She killed Theo in the same way she killed my father. Were it not for Judy Page, my father would have died anyway. But he would have died later.

Of course, it's no defence to murder to say that the victim would have died anyway, later. We will all die anyway, later. But I write that as a son, not a lawyer. As a lawyer, I accuse her of nothing.

★   ★   ★

Concerned about the length of Judy Page's dress, I wrote a note to Eleanor Gorringe, wife of my head of chambers, asking her what length was appropriate for the chambers cocktail party. Her reply — 'Whatever looks nice' — was utterly unhelpful. It was just the kind of waffle one would expect from a founder of the Social Democratic Party.

I feared for Judy Page as I waited for her, prior to the party, in a wine bar in the Strand. I feared for myself. She lacked education and her dress was too short. She, and therefore I, would be a laughing stock.

My fears were compounded by my cold. Judy Page could not have been sweeter, arriving with aspirin and lozenges and vapour rub, saying 'Poor you!', sitting close to me and massaging my thigh, though the cold was in my head. But my cold, in turn, was compounded by bad temper. When she took off her coat, I felt outraged. How could so little material have cost me three hundred pounds?

My mood altered within minutes of our arrival at the party. Judy Page was surrounded by the great and the good. They lapped up her tales of Duran Duran, France, her love of Bach. I was able to hang back from the group and enjoy a dignified solitude.

Chief among her surrounders was Alan Temperley, now, of course, Lord Chancellor, then a barrister of five years' call like me. When she went off to get a drink, he came over to me and said: 'You lucky fucker! What's a girl with legs like that doing with a boring twat like you?'

'Everything you'd expect,' I replied. It was the first time in my life I'd been the object of male sexual jealousy. (Pilkington, vis à vis Ticky, was merely proprietorial.) I was surprised how pleasing I found it, especially as I loathed Alan Temperley and he loathed me.

Alan Temperley was in my year at Oxford. He came fourth in the Bar finals of 1979. (To give you an idea of what that means, I came third.) But law was not his *raison d'être*, any more than it was Mike Bell's. Temperley was a politician. He wanted to be loved by the British People, in order to win their votes. Hence the 'fucker', thus the 'twat' — all the mateyness designed to please pub-goers everywhere. I ask you, though: do pub-goers want their MP saying 'twat'? Wouldn't they rather his manner were remote and his language complex? Wouldn't they prefer it if he ignored them utterly, too preoccupied with matters of state? Don't pub-goers want, in a Member of Parliament, a man who doesn't go to pubs, those parliaments — as they well know — of fools?

An hour later, I found myself at the drinks table with Eleanor Gorringe and Temperley's wife, the luckless Honor. They were looking at their husbands, who were talking to Judy Page.

'What rock was she found under?' asked Eleanor Gorringe.

'I don't know,' said Honor. 'Alan says she's had a hard life.'

'I'm sure the dress is making it easier,' said Eleanor, suddenly devoid of Social Democratic instincts.

'Where's your lady friend then?' she asked, turning to me. 'I'd like to see *her* dress.'

'I can't see her,' I replied, which was true. Alan

Temperley was blocking my view. This was not disloyalty. I simply did not want to embarrass the wife of my head of chambers.

★ ★ ★

In the taxi back to my flat, she was excited.[1] She felt she'd made a connection with Alan Temperley and Gerard Gorringe. Lawyers, she said, had fascinating minds.

It was time, she said, for me to take her to Aldeburgh to meet my father.

★ ★ ★

We arrived on the Friday night.

'Welcome,' said my father, as we entered the kitchen. He smiled benevolently and extended a delicate hand.

'Would you like a drink?' asked my mother, not touching Judy Page but looking at her with her best horse-appraising stare.

'Yes, thank you. I bought you these.' Judy Page gave my mother a box of liqueur chocolates.

'You shouldn't have,' said my mother, placing the chocolates on the draining board.

---

[1] You will wait in vain for more taxi blow jobs. The blow jobs dried up. I did not ask after them, presuming that they no longer had to be done. I don't wish to explore the matter further. But sitting here now, writing this, I *am* exploring the matter further, whether I wish to or not. Truly, there's no safe haven in the mind.

Judy Page looked around the kitchen and remarked on the 'lovely watercolours' of the Martello Tower and the fishermen's huts, knowing they'd been painted by my mother's mother, the (long-dead) Granny P. Then she asked for the 'tour'. My mother dutifully took her round the house, while I hovered as far behind them as I could, without actually being outdoors.

'That's where the wellington boots live,' said my mother, opening a door into a cupboard darker than hell, but damper.

We entered the living room. 'Robert said your house was very special.' My mother winced at her bandying of my name. 'Everything's so lovely and old!' said Judy Page, as she wondered what kind of creatures might live down the holes in our brown leather chesterfield sofa.

'We should eat,' said my mother.

'I'll just get changed,' said Judy Page.

Half an hour later, she came down to dinner, wearing the dress I had bought her for the occasion. It was knee-length and demure. It was worth the money. My mother, still in her golfing clothes, surely admired it.

It was late May. We ate what my father called the Aldeburgh Holy Trinity: asparagus, cod and rhubarb. While my mother clattered about in the background, Judy Page engaged my father in conversation. She asked him what he'd been asked a million times, but she asked it with more eye contact, more nodding, more refilling of his glass, more little laughs: Was it lonely being a judge? Had he ever looked into a courtroom to see a friend of his in the dock? Had he ever regretted a guilty verdict? My father explained, gently, that in jury trials it was the jury not the judge who brought the guilty verdict.

My mother, at the draining board, forked the asparagus, unsure if it was cooked. Then, instead of forking it, she ate it. She ate it and pronounced it, at thirty-second intervals, 'not quite done'. By the time it was quite done, half of it was gone. Judy Page went 'yum yum' as her two spears were presented — a 'yum' for each spear. Her determination to make the best of it had to be admired.

'Won't the long-playing record eventually be supplanted by the cassette tape?' asked my father. She loved the question. My father, the judge, the silver-haired judge, was seeking her opinion. He had the gift of seeming interested. What is politeness, if not that? When he asked her, moments later, who Duran Duran were, he made her feel he wanted to know. He wasn't abasing himself to her level. He was elevating her level to his own.

My mother put the fish plates on the sideboard, then sat back down at the table and said: 'Come on then, old boy.' This was my father's cue to serve the dessert. He waited, as he always did, for my mother to finish smoking her inter-course cigarette. She looked for her ashtray, which she'd left on the sideboard. Thinking and moving faster than anyone, Judy Page got up and fetched it.

'You've got a smashing pair of legs,' said my mother.

'Thank you, kind sir!'

This was a mistake anyone could have made. There is no female equivalent — no 'kind madam' — and of course Judy Page was more used to leg praise from men than women. I hoped the moment would pass. I tried to help it pass by remarking on the excellence of my mother's rhubarb crumble, to which we were all looking forward. But my mother was stuck on Judy's legs. My mother said: 'I bet you have trouble keeping them shut.'

Judy Page flushed. She stared at me, wanting me to leap to her defence. But I was not a leaper. I was rehearsing an argument to make to her later. My argument was that my mother's remark was not an insult but a French-style celebration of Judy Page's sensuality. Regrettably, I could find no evidence to support this argument. My father, with his gift for rising above it, asked Judy Page if she played bridge, explaining that our family liked to play bridge after supper.

'Perhaps Lady Purcell would prefer to play strip poker,' said Judy Page. If she intended, with this remark, to divide and rule my parents, she did not succeed.

'That wouldn't be equitable, would it?' said my father, gently. 'I have shirt, tie, vest, underpants, trousers, socks and shoes. You're not even wearing a tie.' He smiled. She smiled back, beguiled. It was an example of the small miracles that can be achieved by gentility.

My mother cackled.

'Well said, old boy! On with the milky coffee!'

'Would you like coffee?' my father asked Judy Page. 'This is where I come into my own.' With that, he went to the cupboard and produced a tin of Nescafé, large as a gallon of paint.

★ ★ ★

At midnight, in my Aldeburgh bedroom, directly above my parents', Judy Page said: 'Your father's a honey. I'll save you from your mother. Where you going?'

I said I was going downstairs to get a glass of water. She asked me why I hadn't asked her if she wanted one too. I asked her if she wanted one. She said no.

I did indeed want a glass of water, but not for reasons of thirst. I was hoping that if I drank it slowly, she'd be asleep by the time I got back. How dare she offer to save me from my mother, when I hadn't asked to be saved?

As I walked down the stairs, I heard muttering in the kitchen.

'Go on, boy. There's not enough booze in those bloody things to intoxicate a mouse.'

I entered the kitchen to the sound of chomping. With no regard for the creature's metabolism, my mother was feeding the liqueur chocolates to Duncan.

★ ★ ★

Judy Page opened the curtains at 7.30 a.m. She stood at the bedroom window, naked but Hooverless, and surveyed my parents' six thousand square feet of land, which extended to the footpath alongside the allotments. Beyond that were the marshes and the river.

'She doesn't deserve all that, does she?'

Judy Page sashayed to the bedroom door and opened it, halfway. But she didn't leave. On the contrary. She returned to the bed. In the bedroom beneath us, my mother coughed. But it was not a Peter Something-Something cough, not a cough of despair. It was a good old-fashioned smoker's cough, no more, no less.

'They'll hear,' I said.

'Let them,' she said.

After penile encouragements, Judy Page reversed onto me and parked. I'd never felt more alive and I didn't bloody like it. I was glad I couldn't see her face, which I'm sure looked frightening. But I heard her all right.

'Fuck me good!' she shouted, which was worse than Ticky's 'Fuck me!' for being ungrammatical. Duncan wandered in through the half-open door. He looked at her with indifference.

'Piss off!' she hissed. Duncan tensed. I was out of control. Her anger and the shock of the dog made my penis weep. Immediately, Judy Page dismounted and went to the bathroom.

She came back to find me lying on my back in the bed, just as she'd left me.

'So what are we going to do today?' she asked me, sweetly. 'You must show me your Aldeburgh. The sun's in your eyes.' I was, it was true, squinting. With great solicitude, she drew a curtain enough to block the sun.

'I'll go to the bathroom now,' I said, one of

those banal remarks designed to restore equilibrium.

I'd been in the bathroom for less than a minute when there was a knock at the door. I knew it was my mother, for the knock was a firm 'rat-tat-tat' of the kind that has fallen out of favour. People do not knock now, not like they did. They knock, the once, then open the door without waiting for an answer. The knock is no longer a request for permission to enter. It's simply a knuckle-based 'Hi!', as in: 'Hi! I'm coming in now and there's nothing you can do to stop me.'

'Enter!' I said. My mother strode in, followed by my father, who moved more gingerly. My father shut the door.

This was extraordinary. I'd never been in a bathroom with my parents. When I was a boy, there was no 'parenting'. There were parents but it was not their job to hang around the bathroom, having a 'relationship' with you, by spending 'quality' (or quantity) time. Why would they want to spend time with you? You were a child. Your mother would enquire, from a different floor, whether you'd had a bath and brushed your teeth. Your father wouldn't ask. He was reading the paper. He took it on trust that you were having, or would be having, or had had a bath. For more than half the year, of course, you were at boarding school. He was reading the paper a hundred and fifty miles from your bath.

I took my toothbrush out of my mouth.

'No, carry on,' said my father, still standing

near the door. I put the toothbrush back in.

'You've made a mistake, Little Man,' said my mother. 'Everyone makes mistakes, except for your father.'

'Your mother's referring to the young lady,' said my father, firmly, to the towel on the back of a chair.

'The main thing with mistakes is not to marry them. You may think sex is important now. Believe me, it's not. Your father and I haven't bothered with that nonsense in years.'

I looked at my mother and father in the bathroom mirror. That made it easier. It was more like watching a film.

'We were hoping you'd find someone who could play bridge,' my father told the towel.

'She's common,' my mother said, in a voice much louder than his. 'Common girls often use sex to trap a man. It's not your fault. You weren't to know. You're not very experienced.'

'She takes great pride in her appearance,' said my father, wanting to find a good word to say about Judy Page.

'That's cos she's a tart,' said my mother.

I carried on brushing. I thought of Cleo, the Dalmatian we'd had in my teens. One could toss Cleo a bone and not see it again, such was her attack. Nothing was left but a gap where the bone had been. I was brushing my two front teeth as if they were Cleo's bones. If I brushed them much longer or harder, they'd be gone.

'I think we've said enough,' said my father. I was grateful. I hadn't said a word and now there was every chance I wouldn't have to. My father left the bathroom at twice the speed he'd entered it. My mother lingered.

'You and I can have a round of golf. She can go shopping.'

I heard Judy Page, outside the bathroom, ask my father: 'Have you seen Robert?'

I did not want to see her again. I belonged in this bathroom. I didn't belong outside, with her. I'd invested my time and imparted my knowledge. I'd introduced her to the members of my chambers. I'd bought her two dresses and a kilim. She'd bought me — or, rather, she'd helped me buy — a living-room rug (and sofa. Let us not forget the sofa). Why had I allowed her into my life? I hadn't. That's the point. She'd allowed herself.

Judy Page was my mistake. She was my Dick Gage. But I would not do with her what Ticky did with Dick Gage. I wouldn't follow her meekly to the marriage marquee, betraying my parents — my *breeding* — and the spirit of Aldeburgh.

I had to take action. I would not confront her or abuse her. I would do what any gentleman would do: withdraw. I would apply that invisible sword, the sword of withdrawal.

★ ★ ★

Judy Page left my flat early on Monday morning. We agreed we'd speak on the phone. She asked me to get her a key cut. She was fed up with having to ask the 'fat woman' downstairs to let her in. I didn't remark on this description, though Dr Pearson, my downstairs neighbour, was 'fat' only in the sense that she wasn't as thin as Judy Page.

On Monday evening, I wrote a note to Dr Pearson, asking her not to let anyone into my flat, other than the emergency services.

On Tuesday evening, there were six messages from Judy Page on my answerphone.

On Wednesday night, en route to my front door, I met Dr Pearson in the hallway. She asked if I was all right. I said I was and returned the question, putting my key into my lock without waiting to hear her response. I assumed that would be the end of it. That had always been the end of it before. But no. She told me she'd been very concerned by the tone of my note. The reference to 'emergency services' alarmed her. Was I thinking of taking my own life? Was there anything she could do to help? I asked if she were offering to help me take my own life. This was obviously a facetious remark, clearly designed to be amusing. Infuriatingly, she misread it as a statement of intent. She looked me in the eyes. Did I want to come in for a chat about things? We'd never really talked.

We'd spent three years as each other's neighbour. We'd established our universities and professions and, the previous July, we'd agreed to repaint the hall. That was it. Not once had we chatted about 'things'. By 'things', of course, people never mean *things*. They never want to chat about your bicycle pump or your scissors. They're only interested — far too interested — in abstractions like *you* and *yourself*. It is always: 'How are you? In yourself?' It is never:

'How are your scissors?'

If I 'really talked' with Dr Pearson about 'things', there would be no end. Every journey to and from our flats would be fraught with thing-chat potential. Keys would stay in locks for hours. She and I would be the proverbial dentists, unable to enter our surgeries and get on with our working lives.

What was happening to me? Why were women — specifically, Dr Pearson and Judy Page — having thoughts about me without my permission, the one thinking she needed to save me from my mother, the other believing she needed to save me from my death? 'Come on,' she said, seeing my reluctance. 'Just come in for a moment.'

'Frankly, I'd rather kill myself,' I said. She looked stunned. I will never know what she looked after that, as the light bulb above our heads went *ping*. I felt glad my key was already in place, as I heard her scrabbling to locate her lock in the dark.

On Thursday evening, I found a stampless envelope on the hall table. Inside were a note and my key. Dr Pearson suggested I find another keyholder. She asked me not to speak to her again. This was what I wanted Judy Page to ask me. I had achieved the right victory over the wrong opponent.[1]

-----

[1] Dr Pearson and I, as co-owners of the freehold, were jointly responsible for the light bulb in the hall, which therefore remained unchanged. I became adept at unlocking my door with the aid

On Friday evening, I came home and didn't listen to the answerphone. At 11 p.m., however, when I was in my sitting room, reading the *Law Society Gazette*, Judy Page rang the bell.

I didn't answer. I hid behind my new sofa, which was ironic, given that she'd persuaded me to buy it. Already I hated it, hated it for its newness. Sofas are meant to be old. They're meant to bear the stains of history. That is their allure.

'I know you're there!' she screamed from the doorstep. How could I make her think I wasn't? 'You're there, Robert! Your lights are on!'

Yes. Of course. I got up and switched off the lights.

I switched off the lights to prove I wasn't there. Who else but Judy Page could have made me do such a thing? She confiscated my reason.

She put her finger on the buzzer and kept it there. I had no choice but to go downstairs and talk to her through the front door.

'Open the door!' she said.

'You can hear me through it,' I replied.

'How dare you not return my calls?'

'Not returning your calls is an omission,' I replied. 'Acts of omission don't require daring. Climbing Everest takes daring. Omitting to climb Everest takes no daring at all.'

Judy Page hit me. The claim is absurd, given

_____

of a lighted match, a tedious business involving the use of three hands. If, as I did it, I heard a noise from her flat, I whistled some Bach to alert her to my presence, ensuring she didn't come out into the hall while I was there.

the door between us. Nevertheless, I felt her fist on the door — at face height — as if it were striking my nose. I even raised a hand to protect myself, catching the right arm of my spectacles and sending them to the floor. I bent to pick up the spectacles. I could not, of course, see them in the black-as-night hallway. I knelt down, feeling for them. I found them and, still kneeling, put them back on. I discovered that the right arm was no longer there. My spectacles were L-shaped.

Judy Page opened the jaws of the letter box. 'You'll regret this!' she screamed through the aperture. I ducked, so my head would not be illuminated by the light from the street.

I'd known her seven weeks.

★ ★ ★

I'd ignored the dress trousers I'd worn on the night of the Awards. I couldn't take them to the dry cleaner's, given their telltale stain. What tale could I tell when the woman behind the counter asked me to define it? I couldn't say: 'It's a taxi stain.'

Dustbins, in that era, were still metallic. Mine was marked FLAT B. It was parked, in our minuscule front courtyard, next to Dr Pearson's. She came home to find me having a bonfire in my dustbin. With the aid of matches and lighter fluid, I was burning my trousers.

She sniffed as she walked past. She said nothing. I said nothing either. I held my hands in front of the flames as if, though it was a lovely June evening, I craved their warmth.

6
Ridgeon v. Kelly
(1989)

In *Ridgeon* v. *Kelly* (1989), I appeared for Kelly. Kelly and Ridgeon were friends who worked in the same east London electrical shop. One Friday night, they went drinking at a pub in Hackney. At closing time, they came out with two female companions. Ridgeon offered the female companions further drinks at Kelly's flat. The female companions declined. They told Ridgeon he and Kelly had had enough drinks already.

Kelly offered Ridgeon a lift home on his motorbike. The female companions suggested to Ridgeon that Kelly was too drunk to drive. Ridgeon replied: 'Bollocks!' and hopped on Kelly's motorbike. Kelly crashed the motorbike. Ridgeon was killed. Kelly lost his right arm.

The executors of Ridgeon's estate brought an action against Kelly.

Did Ridgeon, the passenger, voluntarily assume the risk involved in accepting the lift from Kelly? If he did, then Kelly was not liable. To a willing person, no injury is done. *Volenti non fit injuria*, as we say.

Counsel for Ridgeon's estate claimed that Ridgeon was far too inebriated to give his consent voluntarily. He couldn't think straight, any more than he could walk straight. He was too drunk, in other words, to see how potentially dangerous a driver my client Kelly was.

It was a question of degree. Ridgeon was inebriated, certainly, as indeed was Kelly. (Prior to this civil case, he'd served four years in prison.) It was my contention, however, that Ridgeon was not so inebriated that he didn't know what he was doing. With assistance from the female companions, I was able to show that this was indeed the case.

I established that when Ridgeon 'hopped on' the bike, the female companions were forty to fifty feet away. They testified that Ridgeon shouted at them: 'Come on, girls. You know you want to. 88 Eleanor Grove! First right, second left!'

Despite the distance and the revving engine, they heard every word. Not a syllable was slurred or incomprehensible. Was this the speech of a man too drunk to know what he was doing? Surely, a man too drunk to know what he's doing is a man deprived of all spatial awareness, incapable of giving accurate directions.

What's more, Ridgeon was speaking through the open visor of his crash helmet, which the female companions had seen him don with consummate ease. Had Ridgeon been as inebriated as my opponent claimed, the helmet would have missed his head.

I won.

★ ★ ★

Volenti non fit injuria. Those who knowingly and willingly put themselves in a dangerous situation cannot sue for their resulting injuries.

I cannot but apply that to my own life. What was Judy Page but a 'dangerous situation' into which I knowingly and willingly put myself? I was not even drunk. It is not good enough to say, as I did only recently, that she 'allowed herself into my life' without my consent. I stepped into that taxi with her of my own volition. I must take responsibility. The blame is mine. I am not a victim.

★　★　★

Ridgeon v. Kelly (1989) was a momentous case, marking the first of my fourteen appearances in *The Times* Law Reports. As I'm entitled — nay, obliged — to open up in these pages, allow me to open up on the subject of those fourteen appearances.

I would simply ask that, when you hear my name, you think of those fourteen appearances. Not my crime, not the sex, not the dog, but my fourteen — an easily remembered number — appearances in *The Times* Law Reports.

Can you do that? No, you can't. That is my complaint.

7

Elizabeth
(1989)

By 1989, I was thirty-three. I was no longer young. This gave me a sense of well-being. It felt like a victory I'd earned. Most men of my age stood at the mirror and cursed the hair that came out with their combs. I, by contrast, would have cheerfully shouted: 'Recede!'

I had not had a girlfriend since Judy Page, six years earlier.

* * *

'Nice one! Brilliant!' This was my client Kelly, after the case, walking towards me outside the robing room. At the end of his artificial right arm, he had a prosthetic hand, for appearance only. He therefore extended his left hand, which pumped my own with agonising force. I guessed it had gained in strength since the loss of its fellow. 'You fought for me. You were well steamed up. Let me buy you a big fat drink.'

Let us leave aside the tastelessness of the 'big fat drink', given he'd lost his friend and his arm on account of his own drunken driving. The jubilant Kelly assumed I cared about him, whereas, dispassionately, I cared only about his case. My dispassion worked to his advantage. A barrister should never be 'steamed up'. One cannot see clearly through steam.

I grant him this: in discussing his case in chambers, over a cup of tea, I identified with Kelly completely. I talked about Kelly in the first person. I *was* Kelly. 'This morning,' I said, 'I'm a twenty-four-year-old man who went out drinking with his mate. I left a pub in Hackney — yes, a biscuit would be welcome, Bill.'[1]

But this identification was not with him, Kelly. It was with his legal essence. In a law examination, on the subject of tort, Kelly would be described thus: 'K'. That would be it. The question would start: 'K and his friend R went out drinking.' As a barrister, I identified with his actions, not his personality or motivations. I was only concerned with what he did, not what he was like. When I said, 'I left a pub in Hackney,' I pictured 'myself' like a toy tank advancing across a map on a war-room table. Why was 'I' so drunk and foolish as to drive that motorbike? The question was of no concern to me. One doesn't look into the soul of a toy tank.

'I fear I must return to chambers,' I said, refusing the offer of Kelly's drink.

'Fair enough, mate. Good luck then. Cheers.'

'I fear I must return to chambers' was a

---

[1] Bill was, for seventeen years, my clerk at 17 King's Bench Walk. Bill took it upon himself to be Keeper of the Chambers' Biscuits. He still sends me a Christmas card, one of the few ex-colleagues who do.

measured and polite response. It was even true, in the long run, given that I had to be in chambers the following morning. I didn't belittle Kelly. I've always been scrupulously gracious in my dealings with the Kellys that cross my path. I'm my father's son.

★ ★ ★

After his 'Cheers', Kelly moved away. Behind him was a young woman, queuing to speak to me. She introduced herself as Elizabeth Webb, an articled clerk with Cheeseman Crick, the solicitors who'd instructed me.

'Congratulations,' she said. Then she blurted: 'I really admired your bearing.' I knew at once she'd given considerable thought to this remark. It was clearly the fruit of many hours of watching me.

I estimated she was ten years younger than I, which proved to be the case. Her admiration and youth I took as gifts, gifts that made me feel even older and more wise. She had long brown hair and a healthy outdoor pallor. She wore a dark blue suit and a white shirt. There was nothing fashionable about her. She was what Granny P would have called a 'true English rose'.[1]

'Thank you,' I replied. 'How long have you

---

[1] Granny P, even in her disturbed dotage, adored the bearing and grace of such English roses as Deborah Kerr, Virginia McKenna and, latterly, Julie Andrews. When she saw them, she sighed. Sadly, our sensibilities have been 'tabloidised'. A

been with Cheeseman Crick?'

'Six months,' she answered, then added: 'Thank *you*.' She blushed, embarrassed by this needless addition. There was a silence, which another man would have curtailed with a charming remark. But, always true to myself, I essayed no charm. Finally, she said: 'I wasn't sure we'd win so I was glad when we did.'

'True,' I replied. I thought that I wouldn't wish to have as a wife a woman susceptible to charm.

Yes. That's right. I believed I would marry this woman. I believed it with the same certainty as, aged eight, I believed I'd go to Christ Church, Oxford. This woman and I would have children, preferably a *d* and an *s*. She would cook for me Afterwards, I'd do the washing-up. She and I would make a fine pair, at tennis as well as bridge. If she didn't love tennis or bridge, I'd understand. She'd learn to love them.

When she found out she was pregnant with our first child, she would give up work. She'd protest. But I'd insist. I'd want to protect her from unnecessary stress. She'd still be busy, though. She'd decorate our house in Highgate. (We'd choose Highgate because it was well placed for the journey from London to Suffolk.) She'd seek out fabrics and furnishings. We'd argue about colours. I'd um and ah. But I'd let her win. Such things would matter more to her than me.

---

woman who sighs is presumed to be thinking of Deborah, Virginia and Julie 'messing around down there'.

'*Hold on, I'll get my wife. The man's here, darling!*' That's what I'd say when the man arrived to lay the new carpet. She'd know how to talk to carpet layers, just as she'd know how to talk to royalty. Given that I was a barrister of ten years' call, firmly planting his feet in his father's footsteps, a father who had met the Queen on more than one occasion,[1] I needed a wife who'd feel at ease not just with Her but with the more socially problematic Prince Charles. Elizabeth, I could tell, from her thoughtfulness, her unfashionability, her outdoor glow, would instinctively side with the heir to the throne against his then wife, Diana, she who would shortly make a Great Exhibition of herself.[2]

Of all this, I was certain. I had certainty enough for two. But I said nothing of it to Elizabeth. I was not a fool. How to proceed? I'd write her a letter, telling her everything, care of Cheeseman Crick. A letter gives the recipient time to reread, reflect in solitude and reach the right conclusion; whereas my voice down the phone, my face next to hers, would give her no time, no space, no dignity.

'Do you know Aldeburgh?' I asked. Elizabeth was surprised. I too was surprised. I had no idea, till I asked the question, that this was the

---

[1] The phrase is entirely justified. He'd met the Queen twice.

[2] It was remarkable, was it not, that her Crystal Palace of Indiscretion was still, somehow, royal. Her bad blood, as spilt over newspapers, as poured over screens, was always blue.

question I was going to ask. It was as if a force greater than I were willing the question from my lips. That force, perhaps, was Aldeburgh itself.

'I do,' said Elizabeth. 'I know Aldeburgh very well.' Marvellously, she went there for a week or more, most summers. She'd done so since childhood. Her parents owned a flat there. I had asked her only if she knew Aldeburgh. I had told her nothing of myself, or myself and Aldeburgh. And yet she asked me, fearlessly: 'Do you know the Pilkingtons?' She might as well have asked: *Do you know we'll get married?* The Pilkingtons question told me I was right. (Never mind my aversion to Christopher of that ilk. She was asking if I knew the Pilkingtons, plural, the Pilkington family.) I was right. I was right about everything. Elizabeth and I, outside the Royal Courts of Justice in the Strand, had found each other.

Was I a fantasist in the throes of love at first sight? No. I can't be bracketed with adolescent poets or soppy girls or the deluded cross-dressing fools in those Shakespeare 'comedies' which always make one regret one has spent £37.50, not including the programme and a taxi.

I was in the throes of something more precious, more durable and, above all, more rational. I was in the throes of marriage at first sight.

★   ★   ★

A week later, I dispatched a note to Elizabeth, care of Cheeseman Crick. I didn't mention the son or the daughter or Prince Charles. It was not that I doubted or even questioned any of the things I'd thought. I simply concluded that, at this point, I would keep them to myself. After all, I had time to tell her. I had the rest of our lives.

By a stroke of luck, Britten's *Peter Grimes* was in repertory at Covent Garden.[1] Did Elizabeth want to accompany me to a performance? With its complex, morally ambivalent hero, its East Anglian marine severity, its themes of isolation, alienation and self-destruction, so hauntingly expressed in the unforgiving beauty of the music, *Peter Grimes* was utterly inappropriate for a 'first date'. As such, it was perfect for my purposes. I did not want Elizabeth to compare me with suitors of her age, who, I suspected, had a first-date formula: 'grab a pizza', 'take in a movie', 'go to a Sex Pistols concert'.[2] I didn't want myself associated with the lightweight, the

---

[1] Britten lived in Aldeburgh from 1947 till his death in 1976. I'm not sure why I mention it. You either know it already or don't care.

[2] Were the Sex Pistols still a group in 1989? They were certainly current some twelve years earlier, when I had the misfortune, for a few weeks, to share a house in Finsbury Park with Mike Bell, among others. He was, like me, fresh out of Oxford. Mike Bell played 'the Pistols' from the moment he woke up, which perforce became the moment *I* woke up. I asked him to desist. He told me, with misplaced outrage, that the Sex Pistols' singer Johnny Rotten had been born in Finsbury Park, not a mile from our

frivolous, the short-term. I wanted her to associate me with a great but difficult work.

Elizabeth proved to be a delightful companion, bright and appreciative and knowledgeable about Grimes. She even quoted from the George Crabbe poem on which the libretto was based. I didn't know the poem so, not wishing to expose my ignorance, kept a dignified silence.

In the interval, I asked her where she'd taken her law degree. 'Durham,' she replied. I respected this. Durham University is the Oxford of the North, as Bristol is the Oxford of the West. Of course, it proved she wasn't my intellectual equal. If she were, she'd have attended, as I did, Oxford, the Oxford of the Oxford, the *Oxfordissimo*. I was not disappointed. I had known from our first meeting that the intellectual balance was weighted in my favour.

At the end of the evening, not wishing to take Elizabeth out to dinner — for fear of keeping her up too late on a weekday night — I offered to share a taxi home. Elizabeth lived in a house with two other girls in Clapham.

'That's miles from where you're going,' she said. This was true. I lived in Canonbury, in north London, many miles in the other direction.

'No, no,' I replied. 'I insist. It's my treat. Then I'll take the taxi on to Canonbury.'

These were sentences of which I was inordinately proud. There was nothing poetic or seductive about them but they conveyed so

house. I was meant to feel I was in Bethlehem, listening to the voice of Jesus.

106

much. I knew Elizabeth would extract and store every ounce of their information. By 'it's my treat', I was conveying that I earned more money than she. Of course I did. She was a young articled clerk, I a barrister in my thirties. 'Treat' told her that my superior wealth was not a problem, any more than my Oxford, her Durham. 'Treat' was in fact a *solution*, an answer to the problem of what to do with that wealth. I'd spend it on her.

'I'll take the taxi on' said: 'This free taxi ride is an act of generosity. It's not an exchange. I do not expect you to grant me an overnight stay. In fact, I'd be extremely uncomfortable if such a thing were offered. You're not some 'taxi tart'.'[1]

As a Clapham park's moonlit, streetlit railings filed past the taxi window, Elizabeth said: 'I play tennis there. Do you play?' I no more didn't play tennis than I didn't know the Pilkingtons.

* * *

Elizabeth had some ability. I wasn't slow to point this out, at midday the following Sunday in that Clapham park.

'Well played!' I shouted, at the end of the first point, as she returned my serve, cleanly and

---

[1] *Peter Grimes*, an intellectually demanding event, was to be followed by a sexless taxi journey. I was systematically expunging the memories of my first night with Judy Page, with its moronic Awards event and sexful taxi journey.

powerfully, into the net. She looked puzzled.

'It was a nice clean hit,' I said. I wanted to show her that winning was not what was expected. What counted, to one who loved the game as much as I, was her appreciation of the way in which a tennis ball should be struck. It was the journey not the arrival of her return of serve that mattered.

I am not a great server. My serve, though left-handed, has none of the boom and boomerang swerve of John McEnroe's. It has accuracy, though, and it foxes the opponent. I give the ball plenty of 'air'. Consequently, its arc is slower and its bounce higher than more conventional serves. Mike Bell says it's like a 'fisherman casting off'. He intends to insult but he flatters. For he is, essentially, describing a lob. A great lobber, like the Swede Mats Wilander, would recognise in me a kindred spirit. He'd simply be surprised and (I hope) intrigued that I employ a lob for a serve.[1]

Fifteen — love became thirty — love, then forty — love, then game. Elizabeth looked frustrated and unhappy. That opening shot, so clean (if misdirected), had given way to nervous

----

[1] In tennis, shortness does not preclude greatness. I adduce Chuck McKinley (five foot eight), Ken Rosewall (five foot seven), Pancho Segura (five foot six). It was not shortness but the pursuit of academic excellence that prevented me spending my formative years on court. What might I not have achieved in the game if I'd been a dunce!

swipes, played with a tight arm and consequently overhit.

Now it was Elizabeth's turn to serve. Her toss was excellent. But, there, once again, was that overanxiety, making her strike the ball too early and send it beyond the service line.

'You shouldn't hit the ball so early,' I said, giving her the benefit of my twenty-five years' Wimbledon-watching experience. She nodded grimly.

Love — fifteen was followed by love — thirty. At love — forty, I made a mistake, a genuine mistake. I did not deliberately hit the ball long to give her a point. That is not my way. I had no intention of lowering my standards. I hoped Elizabeth would raise hers.

I soon led two-games to love, then three — love, then four — love. Her shoulders subsided. Her head drooped. Far from raising her game, Elizabeth was literally lowering it. I was flattered, of course. It was clear how much our match meant to her, how keenly she wanted to show me her prowess. But I knew it was in both our interests for me to conclude the set as swiftly as possible. I could then say something like: 'I'm sorry, my knee's hurting, do you mind if we stop?' We'd leave the court halfway through our allotted hour, saving Elizabeth from further punishment. We'd go back to her house for lunch — she walking, I pretend-hobbling.

As I served for five — love. I thought of Ivan Lendl. Though lacking his power, I had something of the robotic Czech's iron will. Five — love I intended and, Lendl-like, five — love I

109

achieved. One more game and the set would be over.

Elizabeth prepared to serve, I to receive. On the balls of my feet, knees bent, rocking from side to side, I gazed at her intensely. This was the procedure I'd followed for all her first serves, not one of which had landed in; yet every time I paid her the compliment of readying myself utterly. Would this first serve hit the net, be too long or too wide? I might just as well have stood there, knees bent, reading the *Law Society Gazette*.

Elizabeth served. The ball hit the net cord, careered sideways and landed a few inches wide. That was, at least, a new way for Elizabeth's serve to be out.

'Out!' I called, as I always did, dutifully following the proprieties. The poor girl dropped her racquet in despair.

'Come on, you can do it!' I said. 'I know you can. I'm sure you can.' Her second serve thwacked the service line and whizzed past my left ear. The next serve whizzed past my right. In this fashion, varying the ear, Elizabeth held serve. Five — one to me.

What did I 'feel'? That is the question. That's always the question, is it not? I 'felt' proud. I'd helped Elizabeth. For five games, she'd been intimidated by my seniority and inhibited by the need to impress. By stating my faith in her, I'd removed these constraints. I'd allowed her to fulfil her potential.

From five — one down, she fought back to five — five. It was all I could do to stop her winning

110

the set. I won it on the tiebreak, seven games to six.

I felt exhausted. I'd done a great deal of running and was playing an opponent much younger than me. 'Do you mind if we stop?' I asked.

'Come on,' said Elizabeth, 'there's only fifteen minutes to go.'

'All right,' I said. I didn't say that my knee was hurting. (It was, genuinely, hurting slightly.) I insisted, however, on a two-minute changeover, as takes place at Wimbledon. There were no seats, this being a public court, so I leaned against the fence and shut my eyes. Lovers of the sport will recognise the allusion. In his 1975 Wimbledon Final victory over Connors, Arthur Ashe spent the changeovers with his eyes shut, in a sublime and meditative state, while the agitated Connors towelled his face, hair and racquet handle, with increasing exasperation.[1]

I stood there with my eyes shut, for my permitted span, till a giggle from Elizabeth pierced my reverie. Refreshed, I walked back onto the court. A few minutes later, at five to one, two youths — one smoking — arrived at the fence and hovered unpleasantly, waiting to take our place. At one o'clock exactly, I signalled to Elizabeth that, regrettably, our time was up.

The final score was seven-six to me in the first set, and five-love to her in the second. I'd won, by one set to nil.

---

[1] Like me, Ashe wore glasses. He was a wonderfully dignified man.

111

'Are you all right?' asked Elizabeth, as we walked past the swings. 'You're hobbling.'

'Yes,' I replied, 'my glasses are hurting. That's why I played so badly in the second set.'

'You're hobbling because your glasses are hurting?'

I'd meant, of course, to say 'knee'. Elizabeth was vastly amused.

I suggested that, next time, we should play doubles. She could bring her stroke-making to our partnership, while I could supply the leadership, tactical nous, mental strength and historical perspective.

That was, therefore, the first and last time I played singles with Elizabeth. From then on, we were together, on the same side of the net. There can be no clearer metaphor for my relationship with Elizabeth, as opposed to my relationship with Judy Page. With Judy Page, I never felt I was on the same side of the net. I felt I was the ball.

★ ★ ★

We arrived at the house Elizabeth shared with her friends Fiona and Sophie. Elizabeth asked me if I'd like a shower and offered me a towel. I accepted the shower but declined the towel. Anticipating this moment, I'd brought my own. I would not put my manliness on one of her towels, this early in our friendship. In fact, if all went well, I'd never use Elizabeth's towels, even after we married. We'd have His and Her towels, colour-coded, as my parents did. My father had dark blue, the hue of Oxford, and my mother had light blue, though she didn't go to Cambridge, or any other university. She simply liked light blue.

On account of the shower, I was the last to arrive at the table for lunch. Elizabeth was by the sink, making a salad dressing, getting on with things, providing. She carried on making the dressing while shouting out introductions — 'Fiona! Sophie! Robert! — evidence of that uniquely feminine ability to perform two tasks at once. I put my bottle of wine on the table.

Fiona, her large housemate, was overly pleased to meet me: 'Nice to meet you, I've heard so much about you. White or red? I hear you're a barrister. That must be very exciting. Tell us all about it.' Wishing to quell her pointless excitement, I replied: 'Thank you. Red.'

Sophie, meanwhile, ignored me in favour of picking a blonde hair — one of her own — off the shirt of the man next to her.

'And this is Guy,' said Elizabeth. 'Guy . . . Robert.'

'Hi,' said Guy.

Fiona said: 'Known as Guy the guy. For obvious reasons.' But there were no obvious reasons. I'm not known as Robert the Robert. This was the first Guy I'd met who let his name be exploited for a pun.

'You going to a meeting?' asked Guy the guy. He was referring to my tie. Why was I wearing a tie to an informal Sunday lunch?

'I think it's a lovely tie,' said Fiona, helping me where no help was needed.

'A lunch *is* a meeting. A meeting of minds,' I said, with geniality. One fights fire not with fire but water. This emollience, I think you'll find, draws attention to your opponent's fire-starting aggression.

'That's told you!' said Sophie. 'Does anyone else find it hot in here?'

'Shall I open the window wider?' asked Elizabeth, selflessly. (She herself, glowing with tennis-induced health, was clearly the perfect temperature.)

'Why don't you just take your top off?' said Guy the guy to Sophie, who was too thin and sharp, in the same way Fiona was too large and caring.

'I would if I was wearing a bra.'

Elizabeth approached the table. Guy the guy removed my bottle of wine, ostensibly to make more room for the salad bowl. He put it on the sideboard, where it stayed for the rest of the meal.

'God, you're such a fabulous cook,' said Sophie, admiring the salad.

'You all right, love?' asked Fiona of Elizabeth, stroking her arm, as if Elizabeth had just delivered not a salad but a baby.

'Brilliant!' said Guy the guy, apropos of nothing. He tossed his mane of black hair. A split second later, Sophie shook her mane of blonde, as if a fly had flown from his head onto hers.

★　★　★

One speaks of the 'weight of evidence' in a case. In one sense, it's literal. Depositions — claims

114

and counterclaims — can run into hundreds of pages. But I've known the metaphorical weight too. I've sensed, in court, that the evidence in my favour had the force of an avalanche.

Elizabeth needed to leave this house. That was the case I was arguing, if only to myself. As for the weight of evidence, let us begin with Fiona. Her stroking of Elizabeth's arm was meant to show she 'cared'. But I put it to you, as I put it to myself, that it showed no such thing. It showed that Fiona believed she owned Elizabeth. It was an owner's control. Elizabeth was Fiona's to comfort, to praise, to dominate, to stroke. I'm surprised she didn't give Elizabeth a bone.

As for the too-hot Sophie, one could not trust a woman who described the making of a salad as 'cooking'. Sophie did nothing to help in the preparation of the meal. She was too busy drawing attention to her bralessness. I hadn't noticed she wasn't wearing a bra till she mentioned it. I was not surprised to learn later that Sophie owned the house. Her daddy had bought it for her, and much else besides.

Let us turn now to Guy the guy. I could forgive him his hostility. He had the air of someone who'd lunched in this house many times before. Now here was I, older and wiser, usurping his position as the senior man at the table. But I could not forgive him the setting aside of my wine. When I arrived, there were three bottles present. A Piat D'Or red, a Piat D'Or white and a Spanish red whose label I couldn't make out, apart from the word 'Don'.

You will gather that these bottles were scarcely

fine wine. Mine, by contrast, was a Château Haut-Bages Averous 1985, Pauillac. It cost £10.99.[1] I didn't, as I've pointed out, value money for money's sake. I didn't even value the things it brought me. In 1989, at thirty-three, I drove an Audi, not because I craved an Audi, but because Bill remarked one day that the three highest earners in our chambers drove Audis. (I was the fourth.) I valued the Audi, therefore, as proof that I was a high-earning barrister, which in turn was proof that I had *a first-class mind*. (My italics.) Do you see? I bought an Audi not to show off my money or my Audi. I bought it to show off the first-class mind that had procured the money to buy it. Similarly, the Pauillac.

Guy, who regarded me as 'snobby' and 'posh', thought he was bringing me down a peg by removing my superior bottle. But anyone with so much as a third-class mind could see what else he was doing: hiding the bottle so he could enjoy it later, with his girlfriend Sophie and her unsupported bosom.

Elizabeth did not chide him for this, any more than she chided Fiona for the stroking or Sophie for her insincere 'cooking' compliment. Elizabeth had a sweetness to her nature. This left her vulnerable. She needed a white knight in an Audi to take her away.

* * *

[1] What is £10.99 in 'today's money'? Who wants today's money anyway? It's tomorrow's everyone wants.

116

Halfway through the meal, a highly acceptable roast chicken, I excused myself and went upstairs to the lavatory. Post-lavatory, I headed down-stairs. I stopped on the landing. Guy was telling an anecdote. His rhythms suggested he'd told it many times. I heard 'stark bollock naked' and three girls giggling. I walked back upstairs.

I pushed open the door of each bedroom. On the first bed, there was a voluminous blouse, which had clearly contained upper Fiona. On the second bed was a multi-headed octopus of tights and bras, which indicated the bra-centric Sophie.

Elizabeth's room was the smallest. On Elizabeth's bed, there were no clothes. Of course there weren't. My Elizabeth kept her clothes in the wardrobe. Elizabeth's wardrobe was heavy and too large for the room. It reminded me of the wardrobes at High Ridge. It was an old, inherited mahogany wardrobe. There was no sense, as with contemporary wardrobes, that it was 'fun' — a euphemism for 'brittle as Ryvita'.

I approached her bedside table, gingerly, respectfully, the better to see her framed photos. There she was, aged ten or eleven, in a Surrey-ish garden, between two brothers, one grinning, one scowling. She was the eldest. Her expression was grave. This delighted me. It confirmed that she was born to responsibility. She was used to looking after others and, as the sister of two brothers, familiar with the whims and moods of males.

And then she was a grown-up girl in a bikini, with a group of friends on a beach. The aerial angle suggested the photographer was perched on someone's shoulders. Elizabeth was looking up and laughing. Everyone was looking up and laughing, including Fiona, Sophie and Guy the guy. The men were all pale, while some of the girls were (unnaturally) brown. It appeared to be Spain or Greece or Italy but the group was so large — I counted seventeen — that Spain or Greece or Italy was almost wholly obscured.

Elizabeth's smile was a peer-group smile. Here was a young woman who worked in a law firm, lived in a shared house and holidayed with her sixteen closest friends. From others there was no escape. What would happen if Elizabeth said she was going for a walk on her own, to look at the Spanish/Greek/Italian sunset? Sixteen people would agree it was a good idea and go for a walk on their own with Elizabeth. From all this, too, I would rescue her. I would provide her with a home where she was free to be alone.

Finally, thrillingly, she was hugging a dead dog. In the photo, of course, the dog was alive. But Elizabeth was a toddler, a black-and-white toddler. The dog, more than twenty years later, was bound to be dead. That made its presence by her bedside all the more potent. There were no photos of dead humans; only this black poodle. Elizabeth was a dog lover, as I knew she would be.

'Robert?' She was calling me, from the bottom of the stairs. I'd been gone too long. It was the 'Robert?' of someone who missed me and was concerned for me. I was glad to hear her voice. It was wrong of me to be in her room — shades of my father's study — and I was glad her voice forced me to leave it.

I tiptoed to the open doorway which, to a person at the foot of the stairs, could easily pass for the doorway of the bathroom. 'Coming!'

I took one last look at Elizabeth's room before I closed the door. Next to the window was a small pine table, with delicate legs and a single drawer with a copper knob handle. Its placement was strategic. The table was there to distract the eye from the large stain beneath it. The stain, shaped like Ireland, was large, brown and ineradicable. It may well have been coffee.

I decided that next time I came to the house, I would bring a camera. I wanted to photograph Elizabeth's bedroom carpet.[1]

★ ★ ★

As a child, I had a boiled egg every Sunday night I was not at boarding school. I vividly recall my first. My mother asked what I wanted for supper and, without giving me a chance to reply, suggested I had a soft-boiled egg. I eagerly concurred.

As she made it, she explained her method. She placed the egg in a pan of water; when the water

---

[1] This makes no sense now but will later. As a barrister, I regard the making of sense as an obligation. That sense may be time-consuming to detect or, as here, postponed. But, I assure you, it will always be there. Tunnels, yes, but always light at the end of them.

started to boil, she lit a cigarette; in the time it took her to smoke the cigarette, the egg achieved a perfect soft-boiled state.

She brought my egg to the table and showed me how to decapitate it with a knife. She stood over me as I planted my soldier of toast. The soldier bent, from the hardness of the yolk. I was dismayed.

'To hell with it,' said my mother. 'I'll have to smoke faster.'

The next Sunday, I asked, without prompting, for a soft-boiled egg. My mother duly delivered another hard-boiled 'soft-boiled' egg. But this time I was not dismayed. A precedent had been set. Now I knew what would happen, every Sunday night. I accepted it. No — I relied on it.

This was not a childhood trauma. Childhood is not a restaurant one chooses for good food and competent service. Childhood is a home where everything is, or should be, predictable. When I think of my childhood, it's the constancy not the hardness of the Sunday-night egg to which I return and by which I'm comforted.

Constancy. Predictability. These were what I would offer Elizabeth.

★   ★   ★

In the summer of 1989, holidays excepted, I played doubles with Elizabeth at midday every Sunday. Our opponents were Guy the guy and his girlfriend Sophie.

When the four of us arrived on court for our first match, Sophie removed her tennis balls from their tubular container. She then produced what I thought was a small marker pen for branding the balls with her initials. Instead, she applied it to her lips, using Guy's left eyeball as a mirror. To Sophie, the court was a catwalk with a net. Instead of a dress, she wore a white tennis 'suit' with shorts. I can't recall what Elizabeth wore. This, surely, is appropriate. It's her tennis one wants to remember.

Guy the guy always wore black T-shirt, black shorts, black socks and black training shoes. Black was, in some obscure way, the colour of Guy the guy's job. He was an account executive for an advertising agency called Baker Cork Howard Vogel. In the late 1980s, as you may recall, there was a worldwide ampersand shortage.

Guy the guy regarded himself as 'cutting edge'. His black clothes were meant to be 'edgy'. 'Edge', 'edgy' and 'edginess' were words he used a great deal. 'We've got them on edge!' he shouted to Sophie, in his 'edgy' Yorkshire accent, when they won two points in a row.

He was loudly supportive, even when she threw down her racquet in disgust. Why did Sophie, a pat-a-cake player, get so angry when she made a bad shot? She was scarcely 'letting herself down'. At one point, she missed the ball completely, giving the air around it a most almighty thwack.

'You can do it, Soph!' shouted Guy the guy, despite the evidence to the contrary.

Sophie picked the racquet up and prepared to receive my serve. Guy the guy took his place, a few paces from the net. Then, with his back to Sophie, he raised an eyebrow at Elizabeth. His meaning was unmistakable. He was confiding to Elizabeth the strain of being Sophie's partner.

Guy didn't raise an eyebrow at me. From that first lunch, he tried not to look at me at all. When he spoke to me, he addressed his remarks to some invisible monkey on my shoulder. I reciprocated.[1]

I recall the last point the four of us played, some ten Sundays later. I served, Guy returned, Elizabeth volleyed to Sophie's court. Sophie, thinking about her hair, allowed the onrushing Guy to hit the ball on her behalf, drawing him towards the net. It came to me at the back of the forehand court. I reasoned that a lob would win the point and sent the ball soaring over Guy's head. He turned and raced towards it. It landed. Although he had his back to the net, he managed to return it down the line.

Even the greats rarely hit winners with their back to the net. Here was Guy the guy, in a public park, facing a smoking mother on a bench, hitting a shot worthy of Noah, Leconte or Nastase. I watched in disbelief as the ball flew past me and landed, unreturnably, on the line. Yes, it was a magnificent shot. But redundant, as we shall see.

---

[1] When my father, in that Aldeburgh bathroom, addressed his remarks to the towel not me, it was an act of delicacy and restraint. When Guy didn't look at me, it was an act of aggression.

Guy the guy hugged Sophie to his black-clad breast, lifting her off the ground. Airborne, she bent one knee and flicked her heel towards her bottom.

'Out!' I called.

'No!' shouted Guy. 'It was in! It was in!'

'It was in!' said Sophie.

'In!' screamed Guy, at Elizabeth.

'I think it was in,' said Elizabeth to me, with commendable calm.

'Yes,' I replied, with reciprocal calm. 'His shot was in.'

'Thank you!' said Guy the guy, punching the air so hard one feared for its safety.

'My shot was out, though.'

'What are you fucking talking about?'

I looked straight at his invisible monkey.

'My shot missed the line,' I said. 'My shot was out. So your return was redundant.'

'Your shot was in! It was on the line! I was there! I saw it!' He looked at Sophie. 'His shot was in, wasn't it?'

Sophie shrugged, indifferent to any battle not fought over her. He turned back to me. 'How could you see? You were miles away! You don't know what you're talking about!'

'I saw it miss the line by a couple of inches. My shot was out. Ergo, you didn't need to return it.'

'Fuck your ergo! Your shot was in!'

'Let's play the point again,' said Elizabeth.

'No!' said Guy the guy. 'That's the best fucking shot I've played in my life! I won't hit that fucking shot again if I live to be a hundred!'

123

'Let's just play the point again,' repeated Elizabeth.

'Yes, let's the play the point again,' I said, supportively. We had, after all, lost the point. We might win the replay.

'No! Fuck off! Bollocks!' said Guy the guy and stomped off court.

'It's only a game,' said Sophie. She was wrong.

★   ★   ★

At lunch that day, Fiona was absent. She'd gone to see her mother, who was lovely. I know she was lovely because, at previous Sunday lunches, Fiona talked about her mother a lot. Her mother had breast cancer. It wasn't fair that her mother had breast cancer, she said, because her mother was a lovely person. I wanted to point out that disease are neither fair nor unfair, having no concept of fairness; having, indeed, no concepts at all. Had Hitler had breasts, his breast cancer would not have been 'fair'. Hitler's mastectomy would not have been a manifestation of justice, though our boys might have thought so as they sang: 'Hitler has only got one breast.'

Sans Fiona, the four of us sat down in silence. Sophie read the *Sunday Times*, avoiding any sections that contained news. Guy the guy glowered. I helped Elizabeth, but only when instructed, not wishing to make incorrect kitchen initiatives.

Guy the guy put on some music, at extreme volume. Sophie asked him to turn it down. Guy the guy protested. Sophie told him nobody wanted music while they ate.

124

'What about Robert?' asked Guy the guy. 'Maybe he likes it.' It was a shock to hear him use my name. 'Hey, Robert,' said Guy the guy, 'are you into Fine Young Cannibals?'[1]

'I don't know,' I replied. 'This is the first time I've heard them.' Elizabeth turned off the music. Guy, to my surprise, didn't protest.

'Lunch'll be in five minutes,' said Elizabeth.

'Cool,' said Guy. 'Time for a toot. Fancy a toot then, Robert?'

He took out a small polythene bag and propelled a little of its powdered contents onto the table. With karate-like motions of his American Express Card, he chopped the powder up. Then, as if he were a croupier, he raked half the powder towards the edge of the table and sculpted it into a worm-like shape. Finally, he rolled up a ten-pound note. 'Come on then,' he said to me, 'stick your nose in the trough.'

Elizabeth went to the sink and stayed there.

'Leave him alone,' said Sophie.

'No thank you,' I said to Guy.

'Why not?' asked Guy. 'You're not a judge yet.'

'True,' I said.

'You think a policeman's going to look through the window?'

'Given the paucity of policemen on the beat, I'd say that was unlikely.'

'You think you're so fucking clever, don't

---

[1] 'Guy the guy' is as tiresome for me to keep typing as it is for you to keep reading. From now on, I shall call him simply 'Guy'. But I shall *think* 'Guy the guy'.

you?' Disconcertingly, he looked me in the eye. It was all I could do not to answer. That would have been a mistake. A 'yes', though accurate, would have put me at his mercy, of which he had none; a 'no' would have sounded insincere.

'I'm a barrister too,' he said. 'Advertisers are the barristers of commerce.' His remark lacked muscularity. It had the spongy quality of received wisdom. I would guess he'd read it in an 'industry magazine'.

'The comparison doesn't hold,' I said. 'In court, there are two opposing barristers. For your comparison to work, every advertisement would need to be countered by a disclaimer. For every poster saying 'Heineken refreshes the parts other beers cannot reach', there'd need to be a poster opposite saying 'Heineken doesn't even refresh the parts other beers *can* reach, let alone the parts they cannot'.'

'Watch this!' said Guy, with such force that I did. He inserted the note in his left nostril, lowered his head and snorted.

'OK,' he said. 'Did I snort that line? Or did I miss it by a couple of inches?'

I did not answer. Elizabeth burst into tears and rushed out of the room. 'Lizzie!' said Guy. He stood up. Then Sophie said, 'You're such a shit!' and Guy sat down. We heard a door slam, upstairs.

'Go and see her,' Sophie said to me. Yes. I needed to be by Elizabeth's side. And Sophie needed me to leave, so she could fight with Guy.

★ ★ ★

126

I knocked at the door of Elizabeth's room.

'Who is it?' she asked.

'It's me!' I replied. 'Robert!'

'Come in,' said Elizabeth.

She was sitting on the bed, no longer crying.

'Why d'you say 'It's me, Robert'? I know your voice.'

Here was another question I felt constrained not to answer. I stood and waited for her next remark.

'Don't stand over there,' she said. I walked over to the bed and stood closer to her. 'For God's sake!' she said. I took this as an invitation to sit beside her. I sat and looked down. In all the intervening Sundays since my first visit, I had never, in fact, re-entered her room to photograph her carpet. I didn't want to trespass again.

There was a silence, then another. Why, you ask, do I speak of two silences? Surely two silences, divided by no noise, are one? No. It was not like that. At the end of the first silence, I put my arm around her shoulder. That cued the second silence, which was longer than the first. It ended when Elizabeth burst into tears again.

What colour was the carpet? 'Oatmeal'? 'Biscuit'? 'Porridge'? (And what distinguished 'oatmeal' from 'porridge'?) Was it on account of their munchable texture that carpets were named after foodstuffs? 'Crispbread'. That was my last thought before I placed the arm around Elizabeth's shoulder.

'You don't know why I'm crying, do you?' asked Elizabeth.

'I'm sorry,' I replied. 'If a shot is out, you must

call it out, even if the shot's your own. Otherwise the lines serve no purpose. You might as well play without them. You might as well say no shot is out. Anything goes.'

'We've been having an affair.'

When Elizabeth said 'We've been having an affair', I thought she was referring to us. That was irrational. We hadn't been having an affair. I'd fought shy of an affair, knowing, from my affairs with Ticky and Judy Page, that affairs ended, whereas a marriage would be for life.

When I realised the 'We' in 'We've been having an affair' meant Elizabeth and Guy, I felt betrayed, outraged even. Elizabeth, I felt, had broken our vows. That too was irrational. We hadn't made any vows. *I'd* made vows, certainly — marriage vows, too — but only in the privacy of my head.

'It's been going on for two years now, I don't know what I'm doing with him, I don't even like him, he says he likes me more than he likes her, so why doesn't he leave her? It's so painful. They're here every weekend. They're in the next room. But I have to go a hundred miles to see him. I can't go to his flat because she's got a key. I know you hate him but you don't understand him. Guy can be very loving and funny, you just don't see it, he makes me feel so alive. He just needs a lot of attention and love. His parents divorced when he was five. Why don't you say something? He doesn't know what you want, that's why he's so aggressive with you. I don't know what you want either — what do you want, Robert? You don't say anything. The only time you talk to me is when we're on the court.'

My words came out singly, haltingly, as if I were typing them.

'I want you to come for a weekend at High Ridge.'

Elizabeth looked blank.

'My parents' house in Aldeburgh.'

'OK then. I'll come to Aldeburgh. Say something else.'

I looked down at the carpet. My arm still lay across her shoulder, immobile as a branch.

'This may not sound germane,' I began.

'Just talk to me!'

'What colour's your carpet?' Elizabeth tutted. But she didn't get angry. Mine was not a facetious or provocative question. I asked it with quiet dignity.

'I don't know. It was here when I moved in. I think it's called 'putty' .'

There was a third silence, after which she said: 'Guy would never just sit here like this.' I was happy to be told I was doing something Guy would never do. It was clear that Guy was her mistake, just as Judy Page had been mine. I would be the Anti-Guy to Elizabeth's Anti-Judy. There was logic to that. And a pleasing symmetry.

'By now, he'd have got me into bed.'

She cried again. I just sat there again. I did not get Elizabeth into bed.

★ ★ ★

That night, I lay alone in bed in my flat in Canonbury, revisiting what Elizabeth had said to me. I revisited everything and then I settled. I settled on a particular phrase and then, as it were, I settled in it. I dwelt in it, as if it were a cellar in a castle with the drawbridge up.

Guy was conceited, Guy was aggressive, Guy dressed in black, Guy took cocaine, Guy was cruel and unfaithful. What's more, like all unfaithful men, Guy was unfaithful to more than one person: unfaithful to Elizabeth with Sophie and unfaithful to Sophie with Elizabeth. But this was fair enough — *his parents divorced when he was five.*

In the welfare state of Guy's mind, that entitled him to certain character defects. These defects were like vouchers, to spend how he saw fit. He'd cashed in his Divorced At Five vouchers to get Elizabeth and Sophie. Was there a sliding scale, I wondered, as I lay there in the dark, with my eyes open? Had Guy's parents divorced when he was four, could he have had Fiona too? Had Guy's parents killed each other when he was two, could he have had the three of them at once?

★ ★ ★

As I entered the Oxford Street branch of John Lewis, I felt Guy's violation as a burning lump in my throat. He had sneaked Elizabeth into his conference hotel in Manchester, a conference concerned with the 'Future of Advertising', as if that Future contained anything but more dressing in black, more money, more conferences about the future Future of Advertising.

Elizabeth had shown me the flimsy white complimentary bedroom slippers she'd taken from his Manchester hotel room. She'd worn them round the house, as a silent taunt to Sophie, who of course knew nothing of where Elizabeth's feet had been.

Elizabeth was coming to Aldeburgh, the next weekend, the weekend before her birthday. She was coming to High Ridge, the house I would inherit and pass on to my children. Our children. Hurrah. This knowledge was my armour against Guy.[1]

I entered the carpeting department.

'Can I help you?' asked a pleasant woman. No, she couldn't. I wanted to be helped by a homosexual man. Can you understand? I had in my life had sex with two women. Guy had had sex with two women, merely in that *house*. This knowledge melted my armour. I, who was so much less heterosexual than he, craved a man less heterosexual than me. Was there not a homosexual man in every carpeting department?

---

[1] There was no question of my not inheriting the house. By settling, after her Australian sojourn, in New Zealand, my sister Freya had expressed her desire to have nothing more to do with Aldeburgh, England or her family. I would inherit High Ridge. That was the unspoken understanding between my parents and me. Nothing is more set in stone than an unspoken understanding. It cannot be varied or called into question, both of which require speech.

Sure enough, there he was, dealing with a young couple.

'You don't want to sacrifice style for hard-wearingness,' he said, in a voice that teetered on the edge of tears. He had a moustache and his head was as bald as a homosexual egg. I browsed the nearest swatch. When the young couple moved away, I caught his eye.

'I'd like to buy a carpet for my girlfriend,' I said. I'd never called Elizabeth my 'girlfriend' before. I'd never called anyone that.

'Right, sir. What sort of colour?'

'Putty.'

'Putty.' He repeated the word, which didn't give me confidence. Then he said: 'That's a sort of . . . '

'Yes,' I said. And then I had a curious and frightening mental lapse. I couldn't remember what 'putty' was. Was 'putty' animal, vegetable or mineral? Adjective or noun? Small or large? Did one eat it? Or put it in the engine of one's car?

'I'm not sure we've . . . let's look in the oatmeal region.' He picked up a book of swatches and flipped through it with practised dexterity. Finding me unresponsive, he asked if I wanted to take away some samples, which I could show my girlfriend for approval.

'That's not possible. The carpet's a surprise.'

'Ooh, lovely! My wife loves it when I give her a surprise.'

'Why don't you tell her you're homosexual then?' I thought (but did not say). I was glad I didn't say it, since it was illogical. The surprise

132

was not that this man was gay. The surprise was that he wasn't.

'That one!' I said, pointing to a swatch which was unmistakably the colour I'd stared at for so long, as I sat on the bed beside Elizabeth. This, surely, was 'putty', whatever that was.

'Pale sand,' he said. 'I like that one.'

'I bet you say that to all the men!' I said this. Yes, I said it. I gave him a surprise. He had not suspected me of being gay, which I wasn't, or flirtatious, which I wasn't either. I was simply feeling elated.

★ ★ ★

That night, I rang Elizabeth's house. Elizabeth answered. I put the phone down. I rang back. Sophie answered. The next night, luckily, Fiona answered. I told her I needed a key to get into the house, to deliver a secret present for Elizabeth's birthday. Fiona enjoyed our forced intimacy, as I knew she would.

'You dark horse. It's always the quiet ones!' she said. But it wasn't. Guy was loud, yet he was the darkest horse of them all.

I arranged for the estimator to measure up Elizabeth's bedroom carpet on Wednesday. I called Bill in chambers, late Tuesday afternoon, and pleaded a 'heavy cold'. I assured Bill I would be fit as a fiddle by Thursday, but couldn't guarantee that the cold wouldn't return at the weekend, rendering me unfit for Monday, the day the carpet would be fitted.

'My colds tend to be stop-start,' I told him.

'You should get yourself a wife to look after you,' he replied, virtually adding: 'And no mistake!'[1]

I disliked the lying intensely, as it put me on a moral footing with Guy. But I wasn't prepared to tell the truth, which I considered a private matter. I was not due in court on either the Wednesday or the Monday. My conferences could be postponed. No one could accuse me of unprofessionalism, except of the most meticulous kind.

I arrived at Elizabeth's house on Wednesday at nine, collecting the key from under the dustbin, where Fiona had placed it. I took with me a small framed photo of myself, graduating from Oxford. This I put on Elizabeth's bedside table. My photo with her photos: it created the illusion of shared occupation.

The estimator arrived at half past eleven. I stood near my photo while he measured up. I wittered on about the neighbourhood, the incidence of car crime, the paucity of policemen on the beat. Short of greeting him from under the duvet, I could not have done more to convince him I was at home in the house.

I even whistled and put my hands in my pockets, intending to jangle my change. Regrettably, I found I had no change. I flapped my pockets noiselessly.

---

[1] Bill, like many clerks, based his professional persona on childhood memories of the film musical *Oliver!*. I once observed him walking to his Porsche singing 'Food Glorious Food'.

★ ★ ★

'Whisky! You shouldn't have!' said my mother, in the hall at High Ridge, as Elizabeth, arriving for our weekend, handed her a bottle wrapped in white paper. My mother recognised the shape. (The neck of a wine bottle is straight, while the neck of a whisky bottle's bulbous.)

'Oh, you shouldn't have,' she said again. But this time she meant it. Elizabeth, along with her overnight bag, was carrying a pair of riding boots.

'You could have had my Aunt Hetty's boots,' my mother said to Elizabeth. 'She died years ago. But her boots live on.'

'No sense in throwing them away,' said Elizabeth. It was better than a reply. It was a continuation. It was exactly what my mother would have gone on to say. Elizabeth, not yet beyond the hall, was already a twice-admired guest.

After our tomato soup and shepherd's pie supper, my parents, Elizabeth and I left the kitchen for the green baize of the drawing room. We drew for partners. I was paired with Elizabeth. Play commenced. In the first hand, my parents bid three spades. I won the first trick with my king of clubs, then led with the nine of diamonds. Elizabeth won the trick with her ace, then led back with the eight. My mother nodded with approval, as did my father, though technically they were Elizabeth's opponents. I, who'd had a singleton diamond, won the trick with a low trump.

Those who play bridge will understand; others need only know she'd played by the book. In bridge, there is only the book; only signals that demand specific responses, only disciplines to be followed. There is nothing to be gained by going off on a frolic of your own. Freya, aged thirteen, learning the game under duress, was asked by my father why, when he'd led with a trump — the six of clubs — she, his partner, having none, had discarded her spade, the only spade remaining, a potential winner once trumps had been played out.

'I hate spades,' said Freya.

'If you don't play properly, there's no point in playing at all,' he said.

'Good,' said Freya, leaving the table.

Elizabeth didn't leave tables. She joined them. She was a player, a contributor, an unprompted fetcher of the ketchup from the pantry.

When she got up and fetched that ketchup, my mother did not remark on her legs. They were blessedly unremarkable.

★ ★ ★

There was a calm in the house that weekend, a calm ironically induced by ceaseless activity. On the Saturday morning, my mother and Elizabeth went riding at Chillesford. In the afternoon, they played golf. In the early evening, we all walked to Thorpeness and back, prior to queuing for fish and chips, eating them, playing more bridge, then going to bed.

On Sunday morning, Elizabeth and I got up

early (and separately). We began by taking Nelson our lurcher — Duncan the terrier having died — for his walk to the river wall. Then, though it was late September, Elizabeth, my mother and I took a dip in the North Sea, prior to a restorative nip of Elizabeth's gift, followed by sausage, egg, bacon and tomato, fried to a perfect mess by my mother. The Sunday papers were read, not skimped, and then, under my mother's brisk direction, Elizabeth and I peeled potatoes, chopped carrots, picked escaped peas from the back of the freezer compartment, assembled old chutney jars crusty at the inner rim, while the gammon boiled.[1]

At lunch, we talked of Farquharsons and Thodays and Risdons and Pilkingtons and Moxon-Smiths — their births, their engagements, their marriages, their deaths, their rugby wins, their babies, their boats, their cancers, their schooling, their exam results, their disasters or triumphs as Lloyd's underwriters, their participation in the 'Pilkington Putter'. This was an annual golfing tournament invented by the Pilkington family. It was complete with its own amusing trophy: silver crossed sherry glasses on a wooden plinth.[2]

We wolfed down our ice cream and chocolate

---

[1] Back in 1989, bought chutney carried no 'Best Before' date. To this day, the notion of a 'Best Before' date irritates me profoundly. I always think: '*I'll* be the judge of that!'

[2] Elizabeth knew Christopher Pilkington's youngest brother Giles. When he was nineteen and she

cake. We were due on the river. Felicity Pilkington had kindly offered to take us all on the family day sailer, a Norfolk Gypsy. We sailed to Iken and back. Felicity, universally known as 'Ferocity', was widely regarded as one of the best women sailors in Aldeburgh. She loved the river. It was the only place, she often said, where she could truly smoke. (Tony Pilkington was a heart specialist, who wouldn't let her smoke at home.) She told me that Christopher and Ticky were getting on famously. She did not mean 'getting on' with each other — it was getting on with life to which she referred. Christopher was 'doing brilliantly' in the City.

'He works very long hours. Ticky hardly sees him. It's a terrible shame.'

'It is,' I said, thinking the opposite, thinking it a wonderful shame.

It was already dark by the time we got back. I could tell my mother didn't want Elizabeth to leave. When we'd cleared away the kippers and tea, she took the top off the kitchen table. Underneath was a half-size snooker table. She insisted Elizabeth give her a game. I watched Elizabeth and imagined Judy Page. Judy Page, waggling before she took her shot, knowing my father and I were behind her.

They played a frame. Elizabeth won.

'Best of three?' asked my mother.

'The young people want to drive back to

was sixteen, he was her first 'proper boyfriend'. This illustrates both our ten-year age gap and the Aldeburgh 'chain of being'.

London,' said my father.

'Do come again!' shouted my mother from the doorway, as Elizabeth got into the passenger seat of my latest Audi.

'Yes!' said my father. Even Nelson the lurcher licked his lips.

In the kitchen, not two minutes earlier, when Elizabeth was upstairs packing her bag, my mother handed me a scourer to scrape the kipper skin off the plates.

'This one's a goodie,' she said. 'I can see what she's *for*.'

'Yes,' said my father, emptying the tea leaves into the bin. 'She's an excellent choice. Thoroughly appropriate.'

No more needed to be said. I was right, I was right, I was right.

★　★　★

'It was like boarding school,' said Elizabeth as, ten minutes later, I turned left onto the A12 and headed back to London.

'Yes?'

I willed this to be a compliment. I had gone to a boarding school, as had Elizabeth — the Royal Masonic School at Rickmansworth, a more than respectable institution, though lacking the academic distinction of Wycombe Abbey or Cheltenham Ladies College.

'In a good way. So much to do. No time to worry.'

'I'm glad,' I said, not asking what might be worrying her, since we both knew. We hadn't uttered his name all weekend.

'I didn't tell him I was coming here.'

'Right,' I said, looking in the rear-view mirror, as a driver's meant to do.

Elizabeth ejected the Wagner cassette, turned it over and put it back in.

'Ferocity asked me how long we'd been together. I didn't perjure myself. I just said, 'We've known each other a few months.''

I greatly admired this answer. It was a lawyer's answer.

'What do you think? Are we together? Don't look in the mirror.'

Her forthrightness was to be admired, if not exactly enjoyed.

'We can't be,' I said, with difficulty. 'You're Guy's girlfriend.'

'No I'm not. I'm not glamorous enough. I'm his bit on the side.'

I wanted to flatter Elizabeth, while maintaining my position, which was that I wouldn't share her with Guy, any more than he'd share her with me.

'You're a very good person. My parents certainly think so.' Then I said, comfortingly: 'Being glamorous isn't everything.'

'Thanks,' she said, sharply, which somewhat confused me.

'We can't be together. Not at the moment. It wouldn't be fair to me,' I ventured. 'Or Guy.'

'Why would you want to be fair to Guy?'

'Because I believe in fairness,' I said.

I knew, in the short term, Elizabeth would be preoccupied with Guy. Guy's edginess and

140

excitement were just that: short-term. Fairness, like patience, like steadfastness, like dignity, was a quality for the long-term. I wanted Elizabeth to think of me as her long-term prospect.

★ ★ ★

Three hours after leaving Aldeburgh, I drew up outside Elizabeth's house, behind Guy's parked car.

'Do you want to come in?'

'No.'

'Because Guy's here?'

'Yes, I'm frightened of what I'd do to him.'

'What would you do to him?'

Yes. What would I do to him? I'd either be fair to him or avoid him. I couldn't say this to Elizabeth. The floor of my Audi felt like quicksand. I had the intellect and forensic skills to argue my way out of quicksand. But this was not a time to argue. It was a time to emote. Emote how? What? Elizabeth was looking at me. What did she see? I tried to keep my face immobile. I tried, as it were, to park my face, just as I'd parked my car.

'Look at me,' said Elizabeth. She put her hand behind my head and pulled me towards her, as fast as my seat belt would allow. For the first time, Elizabeth and I kissed. I felt vindicated, empowered, reassured. Elizabeth's lips were as wet as the ink on a newly signed contract. Her tongue found my tongue and I let it be waggled. Then she let me go. The kiss — and this is the important thing — was no more than that. No

141

more was presumed or demanded. There was no exciting and terrifying Judy Page-style rush.

I wished her happy birthday for the following day. I told her that when she came home from work, she'd find something rather special.

★ ★ ★

On her birthday morning, at ten o'clock, I let myself into Elizabeth's house to oversee the fitting of the carpet. It felt strange to be entering the house without her, having, only the previous night, failed to enter with her. That strangeness did not last.

The carpet, I explained to the fitters, was 'a surprise for my girlfriend'. Five days earlier, with the estimator, I'd felt fraudulent claiming such kinship. Now, post-Aldeburgh, post-kiss, the claim felt just. The fitters, Terry and Bam-Bam [sic], were very obliging chaps. I made them milky teas. Bam-Bam took three sugars. As a treat, I gave him four.

They followed my orders with good cheer. My orders were precise. They had to be. I wanted to leave no trace, other than the new carpet. Everything had to be replaced exactly as it was: the wardrobe, the bed, the chest of drawers, the bedside table, the chair beside the bedside table. It wasn't hard to replace them per se. The difficulty was replacing the items on top of them. On Elizabeth's bed, for example, there was a present wrapped in glossy black paper. The corner of the present nudged a pillow. I committed that nudging to memory and

142

reproduced it precisely.

In colour, the new 'pale sand' carpet was an excellent replica of the old. I allowed myself to think it was a new carpet for a new era, the era of Elizabeth and myself.

I shook the hands of Terry and Bam-Bam, even though they were dirty. I stood on the doorstep as they drove off in their van. Then I shut the door behind me and replaced the key under the dustbin.

★ ★ ★

That night, in my flat, I waited for Elizabeth to ring, to thank me. I listened to Henryk Szeryng (1918–88) playing the Bach Partita for solo violin No. 3 in E major. Szeryng was a great violinist. He disdained the excessive vibrato so prevalent among contemporary classical violinists, who'd all rather be making a charity record, in a sparkly dress, with Sir Cliff Richard.

Elizabeth didn't ring and didn't ring. Had she not returned home after work? Had she entered her bedroom, seen the new carpet but not connected it with me? (I didn't mention it in my birthday card.) Was there something wrong with the phone in her house? Was there no nearby public phone box that hadn't been vandalised?

A thousand times I'd speculated on a judge's probable ruling, given the material facts of the case. Here I didn't know the facts. I was speculating on the basis of ignorance, which I found abhorrent.

143

* * *

Elizabeth called me the next night, in a state of some distress. Before I could say anything, she said: 'Something's happened.'

She'd arrived home the previous evening to find Sophie holding a present wrapped in glossy black paper. Elizabeth smiled, naturally assuming the present was from Sophie. It turned out to be from Guy. Sophie had walked past Elizabeth's door and noticed it on her bed. She'd gone in and read the (highly incriminating) message on the card. She'd rung Guy. He'd confessed.

Elizabeth was outraged that Sophie had sneaked into her room. She knew I'd be outraged too. I was. I'd entered Elizabeth's room on three occasions. But I hadn't read the private message on the card on the present on her bed. My motives were philanthropic, not sneaky.

'What was the present?' I asked.

'Black underwear,' she replied. Of course. Black underwear, wrapped in glossy black. My present lay selflessly beneath her feet, Guy's wrapped itself round her body. It said: 'I am your underwear.' Guy, that edgy narcissist, had taken the opportunity of Elizabeth's birthday to buy *himself* a present. But his present had cost him the affection of not one but two women. That brassiere, black as the Grim Reaper, had strangled him with its straps and suffocated him with its domed sections.[1]

---

[1] Forgive this approximation. I can't remember the correct term. Bowls?

In tears, she told me, she'd rushed to her bedroom. At this point, I interrupted.

'Did your bedroom seem different?'

'Yes. It wasn't my bedroom any more. Sophie came in and told me to pack up my stuff and leave.'

'What about the carpet?' I asked.

'What *about* the carpet? The carpet wasn't mine. I'm not going to pack up the carpet, am I?'

Elizabeth hadn't noticed. I'd replaced Elizabeth's carpet without her noticing. I'd pulled off a brilliant but utterly pointless carpet magic trick.

She'd gone to her friend Ruth in Wandsworth, from where she'd rung Fiona. Fiona told her she was too good a person to be treated in this way, either by Guy or by Sophie. But they were all basically lovely people. Fiona would do everything in her power to bring them all back together. They'd all get over this, eventually.

Elizabeth changed the subject. 'Fiona said you asked for a key. Was someone meant to deliver a present? Nothing arrived, I'm afraid.'

I had to think quickly. I couldn't say her present was in the bedroom that was no longer hers.

'Yes,' I said. 'I left instructions for the postman. I told him I'd leave a key under the bin, so he could put the present in the hall. I hope you don't mind my trusting him. I was brought up to trust the postman.'

'Yes, no. Oh well. I'm sure it'll come. Fiona can send it on to me. Thank you.'

'Don't mention it,' I said, but that nonchalant

phrase came out wrong. It sounded as if I were ordering her never to mention it, ever.

'What's going to happen to your room?' I asked.

'Guy's going to use it as a study.' I didn't understand. 'He's moving in. Sophie said either he moved in or she'd never speak to him again.'

I carried on not understanding. I do not understand to this day. Sophie was saying, in effect: either I never speak to you again or I speak to you all the time. Where was the logic in that?

'Can I come and see you? What are you doing now?'

'Nothing,' I said. 'You're most welcome.'

★   ★   ★

By rights, the phone call should have made me glad. Elizabeth's relationship with Guy had been terminated by Sophie. But I couldn't be glad. I was mourning the carpet. I'd bought a 'pale sand' carpet for Guy. He'd walk on it in his black shoes, his black slippers, his black socks, his off-white feet. He'd walk on it whenever he entered his 'study'. Why, in the name of the Brothers Saatchi, did an account executive in an advertising agency need a 'study'?

I was now obliged to send Elizabeth a different present, too big for her letter box, thereby explaining the postman's need for a key. I decided on a tennis racquet. What kind of present was a racquet, though, in monetary value, in surface area, in warmth on a snowy night, compared

146

with a bedroom carpet? Did postmen deliver tennis racquets anyway? Wasn't that done by a separate parcel-post organisation?

The bell rang. It had to. Something or someone had to save me from my own thoughts.

★ ★ ★

Elizabeth carried an overnight bag.

'Is it all right if I stay?' she asked. 'I need you to look after me.'

I agreed. I wanted Elizabeth to look after me. I accepted that, in the nature of things, there would be times when I would look after her. That was only fair.

'Shall we go to bed?'

'Yes of course,' I said. 'I'll just brush my teeth.'[1]

It was another of my deliberately banal remarks, designed to restore order and balance. Elizabeth had just been thrown out of her house, to make way for the man who'd mistreated her. She had, in modern parlance, been 'traumatised'. I too. I'd lost a carpet.

In the bathroom, I gave considerable thought to the presentation of my member. Was it only polite to present Elizabeth with an excited member? Or only polite not to? The latter, surely. It also made the journey to the bedroom safer. I had the bathroom and bedroom doors to

---

[1] Using, of course, a manual toothbrush. I cannot bear electric ones, which are like flies on sticks.

negotiate, with their dangerous jambs.

'Come here,' said Elizabeth, redundantly, when I entered the bedroom, as if I were about to bypass the bed and climb out of the window. She sat up and flung back the duvet cover, to make my 'coming there' easier. Her ease with her naked self confounded me. Once again, I was being illogical. Why would Elizabeth not be at ease with her naked body? She'd seen it often enough.

I entered the bed and shut my eyes, opening them when she asked me. She said she was going to make me happy. I said I was glad. She told me that the 'first time' would be for her and the 'second time' would be for 'us'. I nodded. I respected this, whatever it meant. She embarked.

It took her considerable time to rid me of my carpet thoughts. But she managed it. Elizabeth, in fact, proved to be an enthusiastic and abandoned lover, which was worrying. That was certainly not what I wanted from a wife.

I comforted myself. She needed abandonment, to get over Guy. In future, she'd be less excited.

'What are you thinking?' she asked, post-coitally. I explained that this was not a permissible question, since the answer would always be: 'I'm thinking that I wished you hadn't asked me what I'm thinking.'

'God, you're hard work sometimes,' she said.

'Hard work has many benefits,' I replied. She put a pillow over my face and held it there for many seconds. Then, when she removed it, she looked sad.

'You're a loyal person, aren't you?'

'Yes,' I replied with complete conviction.

*   *   *

Elizabeth loved her tennis racquet. She uses it to this day. I handed it to her, three weeks later, having waited for the imaginary Post Office to admit they'd lost the imaginary one in the imaginary post.

For her next birthday, I gave her an engagement ring. My parents were delighted, as was I. It was, as I'd rightly predicted, marriage at first sight.

8

The Wedding (1990)

'Why me, Minibob?'

That was Mike Bell's response when I invited him, telephonically, to be my best man. Print conveys the words but not the tone. I heard considerable (if mocking) affection. How, he asked, had I persuaded a woman to marry me 'without giving her drugs'?

He'd never met Elizabeth, which demands an explanation. Mike Bell and I hadn't seen each other in over three years. I'd invited him, occasionally, to spend a weekend in Aldeburgh but he was always unavailable. I asked him, for example, to come to Aldeburgh for New Year's Eve, 1988. He told me he'd be in Australia. Having tried and failed to produce films, he'd started a company to make advertisements and pop videos — hence his presence in Australia over New Year, reconnoitring a video to be filmed on a beach north of Sydney. The 'artist' was Madagascar Sam.

He was highly amused when I told him that, five years earlier, I'd acted for their record company. It appeared to give us something in common, though on further discussion it did no such thing. He described them as 'a bunch of great guys who are always up for it', to which I could only plead ignorance, not having known them socially. Out of politeness, I asked his opinion of their music. He described it as 'great'. Seeking a point of comparison, I asked if it resembled the Sex Pistols' music to which, I remembered, he was devoted.

'It's nothing like the Pistols,' he said, defensively. 'What Sam do is every bit as good as the Pistols, in a totally different way. I mean, music's a very broad church.'

'When does a church get to be so broad that it's no longer a church?' I enquired. 'When does it become a sort of mystical mall, with a hundred gods, all equally second-rate?'

'I don't know. When does it?' he replied, even more defensively. 'They're a fucking great band and we're going to make a fucking great video. That's it.'

I had, advertently, touched on the distinction between us. I was professionally unbending. I was as dispassionate and authoritative with a record company as I was with a one-armed drunk. Mike Bell was blown this way and that. Am I asserting he was a candle in the wind? No. That suggests a passivity which does him a disservice. He threw himself with fervour into each new prevailing wind. I wasn't cynical about his faith in Madagascar Sam. On the contrary, I believed his belief was genuine. But I also believed it would pass.[1]

---

[1] I can think of only one exception: his unwavering faith in a disc jockey called John Peel. In Andros, in 2003, he informed me with awe that Peel had been in the vanguard of every new movement in music. I asked if one could

Three months later, his partner Luke having decamped to Los Angeles, Bell duly wound up the company.

'I hate watching singers act,' he said, in withering reference to the lead singer of his formerly beloved 'Sam'. 'I want to watch actors act.'

That was why he was unavailable to come to Aldeburgh for Easter 1989. He wanted to spend the holiday in his flat, looking for stories for films.

'Why do we need to see each other, anyway? We know what each other's like.'

This struck me as a splendid barb. It cut to the quick of my friendship with my best friend, Jeremy Hamilton-Wood. I knew what he was like. Why did I need to see him? I needed to see *Current Law Monthly Digest* to keep abreast of changes. With Jeremy, there were no changes. That was the point. That was the *raison d'être* of our best-friendship.[1]

---

trust a man who'd been in more than one vanguard. Wasn't this Peel merely in thrall to novelty? He told me I was talking about the man he loved, which I said was not an answer. Then Bell burst into tears. I was sad. I'd been enjoying our argument. But tears meant the argument was over. One can't argue with blub.

[1] Such changes as there were — new boat, new car, new school, new baby, new extension to the kitchen at the back — were too predictable to be of consequence. Unlike the cases in *Current Law Monthly Digest*, they did not break the mould. They joined the mould. They embraced the mould and were soon mould themselves.

When I called Mike Bell in July 1990, I needed him. A groom needs a best man. So. In answer to his question — 'Why me, Minibob? — I said I could rely on him to give an amusing speech. (He was far more amusing than Jeremy.) He didn't demur but, as always, he doubted he'd be available. When I told him the date, he said he didn't know what he was doing on that day. Then he admitted he didn't know what he was doing on any day. He didn't know where his next meal was coming from. I assured him that, if he agreed to be my best man, he'd know where his meal was coming from on 21st September.

'You'll have to have a stag night,' he said. I agreed and suggested we held it in Aldeburgh on the Saturday before my wedding. We arranged to meet at his flat in Fulham to discuss it.

* * *

His flat, of course, was not his flat. It belonged to his erstwhile partner, Luke. Bell was free to use it while Luke was in LA, until Luke's girlfriend Katie returned from her painting expedition to Senegal.[1] The flat had been 'done' by architects of the Devoid School. It was devoid of cupboards, carpets, picture rails, curtains, wallpaper, Formica, stains, sideboards with open

------

[1] This information is of no interest. Why do I include it? As a symptom of the diseased quality of Mike Bell's life. Nothing held firm. His address and occupation were always gangrenous. How did he fill out a form?

packets of biscuits (the topmost biscuit, flabby from exposure, waiting to be rejected). It was devoid of everything I loved about High Ridge — ubiquitous evidence of the passage of years.

In the lifeless living room was a sofa, a low table and a six-foot lamp with a head too small to cast any worthwhile light. This lamp stood in the middle of the room like a madman in an empty ward, till Bell, tripping over a rogue shoe, knocked it over, denting the head and smashing the bulb.

'Shit! That's bloody Luke's fault. He told me to take off my shoes in here. Do you mind if I say you did it?' I minded very much and told him so. He argued that since Luke and I were strangers, no retribution could ever come my way. In which case, I retorted, Bell should invent a stranger. Why blacken the reputation of a real person, like me? Bell challenged me to invent this stranger's name. I came up with 'Arthur Spottiswoode'. He scoffed. He said he'd never have a friend called 'Arthur Spottiswoode'; anyway, it was not a convincing name for a man who knocked over lamps. I thought this absurd. There was no such category as Convincing Names For Men Who Knocked Over Lamps. What did he suggest? 'Arthur Lampover'?

The argument proceeded like our John Peel debate many years later. Bell reacted emotionally. He felt under attack. Instead of weeping, though, he lashed out. He'd just been hired as a script reader by a famous producer I wouldn't have heard of, because I knew nothing about film. He'd read fourteen scripts in the previous

154

three days. He was an expert on characters' names, what they signified, how they worked, their aptness. I, who lacked imagination, wouldn't understand. Did I know the name of the character Jack Nicholson played in *Chinatown*? I said I didn't but he shouldn't tell me, as the information would clearly be wasted on an ignoramus like me.

'You're right,' he said. 'Jake Gittes. There. I wasted it.'

We'd reached an impasse. He surprised me by saying, in a small voice, that he was happy for me. Whom did I wish to invite to my stag night? I gave him a list of ten typed names, complete with phone numbers, and advised him that the Wentworth Hotel in Aldeburgh would be a suitable location, both for pre-prandial drinks and dinner. Bell said he'd book a table. I told him I'd done that already. Where, he asked, would the post-prandial entertainment take place? He'd booked two exotic dancers.

Bell swept the shards of broken light bulb with vigour. Now he was in his element. This, he said, was what a film producer did. A film producer made things happen. He'd located an Ipswich agency that was happy to supply a suitable dancer, on receipt of a fee plus travel expenses, payable in advance. Bell enquired what the travel expenses were and was told they were 'petrol'. In that case, he said, he'd book two dancers, to travel in one car, thus saving a set of expenses. Bell paused, as if waiting for applause. He put the glass shards into a plastic bag, a highly unsuitable vessel.

I returned to first principles. Why did we need one exotic dancer, let alone two?

'It's traditional,' he said. 'On a stag night, there has to be some kind of sleaze.' I explained that Hamilton-Wood, Hawes, Pilkington, Catto and the others could be relied on to drink too much in the restaurant and sing in objectionably loud voices, arousing the ire of neighbouring diners. Wasn't this sufficiently sleazy? Bell said no.

I told him I was not objecting to sleaze per se. I accepted sleaze was traditional. It was just that I knew the Aldeburgh chaps but did not know these dancers. I simply wanted *foreseeable* sleaze. I wanted to know what would happen.

★ ★ ★

I arrived at the Wentworth Hotel for my stag night at seven forty-five. The invitation was for seven thirty. I thought it appropriate to be the last to arrive. Regrettably, I was the first.

I took a stroll along the beach. The light was fading. I marvelled at the view. The North Sea, without ships, boats or windsurfers, looked as it had in the year I was born, 1956. It looked as it had in 1556. New money could not change it. Though a prime site on the edge of a desirable town, the North Sea remained impervious to property developers. It was houseless and priceless, a marine Boudicca eternally resisting invasion from the shore.

I arrived back at the hotel to find Bell at the head of the table, entertaining Pilkington and

Catto with a tale from the music business. Bell, who didn't then (and doesn't now) own so much as a beach hut, gave the impression of owning this public space, of filling it with his personality. He'd known these men for minutes; it looked like years.

At eight thirty, the hors d'oeuvres began their descent on our table. Pilkington ordered a third and fourth bottle of champagne, hailing the waitress with his gold American Express Card, which he made sure everyone could see. He would have been delighted if the card had come in the form of something wearable, like a gold plastic suit.

At this point, a glamorous woman in a turquoise dress appeared at the entrance to the dining room. She looked around, flustered. Bell got to his feet and waved. She approached.

'Oh God, I'm so sorry, am I all right, only I wasn't sure what time I was meant to be here! There's only me, I'm afraid. Lynn couldn't come. Was I meant to be at the other place?'

'No, no,' said Bell, though the answer was yes, yes. The dancing was due to take place in the Pilkington house.

Within seconds, Bell had wrangled an extra chair and a small table to place at the end of ours. He didn't place her at this extra table, though. He rearranged the seating so she sat in the middle of a line of men. Finally, in true producer mode, he made an extra prawn cocktail happen.

While this was going on, she talked without reason or end. She introduced herself to each

157

and every one of us, in turn, as Annette, as if her name might vary from person to person. She'd had a lot of trouble getting to Aldeburgh. There'd been a big pile-up near Ipswich Hospital. I remarked that this was, in its way, highly convenient. The men ignored me. They had eyes and ears for Annette only. Why ears? What was germane, what was material, in her description of her fellow dancer Lynn's inability to get a babysitter, her usual babysitter, Melanie, being unavailable as her (Melanie's) mum was visiting her (Melanie's mum's) brother in hospital?

Finally, she paused. She couldn't remember Melanie's uncle's name. 'Anyway. It don't matter. I'll do two dances.'

'Bravo!' said Pilkington.

'Bravo!' said Catto.

Within seconds, out of sexual excitement, Pilkington started to sing. It was his party piece, the one I'd heard on many such occasions. The song was called 'Stairway to Heaven' and had no merit other than length. As ever, Catto accompanied him on 'guitar', which he impersonated with two noises: *waah-waah* and *gdug-gdug*. Annette found this hilarious. Bell, to his eternal discredit, supplied percussion, rapping his potted shrimp ramekin with the tines of his miniature fork.

All this was wrong. The singing was meant to occur at the brandy and bill stage, when the other diners could comfort themselves that our departure was imminent. Now, they faced two courses and a coffee's worth of tension. There'd be no release at the end of 'Stairway to Heaven';

just an hour and a half of wondering when the next song would begin.

The song, in fact, ended early, as Pilkington wanted a drink. Annette applauded then asked: 'So who's getting married then?'

'Robert here!' said Pilkington, keen to ingratiate himself by showing his closeness to the groom. He placed his hand on my head and attempted to muss my hair. Instead, he mussed my bald patch, his flesh on my flesh, his palm, greasy from credit-card sweat, capping my skull.

'Here's to you!' said Annette, to me. 'I'll do a special extra dance just for you.'

'Yeah!' said Pilkington. 'He's a really big tit man. And you've got really big tits.'

Annette laughed. She was a simple woman. What excuse did Pilkington have, with his expensive education?

Two dancers could have danced two dances simultaneously. Annette had now promised us three: hers, her proxy one for Lynn, the bonus one for me. She would take off her clothes, then put them back on, then take them off, then put them back on, then take them off again. To what purpose? What man, not suffering from Alzheimer's, could be aroused by three revelations of exactly the same things?

'I don't think Robert would enjoy that,' said Bell. I was touched by this. It was certainly accurate. 'He doesn't want to hang around to watch a lot of dances. He's got too much preparation to do for the wedding.' I nodded. 'In fact, why don't you leave now, Roberto? Wouldn't you be more happy?'

The suggestion was absurd. A man cannot leave his stag night. His friends gather with him to bid farewell to his bachelor state. He can't leave, while his prawns are still in their cocktail. Yet Bell was making this possible, because he'd gone to a comprehensive school, because his father ran a shoe-repair business, because he lacked breeding. He was free to be misguided, to do the wrong thing. That was why it was he, in 2003, who told me to do my crime — my wrong thing.

I got up to leave. I could not pretend to be anything other than grateful for Bell's suggestion. Pilkington said: 'Big hand for Robert!' He and Catto led the applause, which seemed to me heartfelt.

★ ★ ★

I arrived back at High Ridge at 9 p.m. to find my mother in the kitchen at her ashtray, drinking supermarket gut-rot brandy. My father was upstairs, working on the seating plan for my wedding lunch.

I explained my early return to my mother.

'Where's your spunk, boy?' she asked, alarmingly. 'Men have a tart on their stag night.' My mother, in this thunderous form, could not be gainsaid.

My father, having heard my voice, came downstairs. He didn't ask why I was home early. He was beaming. His slippers were twitching.

'I've just counted them,' he said. 'There'll be thirteen knights at your wedding.'

160

Elizabeth's family came to supper at High Ridge the night before the wedding. Her father, Graham, was a bank manager, a large man pleased with what he'd achieved, used to giving orders and having things done for him. His wife, Patricia, twittered and fussed. She couldn't help it. Patricia wanted, and expected, everything to be 'nice'. It was as plain as the red nose on a publican's face that there were areas of High Ridge that my mother kept filthy and areas, 'nice' areas, she paid others to clean. The drawing room was clearly 'nice' (despite its ancient furnishings), while the kitchen was a place of stains and smells and broken-backed chairs. The only immaculate section was the floor in front of the cooker, its spots of gravy and spits of sausage fat wiped clean by the constant application of dog-tongues.

Patricia could not adapt to our kitchen. She couldn't accept that our kitchen wasn't meant to be 'nice'. When Graham took my father's proffered mug of coffee and put it on the kitchen table, Patricia lifted it and asked my mother where the coasters were. My mother appeared not to understand the question. My father went to a drawer which he thought might contain coasters. He opened it, shut it, then returned to the table.

'I'm afraid we don't believe in them,' said my mother. Patricia put the mug down in front of Graham, knowing it would give our table yet another O-shaped brand. She looked as pained as if she'd poured its contents onto the back of her own hand.

'I'll get you some coasters for Christmas,' said my mother. 'You can carry them around in your handbag.' Graham laughed. Patricia didn't.

★ ★ ★

At the end of the night, my father kissed Elizabeth on both cheeks. She was returning to spend the pre-wedding night at her parents' Aldeburgh flat. My mother took Elizabeth's whole head in her hands, as if she were intent on pulling it off. Instead, she pulled it towards her and kissed Elizabeth, rather drunkenly, on her left eye.

'Goodbye,' she said. 'I so enjoyed having your little parents to supper.'

'They enjoyed it,' said Elizabeth, who didn't pause before replying in this most blandly suitable way. She knew my mother intended no offence. She simply intended fact. Had Elizabeth been Northern, my mother would have said: 'I so enjoyed having your Northern parents to supper.' How can fact cause offence? Elizabeth understood that her parents were objectively 'littler' than my own. They had littler backgrounds, littler properties, littler income (not a penny of it unearned). Graham managed a bank, while my mother's brother Tom owned one. Their manners were littler too. They had what might be called a 'coaster lifestyle.'

Let me not be disingenuous. I'm aware we live in an age where people are not grateful to have their littleness, their Northernness, their blackness, their Asianness, their Jewishness, mentioned. They do not wish to be defined by it. I, of all people, understand this, for reasons that will become clear. My mother did not. A black man was a black man and a little woman was a little woman. She did not, like Granny P, harp on these differences compulsively. But she harped on them when she felt like it and she felt like it when she said goodnight to Elizabeth.

Elizabeth accepted my mother as she was. That is the point. Elizabeth knew what my mother was like. She didn't marry me to save me from my mother.

★   ★   ★

Freya, aged thirty-two, flew over from New Zealand for the wedding, with her partner Murray. She had, apparently, been living with him for more than a year. He looked like a sensible man. It was her hat, even more than her sensible man, that made my parents proud of their errant daughter. They had never seen her wearing a hat. It was blue, with a black band, and shaped like a flying saucer.

'Doesn't Caroline look nice?' said my father. 'And Murray looks very pleasant.'

'Doesn't he!' concurred my mother. 'Maybe they'll get married next.'

'Caroline' is not a grotesque misprint. That was my sister's given name. At the age of six, her stair-buttering age, Caroline read a children's book called *Small Fry Freya*. The eponymous

163

heroine was a tiny fish on a very low link of the food chain. Defying the laws of nature, Freya ate only bigger fish. In this way, she grew to be the biggest fish in the ocean. Caroline announced that from then on, she'd only answer to 'Small Fry Freya'. There were no takers; so, in a spirit of compromise, she shortened it to 'Freya'.

Within a week, my mother received a call from Caroline's teacher, asking for confirmation of Caroline's name.

'Her name is fucking Caroline!' said my mother, who was persuaded by my father to write a letter of apology, to avoid harming Caroline/Freya's prospects.

'I'd rather take her out of the school and send her to one that has discipline.'

'I fear it'll happen wherever she goes.'

Remarkably, 'I fear it'll happen wherever she goes' was said by me. At eight, I was not only included in the discussion but adjudged to have made the most pertinent contribution, for both my parents sighed and nodded their heads in agreement.

★ ★ ★

Murray was an accountant from Auckland, some twenty years older than Freya. 'Very good to meet you, Robert,' he said, outside the church. 'Congratulations on the happiest day of your life.'

It would be easy, I thought, to dismiss him as a dullard, because he was an accountant who spoke in clichés. So that is exactly what I did. Just because a thing is easy doesn't mean it's not worth doing. It is easy to breathe the sea air on a summer's day.

Murray was indeed a dullard. But he'd accidentally said something of interest, if only to me. My intention was not to make this the happiest day of my life. I was only concerned with the rightness of the day, its procedural correctness, its predictability, its conformity with precedent, its *facts*, if you will. I was not concerned with the interior states of its participants. 'Happiness' could be a delusion. It was, at best, arguable. How could one agree on 'happiness' with a man whose idea of 'happiness' was to live with my sister?

* * *

In the Dedication of this book, I referred to Elizabeth's radiant appearance as a bride. I had never seen her radiant before our wedding day. I confess that when she appeared next to me near the altar, I thought: 'Who's that?' It was the highest compliment I could have paid her. She'd transformed herself from a person into an archetype. She was a bride.

Though inches from me, her face appeared to be coming from a long way away. Her hair had the most extraordinary rococo architecture, with hair endings I found impossible to relate to hair beginnings. According to Bell, I took a half-step backwards.

I thought again of Murray's cliché. Curiously, it helped me. It reminded me that my wedding day was a *day*. Elizabeth's radiance need only last another twelve hours or so. By tomorrow, she'd be relieved of her 'radiant' duty, as we'd both be of our 'happiest' duty. That relaxed me. Yes, that made me happy.[1]

★　★　★

The marquee occupied most of the garden of High Ridge. There were a hundred and twenty people present. Of the thirteen knights, six were judges, one of whom was Gerard Gorringe, my former head of chambers. My current head of

---

[1] Most of the thirteen knights at the wedding remarked on Elizabeth's radiance. None of them said how happy I looked. But they wouldn't, would they? In 1990, no knight remarked on a groom's appearance, unless the knight (and preferably the groom) were openly homosexual. These days — or so Bell told me in Andros — that restriction doesn't apply. Such personal remarks are routinely made by 'metrosexuals', heterosexual men who aren't afraid of seeming homosexual. Bell encouraged me to commit a 'metrosexual act' by admiring his new wetsuit. I refused. According to him, that just made me a 'metrosexual in denial'. I assured him I was no such thing. That, of course, made me a 'metrosexual in denial in denial'. And so on and so on, till we ran out of retsina and I, being sober and not banned from driving, had to go off and buy some more. When I got back, he was in the swimming pool. What kind of man wears a wetsuit in a swimming pool?

chambers, Michael McAvoy, was also present, as was Alan Temperley, now an MP, and Martin MacDonald, QC, my fellow editor on more than one edition of *Emerson's UK Taxation & Trusts*. (I knew him better as 'Mac'). I could go on and I will. Martin Magnus was there, the senior editor of *Halsbury's Laws of England*, the man who would (I hoped) commission me to work on the volumes relating to Taxation and Trusts. My father had placed Martin next to Jacqueline Birrell, QC, who'd recently been appointed a High Court judge, despite being widely considered both mad and a woman. Geoffrey Noone, my old Director of Studies in Law at Christ Church, had come all the way from Oxford, despite having pronounced himself 'somewhat surprised' to be invited. Of the twelve most senior members of my chambers, no fewer than four had braved the journey to Suffolk. Finally, and most notably, I was honoured by the presence of Lord Whitlock, Lord Chief Justice of England and Wales. He'd been placed on the Top Table, at my father's right hand, to make sure he could hear the speeches.[1]

---

[1] To those of a satirical bent, I should make it clear that Lord Whitlock was not some ancient judge who couldn't hear a thing. Tony Whitlock was old, certainly. And he was undeniably deaf. But that doesn't mean he couldn't hear. Of course he could hear. All judges can hear. He was placed on the Top Table so he wouldn't have to cope with multidirectional sound. That, as we know, is the curse of all hearing-aid wearers.

I wanted, before this august audience, to say something of worth. I didn't want my speech to be floppy with happy-day clichés. My audience had already endured the vicar's address, with its far from searing analysis of what was meant by 'love and honour'. Apparently, it meant not going to sleep on an argument. Also, 'you should never have an argument while one of you is holding a hammer'. I could tell he'd said this many times before. It was his wedding joke. It had been aisle-tested. The joke provoked its customary titter, though it relied, for humorous effect, on the somewhat dated assumption that husbands and wives hit each other with hammers.

I was keen that my speech contain no humour. Humour, by 1990, had come to be the *sine qua non* of all public discourse. From training films to television advertisements, from weather reports to cards in a newsagent's window, everything had to 'use humour' to 'get its message across'. Even Margaret Thatcher had fallen victim. Here was a woman who had risen to Prime Minister because of, not despite, the humourlessness that was her constant companion, correctly seen as the handmaiden to her certainty. Then, at the fateful Conservative Party conference of 1980, she was persuaded that this newfangled humour stuff would endear her to the delegates. To confound those predicting a U-turn on her counter-inflationary policies, she said: 'You turn if you want to. The lady's not for turning.'

There was panic as the delegates twigged,

from her intonation — and the subsequent pause — that the Prime Minister had delivered herself of a joke. Laughter and applause were required, fast. Applause could be easily summoned. It was simply a matter of clapping one's hands till the delegate next to one stopped. Laughter was harder. False laughter sounded false, whereas false clapping sounded true.

Why, anyway, was the joke funny? There was no time to ask. If there had been, one's neighbour could have whispered: 'It's a pun on Christopher Fry's 1948 play *The Lady's not for Burning*. Additionally, the 'you turn' is a pun on 'U-turn'.' Yes, that would have explained the humour. But it wouldn't have made it funny. Nothing could. The most powerful force in the land couldn't have made the joke funny. Self-evidently not. The most powerful force in the land had made the joke.

I noticed, as I stood up to speak, that the guests' eyes betrayed an anxiety which was easily defined. Each guest — save the children and babies — was awaiting (and fearing) my first joke. Within a minute, I'd put them at their ease. I'd made it clear there would be no jokes. The point is this: there are people who shouldn't attempt to endear themselves, whose appeal is precisely their refusal so to do. Thatcher was one. I was another.

As I proceeded, their ease blossomed into concentration and respect. A teenage waitress, with a tray of coffee cups, stood at the edge of my field of vision, unmoving, reluctant to chink and rattle her way to some far-off table.

'That was a great speech, Robert,' said Murray, afterwards. Of course he did. He'd programmed himself with some kind of wedding-day software. Yet I would have to agree. My speech was actually *about* something: continuity; Englishness; family; the flotilla of boats at Aldeburgh Yacht Club as symbols of our community, bobbing about, side by side, private properties in a public place, staying afloat through constant investment of money and care and time, mutually interested in sailing smoothly and avoiding any collision.[1]

I concluded with a tribute to my father, thanking him for his intellectual and moral influence and hoping (but doubting) I could become as distinguished a practitioner of the law as he. This was not lost on the members of the legal profession in my audience. They heard the note of humility and they heard the note of ambition. There are certain sounds only barristers can hear. Sometimes I think we are like intellectual dogs.

I sat down to prolonged and admiring applause, marred only by Pilkington's inappropriate whistling. Then Mike Bell got to his feet.

* * *

---

[1] Regrettably, some guests laughed, thinking this a reference to Pilkington's de-masting of Catto at the Aldeburgh Regatta. It didn't help that Catto shouted 'Hear that, Pilk!' Cleverly, I paused and drank a glass of water, allowing the laughter to die down, distancing myself from its cause and effect.

'Who's your friend?' asked Freya, sitting next to me on Top Table. 'He's so unlike you.'

'Quiet, darling, let him speak,' said Murray.

Freya, though, was right. I had exploited our difference to perfection. After my main course, Bell provided, as I knew he would, a light and fluffy dessert, a soufflé. Now, when it mattered not, was the time for humour.

Without preamble, he launched into his recollection of our first encounter. We met in our first term at Oxford, he said, when he ran back to his college room, having realised, with horror, he'd invited two girls to visit him at the same time. Much to his relief, he found neither had turned up. Then he heard their voices. Evidently, they'd both turned up and, in his absence, I'd seized the opportunity to invite them both to my room. He spied me through my keyhole in a state of high excitement. I was feeding them cucumber sandwiches and reading them my 'favourite bits of the Law of Property Act 1935'. It was, said Bell, the closest I'd get in my three years at Oxford to 'sex'.

There was laughter throughout the marquee. Pilkington pounded the table, causing his dessert spoon to dance in its empty bowl. All I'd say is this: I can state with authority that almost everything Bell said was untrue. His anecdote was shot through with perjury, from the cucumber sandwiches to the high excitement to the date of the Law of Property Act, which was 1925.

It was fiction. But fiction was Mike Bell's solace. He had no job or property or wife. Those were the facts of his life, the nonfiction of his existence. No wonder he took refuge in invention and hyperbole, for his own sustenance and others' amusement.

★ ★ ★

How many grooms are congratulated on their wedding speech by the Lord Chief Justice? Tony Whitlock hobbled over to me and my father and congratulated me thus: 'Excellent speech. Community of boats. I'm afraid I've never been good on boats. Boats are built to make landlubbers sick. Very good speech, though. Very appropriate, with the river only a few hundred yards away.'[1]

'Lovely service, lovely bridesmaids, lovely weather, lovely food, lovely speeches. Everything went like clockwork,' said Amanda Moxon-Smith. This was exactly what we wanted to hear. What's more, it was true.

'You didn't mention the seating plan,' remarked my father.

'The seating plan was you, was it, Michael?' replied Amanda. 'Marvellous. Best seating plan ever.'

---

[1] This was a classic example of the judicial style. The 'judgment' — that my speech was very good — is articulated three times, in different ways, so no one can miss it. The landlubbers remark is an *obiter dictum*, an incidental statement not relevant to the judgment, but opinionated and memorable.

Murray approached and sat down next to us. 'You've made me feel like family,' he said to me, though I'd ignored him for most of the day. Maybe that was what did it.

He produced three cigars from the inside pocket of his jacket.

'Auckland airport,' he said, portentously, as if that were the Antipodean Havana. 'Care to join me, gentlemen?' Neither of us smoked cigars or anything else. But we were, as he'd noted, gentlemen. We would therefore not refuse.

Mine was barely in my mouth before Murray thrust his lighter at the tip, which seemed a long way away. 'Nice lighter, isn't it?' he said. 'Heathrow. You can't beat airports for the things that matter in life.'

We nodded, pseudo-sagely, at this curious observation. He huffed and he puffed like the Big Bad Wolf. 'Damn good smoke, aren't they?' said Murray, moving through his conversational gears. We were meant to be feeling gradually closer, united in our communal stink.

'Freya's a great girl. Free spirit. To be honest with you, sir, I have trouble keeping up with her.' From the *sir*, it was clear he was addressing my father, who appreciated that *sir*, as did I. Murray knew his place.

'She has always been an individual,' said my father, at his most judicious, choosing a word he would have applied to any and every person. He clearly didn't want to discourage Murray from asking for Freya's hand in marriage. The request was imminent. We both knew that. 'Sir' was delighted that Murray was observing the niceties.

173

How imminent, though? Murray went quiet, looking from smoker to smoker. If I left him alone with my father, I could achieve two objectives: A, hasten the marriage request, and B, get rid of my cigar.

'I — '

'No,' said Murray, reading my intention, 'there's nothing I want to say to your father you shouldn't hear too. I'd like your blessing, sir. Would you be happy if I married your daughter?'

'Very happy,' said my father.

'Excellent,' said Murray. 'I'm a lucky man.' He shook my father's hand, then mine. I then shook my father's hand. It was an odd thing to do. I regretted it immediately. It made us appear like medieval peasants, who'd just offloaded a three-footed cow.

'Are you getting married in New Zealand?' asked my father. 'Valerie and I would love to see New Zealand. And of course we'd want to make a financial contribution to the wedding.'

'That won't be necessary, sir,' said Murray. He was, after all, a man of fifty, with his own accountancy firm. He was a buyer of fine airport cigars. Why would he not be keen to assert his financial independence? 'I didn't want to tell you till now, sir. This has been Robert's day. Didn't want to turn the spotlight on Freya and me.' He took a portentous double-puff, signalling an announcement as surely as the *bing-bong* on a railway-station loudspeaker. 'We actually got married a month ago. So today's a kind of double celebration. We'd love you to come to New Zealand. I've extended my house. Put a room above the garage. You and Valerie would be most welcome.'

'Thank you,' said my father. But he said no more. He was too upset to say more. He was upset principally — as I was — that Murray had sought his permission retrospectively. To ask permission to marry one's daughter is one thing; to ask permission to *have married* one's daughter is another.

'We got married in a registry office in Auckland. Photo!'

He handed the photo to my father. Murray and Freya were standing on a street corner. Freya was wearing a brown 1950s dress, from a jumble sale or dead woman's house clearance, that would not have looked acceptable even in black and white. Murray, in dark suit and tie, looked at the camera with a formal expression, valiantly trying to make the photo official. Freya wasn't looking at the camera, though. She was looking at the man between her and Murray. His joyous grin was saying *this is the happiest day of my life*. He had a scrubby salt-and-pepper beard, a T-shirt and a beer belly.

'That's Baz,' said Murray.

'Is he a member of your family?' asked my father, bravely.

'No. He was one of the witnesses. We stopped off at the bus station and asked a couple of strangers. Freya's idea. She didn't want lots of people there. Tell you the truth, sir, I wasn't sure she wanted *me* to be there! Yeah, that's Baz. The other one took the photo.' My father stared at Baz. It was easier than looking anywhere else.

175

I knew, precisely, what he was thinking: he would rather his daughter had not got married than got married like this. The church, the vicar, the bridesmaids, the organist, the congregation, the morning dress, the entrance of the bride and groom — with all heads in the congregation turning to look — the marquee, the lunch, the place names, the tablecloths, the speeches, the thirteen knights: where were they? Where was the seating plan which my father would have so lovingly drafted and redrafted? There was Freya and there was Murray and there was Baz. That was it. They were standing on some nameless street, in no particular order. There wasn't even a *standing* plan.

'Please. It's yours. Keep it.'

'Thank you,' said my father. 'Well, we must go and congratulate the bride.'

He took the cigar out of his mouth and extinguished it in the ashtray. This was uncharacteristically rude. There were four inches of his cigar remaining, as there were of mine. I followed suit. Murray, who had about two inches left, found himself obliged to stub his out too. He had to do as his father-in-law and brother-in-law did. It was a tribute to my father's noble bearing that he made the action appear to be a rule of etiquette. Gentlemen never smoked the last four inches of their cigars. No. Definitely not. In the Imperial War Museum was a splendid collection of Churchill's discarded 'four-inchers'.

We stood up. The teenage waitress hovered, waiting to clear our table. All the other tables had been cleared and stripped of their table-cloths.

'I'm sorry we weren't there,' my father said. 'But may I say this.'

Murray stood stock-still, hanging on his every word.

'Everyone's free to get married in their own way. It's not the ceremony that matters. It's the married state. I'm sure you will be a most loving and considerate husband.'

'I shall endeavour to do my utmost to do so, sir,' said Murray, forsaking all grammar and sense.

★ ★ ★

It was the hat that hurt. When first seen, Freya's hat had given my parents such pleasure, so acceptable was it, so appropriate. A blue hat, with a black hatband, in that flying-saucer shape: as familiar a sight at an English wedding as a dog collar. Why had we not seen that it was too appropriate? She was like the prisoner in the dock who has contempt for the judge, yet knows he must show remorse. So he plasters remorse all over his face, he wears it as undeniably as Freya wore that hat. Who dares call his remorse, or her hat, a mere show of insolence?

She wore no hat for her own wedding. Why did she get married at all? Why, having decided to get married, did she do everything to distance herself from the wedding, short of staying away? Why did my sister always have to be interesting? Was that why she'd married a dull man? To make herself seem even more interesting than she already was? It was perfectly obvious from her wedding photo that she preferred Baz.

★　★　★

The story of my wedding was the thirteen knights, my speech, Elizabeth's radiance and the clockwork excellence of the whole proceedings. Freya and Murray were not the story. On that I must insist. It was my wedding and it is my life. I assert the right to own the story of my life. After all, I'm a man who has read about his 'life' in a tabloid. I know what distortion means.

If that newspaper wished to write about my life, why did they not ask me?

I would have (gleefully) not told them a thing.

9

Contentment
(1991-2001)

Isobel Valerie Patricia Purcell was born on the 21st June 1991, followed by Max Michael Purcell, on 29th May 1993.

I had, as I always knew I would, one *d* and one *s*. My life was succeeding as planned.

★　★　★

'Contentment' sounds quaint. Where nowadays do you find a contented man? The adjective is redolent of pre-war chaps, smoking pipes and doffing hats as they hold doors open for ladies. Nevertheless, contented was what I was, in the years given at the head of this chapter. I distinguish contented from 'happy', that transient, self-advertising state which is the province, as I've noted, of bridegrooms and drinkers.[1]

I was, first and foremost, a contented husband. After all, I was a barrister marrying a solicitor. Both parties knew the elements that go to make a contract of marriage or, for that matter, any contract. They are: offer, acceptance,

---

[1] And those who wish you to know from their face that they've got religion.

intention to create legal relations and consideration.

We all know what *offer* means. The man chooses a knee and bends it. He says: 'I love you. Will you marry me?' We're equally familiar with *acceptance*: 'Yes, oh, my darling, a thousand times yes!' In my case, eschewing cliché, I gave Elizabeth a ring for her birthday, without saying a word. Effectively, I left it to her to ask me if I were asking her to marry me. She duly asked if the ring were an engagement ring. I said: 'If you so wish.' This allowed her to accept the ring purely as a birthday present, if she so wished. 'If you so wish' pre-empted humiliation and embarrassment on both sides. I could be deemed to have asked her to marry me if, and only if, she so wished it.

Elizabeth subsequently claimed she'd had to ask herself to marry me. Quite so. I asked her to make herself an offer on my behalf. She accepted it. Let us move on.

We can take the *intention to create legal relations* for granted. Now we come to *consideration*. This simply means that something of value must be exchanged. In most contracts, money is exchanged for goods or services. A contract of sale and a contract of employment are simple examples of this. What, though, is exchanged in a marriage? A ring is merely given. It's not exchanged for a dowry — not since Victorian times has the bride's family been obliged to provide money or valuables as part of the marriage agreement. I certainly did not seek, or need, any valuables from Graham and

180

Patricia, who'd only have fretted about their getting broken, lost or stained.

At this point, we must admit that the marriage contract's anomalous. It contains no particular conditions, warranties, termination or exemption clauses or provisions for breach (unless both parties draw up a pre-nuptial agreement). What does it contain? It is not even written down. It is a social construct, based on practice and tradition. That brings us to love. Is love the thing of value exchanged in a Western civilisation marriage?

The parties shall love each other. If that's the consideration, the marriage contract isn't worth the paper it's (not even) written on. The lover must die for love, the lover must live for love, the lover must walk into a burning building to retrieve the lover's cigarettes. The rights and obligations enshrined in love are infinite. Love means everything and therefore nothing. 'Love means never having to say you're sorry.' Define that, in contractual terms, terms that are enforceable. How do you make a man or woman 'never have' to say something?

Before we were married, Elizabeth and I lived together for six months. In my Canonbury flat, we defined the terms of our contract. We agreed the contributions each of us would make towards our partnership. I am certain that the thing of value exchanged in a marriage is not *love* but *effort*. The husband makes *efforts* to live with the wife, the wife makes *efforts* to live with the husband. These efforts can be agreed upon, allocated, defined, enforced.

Let us imagine Section 19, Subsection 2 of

our Unwritten Marriage Contract. The subsection's called: *Toilet Rolls, Used, Disposal of.* What are its terms? In that Phoney War and Phoney Peace prior to our marriage, we agreed I was not responsible for *Toilet Rolls, Used, Disposal of.* Elizabeth was. How did we agree this? By omission. Over those six months, I failed to dispose of a single toilet roll. I made no effort. Elizabeth made the effort. She put all the used toilet rolls in the bin. Furthermore, she took care of Subsection 3: *Toilet Rolls, New, Purchasing of.* Further and furthermore, she took on Subsection 4: *Toilet Rolls, Used, Replacement of, by Toilet Rolls, New.*

It is not necessary here to quantify Elizabeth's efforts and my efforts, in a vain attempt at parity. It may well be that Elizabeth made ten domestic efforts to my one. I do not know. Some efforts may be trivial, some great. Prior to our wedding, we purchased a house in Highgate, as I'd always hoped and predicted we would. Elizabeth was *House, Furnishing of.* I was *House, Purchasing of.* Who can compare the effort of earning the money to purchase that house with the effort of furnishing it, with all its shops and swatches and phone calls and its sugaring of coffee for artisans? What mattered was that efforts were made by both parties. Without effort, there can be no married life. If neither party disposes of *Toilet Rolls, Used,* what happens? They remain in the toilet. Years pass. One cannot get into the toilet for the mountain of rolls.

Rubbish, on a Thursday Morning, Putting Out of the: that was me. Do not ask your husband if he loves you. Ask him if he's put out the rubbish. 'I love you' means nothing. 'I've put out the rubbish' means the rubbish has been put out.

★   ★   ★

Why are we here? Because Elizabeth told me to 'open up or die'. When we open up, we don't find contentment, do we? That is wishful thinking. We find trauma, neurosis, guilt, shame, neglect, emptiness. We find childhood secrets long repressed.

Kitchen Cupboard, Care of Shoe-Polish Tins in the. We do not wish to hear of this place of contentment. We do not want to know of my colour-coding system: blacks on the left, beiges, tans and cherries in the middle, browns to the right.

We are not interested in cupboards, except as repositories for skeletons.

The boot cupboard in High Ridge. That's more like it, isn't it? When we look inside ourselves, we open up just such a cupboard. It's dank. It's dark. It smells. What do we find when we root around, feeling with our hands? Nothing reassuring. We touch the slimy head of the penis of a child-abusing priest. Is it a false memory? No. Surely not. In that cupboard where we keep our inner selves we find only what we fear. The 'penis' cannot be the innocent toe of a child's wellington boot. Perish the thought, for it is wishful.

I refuse to be bullied. I think I was contented

183

and I was. I'm not suffering from False Contentment syndrome.

Elizabeth, let us not forget, had been in her own dark place. She'd lived in the shadow of Guy and Sophie. Now she emerged into the light of our marriage. What made me so right for Elizabeth? I would say that, as opposed to Guy, I was the right husband for her because I'm not interested in women.

Compare me with Pilkington. On my stag night, when he saw the waitress, Pilkington altered. He was more alert, more territorial; he made himself bigger in his chair. This is not to say his interest in the waitress was sexual. I would sooner describe it as masculine. When Pilkington waved his credit card, he wanted her to know she was dealing with a man who knew what he wanted (champagne!) and wanted it (champagne!) now. Pilkington needed that waitress to affirm his power, wealth and impatience (champagne!). These were his masculine characteristics.

Bell, of course, was as different from Pilkington as he was from me. I heard Bell ask Annette, as I left the restaurant, how long she'd been dancing. He wasn't fixing her with his masculine gaze. On the contrary, he wanted to learn how it felt to be fixed by the gaze of others. Bell's interest in women was curiously actorish. He wanted to know how it felt to be Annette in order, absurdly, to *become* Annette, play Annette's part. Annette, by dessert, would come to believe there was no distance between herself and Bell.

We cannot discount sexual desire, any more than we can with Pilkington. But Bell's method and intent were different from the self-assertive Pilkington's. Bell sought intimacy with women. He wanted to make, as it were, the beast with one back. Bell loved women.

I was interested in Elizabeth as wife, companion, helpmeet, mother — not woman. I was a monogamist. A man who loves women, by definition, cannot be monogamous. Elizabeth liked to have sex on a Sunday morning, round about nine o clock. I was perfectly happy with this arrangement. It reminded me of my Sunday-night egg. She woke me one October Sunday, playfully pressing the alarm clock against my forehead. The clock gave the time as five to nine. I showed her my watch. It said five to eight. British Summer Time had ended at two that morning. She'd forgotten to put her clock back.

'Oh no!' she said, jokingly. 'That means we have to wait an hour!'

'Yes.'

'Don't be silly. It's five to nine. They're just *calling* it five to eight.'

'No,' I replied. 'It's five to eight. If we tell each other five to eight is five to nine, where does it stop?'

When I was a child, prostitutes were prostitutes. Now they're 'sex workers', like 'office workers' but with car seats for desks. I do not mock the term. It's accurate. Sex is work. There is physical labour, there is repetition.

Like all my fellow countrymen, I'd gained an

185

hour and wished to spend it asleep. I did not want to go to work.

★ ★ ★

We'd planned that Elizabeth would leave Cheeseman Crick when she was seven months pregnant. There was great contentment in making such plans and sticking to them.

The first thing she did after giving up work was invite her old housemates to lunch. There they were, two years after Elizabeth's forced departure from Sophie's house, chatting away on a glorious May Sunday in 1991. After eighteen months of silence, Sophie had got back in touch with Elizabeth, prompted by that honest broker, Fiona. Sophie and Guy were married and Sophie was pregnant. She'd heard from Fiona that Elizabeth was pregnant too. Sufficient water, therefore, had flowed under their bridges and brought them to a similar point.

Fiona was working in housing, either for a local authority or a housing cooperative. (I wasn't listening.) In the two years since I'd met her, she'd got even more caring. She'd also put on weight. It never occurred to me before that lunch that women put on weight in their breasts. Fiona was a walking bosom now, thrilled to have two heavily pregnant women to shepherd from sink to table. At one point, she knelt between them. I feared she was about to pray for their forthcoming babies. But no. She asked Elizabeth and Sophie to place their bumps against her ears. She squealed with delight when she got what she wanted: synchronised foetal kicks.

Sophie, meanwhile, had become even sharper, her bump only accentuating how sleek and honed were all her other parts. She'd tactfully chosen to visit Elizabeth on a weekend when Guy could not accompany her, being away on business. But she talked about him a great deal, making his absence felt. Guy had left Baker Cork Howard Vogel to set up an agency of his own, with his 'best mate' Rick Cooper-Jones — a man, Sophie intimated, we all should have heard of. The relationship between clients and agencies was changing. The flashiness and aggression of the eighties were outmoded. Guy, that connoisseur of edges, had spotted a new cutting edge and decided to place himself on it, with his mate.

'They very much work with the clients,' said Sophie. 'The nineties are about giving clients partnership and friendship.'[1] Accordingly, the two men called their agency Guy & Rick. This was revolutionary. Since what she called 'the dawn of advertising', agencies had been aggregations of surnames. These first names were a 'wake-up call' to the corporate world. Guy & Rick were 'on first-name terms with the future'. Potential clients were intrigued, especially car manufacturers and fashion houses. (As peddlers of fashion, they were of course its first victims.) Something was happening and, whatever it was, they couldn't afford to miss it. In their first year,

---

[1] Anyone who starts a sentence with *The nineties are about* should be shot or given a job as a journalist.

187

Guy & Rick's turnover was in excess of five million pounds. Guy was in Germany as Sophie spoke, setting up a Munich branch. Guy & Rick had taken up residency on the front cover of the advertising 'bible', *Campaign*, though 'Guy & Rick' suggested they should be staring out of *Hairdressers Journal*.

Mercifully — or so I thought — the conversation moved on to kitchen furnishings. Sophie admire our Aga and asked if it was there when we bought the house. Elizabeth confirmed that it was. She'd only replaced the kitchen units, which were hideous. Her decorating principle was simple. If she could live with something, she left it as it was when we moved in. There was no point spending vast amounts of money on carpets, say, when the existing carpets were a perfectly nice brownish-grey and would last another ten years. I excused myself from the table to make more coffee, without first enquiring if there were any demand. This was an avoidance strategy I'd inherited from my father and applied to my own marriage. I confess I found the carpet talk queasy, not wishing to be reminded of my carpeting legacy to Sophie's Clapham house.

Sophie, it transpired, had sold that house. She and Guy had bought a flat in Paddington, just round the corner from Guy & Rick. They'd also bought a building plot just outside a commutable village in Hampshire. Sophie was worried about finding a nanny who'd be happy to whizz up and down the motorway from Hampshire to London.

They were building a house on the plot with

the help of an old friend of Rick's, a 'cutting-edge architect'. (Did we think he'd be friends with a blunting-edge one?) She pronounced herself jealous that Elizabeth had found a house where not much needed doing — she and Guy had bought a plot where everything needed doing.

'This is terrible!' Fiona shouted. She looked on the point of tears.

'What's the matter, Fee?' asked Sophie. Within seconds, the two women were hugging each other, the yin of Fiona's bosom balanced by the yang of Sophie's bump. Fiona was worried that Sophie would spend the last months of her pregnancy getting stressed by plans and site meetings. Sophie assured her she'd let Guy take the strain. Now, of course, Fiona — that equal-opportunity hugger — broke away from Sophie to envelop Elizabeth. Elizabeth, I regret to report, leaned her head on Fiona's shoulder. Then, happily, she straightened and went to baste the chicken. Sophie took Fiona's hand and asked: 'How are YOU though, Fee?'

This was no place for a man. Yes, it was a place for a man like Pilkington, who'd have given the impression he'd created those bumps with his masculinity; and, yes, it was a place for a man like Bell, who'd have touched his own belly in sympathy, then thought about crawling into the oven to see how the chicken *felt*. I left, remarking quietly, so no one would hear, that I had things to do in the garden. Till lunch, I removed the lawn that the gardener had mowed the previous day.

When I looked through the window, though, I

felt — yes! — contentment. This was my house, my garden, my wife. It was nothing like the Sundays I'd spent in Clapham. I could abandon the company of these women, to do some husbandly thing. Leaving them alone was in itself husbandly. A husband, unlike a suitor or fiancé, has no obligation to pretend to be interested in his wife's female friends. There was more. To see my wife with Sophie and Fiona, from the safe distance of the lawn, was to be reminded how utterly appropriate my choice of Elizabeth had been. Sophie and Fiona were everything I didn't want in a wife. The one was sulky, vain, sharp and acquisitive, while the other made you feel she was reaching inside you and slowly, lovingly, fondling your guts.

When I next looked, the women were no longer there. They were coming out into the garden. I couldn't be discovered mowing the mowed. I put the mower on its back and peered at the underside, as if searching for something. Grass, perhaps.

Sophie congratulated Elizabeth on the impeccable state of our garden. She asked if we had a gardener, then bemoaned her own situation: 'We'll have thirteen acres to look after. What are we going to do with thirteen acres? We'll need two or three gardeners. They'll be exhausted.' She shook her head in despair.

'Why don't you build a hospital on it?' suggested Elizabeth. 'Then you could put the exhausted gardeners in the hospital.'

'Sophie doesn't want a hospital in her garden,' said Fiona.

'She knows that,' said Sophie to Fiona.

*　*　*

At lunch, we saw, yet again, the value of a man who isn't interested in women, or emotional matters of the kind that fascinate women; especially three women who've shared a house and formed constantly shifting alliances, the three together, the two together, the one against the two, the different two against the different one. Could Elizabeth's friendship with Sophie survive the hospital remark? Could Fiona bring them together? Or would Fiona's interference cause them both to turn on her? These elephant-sized 'issues' simply sat on the corner of the table, where I ignored them. And so the lunch was able to proceed. The talk was my talk. It was of matters outside our selves. Is that not where mental health lies? I asked vigorous and fascinating questions   about the future of the united Germany, traffic congestion, the resolution of disputes at the Aldeburgh Regatta — then answered them.

*　*　*

When they left, Elizabeth told me she'd decided against hiring a nanny. She wanted to do everything herself. She didn't want to be like Sophie. Sophie was spoilt and acquisitive. She'd forgotten how bad it was.

I said if she wanted to do everything herself, she had my full support. As for Sophie and Fiona, she need never see them again. Our companions would not be the Sophies and Fionas of Elizabeth's past.

I joined Crown Yard Tax Chambers in 1993. My career continued to flourish. I frequently accompanied the set's silks (QCs) to the European Court of Justice and the House of Lords. Personal and corporate taxation, including share schemes, Schedule E remuneration and capital gains tax planning, were my areas of expertise. As first Chancery Junior, I frequently acted for the Inland Revenue. For what it's worth, the directory *Legal 500* described me as 'extremely technically able' and, more colloquially, 'possessed of a brain the size of a football'. As a cricket lover, I was somewhat bemused. Though one didn't wish to have a brain the size of a cricket ball!

* * *

'Hold on, I'll get my wife. Darling! The man's here!' That's what I'd say when the man arrived to lay the new carpet.

You perhaps recall these words, from my first meeting with Elizabeth. In the event, I was right in almost every detail. A man did indeed turn up, ten years after Elizabeth told Sophie and Fiona that the carpets in our house would last another ten years. But I didn't shout 'Darling!' I didn't call Elizabeth 'darling'. I didn't call Elizabeth any pet name, or any name at all. This was not impersonal. Elizabeth had so skilfully and discreetly absorbed herself into my life, allowing me always to hear my own thoughts, that I did not think of her as another person, more as an extension of myself, an indivisible appendage.

'Hello!' I shouted, when he came, in April 2001. 'The man's here!' I didn't say, 'The man's arrived to lay the new carpet.' For 'carpet' would have been a misnomer. I did, as I always knew I would, defer to Elizabeth in domestic matters. The carpet was being replaced with all manner of 'natural flooring', a curious phrase which suggested to me there'd be mud and snakes underfoot. For the stairs, living room, drawing room and bedrooms, Elizabeth had chosen a combination of pronounceables and unpro-nounceables: coir, jute, sisal and seagrass. She assured me they were all dog-friendly, though they didn't look it.

This was not what I was used to and nor was 'the man'. He immediately did not look like the kind of artisan who concerns himself with flooring. There was nothing about him of the tabloid-reader, opening his Thermos in his white van.

'Hi, I'm Anthony,' he said. 'Beautiful house. I love Highgate. John Betjeman lived two streets away, didn't he?'

This was overwhelming. I was his patron, the one who would sign the cheque for his services. He must allow me to patronise him. They understood this perfectly, did Bert the gardener, Billy who 'did' the boiler and all the other servants at High Ridge. My father treated these good men and true with the utmost courtesy, as if they were equals. But they were not his equals and they knew it — that's what made his treatment of them so gracious. Anthony, within a few seconds of our meeting, was not allowing me to treat him as an equal. He was actually asserting he was my equal, with his fund of knowledge and his (unsolicited) opinions.

'I'm Mr Purcell,' I replied, putting him at his unease. 'My wife will be down shortly to give you your instructions.' He nodded. I noticed for the first time that he had a ponytail. Was that to keep his hair out of the natural flooring?

Elizabeth failed to come down the stairs. I was instinctively reluctant to leave him on his own in our hall, in case he took too much interest in our paintings and the family photos atop the hall table.

'I'm sure she'll make you a cup of tea. We have plenty of milk and sugar.'

'I don't take milk or sugar, thanks,' Anthony replied. Of course he didn't. He was far too interesting, in that Freya-like way, to do anything so prosaic. Did he, I wondered, even take water?

'Do you have any lemon?'

From then on, I thought of him as the Lemon Man.

★ ★ ★

Elizabeth came down the stairs to greet the Lemon Man. She'd finally persuaded the seven-year-old Max to stop playing 'short football' in the bath. She'd extracted a promise from his elder sister Isobel not to read in bed for longer than an hour. These, Elizabeth told me, were the two things that always happened at this time, which was seven thirty.

This begs the question: what was the Lemon Man doing, laying his natural flooring at seven thirty in the evening? What could be more inconvenient? We'd have to vacate rooms. There would be noise, which might disturb me in my study. It was all most unusual.

The Lemon Man, I learned in bed that night, was not just a layer of natural flooring and its unnatural forebear (carpet). He was a poet. He liked to write and walk and swim and meditate during the day and was grateful to any client kind enough to let him do his work in the evening.[1]

*　★　★

Once a term, when I was at Oxford, my father would visit me in college, then buy me lunch at the Randolph Hotel. In my first term, as we were leaving college, a Japanese couple asked my father if he would take their photo. He did so and they went on their way. He then remarked,

---

[1] On his third visit, he gave Elizabeth a volume of his poems. It was published by Vervain Press, a poetry publisher with a Glasgow address. That, at least, was in the Lemon Man's favour — he hadn't paid for his own publication. I couldn't accept it as a gift, though. I insisted he accept a ten-pound note, which he did with some embarrassment. I noticed later that the price of the book was £11.99.

wistfully, that it would be nice if there were a photo of us. Accordingly, on subsequent visits, he brought his camera. We found a spot we liked — opposite the college entrance — and waited there, once a term, till a likely candidate for taking our photo walked past, at which point my father would tactfully accost her and offer her his camera, for the candidate was always a 'her'. That became our running joke. Each photographer had to be prettier than the last. Prettiness, of course, is in the eye of the beholder. I deferred to my father's eye. Our Trinity term photo, in the long hot summer of 1976, took a famously long time coming. My father must have rejected about a hundred candidates, till hunger got the better of him and he asked a boy with spots.

In our Highgate house, on the piano, there were eight photos of my father and me in Oxford.

'That looks like Christ Church Meadow,' said the Lemon Man, who was about to fit natural something-or-other on the drawing-room floor. It was a weekday evening in May. He watched as Elizabeth carefully stacked the photos, then put them in my outstretched arms, while she helped him shift the piano.

'I used to love walking to the Botanic Gardens past the back of Merton. I was at Jesus. I hear you were at Christ Church.'

'Not at the same time,' said Elizabeth, saving me from a pointless conversation about when and where in Oxford the Lemon Man and I might have met. He looked about ten years younger than me but seemed even younger, because he was so unresolved. Anthony couldn't answer the question: 'What do you do?' As a professional man, I needed only four words: 'I am a barrister.' What could he say? He'd have to start: 'Depends on the time of day.' Even his hair was unresolved. Did he have long hair or short? A ponytail is a way of not committing to either.

When he left our house for the final time, just before midnight on a Wednesday, he arose from the floor of the downstairs lavatory and walked to the hall. He was uncertain if I were still awake. I was. I was waiting in my study. I didn't like the idea of his being in our house while I was asleep. I came downstairs.

'I'm going now,' he said. 'Thank you for all the lemon tea. Please say goodnight to your wife . . . Elizabeth.'

'I'll certainly say goodnight to my wife Elizabeth,' I replied. Then I added: 'I always do.' He seemed uncertain as to whether this was intended to be humorous. In fairness, I shared that uncertainty.

He gave me an envelope. We both knew it contained not a poem but an invoice.

'Do you mind my saying something?' he asked. Who can object to what has yet to be said? 'You have tension in your shoulders. I think yoga could help you with that.'

The Lemon Man had got it precisely wrong. The tension in my shoulders — which, I grant him, Elizabeth had remarked upon too — was not a barrier to my contentment but a cause thereof. I wanted and needed such tension. It spoke of my concentration and application and intensity of thought. I literally braced myself for work. I'd spent the evening in my study, drafting an opinion on European Community tax relief rules for Marks & Spencer plc. Marks & Spencer was and is a much-loved institution, a national treasure, famous for the care with which it treats its staff, customers and suppliers. Do you think Marks & Spencer gave a 'tuppeny fart' about the state of my shoulders? They cared, passionately, about my opinion, for which they were paying me extremely well. Do you think, if my opinion was misguided, thereby failing to save the company millions of pounds, the chairman would write to me and say: 'Never mind. At least your shoulders were relaxed.'

'I'll bear that in mind,' I replied, opening the front door to speed the Lemon Man's exit. Then, of course, I thanked him for all his hard work. I did not neglect my manners.

'That's OK,' he said and I regret to report that, as he passed me, he placed a gentle hand on my shoulders, thereby doubling the tension.

Subsequently, Elizabeth did indeed attend yoga classes, on a Wednesday evening, and the occasional yoga weekend in Herefordshire. This was no hardship. On the yoga weekends, I would take the children up to Aldeburgh, to allow my mother and father to assist in looking after them. On the Wednesday evenings, Sarah, a local sixteen-year-old, would come to our house to babysit, in case Max or Isobel needed anything while I was in my study.

Sarah was not merely a babysitter, which word connotes a girl watching horror films on a sofa, while her boyfriend, his head lowered to avoid blocking her view, makes her pregnant.

Sarah was a pupil at St Paul's Girls' School, a role model for my daughter. Not once did Sarah bring a boyfriend to our house. She brought always and only homework. I did once surprise her as she watched a video. It was *Hamlet*, the Russian version from 1964, with music by Shostakovich.

10

The Night of My Life
(2001)

I accept that all roads lead to the night of 29th September 2003. It is the reason we are here. But it is not the reason *I* am here.

On 21st June 2001, Elizabeth and I gave a dinner party in our garden. It was the sixth and best of the weekly dinner parties we gave that summer. If one could point at a dinner party as if it were a star and say: 'Look! That's Robert Purcell's life! See how brightly it shines!' this would be the dinner party at which to point.

★   ★   ★

I'd spent the day proofreading the Fifteenth Edition of *Emerson's UK Taxation & Trusts*. Martin 'Mac' MacDonald, QC, my fellow editor, was to be one of our dinner guests.

I deferred to Elizabeth in the matter of the menu. Over the years, she'd become more and more interested in food; motherhood had made her increasingly concerned about its provenance and nutritional value. My mother delighted in ragging Elizabeth on this score. 'I'm

200

afraid Buster's food's not organic,' she'd say.[1]

As well as new floorings, Elizabeth brought new foodstuffs into my life. Without Elizabeth, I might never have encountered chicory, curly kale, chard, all manner of beans not in tins, all kinds of nuts not buried in chocolate with fruit. I remember my first encounter with a chicory. It was swimming in what looked like sea but turned out to be olive oil and lemon juice. In its acrid taste and even its shape, it somewhat resembled one of Murray's wedding cigars.

'This is delicious,' I said.

'Do you really think so?'

'Yes,' I said. She accused me of lying. But I was not lying. I was practising a truth in its incipient stage. I would learn to find chicory delicious. I appreciated how much chicory mattered to Elizabeth and was determined to find it delicious, which I subsequently did. The trick was to eat it quickly and accompany it with an unsuitable wine, a Chateauneuf du Pape perhaps, whose big earthy flavours would fight with the chicory's and win, overpoweringly.

The main course, on that midsummer's night, was an impressively complicated dish Elizabeth had found in a book of sixteenth-century recipes. First eaten at the court of Henry VIII, it involved duck stuffed inside pheasant stuffed inside goose. Perhaps Henry VIII was attracted to it by

---

[1] Buster was an Airedale terrier. It was lying next to Buster, in August 2002, that my mother died. Dog death will loom large, later. It will, I regret to say, loom larger than my mother's.

the amount of beheading involved. It was followed by a summer pudding and preceded by an *amusegueule* of filleted and sliced olives, and a starter of tomato, red pepper and goat's cheese salad, which I kept calling tomato, red cheese and goat's pepper salad, much to my daughter Isobel's amusement. Between the main course and the dessert, Elizabeth inserted a savoury, an exquisite slice of chicory tarte tatin. With the cheese board, we were in for a sumptuous five-course meal.

I finished my reading at twenty to eight, which gave me twenty minutes to complete my allotted tasks: *Garden Table, Laying of; Wine, Opening of; Chairs Round the Table, Putting; Candles and Matches, Assembling.* There had been a time, not a year earlier, when all kitchen efforts, except food preparation and cooking, were made by me; then Elizabeth insisted we buy a washing-up machine, since we were entertaining so frequently. It's important to note that she did this after full consultation; important because it implies that the terms of the marriage can be altered, if the other party agrees and is given notice.[1]

I had never been a great one for dinner parties, or any other kind. But, in my Contented Years, I found that parties could be amusing, provided they were small and one's own. I did

---

[1] I didn't throw away my washing-up gloves. Someone had to take care of the bone-handled knives too precious to be shoved into the belly of that brute of a machine.

not wish to waste my energy on strangers. At other people's parties, I met strangers all the time. Within seconds, I knew *why* they were strangers: they were strange.

In the matter of the guests, Elizabeth deferred to me, knowing I'd invite practitioners of distinction from all branches of the law. That particular night, the guests were: Mac and his wife Alison, Kieran Harris, QC, and his wife (whose name need not detain us here, as they would shortly divorce), His Honour Judge Michael Rodwell and Lady Rodwell (otherwise known as Sheila Gurney, QC) and Alan and Honor Temperley. Alan Temperly, QC, MP, was by this time a junior minister in the second government of Tony Blair. Cordial loathing did not cloud my appreciation of Temperley's achievements nor prevent my welcoming him to my garden on this glorious night. I shook his hand and gave him a glass of champagne.

'Cunt! How are you?' he asked. He was just making a friendly noise and did not expect an answer. In any event, the answer was obvious. Temperley had only to look around to see I had never been better. I had a very capable wife and a thoughtful and gifted and dutiful daughter. To judge from the plethora of footballs on the lawn, I had a son too.

My daughter was, at that moment, bringing a tray of *amusegueules* into the garden.

'Drop it! Go on! Drop it!' shouted Temperley, attempting to amuse her but only embarrassing her. It was Isobel's tenth birthday. As a special treat, we were allowing her to stay up late and, after dinner, entertain the adults.

I was a man of substance, financial, social and even physical, for I had filled out, as was appropriate for a middle-aged man, though I was in no sense obese. My diet was too healthy for that.[1]

---

[1] Once, on a winter's night, with butternut squash, lentils and rice lying in wait for me at home, I stopped off for a burger on the Holloway Road. As I walked up to the counter, I affected surprise, as if I'd been led to believe the place was a library and was puzzled by its lack of books. 'Hi, how are you today?' asked the youth behind the counter, smiling beneath the sparse brown grass of his moustache. In the Guy & Rick style, he'd been trained to be my new best friend. I replied politely: 'Adulterous,' knowing he would not have been trained to reply to my reply. I did indeed feel adulterous. I felt unfaithful to my wife's cuisine. 'What would you like tonight?' asked the youth. I was appalled by the premise of his question, 'tonight' suggesting I was between last night's and tomorrow night's burgers. I replied: 'Your most expensive item.' By describing it thus, I was spared the humiliation of saying 'Whopper' or 'Stonker' out loud. He asked if I wanted to eat it there or take it away. I replied: 'Neither.' From my evident distaste, I hoped he'd assume I was buying it for someone else. But then I ate it in front of him, in an unsmiling, detached way, as if, having bought it for someone else, I were eating it for them too. The experience was — I was going to write 'dreamlike' but that's not correct. In a dream, one's

It was early in the evening. The men were on the lawn and the women were touring the house. I saw them, through the kitchen window, just as I'd seen Elizabeth and Sophie and Fiona all those years before. It was a thrill to see the wife of a High Court judge remove her shoes to paw the new floor of our kitchen. Soon, all the women were doing it, pawing and nodding like horses. This universal approval was a tribute to Elizabeth, though I must say I found the Lemon Man's sisal something of a crumb-trap.

I sat down in my appointed place, opposite Kieran Harris, my old pupil master, and poured him a glass of Sancerre. He'd lost none of his old twinkle.

'You've got yourself a hinterland, young Robert,' he said. I had never thought of it like that. But he was right. I was no longer, as when young, the sum of my intellectual powers, a man alone with his thoughts. Beyond me and behind me were this lawn and these people. Marriage and fatherhood had broadened and deepened me. He watched Elizabeth walking towards us, with a tray of starters.

'Will you look at that! Your wife's had two kids and she's still got her fighting figure.'

---

convinced the events are real. As I wolfed down that burger, I tried to convince myself the events were fictional. I tried to make-believe (make myself believe) that I could distance myself from my actions, look back at myself and state with confidence: 'That's not me.' I tried to have an out-of-body experience. But I just couldn't get out.

'I'm not sure it's a fighting figure,' I replied. Elizabeth was thin but I was keen to defend her from the accusation of sexual allure. She was lean from effort and exercise and excellent diet. Thinness was a by-product, not an aim.

'How did you get a woman like that? Christ, when I met you, you didn't know which end of a girl was up!'

This had never been my sort of conversation, as Kieran well knew. But I decided to allow him to provoke me into indiscretion. I felt unusually expansive.

'I'm not sure that's entirely accurate,' I said. 'There was a girl called Ticky.' I paused.

'Go on,' said Kieran. 'I'm fascinated.' Emboldened, I listed all the women between Ticky and Elizabeth: 'There was the woman who worked in the music business, the woman my mother couldn't stand, the woman who made me buy things for my flat, the woman who hoovered naked.'

Kieran whistled his admiration.

I said nothing. I didn't say the woman was the same woman. I was a barrister addressing a barrister. Kieran could, if he so wished, cross-examine me, thereby exposing my list as a list of one. Instead, he compared my Elizabeth favourably with his own wife, a much younger, orange-coloured stick of a woman at the far end of the table. She looked like she hadn't eaten for a year and would not be resuming tonight. She took a forkful of starter and dropped it on the lawn for her rather repellent sausage dog.

'She bought him because he reminds her of

my cock,' said Kieran. 'Mind you, that was a couple of years ago now.' With every word, he sounded more Irish and mournful. Clearly, this canine simulacrum had supplanted the real thing in his wife's affections. He said he'd married 'a grabbing woman'. Elizabeth, in his opinion, did not look remotely 'grabbing'. She looked, he said, like the kind of woman who could leave a house 'within the hour'. He was right. Elizabeth's lack of vanity meant exactly that. She put on clothes and make-up and we left the house. There was never any agony with mirrors.

'Will you excuse me now?' asked Kieran. 'I need to concentrate on my drinking.'

I turned to Sir Michael Rodwell and asked how his daughter was enjoying St Paul's Girls' School. He said she was enjoying it tremendously, though she found some of the other girls 'a little slow'. She was intending to apply to his old Oxford college, which now accepted women. I felt more and more contented. His Honour Judge Michael Rodwell was in his mid-fifties. He was closer in age to me — I was forty-five — than he was to my father. He had children just a few years older than mine. If I simply carried on, doing what I was doing, I'd be sitting, ten years hence, in this very same garden, telling a guest — maybe Michael himself, now Lord Justice Rodwell — how much my own daughter was enjoying her father's old college. She was, I'd (probably) remark, the only undergraduate in her college whose father was a judge.

I had applied three times to become a QC or

'take silk', in common parlance. (It is from the ranks of QCs that judges are appointed.) On each occasion, my application had been rejected by the Lord Chancellor's office. This was standard. Alan Temperley had applied four times before he was successful.

'Don't worry,' Alan told me, as the goat's pepper salad arrived. 'You'll get there. The fuckers'll see the light.'

He was right. The future was moving towards me. It was simply a matter of waiting for it to arrive.

★ ★ ★

I was the *sommelier* in our household. I took great delight in ordering, cellaring, selecting and serving wine. Elizabeth always said I wasn't so interested in the drinking.[1] That was true. The drinking was over in moment whereas a bottle might lie under one's roof for years. That bottle was not inert, though. While I slept, my wine matured and gained in complexity as, I hoped, did my children.

All guests were possessed of a summer pudding, as I rapped on the table with a spoon.

'Forgive my schoolboy Hungarian,' I joked, 'but allow me to present this Tokaji Aszu from 1975.'

---

[1] Let us not be frightened of that 'always'. There is no marriage without repetition. Repetition in marriage was a friend to me far more than a foe. When I looked for a clean white shirt, I found it. Always.

Even the more extrovert guests — Temperley, Kieran — knew they should quieten down. We all sipped the sweet wine together, apart from Elizabeth, who left the table. It is a wonderful thing when a group of diners takes a long time to imbibe a short drink. We inched — or, rather, we millimetred — towards the bottom of our glass. After every sip, Lady Rodwell gave a little *mmm*, which acted as a musical punctuation mark. I found myself *mmm*-ing with her in unison.

It was dark now. We were starlit and replete.

'Ah! The entertainment's arriving!' said Sir Michael. Elizabeth and Isobel were advancing across the lawn. Isobel carried her cello, while Elizabeth held a music stand in one hand and a torch and sheet music in the other. I fetched another chair for Isobel. Then I asked my guests if they would kindly turn off their mobile phones. No one was carrying a phone except Temperley.

'He always carries two,' said his wife Honor.

'It's a long story,' said Alan. He brandished a phone. 'This one's the PM. He's the only one who's got the number.'

'Wasn't such a long story, was it?' said Honor, to everyone and no one. Alan shushed her. Isobel was seated. Elizabeth turned on the torch.

Isobel played with an understanding and technique far beyond her ten years. Then, some four minutes into the piece, the battery of the torch gave out. Kieran cried out, 'Shame!' Mike Rodwell said, 'Hear, hear!' But it was the ladies, always bastions against disaster, who came forward with practical help. Kieran's wife grabbed the cigarette lighter with which Kieran constantly

209

fiddled; Lady Rodwell blew out two candles and rushed them over to the music stand to relight them *in situ*.

Isobel paused. Of course she paused. She paused for the men's interruptions and the double emission of the wind in Lady Rodwell's cheeks. And then she carried on. My daughter carried on playing the Sarabande in the dark. It was an extraordinary and magical moment — *the* moment — for it spoke of all the moments leading up to it, from Isobel's receipt of a cello on her seventh birthday, to her receipt of this new cello a week earlier, a week before her tenth. (I insisted we gave her the present early, so she'd have time to get used to the instrument before that night's performance.) Isobel had applied herself so thoroughly, had rehearsed this piece so much, that she could play the remainder — some ten or twelve bars — from memory, without losing control of her phrasing. Truly, my nature and her mother's nurture had borne the most marvellous fruit.

Lady Rodwell didn't relight the candles. Kieran's wife flicked the lighter on then off. They realised nothing was needed. Isobel's illumination was coming from within.

* * *

I was not merely proud of, and glad for, Isobel. I was proud of and glad for Bach. For eighteen years, the Cello Suites had not made me think of Bach. They'd made me think of Judy Page, cleaning in my flat.

That night, when I shut my eyes and listened, I finally heard Bach. I didn't hear that roaring suck; nor could I picture that naked form. I had forgotten it. There was nothing in my expression to suggest I was thinking of, and not remembering, the naked Judy Page. How could any face register such a thought? I was therefore unsettled when, an hour later, shaking my hand as he bade me goodnight, Alan Temperley asked if I'd seen her. I told him I hadn't seen her since 1983.

'Great woman,' he said. 'Remember? You introduced us at a chambers party.'

'No,' I said, truthfully. I remembered seeing them together but not the introduction. I would guess she introduced herself.

'Unstoppable. You know? Mad as a snake but went like a train.' I would not be drawn into more of this banter. Let him say that to Kieran. 'Clever, actually. Clever woman. Moved to Greece. Had a kid.'

I stared at my wonderful daughter. I was glad I'd not had a 'kid' with Judy Page. I doubted we'd have had a 'kid' who could play Bach in the dark.

★ ★ ★

Lady Rodwell's letter of thanks, which followed within a few days, made special mention of Isobel's 'talent and fortitude'. I gave the letter to Isobel and told her to put it in her scrapbook. I was surprised to find she didn't have one, as I had a scrapbook when I was her age. I bought her one and made her stick the letter on the first page. I told her that, in years to come, she'd reread it with pride.

At this point, having written about Isobel, I must say a few words about Max. Justice demands that a father treat his children equally, until they are adults and have the right to inflict unequal parental treatment upon themselves. My sister, by emigrating to New Zealand, exercised that right.

But, before I speak of Max, I must reconcile my conflicting obligations. My primary obligation, says Elizabeth, is to tell the truth, for my own sake. But is not a parent obliged to withhold the truth, if it will upset his children? They are (at the time of writing) not only my children but minors. There are explicit sexual details in this book which they might find disturbing. I find them disturbing myself.

I shall reconcile this conflict in the simplest way, instructing Elizabeth not to let Isobel or Max read this until they achieve the age of majority.

I am perhaps worrying unduly. When he was five, Max received a parcel from New Zealand, containing *Small Fry Freya*. Freya's note said it was her favourite book when she was Max's age. But Max has still not read it. He began it, all right. He turned the first page. But, eight years on, he hasn't yet finished. What chance do I have, with Latin and footnotes, where *Small Fry Freya* has a smiley fish and letters two inches high?

★   ★   ★

212

It was soon apparent that my son had inherited his grandfather's frame. I don't refer to my father, a man of slight build. Max had the burly rugby player's build of Elizabeth's father, Graham. He was, therefore, I am happy to report, an Aldeburgh kind of boy, never happier than when riding his bike or engaging in rough-and-tumble games with other boys, at which he could not be bested, even when the other boys were Harry and Tom, the sons of Ticky and Pilkington. When the three of them hurled pebbles into the sea, Max hurled them the furthest.

My father found Max's energy and noise levels somewhat uncongenial. He never criticised his grandson, though. Instead, he tactfully placed himself in a different room, distancing himself from anything that might cause offence. My mother, by contrast, responded to Max in kind. She became louder and noisier. I recall one Boxing Day afternoon at High Ridge, when he was five and Isobel was seven. Elizabeth and my father were in the drawing room, playing Scrabble with Isobel. I was in the kitchen, washing up. My mother was outside, playing snowballs with Max. They were both shouting and laughing as they chucked snowballs and missed. Then my mother caught Max full in the face. She did a little dance of celebration. How many grandmothers in their seventies had such a strong and accurate arm?

Max turned his back on her, fell to his knees and shook with tears.

'Don't cry, Big Boy!' shouted my mother, but

Max carried on shaking.[1] My mother waited a little longer. Then she approached.

'Big Boys don't cry,' she said. 'Come on now. Get up.' When she was just a few feet away, Max got up, turned and, with a manic laugh, threw the snowball he'd secretly squirrelled. My mother spluttered as the ball hit her mouth.

'You little bugger!' she said. Max's face contorted with glee. But he didn't run away, as most boys would have done. He stood there and laughed.

Max was a gifted child and his gift was the gift of fearlessness. That Christmas, I gave him my favourite toy boat, the one my mother had given me, the one I'd used on the Aldeburgh boating pond when I was his age. Max couldn't understand how this could be a present, since it wasn't new and didn't come in a box. Nevertheless, give it to him I did. I wasn't one of those fathers who wanted his children to have what he'd never had. On the contrary. I wanted Max to have *exactly* what I'd had. What stronger evidence can there be of the happiness of my childhood, than my desire to replicate that childhood for my son, in all its colours and detail?

I took him to the boating pond on New Year's Day. By then, the snow had thawed. My boat (his boat) was a yacht with three beige cotton sails, a blue-and-cream hull and a blue rudder on which I'd carved 'RTP'. Max asked me what

---

[1] She'd called me 'Little Man'. Now she called my son 'Big Boy'. I could not help thinking of this as a kind of reverse evolution.

the letters meant. I told him they were my initials. He asked what his own initials were. I told him to try and work them out for himself. After a second, he wailed: 'I tried!'

He stood the yacht on the surface of the pond and shoved it. 'Gently!' I cried. He watched it career, then right itself. He asked why it didn't go faster. We were then distracted, as was everyone else, by the arrival of Pilkington and his younger son Harry.

Pilkington was carrying what looked like a giant red plastic lobster. It proved to be a remote-controlled hydroplane. It was Harry's in name only, since Pilkington wouldn't let him near it, explaining that the boat 'cost more than you did', a remark as offensive as it was inaccurate. It certainly cost more than Max's. Of course it did. It was a vulgar, bought boat, as opposed to Max's heirloom.

Pilkington placed his big red thing at the north end of the pond. Max and I were standing at the south. Pilkington's boat dwarfed every other boat on the pond.

Adjacent to the pond was a Town Council sign: MODEL YACHTS ONLY.

'Model yachts only!' I boomed, conveying the capital letters. Pilkington looked at me.

'Don't spoil our fun!' he said. 'Whoa!' There was barely time for Pilkington to launch the hydroplane before he was obliged to slow it down, to stop it crashing into the end of the pond which, though his boat was plastic and the end concrete, it seemed likely to destroy. Max looked on forlornly. His yacht drifted, happily. I urged him to concentrate on that.

'Isn't it amazing, Harry?' Harry nodded. Pilkington ruffled his hair. Pilkington's hand, which I'd felt on my own head at my stag party eight years earlier, looked enormous. Pilkington was six feet four inches tall. That is a fact as unavoidable as Pilkington himself. He grinned his winner's grin. Why would he not? His year-end bonus for 1998 was the talk of the yacht club. People spoke of it so much, it became something more than a notional pile of money. Pilkington's bonus took on a life. It was, as it were, a body of money, a flesh of fifty-pound notes. I saw it as a being every bit as tall as Pilkington, walking behind him, saying nothing, silently embodying his additional wealth. It ceased to be a Pilkington bonus and became a bonus Pilkington.

Pilkington executed a remote U-turn, sending the hydroplane back in our direction. Max climbed into the pond. He stared fiercely at the advancing boat. From the angle of his hands, it was clear he wanted to grab it, which was ambitious, given its size and speed.

'Hey!' shouted Pilkington. Max was my son, yet he was not my son, not in the way I was my father's son, for I had grown into a short gentleman, just as he wished, one who would never climb into that pond, for the sign, as well as MODEL YACHTS ONLY said NO PAD-DLING, even though my intention, had I now climbed in, would have been to rescue Max from the path of the oncoming vessel, any paddling being pursuant to that rescuing and not the purpose of my entry into the pond.

Luckily, I didn't have to paddle. Max was near the edge, near enough for me to grab him and hoick him out, knowing I would never be able to do it again, for he'd grow bigger while I would not.

I told him he should never have set foot in the pond. I told him it wasn't allowed.

'I didn't know!' he protested.

'Ignorance of the law is no excuse.' I said that, as a punishment, I wouldn't let him use the model yacht again. I was confiscating his Christmas present.

Max said: 'Good!' Then he rushed off to inspect the hydroplane.

The hydroplane had collided with the end of the pond and flown, as hydroplanes will. It landed on the grass, some thirty feet later, entirely unscathed.

'Whoo!' said Pilkington, as if he'd just driven his Porsche through a wall and emerged with no hair unflopped. Why make the accident seem deliberate? Why make disaster success? What a pointless thing charisma was!

Max and Harry Pilkington inspected the un-wreckage. That was the start of their friendship.

* * *

There was a curious alcove next to the front door of High Ridge. It was about three feet wide and six feet tall. Things that were intended to be taken outside and dumped — broken-backed chairs, flea-bitten rugs — often made it no

217

further than this alcove, which was known as 'the mumby'. That New Year, my mother decided it would be a good idea if her grandchildren painted the mumby. She cleared it of all detritus and told Isobel and Max to enjoy themselves. Elizabeth, fearing Max would paint the lion's share, assigned the back of the mumby to him and the sides to Isobel. She then allotted them different times to do their painting. She suggested the theme of 'The Sea'. Isobel painted the sides with fish. They were small, neat fish and they looked like fish. Max painted the rear with one fish, a big red thing which Elizabeth called 'highly imaginative', by which she must have meant he was forcing his audience to imagine what it was. It certainly didn't look like a fish. I believe it began as a fish and ended up as Harry Pilkington's big red hydroplane.

My mother put all the detritus back into the mumby, thereby obscuring the children's handiwork.

The mumby's gone now. But I mustn't get ahead of myself.

★   ★   ★

After Isobel finished playing the Bach, there was a loud and long ovation. In Kieran's case, it was a standing ovation, with a little lurch at the end. There was then a loud crack, like a pistol shot. It seemed a bullet had flown over our heads and struck the garden wall. Lady Rodwell arched backwards in her chair, as if she believed herself hit.

I knew what had happened. I looked up to see a pyjama'd Max leaning out of his bedroom window. He retreated as soon as I caught his eye. No one else — apart from Elizabeth — was aware he was responsible.

'I'm afraid our son threw a stone against the wall,' I said. Max collected stones from the beach at Aldeburgh and brought them back home to London. I urged him to collect stones of interest — jasper, cornelian, jet — but the fact was, he just liked big ones.

Kieran, alerted by the shutting of the window, looked up at Max's bedroom and then round to the wall.

'The boy's got a strong arm,' he said.

'That's right,' said Elizabeth. 'He won the Throwing the Cricket Ball on Sports Day.'

This was extreme maternal loyalty. It had to be counterbalanced with condemnation.

'That was very wrong of him. I'm sorry. Are you all right?' Lady Rodwell waved a hand, urging me to say no more about it. But I did.

'That stone could have hit you.'

'Only if I'd been standing on my chair.'

'I'll deal with him in the morning,' I replied. 'Let the punishment fit the crime.'

'What's that mean?' asked Alan Temperley.

'Will you be stoning the boy?' asked Kieran. They laughed. These men, one a gleeful cynic, the other a shiny politician, had enjoyed outstanding careers in the law. But they did not believe in the law as I did. They did not abide by it. It was a means, not a value.

It was true that I was uncertain what a fit

punishment would be. Nevertheless, I didn't regret saying what I did. I wanted Sir Michael and Lady Rodwell to know I wasn't 'soft' on stonethrowing. I turned to Isobel, whose conduct pleased every adult she met.

'Say goodnight, Isobel. You've done us all proud.'

'Goodnight,' said Isobel, and rushed across the lawn into the house as fast as her cello would let her.

'We better say goodnight too,' said Lady Rodwell, getting to her feet, completely confident she could do so without being hit. 'It's been a memorable evening.'

★ ★ ★

It had, indeed, been a glorious night. Nothing could make it otherwise. In my Contented Years, you see, I thought not of the stone hitting the wall, but of the wall itself. How many people owned a walled garden in Highgate?

When Elizabeth, at the end of the night, told me she was exhausted and couldn't carry on making five-course meals for me and my 'important legal friends', I didn't allow her remarks to alter my contented mood. Instead, I addressed them, manfully. I didn't want Elizabeth to suffer, not one whit. She was my wife, my companion, my rock.

First, I assured her that our guests had not been my important legal friends but *our* important legal friends. Kieran, for example, had complimented me on her. (I didn't relay his exact compliments — the fighting figure, the speed in leaving a house — as I could not give them their due Irish brogue.)

As to the five-course meal, I said I understood how exhausting it must be to make such a thing. 'Do you?' she asked. At this point, as any husband will tell you, an argument can race from the particular to the general with terrifying speed. We were arguing about duck and pheasant and goose and goat's cheese and summer pudding. These were real things. One could *eat* them. Let us not go from them, in an instant, to psychological candyfloss made from spun nothings. Please, I beg you, let us not go from goat's cheese to What My Mother Did To Me As A Child Which Made Me An Angry Person.

This, I submit, is what made me strong and our marriage strong: I stuck to the point. The point was that Elizabeth was exhausted from making too many five-course meals. What was the solution? Her well-being was more important to me than a hundred chicory tartes tatins.

'No more five-course meals,' I said. 'From now on, we'll do with four.' Elizabeth seemed shocked by my simplicity.

'Does that include cheese?' she asked.

'Yes!' I said and triumphantly turned off the bedside light.

*   *   *

I woke up clear in my mind what Max's punishment should be. I would make him write a letter of apology. This neatly combined punishment with rehabilitation, since he didn't like

221

writing or apologising and needed help with both. First, there was the small matter of getting him to sit down. That took, in the end, forty-eight hours. I had to promise him that, once he completed the letter, his mother would go in goal.

He took a piece of lined paper from his exercise book. He picked up his big fun biro. Then he looked at me for further instruction. I tried to make him understand that the words should be his. What did he want to say to Lady Rodwell about his actions of that Thursday night? He didn't, he said, want to say anything. What did I want him to say? I wanted him to say he was sorry for what he did. But he must feel sorry. Did he not feel sorry? Surely he did. He would have been hurt and upset and angry if someone had thrown a stone at *him*. He claimed he hadn't thrown a stone at anyone. He'd thrown a stone at a wall.

I asked him what he thought Lady Rodwell felt when she heard the crack of stone on wall. He said: 'Surprised.' I asked him whether 'shocked' might not be a better word. He agreed. I asked him if old ladies like to be 'shocked'. He said he thought they didn't. Then he qualified that. Old ladies who liked horror films liked to be shocked.

Why did my son not just write the letter? Why was my telling him to write the letter insufficient reason to do so? Was I not being sufficiently stern and remote? I would have written such a letter if my father had told me to write it. But *I* would not have thrown that stone.

222

During these despairing thoughts, I stared at Max wordlessly. Perversely, this despair advanced my case more than my cogent arguments. Max was getting impatient. He wanted to go out to the garden and play football with his mum. He asked me how to spell 'Rodwell'.

I sat down next to him as he wrote his first words: *Daer Lady*. I explained that before he wrote her name, he must write his address at the top right-hand corner of the page. He asked why. I explained that this was the correct way to write a letter. He repeated his question. Why did he have to write his address, when Lady Rodwell had just been to our house? She already knew where we lived.

I could not counter his arguments, because they weren't arguments; they followed no rules, they had no logic, they paid no regard to the premise of the question or statement to which they were nominally a response.

Daer Lady Rodwell. He'd made a start. I agreed no address was needed.

Half an hour later, I stood at his window, watching him take penalty after penalty, hearing him shout 'Goal!' and 'Goal!' and 'Goal!', punctuated by the occasional heartfelt 'Great save, Mum!'

I returned to his desk to reread his letter. To save time, I'd agreed to write the envelope myself.

Daer Lady Rodwell, he'd written, *I'm sorry I shocked you when I threw the stone against the wall. Yours sincerely, M. M. G. Purcell.*

Let us not dwell on the initials. Ever since I'd

explained, at the boating pond, the concept of initials, Max had written his name in this fashion. It was the *I'm* that cut me to the quick. The *I'm* was not his first attempt. There was *Ime* and there was *Im*, both crossed out. Most of his words were second or third attempts. The letter was, in essence, a series of corrections, which corrections would only draw Lady Rodwell's eye to the underlying mistakes, which were covered in large black spots. I'd not had the stamina to make him write a fair copy.

From the room below — the drawing room — I heard Isobel practising her cello. From next door's conservatory came the theme tune of *Desert Island Discs*. It was 11.15 on a June Sunday morning. All was right with the world and, where it was not, I would make it so.

Isobel would always remember her letter of congratulation from Lady Rodwell. What memories would Max have of that night? A letter not from but to Lady Rodwell. A botch of crossings-out. Words that took off from the lines on which they were meant to be grounded. A page covered in black spots, as if his young life were plagued. Was this what I wanted for my son?

I took another piece of paper from Max's pad. With my non-writing hand — my left — I picked up the big fun biro, the one that allowed him to make mistakes in six different colours. I brought the biro down onto the page and wrote our address in the top right-hand corner, with great difficulty, hoping that a wrong-handed father would write like an eight-year-old son. But my letters were too large and spidery. They looked like the work of a loon. I scrunched up the paper and threw it away. I started again, with my right hand, making each word an aggregation of unconnected letters. I took pains. I put a big loop on every little y. Oh yes. This was more like it. Two versions later, everything was under control.

I heard Elizabeth, outside, telling Max she'd had enough. I heard him say he'd had enough too. I finished my *M. M. G. Purcell*. I walked out of his bedroom as Max came running up the stairs.

'I'll post it now,' I said as I passed him on the landing.

'Yeah!' said Max, uninterested. The letter was forgotten. He lived in the present tense.

I went to my study and reread it. There were no mistakes. Of course there weren't. When did I make mistakes? I resolved that, before I put it in an envelope, I would insert a mistake. I put a rogue *e* in *sorry*, between the second *r* and the *y*. Lady Rodwell would notice this mistake and conclude that Max had written the letter without my supervision. She'd be impressed by his maturity and, ironically, by his spelling. Look at all the words he'd spelled correctly. Look at the spelling Everests he'd climbed: *sincerely, against*.

I wrote the envelope, in my adult hand, and put the letter inside. I affixed a stamp at a jaunty angle, as if I'd written the envelope but Max had youthfully applied the stamp. I whistled as I walked out to post it. On my way, I passed my son and daughter's prep-school blazers, hanging on their pegs in the hall.

What was the point of my education, my breeding, my status, my intellect, my wealth and contentment — if not to make everything right?

11
Mike Bell
(1993-2002)

When Max was born, I decided to invite Mike Bell to be his godfather. Elizabeth was surprised. She'd only met Bell once, on our wedding day, and found him 'flaky'. Might he not have a bad effect on Max?

I explained I wanted Bell to be Max's godfather for Max's effect on Bell. Bell had no children. He did not even have a wife. My impulse, therefore, was charitable. I wanted Mike Bell, who had no family, to share in my contentment. Elizabeth didn't understand the logic but deferred to my conviction.

When I rang him, he was surprised. He was always surprised.

'You serious, Robbo? Me? Again? What do I have to do?' I told him he had to attend a church ceremony and promise to renounce the Devil. I did not mind if he perjured himself. A church was, in my opinion, a court of law in which the judge did not really exist.

'What about presents?' I said it would be appropriate, initially, to give a long-term present, a crate of burgundy or a standing order for a savings account, to accrue when Max was eighteen. He greeted this with such silence that I instantly let him off. I told him he need only give Christmas and birthday presents. He said he would rather do that than come to the christening. Since my invitation was, apparently, a negotiation, I let him off the christening too. Max's godmother, Fiona, was happy to coo and fuss for two.

Bell was meticulous in sending a birthday and Christmas present, in the second year of Max's life. After that, he was lax. When Elizabeth complained, I defended him. His life was chaotic. He'd probably forgotten the date of the birthday. It was, however, difficult to claim he'd forgotten the date of Christmas.

Then came my vindication. Mike Bell rang me up to invite himself down to Aldeburgh, for the weekend of Max's seventh birthday, in May 2000. He also asked to see 'the big man and his henchman' whom he'd met on my stag night, a reference to Pilkington and Catto. I was touched by this nostalgia. I gave him Pilkington's number. (Catto had gone to live in Florida.)

'I thought he was meant to be a film producer,' said Elizabeth, as Bell drew up outside High Ridge in an old Ford Escort. I explained that he was a film producer who'd yet to produce a film. She asked why he called himself a film producer then. I told her that, in Bell's world, you had to say what you were in advance of being it, in order to become it.

Bell greeted Max, holding up the palm of his hand for Max to punch. Max went for it. Bell moved it at the last moment, causing Max to punch thin air. Max laughed, had another go and was similarly bested. Finally, without waiting for a palm, Max punched Bell in the stomach. Elizabeth berated Max. Bell fell to the floor in mock agony, mixed, I think, with the real thing. It was all going rather well.

Then Bell reached into his overnight bag and got out Max's birthday present, which was the size and thickness of an A4 envelope. Max ripped off the wrapping paper eagerly and, sure enough, uncovered an A4 envelope. He ripped that open too and, baffled, extracted a set of keys.

★ ★ ★

'We can't give it back,' I told Elizabeth. 'That would be ungracious.' It was lunchtime. Bell had gone off to meet Pilkington in the Cross Keys. 'You've always said he's mean, so you can't complain when he's generous.' She thought it was confusing to give a seven-year-old a Ford Escort. I countered that it was a long-term present, a belated christening gift.

We discussed, at length, the practicalities. It would live in the drive of High Ridge. As the registered owner, I would tax it (as an off-road vehicle) and take it for the occasional drive to keep the engine turned over, barely adding to its seventy-four thousand miles. These were impositions, but minor.

★ ★ ★

It was a free gift, in the sense that Bell hadn't paid for it. He'd been given it by the previous owner, one Tina Hollerbach. Who was she? He called her his 'kind of' girlfriend. They loved each other but no longer lived together, were no longer partners.

We sat on the sea wall, Bell and I, he with a pint, me with a half, while he told me about Tina. She was a set designer who lived in Richmond with her children, Marc and Emily, just two doors down from her ex-partner, a commercials director called Dan. Dan was still an occasional lover of Tina, who was also Bell's occasional lover. What the occasion was, and how a Dan occasion differed from a Bell occasion, were mysteries to a contented monogamist like me.[1]

Dan was the father of Marc, Tina's first child. Dan and Tina had lived in Bethnal Green till Marc was three, at which point Dan moved to the Richmond house of his new partner. (It is not necessary to follow all this. You merely have to understand how much there was to follow. I suggest you read the following paragraph at double or triple speed, to experience, as I had to, the nauseating dizziness of Bell's private life.)

The father of Emily, Tina's second child, was an American called Lou, from whom she was now divorced. (Why did she marry Lou but

---

[1] On the strength of directing some building society commercials, Dan bought his occasional lover Tina a new car, presumably as an occasional love token; she gave her old Ford Escort to Bell, who gave it to Max, because he couldn't afford to run it. He didn't say this explicitly. One knew.

230

not Dan?) When Lou left Tina to return to his native Chicago, Tina found herself alone in the Bethnal Green house with two children under six. Wanting Marc to be near his dad (Dan) whom Tina had 'never stopped loving', she bought the house in Richmond two doors down from Dan and his partner. When Lou first flew back to England to see his daughter Emily, he stayed at Tina's, which made her uncomfortable, as she'd definitely stopped loving Lou. The next time, Lou stayed two doors down, with Dan and his partner. This arrangement proved 'amazingly convenient'.

Attempting satire, I asked why Tina hadn't, for the sake of neatness, had a lesbian relationship with Dan's partner. That was easily answered. Dan's partner was a man called Steve.

At this point, I fear, I became angry. Was Bell deliberately contriving all this to annoy me? The notion was absurd. No man would dwell in this labyrinth of confusion just to infuriate me. That, nevertheless, was how it fclt. It was more than twenty years since we'd left university, yet Bell was still a man with two girls in his room, who wasn't even in the room. He was without clarity, without which there can be no contentment. I had a wife and two children. He had an occasional lover, with whom he didn't live, to whose children he had never been a stepfather. What had he been, then? How do you define the relationship between the 'partner' of a woman and her children? He is the man in the house, as their father once was. He is their *houseman*.

Now let us turn to his professional life.

★ ★ ★

He told me about *Strong* when I rang him to ask him to be my best man. The eponymous Strong was a singer in a group. The film was the story of his rise and fall. It was 'very much a London film' that 'took its energy from the streets'. Bell had written the script with Luke, his former partner in the video production company. FilmFour, the potential backers of the film, were 'incredibly excited'.

I opined that this was bad news. If FilmFour were incredibly excited, they would shortly be incredibly unexcited. That was the pattern with excitement. I told him about my parents' much-missed terrier, Duncan. Every Monday morning at eight thirty, when the cleaner entered the house, Duncan was always overcome with excitement. By eight thirty-three, he'd forgotten all about her.

'How many films did Duncan produce?' asked Bell, with irritation.

'None,' I said. Sure enough, 'none' was the number of films Bell produced for FilmFour.

Now, as he sat on that sea wall, ten years later, he was developing a film for Pathé. It drew, he said, its energy from the streets. I reminded him he'd said the same about *Strong*. This didn't deflate him. If anything, he was flattered — I'd detected the theme in his unmade work. Anyway, his new film drew its energy from Leicester streets, not London. *Man Curry* was about five young Asian men made redundant from a textile factory. They decide to set up their own business. How can they fund it? How can they make money fast? The men start an escort agency, concealing the true nature of their work from their families. In the 'third act', the five men end up naked in the bed of a millionaire businesswoman. They earn enough, on that one night, to fund their business. Word of their escapade spreads throughout Leicester, affording them legendary local status.

I was no fan of English cinema, believing it to have reached its peak with *Kind Hearts and Coronets*, though I'd much enjoyed *Four Weddings and a Funeral* and *Notting Hill*. Elizabeth had also forced me to see *The Full Monty*, a film about a group of unemployed Sheffield men who raise money by putting on a striptease show. Word of their escapade spreads throughout Sheffield, affording them legendary et cetera.

'Isn't it,' I asked, 'rather like an Asian *Full Monty*?'

'Yeah. That's right. Brilliant, Bobo!'

I couldn't understand his elation. I'd told him he was making *Full Monty We Are Not*. Was this not an insult? No. I'd divined his successful 'pitch' in all its parasitical glory. The time was right for an Asian *Full Monty*.

Bell finished his pint and went to the lavatory. He came back in a state of outrage.

'God, the people in this town. They're so fucking arrogant. I don't know how you stand it. There were two braying men pissing next to me, going on and on about builders. Builders were lazy, builders were thieves. How did they know I

233

wasn't a builder? I'm real. You know? I grew up with nothing. I could have shot them, then and there. It was like a scene from a film called *Pub Bog*.'

'Please don't make a film called *Pub Bog*.'

'OK,' he said, 'I won't.'

He said it with melancholy, as if he knew he'd never make a film of any kind.

★ ★ ★

The next time Bell rang me — a rare event — *Man Curry* had indeed died. It was 2002. The time was no longer right for an Asian *Full Monty*. The time was no longer excited.

Although *Man Curry* hadn't worked out, I'd 'got' it. I'd 'got' its potential appeal. I had, Bell said, a feel for the film business. How would I like to invest in his latest project? He was looking for a small number of 'players' to invest between ten and thirty thousand pounds. He didn't want impersonal corporations. They were 'all muscle and no taste'.

He told me the film was called *Big Ben*. It was a gangster movie set in the East End. Was I interested? Yes. Bell was my friend. I was interested in helping my friend. And I was lucky enough to have the wealth to do so, though the cause of that wealth was not luck but intellect and application.

12

Unforeseen Events
(2002)

One summer day, when we were children, in the Aldeburgh house of Pilkington's parents, Orlando the Pilkington cat found its way upstairs to the children's playroom. Boo Risdon and Ticky Moxon-Smith screamed. In its mouth, the cat had a not-quite-dead bird.

Pilkington grabbed the cat and held it out of the window. The dog-snogger was now, it seemed, a cat dropper.

'No!' shouted Boo Risdon.

'I'm not dropping it, you spazz! It'll let go of the bird!'

For once, I was on Pilkington's side. I too thought the cat, suspended sixty feet above Death, would yowl in protest, thereby unclenching its jaws and releasing the bird. But no. It held on. It would rather die with its prize in its mouth than let the prize go.

Similarly, on that April morning in 2002, I wouldn't let the letter go. I clutched it as Isobel put her cello in the boot of the Audi, that most cello-friendly of cars. I clutched it as Max put his sports gear on top of the cello. I clutched it as Elizabeth moved his sports gear off the cello and slammed the boot.

All three of them waved, surprised to see me at the gate. I, who prized normality, normally stayed indoors when they left for school. But, that day, I wanted them to bask in my bonhomie as long as possible. 'Tell all your friends the news!' I shouted at Max and Isobel. They nodded.

Elizabeth drove off. I walked into the road and waved at their departing rear window, as they headed for Isobel's school (Channing) and Max's (UCS). Isobel had won a place at St Paul's Girls' School. She would go there in September. It was the best girls' school in England and was not frightened to be known as such. Why should it be frightened? Why should it strive for false modesty?[1]

I stood in the middle of the road and read the letter again. The letter was from the Lord Chancellor's Office, informing me that my application to take silk had been successful. I was a QC now. I was one large step from a judge.

'Car coming!' shouted my neighbour, Alison, former wife of the British Ambassador to Cairo. She wanted me to carry on living, probably so she and I could continue our boundary dispute.

I heard the engine. But I didn't move. Let them slow down. Who dares run over a QC?

* * *

---

[1] Let me assure you of this: if the school decided to be falsely modest, it would be the best at false modesty.

The QC letter had been due that morning, Thursday 11th April. So I waited in the hall from eight twenty-five, hoping the good news would arrive before Elizabeth, Isobel and Max departed. (If it were bad news, I would simply not tell them.)

'Oh. There you are,' said Elizabeth, from the kitchen doorway, looking at me hovering on the doormat. 'You look like you want to be taken for a walk.' Happily, the letter landed just after she spoke. I read it and reread it. I scanned it for a previously unnoticed *not*. But there was no *not*. I was not *not* a QC. I was a QC. I relayed the marvellous news to Elizabeth.

'Congratulations,' she said. 'You've worked for it.' And then she was gone. In the kitchen, Max turned up the radio to maximum volume. A fat-voiced disc jockey spread his ooze throughout the house. He didn't disturb me. I was in a state of grace which no one could disturb.

★   ★   ★

In chambers, I enjoyed the congratulations of all the other new silks; and the studied indifference of those passed over. I left messages for Lord and Lady Rodwell, Mac, Kieran Harris, Gerard Gorringe and Alan Temperley. Then, at lunch-time, when I knew they'd both be there, following their morning constitutionals and my mother's round of golf, I rang my parents, in High Ridge, where they lived full-time. They were now in their eighties. My father had been retired from the bench for nearly ten years.

'You have my heartfelt congratulations,' he said. 'This is an accolade that's richly deserved.' With age, his words appeared more slowly. Each was polished, as it had been since I first heard him speak. It was simply that the polishing took longer. He passed the phone to my mother.

'Well done, Little Man. I expect you've spent the whole day crowing.'

'Not crowing. Just passing on the good news.'

'Well, I can't remember anything and I keep falling over. That's *my* good news.'

I laughed. I told her that Elizabeth and I would invite them to a celebratory dinner, the date to be confirmed.

'Don't worry about the dinner,' she said. 'Just make sure there's plenty of booze.'

I laughed again.

My mother said: 'I'm saying goodbye now.' I assumed this would be followed by her saying 'goodbye'. But no, it was followed by silence. She'd said what she wanted to say. Her pride in my achievement shone through.

★ ★ ★

That night, after Elizabeth put the children to bed, I performed my nightly task. To stop Max getting up after lights-out and playing on his computer, I placed a chair beneath the fuse box in the hall and flicked the switch that regulated the flow of electricity to his room.

'My light wouldn't come on in the night,' he'd said, after I first did this.

'Sorry,' I replied. 'I've contacted our electricity

238

supplier. They say they can't do anything about it.' He nodded. He never complained again.[1]

I returned to the drawing room and replaced the chair at the table. Elizabeth was watching television, as she usually did after children's bedtime. She was tuned to her favourite programme. Each week, a couple was filmed in the process of redesigning, or building from scratch, their 'dream home'. The presenter, a knowledgeable and educated man, asked the couple many questions about materials and lighting and doorways and furnishings and stairwells. He was fascinated, too fascinated for my liking. Was he intending to move in with them, given that his interest in their interior was obsessive to the point of proctology?

I waited, politely, for the programme to finish. I had spent the evening hoping Elizabeth would suggest a drinks party in my honour. (My mother was right. Dinner was unnecessary. And one could invite more people to a drinks party.) *Elizabeth Purcell. At Home. For Robert.* That would be the invitation. Or was that overly discreet as to the cause for celebration? *Elizabeth Purcell. At Home. For Robert Purcell*, QC.

---

[1] Incensed readers may feel a Dickensian urge to complain on the mite's behalf. What if he were frightened in the night? Where would he turn, for instant comfort, if not to electric light? How would he see to get out of the room in the event of fire? Let me therefore add that Max was provided with a pillowside torch. Let me also add that when there's a fire, one sees one's way out of the room by the light of the fire.

I couldn't wait any longer. As soon as the programme finished, I proposed it myself. Who did Elizabeth think should be on the guest list?

'Not me,' said Elizabeth.

'Of course not. You're the hostess.'

'How can you be so dense, Robert?'

On the television, an ugly woman on an ugly estate was opening her front door. Outside stood an unreasonably good-looking policeman. He was grave.

'Mrs Harvey?'

'Yes. What is it?'

'I'm afraid I've got bad news.'

Elizabeth turned it off. Rightly so. It was a third-rate drama from a commercial channel. But the turning-off was not just a matter of aesthetics. Elizabeth was embarrassed by the coincidence. I was the housewife, was I not, and Elizabeth was the policeman. The preamble — *Mrs Harvey?/How can you be so dense, Robert?* — was not a preamble at all. It was the bad news, in all but specifics. (Which member of Mrs Harvey's family had died? What terrible thing had I not understood?) It was an auditory bullet. One braced oneself for impact but impact had already been made.

As Elizabeth said *How*, Mars entered and sat between us, his head facing the screen, which Elizabeth then rendered blank.[1] Mars carried on

---

[1] It was Isobel who'd given Mars his name, not simply because he was a chocolate Labrador but because he reminded her of the Roman god of war.

watching. He always sat on the sofa between us, around this time, hoping to be taken for a walk. We spoke the word in code so as not to excite him. The code was simplistic. We spelled it out: 'W-A-L-K'.

Elizabeth was leaving me for the Lemon Man. She'd been having an affair with the Lemon Man for the last nine months.

How did Mars react? He didn't. Of course he didn't. He'd have reacted only if Elizabeth had said she'd decided to 'walk'.

Mars was the same before she said it as he was after. Rightness, continuity, duty, constancy: Mars embodied them. I stroked him and carried on stroking him for the next two hours.

★ ★ ★

Elizabeth was leaving me for the Lemon Man and hoped, for the sake of the children, that I would consent to our living apart for two years, after which we could proceed with a 'no-fault' divorce.

This was the barrister's nightmare. I was unprepared. I didn't know the material facts. I depended, for all my information, on what I heard, now, from the other side. (Allow me that courtroom metaphor, since Elizabeth was literally sitting on the other side of Mars.)

'I want you to understand why I'm doing this,' said Elizabeth. Was it not obvious? She had fallen in love with this Lemon Man. She had made a mistake. She was asking me to understand her reasons for making a mistake.

'I thought if I married you, you'd change. But you haven't. You're exactly the same as you were when I met you. I'm not. I was twenty-three. I'm thirty-six now. I want different things.' This was admirable in its clarity, except for 'different things', which I took to be a euphemism for Anthony, which I regarded as a euphemism in itself, for the Lemon Man.

The effect of her speech was not what Elizabeth intended. *You're exactly the same as you were when I met you* was meant as a complaint. I took it, however, as a compliment. Did it not vouch for my integrity, my knowledge of who I was and always would be? Imagine that the contract of marriage were a contract of sale; that the bride, instead of taking a man for her husband, took a tin of baked beans. Imagine that, more than eleven years later, this tin of beans was the same tin, miraculously preserved, the tin not rusted, the beans as nutritious and bean-coloured as they were when she first held the tin. Imagine, further, that the wife ate those beans, three times a day, for eleven and a half years; yet the beans always replenished themselves. The tin always reverted to its original contents, the beans tasting and numbering the same as they did when she first caught sight of that tin and knew it had to be hers. Was that not the purchase of a lifetime?

'You're still remote. You're still incapable of real intimacy. I need intimacy, Robert. I want to be loved.'

The key word here was *still*. I was *still* the man she married, with the faults she married. To steal a phrase from an advertising slogan I find hard to resist, I had done exactly what it said on the (my) tin. And let us not forget our old friend *Ridgeon* v. *Kelly* (1989). To a willing person, no injury is done — *volenti non fit injuria*. In that case, a man gets onto a friend's motorbike, knowing the friend is drunk. A woman gets married to a man, knowing the man is remote.

'Anthony's kind and he loves me.'

I could not possibly comment on the Lemon Man's treatment of Elizabeth. I could — but did not — comment on his treatment of me. I thought back to his act of kindness at the bottom of the stairs, when he recommended yoga for the easing of the tension in my shoulders. Was he being kind because of or in spite of his affair with my wife? Let us give him the benefit of the doubt. Let us say that when he made that shoulders remark, he was not yet having, nor even contemplating, an affair with Elizabeth. The remark was still as cruel as it was kind. He took pleasure in offering a solution. But he took equal pleasure in pointing out the problem. I sensed that he revelled in my tension, which he, as an artist and a spiritual person, saw as the consequence of a coat-hanger-shouldered life-style he disdained, with its overt ambitions and achievements. He pretended to be straightforward and caring but I could see how complex he was. Compare him with Elizabeth's friend Fiona. She was genuinely, if appallingly and invasively, kind. Fiona wasn't complicated, not in the least. The Lemon Man was. What kind of man *smiles* when he tells you your shoulders are tense?

'I've developed, Robert. You haven't. You haven't had to.'

There were, thus far, two prongs to her argument: Anthony's virtues and my shortcomings. Now came the third prong, the prong she applied to herself: 'My mother always ran around after my father, because he was the breadwinner. And I've done the same for you. I even did it for Guy. I hung around hotels while he had his conferences. It's like I provide a service for high-achieving males. That's my destiny.'

Once again, this did not have quite the intended effect. To my ears, it sounded like a perfectly acceptable destiny, provided one chose one's high-achieving males carefully. They certainly sounded preferable to their low-achieving counterparts, like Anthony.

'I should never have given up work. I think I've got a lot to offer as a counsellor so that's what I'm going to do. I just don't think we have the same values.'[1]

This was vague. This could not hurt me. Then she swooped and stung.

'You can't give a little girl her birthday present a week before her birthday, just so she can practise for Lady Rodwell. Is that what my life's about? Making my children perfect for Lady Rodwell?'

---

[1] At first, I heard 'councillor'. I thought Elizabeth, in a spirit of public service, wanted to stand for the council. But nobody wants to do that, do they? We'd rather stick our noses into others' private lives than spend our time saying 'yes' to Tesco.

Lady Rodwell was the wife of a judge. She was a distinguished barrister in her own right. She was a member of the Law Commission and had served on the Committee of Inquiry into the emergence and identification of bovine spongiform encephalopathy (BSE) and variant Creutzfeldt-Jakob disease (vCJD). She was a talented horsewoman. Every year, in the garden of her Hampshire home, she erected a marquee and staged a Mozart opera. I didn't understand. Why would one not want to make one's children perfect for Lady Rodwell?

Elizabeth got up and went to the drawer in our telephone table. Mars followed but was disappointed, for that was as far as she walked. She came back with a piece of paper.

'That's your handwriting, isn't it? You wrote that.' It was an early version of my letter to the aforesaid Lady Rodwell, written in my own hand but in the style of Max. *Children's Bins, Emptying of, into Black Plastic Sacks*. Elizabeth had found my forgery and kept it.

'Why are you looking at it like that? You know you wrote it.' She was right. This was the smoking gun of courtoom legend. 'You wrote it for Max. Don't you think that's weird? What else have you done that you haven't told me?'

This was an extraordinary question. I would never have asked that question, not unless I'd known what the 'what else' was. Perhaps that is a fundamental difference between solicitors and barristers. We barristers try never to ask a question to which we don't already know the answer. *Did you, on 17ᵗʰ June 2002, purchase* twenty-four thousand shares *in Magenta Hold-ings?* That is not a question. That is a statement, in the form of a question. We are not curious to find out. We do not ask: *What did you do on 17th June 2002? I'd really love to know!*

What else had I done that I hadn't told Elizabeth?

'The carpet,' I said.

I took her through the story, stage by stage: the struggle to define her carpet colour, the discovery of the putty-like 'pale sand', the borrowing of the key from Fiona, the meeting with the estimator, the morning with the fitters, the removal and replacement of Elizabeth's furniture, her failure to notice the new carpet, the hijacking of the carpet by Guy. At this distance, the events were farcical, curious and not a little sad. But they manifested my generosity and my desire to get everything right. It was, I felt, the kind of story that would make a wife change her mind about leaving a husband.

Elizabeth, however, responded in quite the wrong way. She harped on the curious, not the generous. She made another reference to 'weird':

'I can't believe you went into my room and moved all my things. So weird. It's like you're a ghost.'

'There was a great deal of effort involved,' I said, hoping she would harp on the effort.

'Why would you do all that for me and then not tell me? It's like you weren't doing it for me at all. You were doing it for yourself. It's like I don't exist or something. I find it rather sinister.'

'Why would I tell you, when it all went wrong?'

'You just would. I can't explain it. You just would, cos it's weird not to. What I'm doing isn't weird. I've fallen in love. That's not weird. That's what happens. That's what people do.'

The injustice of this was hard to bear. How could my failure to tell her about the carpet be 'weirder', be worse, than her affair with the Lemon Man?

'Why didn't you notice I was in love with him? He was here, in the house.' This was weirdness upon weirdness. Now I was being accused of not noticing an adultery, as if that were somehow an offence on a par with adultery itself.

'Don't hurt him!'

She was right. I was rubbing the poor dog's head off.

'Don't get angry with Mars, Robert. Get angry with me. I'm leaving you.'

Elizabeth wanted me to be angry, as if that would prove something. But I was not an angry man. She hadn't married an angry man. Nowhere on my putative tin did it say: May Contain Anger. I took my hand away from the dog.

At such a moment, a man must be true to himself. If not then, when? My father taught me, from the beginning, when Pilkington punched me after snogging my dog, to 'rise above it', be detached when one was meant to feel at one's most attached. I was a participant in this drama, not an observer. Yet that was the reason to stay calm. Anger only spawned more anger. It spawned 'crimes of passion', that nauseating (French) formulation whereby the crime was excused by the passion, as if a crime of passion were less of a crime on account of its motive. Was the victim of a crime of passion less dead than the victim of a yawning hitman, who was just doing it to pay the mortgage?

It was not just a matter of being true to the principles in which I'd been schooled. Let her follow her heart. I would not get angry or try to stop her, because her heart would lead her to disaster, which disaster would in turn lead her back here, to me, to hearth and home. When it went awry with this man, as it would, she'd remember me as I was now: a civilised and measured man, a man to come home to. After the turmoil, she'd crave my calm. It was my *best point*.

I thought of our children, their blazers by the door, the cello by the piano, the footballs on the lawn. I wanted my children's lives to carry on as normal. How to make the abnormal normal? That was my mission now. I would move out of our house and let her conduct this affair in peace, until such time as she got sick of the Lemon Man, at which point I would move back in. The Lemon Man and I would pass each other in the hall, he leaving, I returning, and I'd be gracious, holding the front door open for him and his suitcase, promising to return any possessions of his I found. Oh yes, I'd be annoyingly gracious.

'I'm not angry,' I said. 'I'll find a flat to rent nearby. Then I'll leave you two in peace.'

'No,' said Elizabeth. 'You're staying here. We're doing the leaving. We're moving to Herefordshire.'

My wife and children and the Lemon Man were going to live, rent-free, in the annexe of

Guy and Sophie's new house, near Hereford. I was to stay in our house till we'd sold it; then Elizabeth and I — Elizabeth, that is, and the Lemon Man and I — would buy two separate properties, each with enough accommodation for the children.

'You've never said you loved me. I don't know what you want. What do you want? Don't just sit there. Tell me what you want.'

'I want what I have, Elizabeth.'

I was pleased with this. There was something yoga about it, something Buddha-like, something non-acquisitive, something natural flooring and Lemon Man which ought to please her.

Equally, 'I want what I have' was proudly conservative.

⁂

Hereford. Yes. I understood. I'd read an article in the *Evening Standard*, only a week before.

Guy and Rick had sold their advertising agency to a 'media conglomerate' with three important initials. Guy was now a multi-millionaire. There is, these days, no other kind. Those with a single figure of millions keep it quiet, for fear of being thought 'losers'.

The Guy of Guy & Rick was now the Guy of Green Guy. Green Guy made organic yogurts on Guy's Herefordshire farm. But that, he'd told the *Standard*, was only the beginning. His ultimate goal was the happiness of the planet.

'If we make the planet happy, we'll make ourselves happy,' said Guy, that two-timing bastard,

249

that tennis player racked with court rage. He intended to be 'the organic Branson' with a 'green consumer portfolio' of everything from organic milk chocolate to organic electric cars, which would be the people's electric cars just as, once upon a time, Branson's Virgin had been the people's airline. For green and obvious reasons, Guy wouldn't start an airline. 'I might do a Green Guy pogo stick, though. That takes off and lands, doesn't it!' With such puppyish remarks, Guy made the readers of the *Evening Standard* feel he belonged to us (the people) and not to them (the them). 'I want to make products that people love and products that love people,' said Guy. This was madness. Guy wanted to make yogurts that loved people. This was Green Jesus weirdness, infinitely weirder than the carpet weirdness of which I'd been unjustly accused.

What, in any event, did Green Guy Organic Natural Yogurt have to do with Guy? I was a man who put his name to legal opinions that were based on his own research and experience and intellect and knowledge, gained from twenty-three years at the Bar. Green Guy Organic Natural Yogurt suggested a product Guy had manufactured, a product to which he was intimately related. Had he milked his own nipples? No. Guy's relationship with his yogurt was nebulous. He'd bought the business from a Welsh couple who'd first made the stuff in their farmhouse kitchen. Megan's Farmhouse Yogurt was now Green Guy's. That was it. Guy had no yogurt on his hands.

This was how he was saving our planet. He

was buying up small businesses and rebranding those businesses as his own, with infinitely better distribution and publicity. What was this *Evening Standard* interview but publicity, with its yogurt-selling photo of Guy (handsome, not yet forty) and his pretty wife Sophie, ten-year-old Jasper, eight-year-old Nina and Henry the lurcher, outside their Herefordshire coach house, with a croquet lawn and a tennis court and land that ran down to the River Wye, and a 'granny annexe' which Guy's parents had not yet moved into because 'they didn't feel old enough!'?

That was the very annexe where Elizabeth, Isobel and Max would live, with the Lemon Man. How had this happened? I thought I'd rescued Elizabeth from Guy. Now he and Sophie, evidently, were rescuing her from me.

'We've had our ups and downs but they're my friends,' said Elizabeth. 'They want to be nice to me and help me.' Why? I could not accept that Guy was nice. He was a capitalist. He would only be nice in a proprietorial way. He was rebranding my family as his own.

'What about schools?'

'There are schools in Herefordshire.'

I was shocked by the banality of this statement. It sounded so innocuous, so true. Of course it was true. But it was true for others. It was not true for my daughter. There were no schools in Herefordshire, nor Hampshire nor Hertfordshire, for my daughter Isobel. There was only one school for my daughter: St Paul's Girls' School, the finest in the country, the one where she was due to start in September, a mere five months hence. We have all heard, hundreds of times, from hundreds of different parents, that their daughter is 'so beautiful/so clever/so talented/so gifted'. The statement has all the authority of a greetings card, except in the case of my daughter, Isobel, where it was fact. She was not so beautiful — for beauty might divert her from fulfilling her academic potential — but she was so clever, so talented, so gifted that to send her to a school other than the finest was wicked and perverse.

'They'll go to the local state school. We've looked at it and it's fine.'

'Do Guy and Sophie's children go to the local state school?'

'No. They go to boarding school.'

'A-ha!' Yes. I confess. I emitted an *A-ha!* — that crass ejaculation of those fictional detectives, Clouseau and Poirot, so loved by my mother.

'But that's them,' said Elizabeth. 'They equate the best with the most expensive. I don't necessarily share their values. I don't want Guy to feel he owns me.'

What could I say? How could I argue with something with which I agreed?

'Iz will shine at any school. She's a naturally schooly girl. And we know Max isn't academic. What matters is, he's happy.'

'But state schools don't play rugby.'[1]

---

[1] This was a bluff. I didn't know whether state schools played rugby or not. I didn't know anything about state schools. And I wanted to keep it that way.

'I've put him down for a trial for Herefordshire Colts. He'll train on Saturday and play on Sunday.'

'What about tennis? Don't tell me state schools have tennis courts.'

'Guy and Sophie have a court. He'll have a court in his back garden. What could be better? Even when we move out, he can use their court any time he likes. He and Jasper have already played each other. Jasper's slightly better than Max, which is good. It'll make him raise his game.' Then she added, with deceptive gentleness: 'Mike Bell went to a state school.'

'True.'

'And you like Mike Bell. You're always more excited to see him than you are to see me.'

'That's because' — and here I paused. By saying 'That's because', I had already conceded the point — 'That's because I see him less than I see you.'

Of what was I guilty? Is not every human being more excited by those he or she sees less? Elizabeth let the remark hang in the air. I could hear her silent *A-ha!*

Here was my wife, leaving me. Yet I could not help admiring her at the *advocacy level*. She had marshalled and presented her arguments with considerable skill. Her case, objectively, had no merit. She was taking my children to Herefordshire, to disadvantage them while she wasted her own time on a fool. And yet, and yet. Consider the way she exploited the smallest detail: Guy's son Jasper was 'slightly better' than Max, which would make Max

253

himself a better tennis player. What kind of husband wants to stop his son getting better at tennis?

The sharpness of her advocacy confirmed, if confirmation were needed, that I had married a capable woman, who'd absorbed many of my finest qualities.

'You'll find someone. I know you will. If you want to. I'm not sure you *do* want to, really.'

No. I had found someone. I had found Elizabeth. She would see the error of her ways and come back to me.

'This is goodbye then,' I said. I knew this was what she wanted to hear. But I knew, equally, that it wasn't true.

I didn't perjure myself when I said this goodbye. I knew, of course, that Elizabeth would hear, but I actually addressed my remark to Mars, who was leaving me too.

★　★　★

How would I explain the situation to my children? In the event, it wasn't necessary for me to explain anything. The very next morning, Max said: 'We're going to live in a place with a tennis court!'

'Yes,' I said, making the best of things. 'I'll come down and play you.'

Max thought about this. 'It's OK. You don't have to. I can play with Jasper. He's better than me. That'll make me praise my game.'

'Raise your game,' corrected Elizabeth.

A few minutes later, by the front door, I found

myself alone with Isobel as she put on her blazer.

'Does this mean you don't love Elizamum any more?' Isobel never used 'Mum' when talking to me about Elizabeth, since Elizabeth was not my mum. Hence her coinage of 'Elizamum'.

I helped her on with her blazer, which I didn't normally do. She had difficulty getting her right arm into the sleeve. Finally I said: 'I feel the same about Elizamum as I did when I married her.' This was true and I hoped it would satisfy her. But it didn't.

'That's a bit ambiguous.'

I felt like weeping. Isobel, not quite eleven, knew what 'ambiguous' meant and used it with confidence. Of how many state-school pupils of her age was that the case?

I didn't reply. Of course I didn't. What purpose would be served?

I went out with her and hovered by the boot of the car. I watched Max and Elizabeth come out. Elizabeth opened the boot and put their school bags and the cello inside. She shut the boot and told the children to get in the car. Then she turned to me.

'Go on,' she said. 'Say it. Be quick, though.'

'I'm happy to pay your Hereford expenses. I don't want you and the children lacking for anything.'

'That's fine,' she said, ambiguously, for she meant she was fine for money and didn't want mine. She told me, hurriedly, that her parents would help her and Anthony had been promised work by his brother, a builder who lived in

Kington, near Hereford.[1]

'Is his brother a poet too?'

'No,' said Elizabeth. 'He's a sculptor.' Of course he was. He was a builder and a sculptor. No doubt he could build you a conservatory in the shape of a naked woman.

'At least let me pay for the cello lessons.'

'We'll talk about it tonight,' said Elizabeth. But we never did. That night, I went to a meeting for potential investors in Mike Bell's film, *Big Ben*. The meeting was in a drinking club in Whitechapel.

---

[1] 'Near Hereford' amused me. Nowhere was 'near Hereford'. It was virtually Wales. Herefordshire was full of poets and sculptors and potters and woodturners who took refuge there because they craved a solitude I was only too happy to give them.

13

The Investment
(2002)

My journey to Whitechapel was not without precedent. Precedent was more important than ever. It provided equilibrium, after the unbalancing events of the previous night.

Whitechapel was the home of my father's friend Maurice. Even though he was old and no longer lived in London, my father still made the journey to see his friend. The round trip from Suffolk — by taxi, rail, Underground, bus and foot — must have taken him a day. Bell was, we know, my Maurice, the friend whose life had been less privileged and successful than my own. I was walking in my father's footsteps.

The drinking club, Jimmy's, was below an Indian restaurant on the Whitechapel Road. Smoking appeared to be compulsory, possibly to kill off the odours from above. I was, of course, on time. Bell, of course, was nowhere to be seen; and none of the other denizens of this deep looked like an investor in the arts.

Jimmy, the proprietor, was a tall, stooped man in his seventies. He was not only behind the bar but in almost all the photos on the wall. Many of them dated from the sixties. In those days, Jimmy wore heavy black-rimmed glasses. Now, they were wire-rimmed and light. It was a familiar optical evolution — he'd gone from Michael Caine glasses to *Sir* Michael Caine glasses. Indeed, there was a photo of the two men together, in their black-rimmed days. Jimmy was smiling. Caine was not. Good for him.

Next to it was a photo of the Kray Brothers. Ronnie and Reggie were standing behind the bar with Jimmy. Their presence behind this bar was curious. They were certainly not barmen. Had they been helping themselves to the till?

'Scuse me,' said Jimmy, who'd travelled from behind that bar just to speak to me. Why? I tensed as I recalled Alan Barnes, punched by a drummer for looking at his drums 'in the wrong way'. Had I been looking at these photos of Jimmy in 'the wrong way'?

'You looking for Mr Bell?' asked Jimmy. I nodded. I thought it best not to speak in case he felt patronised by my accent. He directed me to the back room, where 'Mr Bell' was waiting. I was not the first to arrive but the last.

★ ★ ★

In the back room, there were only men. Two were playing pool, that snooker for idiots. Otherwise, the men were seated at tables. I walked, gingerly, towards Bell, who was having an intense conversation with a bulky man. Bell got up and hugged me. I didn't reciprocate. He was only doing his job. Hugging, for a film producer, was a professional preliminary, as prosaic and quotidian as my donning of a wig and gown.

258

'Good to see you. I think you know this man here!' It was Pilkington, sitting with a group of similarly shiny men.

'Robert!' said Pilkington, who found a chair and placed it next to himself. I could scarcely ask whom the chair was for. He then introduced me to his City colleagues; I made a point of not remembering their names. They burbled with approval when Pilkington told them we'd known each other since childhood. I was, apparently, a 'top barrister'. He added that I had a 'really great wife'. But, happily, he didn't ask after her. This was the great advantage of spending the evening with men. What man ever said, to another man: 'And how is your marriage?'

The man to his right said that Pilkington had a really great wife too. This was merely a conversational reflex and needed no further comment. But Pilkington was crass enough to argue. 'The Ticky's all right,' he said. (What kind of man inserts a definite article before his wife's name?) 'But she's a hell of a whinger.'

Bell shouted, 'OK, gentlemen! Shall we start?' Many of the men carried on chatting. Bell's bulky neighbour looked displeased. He was an ugly man in his sixties, with a nose like an aubergine, a word, I suspected, he wouldn't be able to spell, pronounce or define. He wore a ring inlaid with two gold dice. He gave a loud shush and, one by one, everyone stopped talking. Everyone, that is, except a shaven-headed young man at my table, who was ranting to his friend. Neither looked like an investor. They looked like locals, like regulars.

'And I'll tell you another fucking thing,' said the Ranter. His friend listened patiently, chewing all the while. He poured the Ranter and himself two glasses of champagne, then raised his glass to his lips. I waited for him to take the gum from his mouth. But no. I saw it as clearly as if his jaw were glass: the champagne flowing into his mouth and fizzing, en route to his gullet, the grey barnacle of gum. What right had such a man to buy champagne? He could not be trusted to safeguard the taste of *gum*.

'You don't give a smackhead more than one last chance,' said the Ranter. The Chewer chewed on this piece of wisdom as if it were from the Bible. But the bulky man had heard enough. He sneaked up behind them. He placed the flat of his hands on their temples and knocked their heads together.

'Sorry, Bernard,' said the Ranter, more humiliated than hurt. The Chewer said nothing. I was pleased to see that the shock had made him swallow his gum.

Bernard returned to his table, his presence felt by all. He was, it transpired, the guest of honour. Bernard Brown, Bell told us, was the inspiration for *Big Ben*. One night in 1957, in this very room, the eighteen-year-old Bernard had been approached by a stranger. The stranger introduced himself as Ronnie Kray. Ronnie gave Bernard a ten-bob note and told him that, if anyone asked, he — Ronnie — had left the club at 10 p.m. Bernard nodded, to show he understood. Ronnie left. It was just before nine.

Pilkington nodded, keen to show that he too

understood. Then he made a kind of grunting noise, to make his nod audible. This alerted Bernard, who looked Pilkington in the eye. A bond was formed.

Though the plot of *Big Ben* was fictional, said Bell, the incidents and details were derived from hundreds of hours of interviews with Bernard. He was the source for both the main characters: Ben Morris (the Mr Big character) and his young nemesis, Jake. Bell said that, as potential investors, we should listen to what Bernard had to say about the script. It was worth more than anything Bell could say.

Bernard began by praising Bell. His enthusiasm and determination had greatly impressed Bernard. Bell was a man who had a feel for what life was like on the streets. The screenplay reflected that. It was 'authentic, authentic, authentic'.[1]

Here Bernard picked up his script. He'd managed, though it must have been a hundred pages thick, to roll it into a tubular shape he could grip in his fist. Brandishing it like lead piping, he asked, rhetorically, why it was so

---

[1] This was a homage, whether conscious or not, to the Prime Minister. On achieving office in 1997, he'd said that his three main priorities were 'education, education, education'. In repetition, repetition, repetition lies truth: I've availed myself on many occasions of that particular oratorical stratagem. Let us not forget that Tony Blair was a member of the Bar. He was the Prime Barrister.

authentic. It was authentic because it was a man's life. He should know. He was that man.

From this point, he literally departed from the script. He stopped canvassing the film and started selling us — the assembled bankers and venture capitalists, the Ranter, the Chewer and me — his life itself. It had been a life of poverty, graft, riches, loyalty, disloyalty (of which he was always victim, not perpetrator), imprisonment, violence and yet more violence.

'You never rest in my game. Cos you don't know what's going to happen. You get knocked down. And you got to get right back up again.' What was this vein in which he carried on? It was sentimental and brutal, a vein through which ran only bad blood. 'Who do you turn to? Who can you trust? In the end, the only person you can rely on is yourself.' Here was the self-righteous victim as hero, buffeted by Fortune but praising himself for his constancy and resilience. Where had I heard this before? It was a cross between 'Candle in the Wind' and 'My Way'.

Who could stop this man and his 'Candle in My Way'? Pilkington, of all people, interrupted. But the interruption was not prophylactic. Pilkington only increased Bernard's dirty flow.

'What's the worst thing you've ever done?' he asked.

Bernard looked pensive. 'I've retired, son. These days I spend most of my time with my vegetables.' Was I alone in picturing these 'vegetables' as members of Bernard's gang, whose brains he'd personally damaged?

'All right, then. I'll tell you.' (I'd never seen reluctance so obviously feigned.) He shook his head. 'It's bad,' he said, 'it's very bad.' The massed investors, as he knew they would, advanced their expensively accoutred buttocks to the edge of their seats.

'It's all in the script, isn't it?' said Bell, neatly reminding us why we were here.

'Yeah,' said Bernard. 'There's a few going to faint when they watch that scene!' He looked Pilkington straight in the eye. 'Ever seen a man with his cock in a vice?'

Had Pilkington ever seen a man with his cock in a vice? Pilkington wouldn't commit. He didn't want to be outdone. He thought long and hard. Why? Was he spooling through his memories of his boarding-school woodwork room? Finally, he shook his head.

'There was a man called Dave. Used to do errands for me.' Bernard stopped. Pilkington's mobile was ringing. Pilkington answered it and told the caller he'd call him back.

'Will it still ring when I shove it up your arse?' asked Bernard.

'I hope so, the amount I paid for it,' said Pilkington. Nobody laughed.

'Is that meant to be funny?' asked Bernard. Brilliantly, he asked it of Bell. He asked Bell to explain his friend, demeaning them both.

'Please carry on,' said Bell to Bernard, in a voice I'd never heard him use, like a headmaster sweetening a bishop.

This is a book of my confessions, not Bernard Brown's. I will therefore ruthlessly edit his story of the man with his cock in a vice.

Dave, Bernard's errand boy, had made the mistake of 'suggesting bed' to Jackie, Bernard's girlfriend. One Friday night, at Bernard's house, Bernard asked Dave to give himself an erection. Dave, not unnaturally, asked why. Bernard told Dave the erection would facilitate the placing of Dave's penis in a vice. Dave, despite the gun at his head, failed to get an erection. A sensitive soul, he didn't find the prospect of his penis in a vice sexually arousing. Then Bernard had a brainwave. Jackie! Of course! Bernard rang Jackie. Jackie came round. Bernard told Jackie, his own girlfriend, to arouse Dave's offending penis. Jackie demurred. Bernard insisted. Jackie refused to touch it. Bernard gave Jackie his gardening gloves. Of course. His gardening gloves. For Bernard Brown, when not a psychopath, spent time on his allotment with his veg.

'She's done the business. He's stuck it in the vice. I start to turn the handle.'

I looked from the rapt Bell to the rapt Pilkington. I saw only weakness. Pilkington was revelling in the power of Bernard. Bell looked to Bernard as his saviour, his ticket to a feature film production. More than his fictitious Anglo-Asians, this repellent individual was 'authentic'. 'Authenticity', apparently, meant only poverty and hate. A June evening in a walled garden was not 'authentic', unless one spent it with one's cock in a vice.

Who could resist Bernard Brown? What City investor, with his floppy hair, his holiday house, his nest-egged parents, could refuse to invest in this hard man, blackmailing all of us with the darkness and deprivations of his past?

'He's crying out. He's screaming. But I can't stop. I crank it up even more.'

Elizabeth had betrayed me. There was a word I hadn't said to her, a simple word: 'wrong'. What she had done was wrong. What Bernard Brown had done was wrong. I am not suggesting a moral equivalence between Elizabeth's adultery and Brown's crime. I am asking if there was anyone in the back room of that drinking club who believed in right and wrong, whose moral compass had not been destroyed by greed or ambition or irony? For nothing was bad or good now. Everything was entertainment. There was bad or good entertainment, certainly, but that was not a moral judgement.

I felt alone. I felt so alone.

Back in the vice, Dave had fainted. Bernard was looking at me as he said this. I blinked. Bernard did not. I had never seen a man go so long without blinking. Now Bernard was turning the handle of the vice, anticlockwise. He was releasing Dave from the vice. Dave fell on the floor. Jackie cried as she looked between his legs.

'I had another fellow who worked for me. Barry. Welsh Barry. Always carried a bottle of lighter fuel. Cos you never know, do you? So I say, 'Barry, it's getting chilly in here. We could all do with a bit of warming up. Specially Dave. He's white as a sheet. Pour some fuel on his chilly little cock.' So Barry splashes some fuel on his cock. I light a fucking match. Then I kneel

265

down and I hold the match an inch above his cock. Then I — '

'Enough!' I shouted. I stood up. 'This is wrong!' I was shaking. For the next few seconds, I couldn't speak.

'This man is disgusting. He's a criminal. He should be ashamed of the things he's done. Why's he boasting about them? And why are we listening? This is wrong. This must stop.'

Bernard sat down. I had crushed him. There was silence. Of all the silences I've ever heard, this was the most impressive. I had shamed every man in that room into silence. Such was the power of my silence — for I think I can justly claim it as mine — that the men at the table stopped playing pool. They were bystanders. They had nothing to do with it. But they didn't dare make a sound.

'Thank you,' I said, with grace and modesty. Then I too sat down.

Bell got to his feet. 'Yes!' he said, punching the air. Then he hugged Bernard Brown, though he was standing and Brown was sitting down.

'Gentlemen, this is the brilliant actor Alf Stone! Alf is creating the character of Ben in my film *Big Ben*. You've all just seen what a great actor he is. This is your chance to invest in a great actor and a great film!'

Pilkington stood up and started the applause. Soon everyone in the room was applauding, except Alf Stone and me. Bell raised and lowered his hands to silence the applause.

'Can I also introduce Michael McAdam, who's Jake, and Tony Alexander, who's Headcase!' The

266

Ranter and the Chewer took their applause like divas, extending their arms towards Alf Stone, as if to say, no, no, please, no, we're nothing without the maestro.

And then Bell was upon me again, hugging me even tighter: 'You were fabulous, Bobby, you made the whole thing work. Magic! When you got to your feet . . . electric! Thank you! Thank you!'

Now I, through this hug, was made to feel a co-conspirator in his deception. My humiliation was complete. Or was it? I have learned, as we shall see, that humiliation is never complete. There is always more. Humiliation replenishes itself, like that magical tin of beans.

Then Pilkington was hugging Bell: 'You bullshitted a bullshitter, mate. I respect that. I'm getting out my chequebook.'

* * *

I had expressed my belief in right and wrong. Yes, the wrong was an actor's fabrication. But I didn't know that. I believed I was listening to the truth. I stood up and was counted.

Why then, not fifteen minutes later, did I invest twenty thousand pounds in *Big Ben*? Was it simply because Pilkington had invested fifteen? No. Yes and no. That morning, Elizabeth had rejected my money; that night, my friend Bell sought it and was grateful.

Do not mistake me. I did not, in that hour, bend. I remained rigidly opposed to the film. It deserved to fail, pandering, as it did, to the

267

basest instincts. Unique among the investors that night, I wanted from the noblest motives to see no return on my money.

I did not spend a penny of Elizabeth's money, since it came from an account that was in my sole name.

14

A Man Alone
(2002)

One Saturday in early July, I departed for Aldeburgh at seven in the morning, not wishing to remain in my house while unknown men loaded my wife's, daughter's, son's and dog's possessions into a van. How long before those men noticed that my shirts — white as ghosts — remained unmoved?

I arrived in Aldeburgh by half past nine. I drove past the golf course, past the Hamilton-Woods' house, past Margaret from the off-licence walking her whippet,[1] past the roundabout and then, instead of turning into the private road that leads to High Ridge, I took a detour via the High Street. I wished to see that things were as they always had been. Sure enough, Geoffrey Moxon-Smith, in his yellow-gold corduroy trousers, was emerging from the butcher, while a few yards further on, his wife Amanda stood outside the Co-op with her charity collection box, receiving

---

[1] I recognised Margaret immediately, which is a tribute to her (and her whippet). Usually, with people who work in shops, I don't recognise them when they're not behind a counter. I'm just not accustomed to seeing them with legs.

money from other ladies, in exchange for gossip. The old outnumbered the young. Sailors outnumbered tinkers, tailors, soldiers and beggarmen, of whom there were none. Deck shoes outnumbered trainers. Dogs outnumbered people from the working class.

I parked my car in the drive of High Ridge, next to the white Ford Escort. (It was now only eight years till Max could take his test.) Before entering the house, I strolled over the road, to salute Bert Gage, who was gardening for the Thodays.

'Morning, Bert!' I called. He was eighty. His gardening, now, was sponsored pottering about. He appeared to be deadheading a delphinium, though he may have been merely leaning on it.

'How are you, Bert?' I asked, with just the right level of enthusiasm, neither so little as to offend him nor so much as to make him wonder why I cared.

'I shall be joining the compost heap soon,' said Bert. It was what he always said, at this time of year. In winter, he said, 'I won't last another winter.' What more could one ask of a gardener than seasonal remarks?

I walked back to my parents' house. I longed for the smell of Nescafé and dog. I unlocked the front door and was rewarded.

'Hello! I'm just pouring the coffee,' called my father from the kitchen.

'Don't spill it,' shouted my mother from the drawing room.

My parents emerged into the corridor, simultaneously. My father took my hand, which

270

he'd taken, in his later years, to sandwiching between his own instead of shaking. My mother, as always, spoke her greeting as opposed to conveying it with touch. Since I'd last seen her, she'd shrunk. When did it happen? In the night? Was it happening, infinitesimally, as she spoke?

My mother, blatantly, was close to death, yellow-grey and short of breath. I was therefore determined that death not be mentioned. Nor did I want my separation to be mentioned. Let's face it: I wanted nothing to be mentioned.

I put my bag down next to the mumby, which was stacked with empty brandy and whisky bottles. Through them, I could see part of the big red thing painted by Max.

'There's only me, I'm afraid. Elizabeth has taken the children to Hereford. She's got some friends there. She wanted a break.' That was the fruit of my journey's labours. That was the statement I'd drafted on the A406, redrafted on the M11, honed on the M25, polished on the A12 and the A1094 to Snape and Aldeburgh. It said everything yet nothing. It mentioned nothing.

'It's all right, Little Man. Elizabeth wrote to us.'

'On what subject?' I asked. I would not give up easily. Elizabeth might have written on the subject of my mother's health.

'On the subject of her leaving you,' boomed my mother.

'Let him have a cup of coffee,' said my father.

'That won't bring her back.'

★ ★ ★

'Women want love and sex now. Golf and sherry aren't enough. Not like they were for me, eh?'

'Are for you,' said my father, evenly. 'You're very much still alive.' My mother looked at me with her filmy eyes.

'Your father and I have been married for fifty-two years,' she said. Why was she telling me what I knew? 'Your father's very clever and extremely polite. But I don't have a clue who he is.'

My father said: 'Perhaps that's a cause of our longevity. If you knew who I was, you might not like me.'

'Top me up, Old Boy.'

He was glad of this request, which allowed him to leave the table, since the bottle was on the sideboard. He returned with the bottle for my mother and a scrap of paper for me. On it he had written eight names: Goldman, Laurence, Carne, Turner, Priday, Driscoll, Benton, Blundell. They were judges. I did not know what else united them till my father explained.

'Divorced members of the bench.' Then he added, with a kind of sad sweetness: 'Divorce is not a crime, Robert. You can still be a judge. Arnold Benton is one of the finest legal minds we have — and he's been divorced twice.' I was moved. My father was acknowledging the difficulties in my private life, while reassuring me that my destiny was unimpaired.

'Is Rodwell on that list?' asked my mother.

'No,' said my father. 'Michael Rodwell's never been divorced.'

'No. He just killed them.'

272

My father was upset by her loose use of language. 'Them' was a reference to Michael Rodwell's previous wives. (Sheila Gurney, QC, was his third.) His first wife, a doctor, had committed suicide. His second wife, an actress, had committed suicide too. These were stressful occupations. Doctors were subject to overwork, actresses to its opposite. Lord Rodwell had not 'killed' his wives. On the contrary, as my father now pointed out, they'd killed themselves.

'That's one way of leaving your husband, eh? Without going to Hereford. Without going anywhere, eh? I'll find out soon enough.' I fingered the chip in my mug and waited for her to finish. 'I'm sure you did your best, Little Man. Hard to keep a younger wife. Next time, pick on someone your age. She'll have lower expectations.'

'Elizabeth hasn't left me, Mother. She will return. Now can we proceed with the business of my stay.'

'Ha! I've never heard it called that before.'

With difficulty, my mother got to her feet and cleared the table of our coffee cups. She dropped two, each eliciting a double 'Bugger!' My father and I did not speak. We went to the cupboard under the sink and found a dustpan and brush together. (It is we who were together. The dustpan and brush, typically, were far apart.) He took the dustpan, I the brush. Together, we knelt and got the job done. Then we repaired next door. Normally, of course, there were four of us: my father, mother, Elizabeth and I. On this occasion, adapting to circumstance, we played three-handed. My father partnered my mother and I partnered the absent Elizabeth, walking round the table to do her bidding and play her cards.

★ ★ ★

Our house in Highgate was worth nine hundred thousand pounds. Everyone agreed: Cheryl from Peete's, Barry from Hill Coates, Mona from Capital Homes. Which agent should Elizabeth and I choose?

Barry was engaging and straightforward. But, in the circumstances, his ponytail ruled him out. Cheryl was intelligent and polite. Mona had no qualities. She was greed and vulgarity personified. She wasn't interested in selling our house for what it was worth — she was, she told us, 'about selling houses for more than they're worth'. We should put it on the market at one million, three hundred and fifty thousand. Mona knew 'in her waters' — I do not misquote — that someone 'out there' would snap it up. At this point, appropriately but alarmingly, Mona's waters played 'Big Spender'. She reached into the pocket of her jacket and pulled out her phone.

Elizabeth, naturally, wanted Cheryl. She could not understand why I, of all people, insisted on Mona. Nine hundred thousand was a fair price. We'd probably find a buyer in two days. Why protract the sale by putting it on the market at Mona's inflated price?

I explained to Elizabeth that I wanted her to

get as much money from the sale as possible, not as much money as was probable or fair. I appreciated that she and Anthony were not materialistic. Nevertheless, he might one day wish to set himself up in his own business. It was, I suggested, in the interests of our children that Anthony be fulfilled and contented and financially secure.

Elizabeth was impressed. Her husband, whom she was leaving, was arguing for the happiness of her lover, albeit from the desire to secure the well-being of his children. She couldn't find the flaw in my argument. In truth, there was no flaw. It was simply that my motives were not as stated. I *wanted* to protract the sale. I reasoned that if we held out for this overinflated price, we might spend four or five months not finding a buyer; by which time, my waters told me, Elizabeth would have realised the error of her ways and returned, with the children, to the house, which we'd then take off the market.

I was fighting for what I believed to be right.

★   ★   ★

We wrote the letter to the High Mistress of St Paul's Girls' School together, regretting that, 'owing to a change in our circumstances', our daughter Isobel would not be able to take up her place in September. We said this was a matter of great regret. We had infinite respect for the school's ethos and appreciated the vast and significant contribution made by former pupils to the law, the arts, academia and government.

275

We noted that the current Solicitor General, Harriet Harman, was herself a former pupil and, while we did not share her political views, we admired her achievements.[1]

I walked to the postbox with the letter. Then I walked back again. I took the letter for a walk then I burnt it at the bottom of our garden. I was not prepared to throw it away. Look what happened to the draft of my Max letter to Lady Rodwell. I'd burnt nothing — other than firelighters, kindling and logs — since I'd disposed of the taxi trousers, nineteen years before.

Then I went into my study and wrote my own letter to the High Mistress of St Paul's, regretting that, 'owing to a change in our circumstances', our daughter would not be able to take up her place in September. Could they kindly defer her place till the spring term, commencing in January 2003?

Elizabeth and the children would be back by Christmas, surely. People go home for Christmas.

* * *

---

[1] Elizabeth found this embarrassing. But she let it pass. After all, this was merely a goodbye letter — what did it matter what we said, as long as we said goodbye? She resented the reference to 'our' not sharing Harman's New Labour political views. Elizabeth claimed she was no longer a Conservative. She would probably vote Green at the next election. Green! Of course. The party for people in love.

I confess that, in the week after the departure of my family, I made some mistakes. They were the right sort of mistakes, made for the best reasons.

On the first Monday evening, I went home with a burger in my briefcase. Regrettably, I found myself heading for the house at the same time as my neighbour Alison was heading for hers. I stopped a few paces short of my gate, to deny her my burger perfume.

'Hello, Robert,' she said. 'Lovely evening.' We'd been engaged in our border dispute for over five years. For once, though, she was pleased to see me. The reason was plain. Reigning over my front gate was a For Sale sign. I was doing the one thing guaranteed to make her happy. I was leaving.

She pointed at the sign. She pointed as crassly as *pointedly* as a child in a nativity play extending its forefinger towards the Star in the East.

'I see you're selling your house,' she said.

'No.'

'There's no need to be sarcastic.'

I was not being sarcastic. Did Alison but know it, I was asserting the best interests of my family, who'd one day return to the house. My 'No' was not said to annoy Alison. That it did so was merely a bonus.

It was the burger, not that encounter, which was my first mistake. To eat a burger from the Holloway Road, in my own house, when my family had gone, was a lapse into self-loathing, akin to bringing a prostitute home.

The burger mistake, however, didn't end with

my eating the thing. Next morning, in chambers, Terry, my clerk, remarked that my papers 'smelt of relish'. I found myself saying that my son Max had one Big Mac a week. My wife and I called it his 'junkfood allowance'. Terry looked surprised. I was not one of those members of chambers who vouchsafed details of his family life. But now I was deprived of that life, I spoke of it, ironically, at great length. Terry became familiar with my wife's yoga lessons, my son's rugby triumphs, my daughter's musical gifts. On the Wednesday morning, he remarked on my cheerful disposition, which was a consequence of my appearance (my twelfth) in *The Times* Law Reports.

'You're in a good mood,' said Terry. 'Wife give you one last night?'

I did not need to look at him to make him go red. The very air around us seemed hot. Terry had made a mistake. But so had I. I had been foolishly 'matey'. It was I who had given him the licence to be presumptuous.

On the Wednesday evening, I went to the supermarket. I hadn't shopped for twelve years. *House, Purchasing of.* Not *House, Shopping for.* When I approached the till, with my Liver and Bacon Meal for One, my bottle of Chilean Merlot (to last the rest of the week), my multipack of kitchen roll, which I took from the shelves in the mistaken belief it was toilet paper, I felt humiliated by the nature of my 'bachelor basket'. I resolved that the next time I approached the till, it would be at the head of a trolley, in paterfamilias-style.

And so, on the Saturday morning, I made my biggest mistake. I approached the till with my trolley, for all the world like a family man. I paid. I exited. I pushed the trolley to my car in the Sainsbury's car park. I unloaded my shopping into the boot, save for one purchase, which had served its purpose. Now I wished to be rid of it. I did not wish to take it home.

Accordingly, I returned to Sainsbury's, single carrier bag in hand. Looking neither left nor right, I went straight for the toiletries shelves and replaced the nappies I'd bought to give my trolley its 'family' look. I then turned round and — here was my mistake — ran towards the exit.

Two minutes later, I found myself in the head of security's office, furnishing her with my receipt as proof of purchase of the nappies. I reassured her that there was nothing for her to worry about. I'd bought the nappies and decided to return them. She asked why. I explained, clearly and confidently — for why would I not be confident, since I'd done nothing wrong? — that I had no reason to take the nappies home, as I did not have a baby.

She asked me why I'd purchased the nappies if I didn't have a baby. I explained that they were for my own use.

'They wouldn't fit you,' she said. Then, to appraise me of her reasoning, she added: 'They're too small.' She was a large woman, of West Indian origin, with the wary authority of a matriarch.

'I didn't buy them to wear them. I bought them to give the impression in your store that I

279

was a husband and father. Once I'd left the store, they'd fulfilled their purpose. That's why I returned them.'

My answer, truthful in every detail, was too complex for a woman used to morons mumbling: *I put it in my pocket and forgot.* She stared at me.

'Say again?'

'Never mind,' I said. 'I wish to be judged on my actions, not my motivations.[1] I bought the product lawfully and returned it lawfully. Really, you should be thanking me. I mean, if every customer returned their purchases to your shelves, you'd overtake Tesco in minutes.'

I thought she might enjoy this. She didn't. She studied the packet again. She gazed at the photo of the baby.

'Sir, did you tamper with this pack before you put it back on the shelf?'

'No,' I replied. It was a worthwhile question. Was I a blackmailer who'd placed a shard of glass in a pack of nappies?

'You can go,' she said.

'Thank you,' I said. I meant it. This woman was saddled with a difficult and repetitive job. I was glad to have brought some variety into her working day. I would go so far as to say I identified with her. In Sainsbury's, this woman was the law.

'I propose to write a letter to the manager of the store, commending you for your thoroughness.'

---

[1] So pleased was I with this formulation that I used it again at my criminal trial.

She looked at me with an expression I hadn't seen before but would see many times thereafter. She looked at me as if I were the long-term occupier of an institutional bed.

'You must understand,' I said. 'I'm on your side.'

★　★　★

Elizabeth, Isobel, Max and I traditionally spent August in Aldeburgh. We something went the whole summer without going abroad. Aldeburgh was our summer. When necessary, I commuted to chambers from Saxmundham station, leaving for London on the 06.24.

That August, Isobel was scheduled to have taken the Aldeburgh Yacht Club sailing course. Max was scheduled for the tennis course, the golf course and the sailing course. That, plus bike rides, crabbing, marine horseplay and shouty games with his best friend Harry Pilkington, would have been just about enough to make Max tired. Now Max and Isobel would be spending their summer in Hereford, denied the Aldeburgh summer that was their birthright.

I went up to Aldeburgh alone, on their behalf. I could, of course, have insisted they visit their sick grandmother. But I did not wish to be heavy-handed. Gentleness now would be rewarded later. In any event, I was terrified my mother might say something. What might she say? I didn't know. She herself wouldn't know, till she said it.

★　★　★

How did I prepare for my first visit to Hereford? I looked for certainties. Hereford Cathedral housed the marvellous Mappa Mundi, a medieval map that placed Jerusalem at the centre of the world. The Ace Guest House advertised itself as 'five minutes' walk from the city centre'. All its bedrooms had 'en suite or private washing facilities'.

On the Friday evening, therefore, as I drove down the A40, I was certain I'd walk to see the Mappa Mundi on the Saturday morning, having privately washed myself beforehand.

To these certainties, I added more, visit by visit. Elizabeth would bring the children, at ten, to the parking space nearest to the travel agent in Castle Street.[1] We would eat at the Italian restaurant in Broad Street. We would go for a walk on the River Wye towpath. While Isobel and I were in the cathedral, Max would run round the outside. At some point, we'd find ourselves walking past the Hereford Museum. I'd suggest, in my best 'fun' tones, that now we were passing, we might as well 'pop in'.

I feared, before the first visit, that I'd have to ask them questions of my least favourite kind: ones to which I didn't know the answers. They were in a new house in a new town with a new family. What were the details, the excruciating

---

[1] She understood that she had to bring the children to me. I would never come and pick them up, not from a house occupied by the Lemon Man and owned by her ex-boyfriend Guy. Sadly, this meant that I didn't see Mars.

details, of life with the Lemon Man, in Guy and Sophie's annexe?

I needn't have worried. They were children. What were we doing? Where were we going? When would we have lunch? Was there a shop where Max could buy removable tattoos? That which had happened in the two weeks since I'd seen them was archaeological; it was buried and would only be remarked upon if evidence were uncovered. In the Italian restaurant, on that first visit, Max took from his pocket a short offcut of frayed thick rope. It was clearly a memento of his new life. I was obliged to ask him its origins.

'Me and Tony have been building a rope ladder down to the river.'

'It's not a ladder,' said Isobel. 'They've put in these poles about so high and strung the rope between them. You hang on to the rope when you go down to the water.'

'Ah. It's more like a banister,' I said.

'Yes,' said Isobel. Max, unconcerned with semantics, swished the rope against the salt and pepper, successfully knocking them over.

'How old's Tony?' I asked cheerfully, pleased Max had found a friend with whom he could engage in outdoor activity.

Max looked puzzled. I couldn't help but feel exasperated. What was so hard? Was age not the first thing boys established?

'I don't know,' he said. 'He's quite old.'

'Ten? Eleven?'

'Tony,' said Isobel.

'Tony's my mum's new partner,' said Max. He'd been trained, I could tell, to say it loudly and clearly. Let the waitress hear. Let the waitress know it was nothing shameful.

'Is everything all right?' I had, inadvertently, looked at the waitress. She meant 'your pasta' but she said 'everything'. How could 'everything' be all right?

★   ★   ★

The repetitions of marriage were replaced by the repetitions of separation. When we spoke on the phone, Elizabeth asked if I were looking after myself. Was I burying myself in my work?[1] I always asked: 'How's Tony?' She always told me, cautiously, that Tony was fine. But eventually the repetition wore her down. I was rewarded for my solicitousness.

Elizabeth knew I deserved to hear that Tony was not fine.

'It's not always easy for him,' she said. 'We're living next to a multimillionaire. It's not what Tony's used to. Guy's so competitive. Tony daren't even play tennis with him. We were talking last night with him and Sophie about giving away what you don't need. Even *that* was competitive. They're going to give away one of their cars. How do you think that makes Tony feel?'

Here was overwhelming evidence that her alliance with the Lemon Man was doomed.

---

[1] In my case, this cliché was precisely wrong. I never buried myself in my work. I came alive in it.

Tennis, riches, competition: this was the world from which Elizabeth came. She'd crewed for Pilkington in the Laser and Laser Radials class, in the previous summer's Aldeburgh Regatta. They'd finished second. Pilkington was inconsolable. That was the degree of competitiveness to which Elizabeth was used. I did not believe she could get unused to it.

'It must be difficult for him,' I said, and meant, though I still wanted to strangle him with his own ponytail.[1]

'How's Mars?' I asked, as she delivered the children, on my third visit, in mid-August.

'He's really taken to it,' she said. 'He sends his love.' Why would she send the dog's love? The dog's love, surely, was a proxy for her own.

'Have you found a cello teacher yet?' I asked.

'It's summer. Isobel should be outside.'

Max slammed the car door. On the way to the cathedral, he barely took his eyes off the paving stones. Why, he moaned, did we always have to go to the boring cathedral? This was rich, from a boy who'd never been in it, always staying

---

[1] I never attempted to do this. It is curious, is it not, that we regard an attempted murder as less reprehensible than a murder. (Try hissing 'Attempted murderer!') If I try to strangle you, I have the *mens rea* — the guilty intent — of a murderer. Yet people will not condemn me to the same degree. They'll regard me with disdain and perverse amusement. I tried. I failed. The ponytail wasn't long enough. I am that lovable English type, a bungler.

outside to run round it, thereby curtailing the time Isobel and I could spend inside.[1]

'After that, I spose we'll go to the same old boring museum.' The museum was not particularly boring, though it was fair to say that, with each visit, it became slightly more so. 'I'd rather you were bored by a good museum than something less worthwhile.' As I said this, I experienced a revelation. I'd thought that by going to the same old cathedral, museum, restaurant, towpath and tea room, I was satisfying my need for certainty. Now, belatedly, I saw there was more to it.

I did not want my children to get used to their new life. I wanted them to hanker after the old. Logically, therefore, *I should make my visits boring*. There is an analogy here with prison. My children had been sent to Hereford, for an indeterminate sentence. It is axiomatic that imprisonment at its best should be less desirable than liberty at its worst. From the prison of Hereford, I wanted them to long for the liberty of home, their home, our London home. That they should live contentedly in Hereford, looking forward to my visits: this was what I wanted to prevent.

I would save them from their Hereford life,

_____

[1] I instructed him not to stop for anyone when he ran round the cathedral. He understood. At nine, the longest word Max knew was 'paedophile'. What does that tell us about our society? And why does 'the paedophile hung around the cathedral' sound so utterly plausible?

though I did not yet know how.

'Aren't you supposed to bring us presents?' asked Max, as his fortnightly American Hot pizza landed on our table. I didn't know what to say. Isobel, as so often, came to my aid.

'You only get presents if your parents are divorced.' Then, for my benefit, she added: 'He wants presents cos we made him give his old Game Boys away. We're giving away what we don't need.'

'They're going to poor children,' said Max, giving the impression that, should he meet these children, he'd ask for his Game Boys back.

When his fruit salad and ice cream came, Max asked: 'So are you getting divorced?'

'No,' I said. I thought it best to say no more.

Isobel looked embarrassed. Max shook his head. Over the years, I'd come to understand what his headshake meant. He wished his father played contact sports. He wished his father were taller.

★ ★ ★

Before my next visit, Elizabeth told me that the children were going to bring the dog. I agreed, with my usual grace, delighted to be reunited with Mars. Max grinned as he pushed Mars out of the car. This visit was bound to be different. You could not take a dog into a museum, not unless you were blind.

Generally, I stood outside shops with Mars, while Max went inside with his sister. Once, for variety, I went into a shop and left the children

287

and Mars outside, returning with some biscuits which I entrusted to Max. He ate one, pronounced it disgusting and threw the rest over a wall. How could he not have noticed that the biscuits were for the dog? His concentration levels had worsened. Tony, I was sure, was not disciplining him. Tony would see discipline as an undesirable competition between discipliner and disciplinee. In any event, what moral authority was vested in a *houseman*?

On account of Mars, we did far more walking than on my previous visits. We headed further down the towpath than ever before. Isobel held the lead. Max hung back, playing a game on my mobile phone.

'That's our new school,' said Isobel, looking back at the town. 'Where?' I asked. She pointed, again, at what looked like a block of flats on an industrial estate.

My phone made two bleeping noises. In my ignorance, I thought these a part of Max's game.

'You've got a message,' said Max.

'Thank you,' I said. Max pressed something that turned the phone into a small radio. I heard my father's voice: 'This is a message for Robert Purcell.'

My father had never left a message for me in his life. *How can you be so dense, Robert?*

My mother had died of a heart attack at nine fifty-two the previous night.

Isobel, sweetly, looked sad and hugged Mars. This was exactly what I would have done, had I been in her position.

'I'd like you to play at the funeral,' I said.

'Cello Suite Number One. The second minuet.'

'I'm not playing any more,' said Isobel.

'Tony gave Isobel's cello to Africa,' said Max.

'I see,' I said. Then I burst into tears. Isobel explained this was 'delayed shock'. Max nodded. He wasn't sure if he should go back to his game or not.

★ ★ ★

Elizabeth rang late that night, to check I'd arrived safely in Aldeburgh. She had already rung my father to give him her condolences. She'd also rung Ticky Pilkington (née Moxon-Smith), both to tell her the news and ask if she and Isobel and Max might stay at the Pilkingtons' house for the funeral. Elizabeth hoped I would understand that she didn't want to stay at High Ridge with me and my father and sister. She wouldn't bring Tony, as that would be inappropriate.

This was Elizabeth at her best. We did not even know the day of the funeral, yet she'd made arrangements. This was practical and tactful and *wifely*. Ticky had rung her mother Amanda. Amanda Moxon-Smith, that ageing loudmouth, had rung everyone she knew who knew my mother and doubtless many who didn't. Then Amanda had rung my father and me, with a list of the people she'd told. There were seventeen. Amanda had saved us the agony of seventeen phone calls. Elizabeth knew this would happen. That's why she'd rung Ticky, setting it in motion.

There was more and better. By weeping on the towpath of the River Wye, I'd endeared myself to Elizabeth. Isobel had told her mother all about it. She'd never seen me cry. Elizabeth, who'd never seen me cry either, regarded it as evidence of my progress.

'You should cry more,' she told me on the phone. 'It's good for you. I'm glad you did it openly.'

'Thank you,' I said.

'I still care about you.'

This was glorious. I had no desire to exploit my mother's death. Nevertheless, the fact was the fact. My mother was dead. Tony's mother was alive. Bad luck, Tony. Had Tony's mother died, had Tony wept on the towpath, Tony could have had the admiration and respect that were now accruing to me.

I didn't say that my tears were not for my mother. My mother was eighty-three. What did one expect of an eighty-three-year-old who had, for months, been dying? My tears were for my daughter's cello. Tony the Lemon Man had given away my daughter's cello — the Chinese cello I'd bought her for her tenth birthday, at a cost of eighteen hundred pounds, plus an extra three hundred to set up the instrument correctly, reshaping the nut and refitting the sound post, and fifty pounds to have the black leather case embossed 'I.P.' for Isobel Purcell.[1]

Tony gave the cello to a woman he'd met at

_____

[1] The money was not the issue. I only mention the money as an index of the quality of the cello. Isobel was a gifted cellist who deserved the best.

the Hay-on-Wye Festival. The woman ran a charity that donated musical instruments to African children. I, of course, was meant to feel this donation was natural and right. What kind of father failed to give his daughter's cello to African children? What kind of devil dad thought, as I did: how are they going to eat it?

'Don't worry about the cello,' said Elizabeth. How did she know, down a phone line, what I was thinking? Because she was my wife. My wife. Not three months earlier, I'd walked into our living room and said: 'I.' That was it. 'I.' That was all it took — 'I' — for my wife to say: 'They're on the mantelpiece.' And they were, too. My glasses were on the mantelpiece.

'Isobel's living in a new place, she's going to a new school, we just wanted to take some pressure off her. She can always come back to it later. It's not as if she's going to be a professional cellist.'

'I understand,' I said, as blandly as I could. Now, more than ever, I had a cause. I wouldn't rest till Isobel held a cello in her arms again.

★ ★ ★

Three days later, I received a letter from Tony. I didn't recognise his handwriting, which I'd only ever seen on an invoice. First, I looked at the signature. Then I read the opening sentence: *I'm sorry about your loss.* I don't know what else he wrote. I threw it in the bin. My loss? What rampant egotism made my mother's life mine to lose?

Late that night, on my lonely way home from a concert at the Wigmore Hall, I saw a classic London sight: a single black glove, skewered on a railing. Somewhere, the owner of that glove was walking round with one hand in his pocket. *That* was a loss.

15

My Mother's Funeral
(2002)

There were seventeen knights at my mother's funeral, four more than at our wedding, twelve years earlier. Of the knights at our wedding, three had died; but seven of our wedding guests had since been knighted, leaving us in, as it were, titled profit.

In the church there was standing room only. Regrettably, one of those standing was the vicar, who had met my mother only once. His address, based on hearsay, ignorance and a brief, uncomfortable interview with my father — 'Would you say she suffered fools gladly?' — sounded like something he'd copied off the Internet. It did not matter. The vicar was the price of entering the church, as a cabby is the price of entering a cab. We were obliged, socially, to have a church service. After the service, we'd take her to Ipswich to be cremated.

What mattered was that all the Aldeburgh families were there: the Holts, the Pilkingtons, the Risdons, the Thodays, the Moxon-Smiths, the Farquharsons, the Hamilton-Woods. Rita who nursed my grandmother was there, as was Margaret who cleaned High Ridge, Bert who was its gardener, Eric who added its conservatory in

1968, Billy who 'did' its boiler.

These servants, with a combined age of several hundred years, were determined to get to the church, by hook, crook or Zimmer, all of them armed with the same phrase — 'I'll be next!' — followed by a little laugh.

The most important Aldeburgh family to be there was my own. It was the first time since their flight to Hereford that my wife, my son, my daughter and I were united in public. (I didn't count Castle Street, near Hereford Cathedral, where we united only to get children in and out of a car.)

We stood in a line, outside the church — my father, myself, Elizabeth, Isobel and Freya — greeting the mourners as they came out at the end of the service. My father, as ever, had the right word for everyone. My role was merely to second his words and thank each guest for coming. But our verbal skills were not enough, not in these tactile times, where women under fifty (and even some men) feel the need to hug. All the guests, without exception, were reluctant to touch my father. He was, though retired and bereaved, a judge. I, not yet a judge, had inherited the untouchability that every judge must have. Where, then, would we have been without Elizabeth? Elizabeth allowed herself to be embraced a hundred times or more. She was enveloped. She was cried on. But she soldiered on. No one could have failed to be impressed that my wife was by my side, nor that my daughter bravely held her mother's hand.

When the last guest had passed, I looked for

Max. There he was, with Harry Pilkington, shouting: 'I win!' He and Harry had just raced each other round the church. This pained me. Lapping religious buildings was a skill he'd honed in Hereford. At least he was exercising that skill in Aldeburgh, where he belonged.

Elizabeth and I walked to my Audi. I was to drive her to the cremation, which would be followed by drinks and canapés at High Ridge, from six till eight. We left the children in the care of Ticky Pilkington, née Moxon-Smith.

You will forgive me if I type that paragraph again. The rightness of it gave me such pleasure.

Elizabeth and I walked to my Audi. I was to drive her to the cremation, which would be followed by drinks and canapés at High Ridge, from six till eight. We left the children in the care of Ticky Pilkington, née Moxon-Smith.

★　★　★

At the drinks, Pilkington asked where Mike Bell was. I told him Mike Bell hadn't been invited. He expressed surprise. Mike Bell had been best man at my wedding. I acknowledged this but countered that there was no best man at a funeral. I added that my father had not invited his oldest friend Maurice, fearing Maurice wouldn't know anyone. Pilkington said he didn't know Maurice. We stood there, at the funeral of our dead conversation, not knowing what to say.

'Mike called me a couple of days ago. He's got most of the money now. Should be shooting in the autumn.'

I was somewhat miffed that Pilkington knew this and I didn't. There is status in friendship. I had known Bell for twenty-five years. It was not for his new pal Pilkington to give me news of Bell.

Pilkington looked at our wives, who were talking intensely to Freya. Please, no reference to the return of Elizabeth, for that would imply she'd left me. Let us have no personal remarks about my 'situation'.

'Elizabeth's a good woman. You must miss her,' said Pilkington.

'Not really,' I said. 'She's just over there. Excuse me.'

* * *

After the drinks, Elizabeth and the children went back to the Pilkington house.

My father said he was going to bed. He was glad that he and my mother hadn't slept in the same bed for forty years. It made going to bed on the night of her funeral easier. This was an unusually intimate remark but, in the circumstances, understandable.

I followed him up the stairs.

He asked how long I was staying. I said I had to get back the next day — Saturday — as I was in the High Court on Monday.

'Concerning?' he asked.

'I'm seeking a declaration that a trust deed transferring a beneficial interest is void.'

'Insolvency Act,' he said. '1986. Section 323.'

He was my father. I admired him more than

anyone. He had just endured his wife's funeral., Nevertheless, it was my duty to tell him the truth.

'It's actually Section 423.' He thanked me, genuinely, for correcting him, then bade me goodnight.

It was too early for me to go to bed. I had no choice but to go downstairs and be with my sister.

★ ★ ★

I'd seen Freya once since my wedding. Two years later, she and Murray flew their newborn twins to England to meet their grandparents. This was an admirable gesture of reconciliation, which unfortunately involved more cigars.

Motherhood had transformed Freya, if you accept that people can be transformed, which I do not. She had done a course at the Auckland College of Classical Homeopathy. She wrote articles about diet and nutrition and health for a paper called the *Remuera Age*. Yet, in the kitchen of High Ridge, she smoked and smoked in that contrary way she'd mastered in her Top Shop/heroin-addict boyfriend years. She rolled her own, handling the brown stuff with delicacy, as if tobacco were a plant that deserved her affection and would reward her with its own, in the Green Guy style of the loving yogurt.

She was now an expert on love, as I was on Section 423 of the Insolvency Act, though I *am* an expert on that, holding a first-class degree in Law, whereas, at the University of Life, there are only conflicting claims to expertise. You award yourself your own degree.

My sister had become what is known as an 'Earth Mother', loudly smothering Murray and the twins, Keisha and Alastair. Murray had told her she'd taught him how to love. She'd made him feel more alive. My best point, which I withheld, was that Murray had died the previous November. The poor man had had a heart attack, aged sixty-one. There was no doubt in my mind that he'd died of Freya, the quixotic, exhausting and terminal Freya, just as one day my father would die of Judy Page.

After his death, the Earth Mother was an Earth Widow too. Inheriting our mother's energy, she'd parlayed these states into a career. The *Remuera Age* gave her a column called '*Learning to Love*'. On Friday evenings from seven till nine on Radio Auckland, she had a phone-in for people with emotional problems. My sister pronounced on strangers' emotional problems, in public, like a cabby with a microphone. What was her qualification? Only that she was an emotional problem herself.

Why had our father never talked about his own dead mother? Why had he never shown us a photo or told us what she was like? Why wasn't his best friend at the funeral? Why didn't our father kiss and hug us? Had his own mother never kissed and hugged him?

I asked my sister not to broadcast these questions in my father's own kitchen, on the night of our mother's funeral. It seemed indecent. Regrettably, she turned her emotional torch on me. There was nothing she hadn't found out, by embracing Elizabeth at the funeral drinks and not letting go till she'd squeezed out all the information.

I was not to worry. That was the good news my sister gave me, as I ostentatiously opened the kitchen window, to expel the fug of her smoke and, I hoped, let the love out.

There was still time, said Freya, for both of us. But she wasn't referring to Elizabeth and me. She was talking about my father and me. According to her, we still had time to express ourselves sexually and emotionally. We still had time to learn how to love.

★ ★ ★

An hour later, following me up the stairs, she told me I must go round to the Pilkingtons' house 'now!' and have a 'passionate outburst'. I must tell Elizabeth I loved her. I must express, not repress, what I truly felt. I was suffering from what she called the 'English disease'.

'I'm not that kind of Englishman,' I said. 'You've lived in Australasia so long, your idea of Englishness is now derived from films.' I took the opportunity, on that landing, of lecturing her, as she'd been lecturing me. My subject was that celebrated Englishman, Hugh Grant.

I explained that Hugh Grant was an Englishman who suffered from low self-esteem and took refuge in self-mocking irony. I had never suffered from low self-esteem. Why should I? What Hugh Grant needed, in such films as

299

Four Weddings and a Funeral and *Notting Hill*, was an American or an actress (or both) who would help him release his long-repressed capacity for undying love and lifelong commitment. I needed no such thing. I had no capacity for undying love and — the italics are mine — *nor did I ever claim to have such a capacity*. I certainly had a capacity for lifelong commitment. But that did not need to be — and could not be — expressed in a 'passionate outburst'. Commitment wasn't passionate. Nor did it burst out. On the contrary.[1]

---

[1] In this paragraph, I've conflated Hugh Grant with the character created for him by the writer Richard Curtis. If Mr Grant believes I've libelled him, so be it. I shall see him in court. I hope I shall see them both in court. They are, like me, Oxford men, though Mr Grant, being four years younger, went up after I came down. I was, in fact, a contemporary of Mr Curtis at Christ Church. I never spoke to him but knew of his reputation as a scholar and delightful man. I recall, from proximity at dinner, that he had the most beguiling gurgle of a voice. Once the case is over, win or lose, I shall seek Mr Grant's autograph (for Isobel) and take the opportunity to show both men the photos of my father and me outside Christ Church. I want Richard and Hugh (if I may call them that) to remember me as a civilised man. I don't want them to remember me, if at all, as a man who committed a crime sensationalised in the tabloids. Hugh, in particular, will understand. The tabloids feasted,

In the event, when I went round on Saturday lunchtime to say goodbye to my family, there was indeed a passionate outburst.

The Pilkington family house was on Crag Path, abutting the beach promenade. The door was open. Out came Max with Harry and Tom. They were off to the fish-and-chip shop to buy lunch for all. Max, who was with his 'troops', didn't want to engage with his father. I extracted a 'hello', followed by a 'bye'. That was it.

Pilkington sat in the small front garden, reading the *Financial Times*. He nodded at me but ignored the children completely. Ticky came running out to ask him if they'd 'written it down'. She was followed by Elizabeth.

'What?' asked Pilkington.

'Did they write down the fish-and-chip order?'

'WHERE THE F*** IS THE CORKSCREW?'

This was not Pilkington's reply. This was what was written on his T-shirt. Pilkington, in fact, made no reply. So Ticky repeated the question.

'Did they write down the order?'

'I don't know.'

'Well, run after them and check.'

---

nay, sickened themselves on his brief and unfortunate association with a 'hooker' called Divine Brown, as if she were Divine Retribution for his talent, success, wealth and Oxford education. Let us agree: a man should be remembered for his body of work, not the work of his body. (Yes. I rather like that.)

'You run after them.'

'Why should I run after them? You're sitting there reading the paper.'

'Go on. Run after them. Might lose some weight.'

'You fucking shit! I hate you!'

'I work two hundred hours a week! I work two hundred thousand fucking hours a week!'

To stand there with Elizabeth, witnessing this, was not without its rewards. While they abused each other, Elizabeth and I were deeply embarrassed, together. Elizabeth was surely thinking, as was I, that in all our years of marriage I had never raised my voice.

We walked to the sea wall, to get away from the noise. She asked about my father. I told her he was bearing up. I thanked her for all she'd done at the funeral.

'I was glad to help. I wanted to help. But you're looking at me as if we're together again.'

'We're together now,' I said.

'Have you seen Isobel?' she asked, briskly. 'She's reading on the beach.'

'She's enjoying it while it lasts,' I remarked, portentously. It was nearly September. I was keen to remind Elizabeth that the holidays were almost over; which meant there was still time for her to think of the Hereford adventure as a holiday.

'Isn't it time Isobel went back to the cello? We could always hire one, if we don't want to buy her another.'[1]

---

[1] You will note that I twice referred to us as 'we'.

'You should talk to her about it. I just don't want to put pressure on her. Maybe she could just play for fun. Tony doesn't believe in music as a competitive thing.' Elizabeth didn't look at me. She didn't dare.

I had an inkling that Elizabeth was on my side, in the matter of the African cello. It was Tony who'd argued for the giving away of the cello. They had, perhaps, fought about it. Happily, at that moment, Ticky grabbed Pilkington's *Financial Times* and started tearing it up.

There was a divide, perhaps, between my wife and Tony, concerning the lost cello. I would probe that divide, probe and probe. To be crude, I'd drive a big truck through that divide, then reverse it, then drive through again, to make sure.

⋆   ⋆   ⋆

I found Isobel, heavily sweatered, reading *To Kill a Mockingbird*. I suggested we go to a concert. There was bound to be a cello concert in Hereford, in the autumn. If not, I would take her to Worcester or Gloucester. We would seek out the music of the cello. Isobel agreed.

⋆   ⋆   ⋆

'What am I supposed to do now?' asked my father as I left High Ridge. I had the answer. It had been provided, the previous evening, by Amanda Moxon-Smith. She'd told me she and Geoffrey were going to see the matinee of

303

Genevieve at the Aldeburgh cinema at 3 p.m.; I should persuade my father to accompany them.

'He's probably seen it a million times,' said Geoffrey, embarrassed, as always, by his wife's pushiness.

'Then he won't mind seeing it a million and one!' said Amanda.

It was now twenty-five to three. I told my father to walk, slowly, to the cinema. He looked uncertain and a little afraid.

'Freya says I have to learn how to love.'

There we had it. Of his two children, who was helping their father more? The one advising him to go to the cinema to see *Genevieve* or the one advising him to learn how to love?

16

The Concert
(2002)

In early October, Mona called. On Saturday at ten, a couple called Andy and Sonia were coming to see our house. It would, she said, be the thirty-third viewing. No one had offered more than nine hundred thousand pounds. Mona felt we were wasting our time holding out for more. As she'd been saying since the tenth viewing, we had to listen to the market. The market had spoken. What about her waters? I asked, as I always asked. Hadn't they spoken too? Hadn't they shouted from the rooftops that our house was worth one million, three hundred and fifty thousand pounds?

Mona asked if she could be 'very truthful'. If Andy and Sonia didn't offer the asking price, and I refused yet again to reduce it, Mona felt she'd have to let me go. Mona, my estate agent, was threatening to fire me. To be fired by one's estate agent is akin to being swatted by a fly. Nevertheless, I didn't object. If Mona fired me, so be it. I would simply tell Elizabeth she'd failed to find us a buyer. It was not a question of lowering the price but finding another agent. In this fashion, I'd waste a few more weeks, as we sought another agent who'd agree to the implausible price.

In the event, I was in trouble from the moment I opened the door. I have never wanted to compensate for my shortness with an oversized personality. Andy most certainly did. I could tell by the way he wiped his feet, which is to say he didn't wipe his feet, but entered our house as if he already owned it and could cover its surface with his own shoe-dirt if he felt like it, which he did. Sonia wiped her feet, though. She was demure, blonde, and taller than Andy. Of course she was. Andy wanted the world to know he'd scaled a taller woman. He had ascended Sonia on his path to the top.

'What d'you think, babe, it's fantastic, isn't it?' Since they'd got no further than the hall, Sonia sensibly reserved judgement. I showed them round the ground floor. Andy made satisfied clucking sounds and tapped his foot with impatience if Sonia spent too long in a room.

'You always know with houses, don't you?' he said, his little eyes level with mine.

'There's an upstairs too,' I said. He ignored me.

'We should buy it, shouldn't we?'

Sonia nodded.

'How much you asking?'

'One million, three hundred and fifty thousand pounds.'

I spoke it, as always, in my best judicial manner. I gave it as a verdict with which there was no negotiation, any more than the prisoner in the dock could say: 'Ten years, Your Honour? You can't be serious. I'll offer you six.'

* * *

Fifteen minutes later, Andy and Sonia were standing on my doorstep, discussing what colour to repaint my front door. Sonia, I thought, was my only chance. I explained that my wife and I were not prepared to accept anything less than the asking price. They should take their time.

Andy stepped in front of her. He actually interposed his body between Sonia and me.

'We don't need time. We'll pay it.'

'Subject to survey,' said Sonia.

'Subject to survey,' said Andy, from lower down.

In the road, a car door slammed. My neighbour Alison was returning to her house. Discreetly, I motioned Andy and Sonia back into my hallway. I closed the front door.

'I'm duty-bound to tell you I'm in dispute with my neighbour.'

'What's it regarding?' asked Andy.

'The angle of a wall built by the previous owners. She believes they pirated an extra strip of land at the bottom of her garden. About thirty square feet.'

'In that case, we don't care,' said Andy. 'We'll give it to her. We're nice.'

'I don't think you quite understand,' I said. 'She puts excrement through my letter box.'

'We'll give her what she wants and she'll stop.'

'I'm not sure I want to live next to a woman like that,' said Sonia. Encouraged, I said: 'It's different excrement every time.' I wasn't sure what this meant. But I knew it sounded bad.

* * *

Half an hour later, Mona was on the phone. What was all this about excrement? I apologised. I said it hadn't occurred to me to mention it before. Mona asked if my wife knew about it, as she was about to call Elizabeth with the fantastic, brilliant news that Andy and Sonia were going to buy our house for one point three five million pounds, subject to survey and subject to clearing up this business about the excrement.

I was shaken. I didn't want Mona to tell Elizabeth about the excrement, which was phantom. Elizabeth wouldn't understand. She'd think it a lie. But it was not a lie. It was a much more noble thing. It was a tactic for saving our marriage, which Elizabeth was misguidedly trying to destroy.

Mona went in for the kill. A partner in a 'broken relationship' — her words not mine — often tried to block the sale of the marital home, out of spite or an obstinate refusal to face the truth. Mona knew where I was 'coming from'. She'd been divorced herself, twice. She understood that, in times of stress, people said things that weren't true.

I asked her whether she was accusing me of making up the excrement. She said she wasn't accusing me of anything. She was just asking me what she should tell Elizabeth. Basically, I had a choice. I could send Mona an email explaining that the story wasn't true (which she could forward to Andy and Sonia) or I could back up my story by biking Mona some excrement.

Elizabeth rang me an hour later, delighted by the news. I suggested we instruct Geoffrey Moxon-Smith to deal with the conveyancing. Elizabeth was reluctant. Geoffrey lived in Aldeburgh. Why not hire a local London solicitor? Or let Elizabeth, a solicitor herself, handle the sale? I explained that Geoffrey was one of my father's oldest friends. It was a question of loyalty. Elizabeth accepted this.

The following Monday morning, I called Geoffrey at his office. He wasn't there. The girl told me he'd just called to say he wasn't feeling well.

Geoffrey, that genial, plodding man, worked two days a week and was eighty. I had hoped this would delay the sale. So far, he had played his part to perfection.

I told her to give Geoffrey my best wishes for a leisurely recovery.

I was fighting to save my house and my marriage, the bricks and mortar of my life.

★ ★ ★

My father was not alone. There were many old widowers in Aldeburgh, as well as old husbands, old wives, old widows, old spinsters and, yes, old bachelors. It was one of the last places in England where an old bachelor could walk down the street without being 'outed'. In fact, he would be 'inned' — his private life, forcibly revealed elsewhere, would in Aldeburgh be

309

returned to him for safe keeping, for keeping in.

As I walked down Aldeburgh High Street, on a Saturday morning in late November, I too had the sense that my privacy was inviolable. I waved to Ping Mottram (née Farquharson) and reviewed the weather with Boo Priday (née Risdon). Both would have known that Elizabeth had left me, four months earlier. Both would have known we'd accepted an offer on our London house. Yet no reference was made to these events by Ping or Boo or Pidge Holt — that much-admired, unmarried godmother and aunt — as, bending at the knee, she said *yes yes yes yes yes* to Buster, my father's Airedale terrier (formerly, my mother's). Poor Buster needed all the sympathy he could get. He was old and on the verge of immobility. He spent hours with his head in my father's houseplants, comforted by their smell and texture.

Pidge, of course, asked after my father. They all did. Death, with its funerals and announcements in *The Times*, was scarcely private. I told them he was bearing up well.

It was not that my father was bearing up well to my mother's death; rather, he was bearing up well to the punishing schedule imposed on a widower by his fellow old folk. There were coffees, there were sherries before lunch, there were lunches, there were teas, there were sherries before supper, there were sherries before sherries. There were morning concerts, afternoon concerts and evening concerts: three square concerts a day. There was twenty-four-hour bridge. He could not, he said, have an afternoon nap without being woken by an invitation to bridge.

A week earlier, at the Farquharsons, Amanda Moxon-Smith had led a heart and my father, thinking he had no hearts, trumped it with a low club. Then he espied a singleton heart, hidden in his hand behind a diamond. He'd inadvertently cheated. He snatched back his club and hurriedly attempted to replace it with his heart. This in itself was further cheating, since a card, once played, cannot be withdrawn. Doubly embarrassed, he jabbed his thumb at high speed on the edge of the table. My father had what can only be called 'a bridge accident'. His dislocated thumb was now in a cast.

Sadly, the thumb was on his dog-walking hand. (Each of us has a preferred hand, don't we?) Hence it was I, not he, proceeding down the High Street with Buster, certain I'd be asked about Buster and my father and my father's thumb, but equally certain I'd not be asked about me.

* * *

'I was young and thin and gorgeous once. Do you remember? I should have held on to you. You're reliable. I've had enough excitement to last a lifetime. He hates me now — that's why I eat all the time. I'm really sorry about you and Elizabeth but she told me that Tony's very good with your kids. That's some comfort, isn't it?'

All I'd said to Ticky was 'Morning'. Now this. Let us disregard the breach of my privacy: *I'm*

311

really sorry about you and Elizabeth. She'd begun by breaching her own privacy — *He hates me now — that's why I eat all the time.* Did I not have a negative right, a right not to have her breach her own privacy in my presence? Let Ticky and Pilkington fight their own battles. And let me not, against my will, be dropped between their trenches.

'I don't know what he did on your stag night. I know he did something. You weren't even there, were you?'

'My stag night was twelve years ago,' I said, irrelevantly. Her floodgates were open. Past, present and future all rushed through, scummy and undifferentiated.

'I'm going to leave him. You mark my words. What's the date? Where are we?'

'Twenty-third of November. We're in the Co-op.'

'He's got no respect for me or himself or anything. Did you know he threw a phone? He yanked the phone out the wall in his office and he threw it down the stairwell. Fourteen floors. He should have himself seen to.'

Ticky fell silent.

'Why don't you take me out to dinner? Are you worried I'll drink too much? Or are you worried I'll eat too much?'

'I'm not worried,' I said, which was true, but did not amount to a statement of intent to take Ticky out to dinner. I had already taken her out to dinner, some twenty-three years earlier. There was no need to take her out to dinner again.

* * *

Geoffrey got better. Contracts were exchanged. What could save me now?

Right could save me. I had right on my side.

* * *

The concert was at Great Witley Church, near Worcester, on a Saturday evening at seven thirty. Penelope Orchard (cello), accompanied by Graham Burtenshaw (piano), were playing Bach's Sonatas for Cello and Piano. Never mind that the programme was padded out with piano sonatas by Debussy, that fatuous French burbler.

I asked Elizabeth to get Isobel to the church for six thirty. I wanted us to have time to enjoy the paintings and the windows and the organ, not to mention the exterior, which I hoped would be illuminated. The church, according to my researches, was the only one of its (late baroque) kind in England.

I was surprised to see Isobel get out of my Audi with Tony.[1] Elizabeth was busy at home, he said, cooking for Guy and Sophie. Things were quite stressful. It wasn't every night a

---

[1] That's right. I'd let Elizabeth take my Audi to Hereford, while I struggled in London with public transport and drove hired cars to Aldeburgh. Elizabeth, the children and Mars loved my Audi. I hoped it would remind them of me. I didn't like the way Tony parked it. I don't trust a one-handed parker.

313

multimillionaire came to dinner! But she was coping fantastically, as always.

Why wasn't Tony cooking? Elizabeth had referred to his culinary abilities. I knew, for example, that he made 'great curries'. I feared she'd dispatched him — or he'd dispatched himself — so we could get to know each other better. Already, he'd commented on Elizabeth's fantastic coping, as if it were something we both admired which, to be fair, it was. Conspiratorial, too, was his pejorative reference to the 'multimillionaire'. Tony was uniting with me against our common enemy. In such ways does a greater enemy, like Tony, lay claim to be one's friend.

I emitted some polite noises, then expressed my concern about Isobel getting cold. Tony said we shouldn't all hover by the car, 'freezing our bollocks off'.[1]

I hurried towards the church with Isobel. Graciously, I turned to give Tony a farewell wave, only to find he was following us. The 'we', apparently, was the three of us. Tony, with a sensitivity that of course annoyed me, asked if I

---

[1] That was chummy, too. Swear words are friendly these days. When I was a boy, 'fuck off, you bastard' was abuse. Now, more than likely, it's the preface to a hug. Note that he made 'bollocks' inclusive, applying the term to Isobel too, not wanting to discriminate against her on gender grounds. He would rather be politically correct than biologically so. I detested this. It was the triumph of attitude over fact.

minded his accompanying us inside. He'd read about this church and had been looking forward to seeing it. I agreed, of course. How could I not?

We entered the church. I looked up at the ceiling.

'Descent from the Cross ... Ascension ... Nativity. Antonio Bellucci. 1654 to 1726.'

'Did you get that off Google?' asked Isobel. I was upset. It was not like Isobel to cheek me in this way. Yes, I had got it 'off Google'. That was not the point. I had got it and I was disseminating it, for which I hoped she'd be grateful, yet here she was, disrespectful not just of me but of knowledge. Had her state school made her wary of displays of learning? And/or was she embarrassed? Was I older, more scholarly and less exciting than Tony? If so, I was proud to be all three.

'Tell us more,' said Tony. I resented his coming to my rescue. Nevertheless, my knowledge could not be contained. I led him and Isobel to what I knew to be the Foley Monument by Michael Rysbrack, a sculptor born in Antwerp. I told them it depicted the first Lord Foley, his wife and five of their children. The scale of the monument provoked Tony, who gave us the benefit of his views on the patronage of artists by the aristocracy. His views were just that — views. They were not knowledge. However, he was concerned to impress them upon Isobel. Patronage, he opined, was the death of artistic integrity. He gave Isobel the impression that this was a matter of urgent personal import, as if

315

Prince Charles had been pestering him with cheques in the hope of getting poems in the post.

At this point, in preference to listening to him, I looked at him. Who was he? He looked different from the man who had come to put new floors in my house. He was, of course, not dressed for flooring. His clothes were surprisingly expensive, for a man who was supposedly neither materialistic nor rich: a three-quarter-length black coat and a cream linen suit. He wore these clothes as if they were bohemian but I thought them 'smart casual'. He would not have looked out of place in a magazine.

There was something else, though. What made this Lemon Man different from the one I'd met? Did he now have a beard or a moustache? No. He'd gained nothing. What was new about the Lemon Man was a loss, a sorry loss. Tony had cut off his ponytail. I'd been in his company for many minutes, yet only now had I noticed. What could be more disconcerting than one's enemy changing shape?

Five months had passed since Elizabeth and the children had left me. *Tony's my mum's new partner*. That's what Max had been trained to say. Now, I was sure, he wouldn't say that. Too much time had passed. The *new partner* had a ponytail. The *partner* did not.

★ ★ ★

Fifteen minutes later, as the audience arrived, Tony prepared to depart. He promised to return at half past nine to pick up Isobel. I apologised for the disruption to his evening. He waved this away, needlessly adding that 'a little Guy and Sophie went a long way' and Isobel was a 'great kid' whom he'd be happy to come back and fetch. With a mateyness that was positively punchable, he said that the next time I came down, he'd cook me one of his 'famous curries'. I told him I'd do everything in my power to avoid this. He laughed, assuming, as I knew he would, that this *fuck off, bastard* was really a *hug* in disguise.

★　★　★

Isobel was no longer torn between Tony and me. She was alone with her father and wanted to please. She told me, just as her mother had, that she was thinking of resuming her cello-playing but not taking more exams. She wanted to play for pleasure. I replied that exams weren't exclusive of pleasure. My heart had leapt every time I'd turned over a law exam paper.

Isobel went quiet. Soon the cellist would appear, between the piano and the altar. I wanted to talk to my daughter while there was still time.

'Is your bedroom nice?' I asked. She said it was. She went on to say that Tony had had a brilliant idea. Every time anyone turned off an electrical appliance, they put money into an Oxfam box — ten pee (for Elizamum and Tony) and two pee (for Isobel and Max). In this way, they were saving the planet from global warming and famine. They were saving the planet twice.

317

I reminded her that, in London, I'd turned off the electricity supply to Max's bedroom at night.

'That wasn't to save the planet,' she said. 'That was just to stop Max playing computer games in the night.' That was true. Isobel was right. But wasn't I saving the planet too, even though that was not my intention?

Penelope Orchard walked down the aisle, carrying her cello. I applauded, lifelessly. I was, unusually, in the grip of self-pity. Too many forces were weighed against me: Elizabeth, Tony, Isobel, Max, Guy and Sophie, Mona, Andy and Sonia, the passage of time itself.

★　★　★

Like many cellists, Penelope Orchard was greatly influenced by Jacqueline du Pré. Of course she couldn't match her phenomenal technique. But in texture, colour, flow, *glissandi*, Penelope Orchard was more than a match for Jacqueline du Pré's hair. It rippled, it flicked, it bounced, it flew. It did everything but leave her head. Critics, hair critics, might have carped. In the *Adagio* of Suite Number One, they might have wished for a little more *adagio* from the hair, which was at best *allegro* and at worst *vivace*. Was her hair incapable of slow movement?

Why did I seek to belittle her with these thoughts? Was I haunted by the Lemon Man's departed ponytail? I felt incapable of noble sentiments. My mind was a poisoned well.

Then Isobel tapped me on the arm and whispered: 'Her cello's just like mine.'

318

The *Adagio* ended. Before the *Allegro ma non tanto* began, as the good burghers of Great Witley enjoyed a winter cough, I told Isobel I'd be back in a minute and sidled out of our pew.

★ ★ ★

I walked towards the doors of the church. Penelope Orchard, like a bride, had walked down the aisle from that direction. Somewhere near the door, I might find what I sought.

Sure enough, by the shelf of Bibles, next to the chair on which lay her coat, I saw it.

The *Allegro ma non tanto* began, before I had time to return to my seat. Isobel looked anxiously over her shoulder. She spotted me. I smiled. I indicated I'd stay where I was, so as not to disturb Miss Orchard or the audience.

At my feet was a black leather cello case monogrammed 'I.P.'.

★ ★ ★

I was right, I was right, I was right, I was right. Tony, with his assassin's grin, was a man not to be trusted. He hadn't given Isobel's cello to charity. He'd sold it. That linen suit and three-quarter-length coat were bought with the money he'd made by selling my daughter's tenth birthday present, for which I'd paid over two thousand pounds, including the refitted sound post and the monogrammed case.

I stood listening to Bach. Not once did I look at the hair. I felt an intense loyalty to the things

319

that had brought me here: a profound respect for Bach, a love of church architecture, the wish to instil in my daughter the noblest values.

At nine thirty, Tony would re-enter the church. I would present him with the evidence. That was a principle of natural justice. I'd give him the freedom to defend himself. Then I'd denounce him. But I wouldn't denounce him to Elizabeth. No. I'd never say a bad word about him to Elizabeth.

Isobel looked over her shoulder again. The *Allegro ma non tanto* was over. With a surge of rightness, I rushed back to my pew.

'Everything all right?' asked Isobel, sweetly.

'Yes, my darling.' She looked alarmed. I'd never called her that before.

★ ★ ★

By the Debussy, doubts had set in. Principally, I blamed Mike Bell. The last time I'd publicly denounced a wrong, the wrong had been committed by 'Bernard Brown', who turned out not to exist. Bell had made me doubt my best quality: certainty.

Tony could have given the cello to charity, just as he claimed. Someone from the charity could have fraudulently sold it to Penelope Orchard, or the dealer from whom she'd bought it.

Why, though, would a dishonest person work for a charity? It was the last thing one would expect a dishonest person to do. Therefore, it was the first thing a dishonest person would do. Dishonest people exploited and confounded decent people's expectations.

A vague and watery unease ran through me, a very Debussy unease. I comforted myself with this: if the Lemon Man were innocent, I would know it from his face. A guilty face tightens, anxious to betray no guilt. An innocent face is openly confused.

I longed for nine thirty, when he'd return. I was spoiling to see that face. I willed the pianist to speed up the concert. Such were the depths of illogicality to which Bell had made me sink. No matter how fast he played that piano, nine thirty would arrive, precisely, at nine thirty. The pianist couldn't speed up Tony's return. He could only hasten the end of the concert. That would mean Orchard and her cello would have gone before Tony arrived.

⋆　⋆　⋆

The concert finished at nine thirty-five. Tony had not yet arrived. The audience filed out. Penelope Orchard and the pianist talked to some ladies. The ladies, as ladies will, chattered away. Tony did not arrive. The pianist, to judge from his protective stance, was Penelope's boyfriend or husband. He touched her arm and said something. She nodded. She smiled at the ladies, who said their goodbyes and withdrew. Penelope Orchard walked down the aisle, towards her coat and her cello case, carrying her cello. But Tony did not arrive.

'Let's go and talk to them,' I said to Isobel. She looked worried. Talking to strangers, like calling her 'my darling', was not the kind of thing I did. She hung back while I advanced.

Now was the time for the charm I'd never possessed, nor craved.

'May I say how much my daughter and I enjoyed the concert? Especially the Bach.'

'Thank you, kind sir,' said Penelope, prettily, able, as only women are, to put a cello in its case while talking. The pianist didn't comment. Doubtless, he thought my remark an insult to his Debussy.

'You have a splendid tone. It's a wonderful instrument. Chinese, I think.'

Penelope spoke less prettily now and with more respect. 'That's right. Do you play?'

'My daughter plays.' I nodded at Isobel, who was looking towards the doors. 'May I ask where you bought it?'

'Oxford.'

'Oxford! I'm a Christ Church man myself. I hope Isobel will be too, one day.'

Penelope snapped the clasps on the cello case. Tony had still not arrived, though Isobel was now standing by the door, willing him to do so, so she could get away from her embarrassing father.

'Nice to meet you,' said Penelope, putting on her coat.

'And you!' I replied. Graham the pianist flinched as I turned to him. 'I expect you wish you could put *your* instrument in the boot of the car.'

'No,' he said, unhelpfully. I glanced at the doors. Tony, yet again, failed to arrive. I turned back to Penelope. I could not let her leave. I had to see him see her case, which she'd now picked up.

'May I ask you something?'

'Yes,' she replied, without enthusiasm, edging away from the shelf of Bibles, towards the door.

'Where do you get your hair done?'

The pianist bristled. He'd doubtless encountered this before — the man who admired Penelope's tone as a way to Penelope's hair.

'London,' she said. And now she wasn't edging any more. Penelope Orchard was moving.

'Any salon in particular? It's for my wife.'

'We have to go now,' said Penelope.

'What about shampoo?' I struggled to find the name of a shampoo. 'Do you use Ronseal?'

'That's not a shampoo,' said Graham. No. Of course. That was the sealant that did exactly what it said on the tin. That was the stuff of me, the human Ronseal.

Tony entered. He was breathless. 'So sorry I'm late.'

'Tony, this is Penelope Orchard.'

Penelope smiled at Tony. Here was a man with genuine charm.

'And this is her cello,' I said. 'She bought it in Oxford.'

Tony, who'd never been introduced to a cello, failed to look at it. Of course he did. He looked at Penelope.

'Hope you had a good concert,' he said. 'Sorry I couldn't be there. We had people to dinner.'

'Ooh, what did you have?' asked Penelope, simpering. Now the pianist bristled in Tony's

323

direction, as Tony talked of Welsh mountain lamb and its perfect partner, chicory, which he loved. Tony was talking about my wife's favourite vegetable as if it were his own.

'That's my cello case,' said Isobel suddenly, as I knew she would.

'How do you mean?' asked Penelope. 'The cello case came with the cello.'

'Oh Jesus,' said Tony, touching his hair. Why did he touch his hair? Why this motif of hair? I think, perhaps, he was missing his ponytail, which he once used to tug, for comfort.

'That's such fucking bad luck.'

'I shall say nothing of this to Elizabeth,' I said. 'I'll leave that to you.'

Penelope Orchard was excited. 'What's this about? I bought it from the Oxford Music Shop.'

'Come on, let's go,' said the pianist. 'This has nothing to do with us.'

He was, in legal terms, absolutely correct. I could not demand the cello back. Penelope Orchard had bought the cello and its case in good faith. She was what is known in Equity as *a bona fide purchaser for value*. I had no claim against her. My claim was against Tony.

'Thank you,' I said to Penelope. 'You've performed an invaluable service.' As she left, I said — though I don't believe she heard — 'I apologise for asking about your hair.'

★   ★   ★

'I thought you'd given it to Africa,' said Isobel. Tony shook his head and said nothing more. We

324

were hovering by the Audi again, shivering. I explained, on his behalf, with all the regret I could muster, that Tony had sold her cello and 'pocketed the proceeds'. I enjoyed the louche-ness of that phrase. I pictured his pockets bulging like a fat boy's cheeks.

'That's wrong,' said Isobel to Tony. I was proud to hear her say that, so simply. Here was my daughter, grave and true. Here were my genes.

Tony told her how sorry he was. To me he said: 'Don't judge me till you understand me.' I didn't need to reply. I was not the judge in this case. It was Elizabeth who would pass sentence.

I drove Isobel back to the Hereford house in my hired car. I did not want her to be alone in my Audi with Tony the cello-selling cheat.

We followed him, though. We had to. He was the only one who knew the way. When we arrived, I didn't get out. Guy, Sophie and Elizabeth, in winter coats, were playing tennis on the floodlit court.

'Out!' shouted Guy.

★   ★   ★

Three days later — a decent interval — I wrote Elizabeth a letter. It read, in its entirety:

Elizabeth,
Come home to London and Aldeburgh where you belong.
Robert

Note that I made no reference to myself, other than in the signature. Note that I did not refer to Tony either.

★ ★ ★

Was it coincidence? Was that why we — Tony, Penelope Orchard, her cello, Isobel and I — found ourselves in Great Witley Church together?

Coincidence, according to the *Concise Oxford Dictionary*, is the *notable concurrence of events or circumstances without apparent causal connexion.*[1]

No. In this case, there was an *apparent causal connexion*. I know. I supplied it. I caused Penelope Orchard to be there at the perfect time. I caused this with my actions and my attitudes and my values, my deprivations and my forbearance, my dogged faith in the rightness of my marriage, my nine breakfasts at the Ace Guest House in Hereford. Others might think this far-fetched. They're entitled to their (wrong) opinion.

I concur with the man I heard on Radio 4 this morning, at eight twenty-eight, in the sports report on the *Today* programme. I didn't catch his name. It was drowned by the sound of a lone

---

[1] Fifth Edition, 1964. Doubtless, the definition has since changed. No twenty-first century dictionary compiler would use an elitist word like 'connexion'. The current definition probably runs: *Thing that makes you go: 'Wow, amazing!'*

piece of toast popping up in my toaster — *Ker-ching!* The man was a football manager. That much I heard.

'In this game, you make your own luck,' he said.

I would say, in less demotic fashion, that one is responsible for one's history. One makes the story of one's life.

★   ★   ★

On 5th December 2002, Elizabeth wrote back to me. Her letter read, with sublime understatement:
OK

17

The Return
(2002)

I rang Geoffrey Moxon-Smith and told him we were taking the house off the market, though contracts had been exchanged.

Then I rang Mona. She could not conceal her anger, though one might have considered it her professional duty so to do. I told her to remove the For Sale sign, which I'd pulled up already. She said the sign belonged to Capital Properties and I had no right to touch it. Thus did I further trouble her waters.

Two days later, a note arrived from Andy of Andy and Sonia. It was attached to a bag of horse manure placed, overnight, on my doorstep along with a packet of envelopes. Andy apologised — he didn't have time to 'stick the excrement in the envelopes and shove them through your letter box'.

Here was the culture of the somethings in the City, writ large. My excrement was imaginary, his literal. Mine was conceived from the noblest of motives, his was the stinking product of a vengeful urge. Mine was free; his was expensive. Disregard, for the moment, the cost of the manure and the envelopes. How much of his time-is-money working day had he devoted to thinking up the prank? Would the price of those man-hours be deducted, come Christmas, from the huge excremental mulch of his year-end bonus?

Andy meant nothing to me. The High Mistress of St Paul's was a different matter. I wrote to her confirming that Isobel would indeed take up her place in January. Then I emailed her and called her too. Why stint? As for Max, he would have his heart's desire. He'd attend the same boarding school, Orwell Park, as his best friend Harry Pilkington.

I drove up to Aldeburgh and told my father the wonderful news.

'Normal service will be resumed as soon as possible,' he said, with delight. It was one of our favourite expressions. BBC announcers said it when a technical fault made one's television screen go blank, back in the 1960s, when announcers still sounded as if they were properly dressed.

From my bachelor house, soon to be a family house once more, I took to High Ridge a handsome present for Buster. Several handsome presents, in fact: all the Sainsbury's pre-cooked meals in the freezer. I had no need for them. Elizabeth was returning, with her home-cooking.

Those meals served Buster well. The Steak, Bacon and Red Wine Pie was the last thing he ate before he died. There was no causal connexion, though. My father and I agreed that Buster, mourning my mother, died of a broken heart. That was the kind of thing we said about a dog. About the human heart, we were silent.

I sought no revenge. I wanted the restitution of my family, not my two thousand pounds nor the head of Tony. I didn't even mention Tony. Instead, I allowed Tony to be mentioned to me. Elizabeth thanked me for my lack of vindictiveness then, touchingly, corrected herself. She didn't want to thank me for a lack of anything. She wanted to thank me for what she called 'the positives'. I'd been so 'actively dignified'. She couldn't think of any other man who'd have behaved like me. I'd treated her with courtesy throughout. I'd kept an even temper. I'd allowed her to make her mistake and then I'd asked her to come back. I'd shown tolerance and restraint. By asking her to come back home, without gloating or condemning, I'd shown her I knew how to forgive.

She wanted me to know why her relationship with Tony had to end. Tony had forfeited her trust and the trust of her children. He'd done a dishonourable thing, the kind of thing that made her feel he was a stranger. She couldn't stay in Hereford without him. Hereford was a joint venture. Without him, it was over.

I told her that, as far as I was concerned, the matter was closed.

At this point, we were standing in the road, by the gate, my returned wife and I. The children were inside. The estate agent's flag no longer flew over us. I had given the bag of manure to our neighbour Alison, as a gift she neither expected nor wanted but did not know how to refuse. The removal men emerged from our family house for the last time, their mission accomplished. Elizabeth thanked them and bade them farewell.

When they drove off, something gave way in Elizabeth. She put her arms round me and rested her head on my neck. I found myself, much to my embarrassment, in a public embrace. I did not want to give the impression, to neighbours or passers-by, that this was a dramatic reconciliation. I wished it to appear a low-key embrace, of the kind to which any married couple might publicly subscribe. Unfortunately, I'd never embraced Elizabeth publicly. At our wedding, obviously, I'd kissed her. But I'd kept my hands to myself.

I had to make our first pavement hug seem as casual as our thousandth. I placed my crossed palms on her shoulder blades and hoped for the best.

* * *

On Saturday 14th December 2002, I woke up without a family and went to bed with a family restored. As I switched out the lights in the kitchen, I smelt something I hadn't smelt since July: Labrador. Mars was back in his basket in the corner, sharing his canine dormitory with the old cherry-red checked tea towel that had once been mine. Before the arrival of the washing-up machine, I walked round the kitchen with that tea towel on my shoulder, showing Elizabeth the tool of my husbandly trade. Now it absorbed Mars's slobber.

In bed, Elizabeth lay with her eyes shut, in a pose that informed an experienced husband that his wife was still awake. I enquired after her well-being. She told me she was exhausted. I got into bed. I told her that when she woke up it would be Sunday morning. I would be available if she wished to exercise her conjugal rights. In the event, she didn't. Elizabeth was still the lawyer I married, one who understood the difference between a right and an obligation.

★ ★ ★

We agreed that, at this late stage, we wouldn't alter the Christmas plans we'd made, back in the Hereford era. Elizabeth would take the children to her parents, while I'd spend Christmas in Aldeburgh with my father. This meant that the few and breathless days leading up to Christmas were more of a prelude to a reconciliation than the thing itself. Peace had been declared but there was no time to enjoy it. It was a Phoney Peace, prior to the sustained one that would follow in the New Year.

Elizabeth, in her exhausted state, was engaged in every mother's battle with Christmas. I did not add my own demands. I am not a monster. I accepted that, in terms particularly of laundry and cuisine, normal service was yet to be resumed. I looked, in Elizabeth's phrase, for 'the positives'. And so it was that when I sat down to Sunday lunch on 22nd December and saw Elizabeth approaching the table with two oven trays of bubbling pizza, I asked, with genuine interest, if they were from the Sainsbury's 'Taste the Difference' range. Elizabeth told me they were. I remarked, with genuine fervour — since I'd fully explored the range — that a Sainsbury's 'Taste the Difference' pizza was one of the finest bought lunches a mother could provide.

Thinking herself, quite mistakenly, under attack, Elizabeth said she hadn't noticed my cooking us an 'unbought' lunch. Then she let the oven trays fall from her hands. One landed on the table, one on the floor. I went into action immediately, taking Max into the garden for a game of football. On the lawn, he asked, as he had in Hereford, if his mother and I were getting divorced. I told him we weren't. His mother was tired. Soon she would not be tired and everything would be as it was. He replied, if reply it was, that I was not as good at football as 'Tony or Granny'. This cannot have been a reference to Elizabeth's mother, who never played rough outdoor games. It was therefore a reference to my late mother. I told him his comparison would only spur me on.

★ ★ ★

The matter — the matter of Tony — was not closed, even though I, the injured party, had magnanimously declared it so. I'd (inadvertently) reopened it with my lunchtime remarks. That night, at bedtime, Elizabeth talked and talked. She was, unfortunately, far from exhausted where the Tony matter was concerned. He was now in the last place I wanted him to be: the marital bed.

Tony, for five months, had lived with Elizabeth and shared all the cooking duties. As well as Indian, he was adept at African and West Indian cuisine. He called himself, modestly, a 'world cook'. He cleaned too. He understood the rudiments of plumbing. Domestically, said Elizabeth, he was a 'shining light' — an unfortunate, religiose image. Tony gave generously of himself, apparently, doing unto others in the home as he would be done by. He'd constructed, with Max, a rope banister down to — here I stopped her, explaining that I'd heard all this from the children. Did I also know that he collected the children from school on the days when Elizabeth attended the Herefordshire College of Technology, for the counselling course about which I'd asked her nothing?[1]

She then turned to the night of the Great Witley concert. Did I know he'd helped her prepare supper, then taken Isobel to the church, then returned to eat the supper, then left before the dessert to collect her? Did I appreciate how much driving and 'self-sacrifice' that entailed?

Tony had asked me not to judge him till I

---

[1] This was true. I'd not asked Elizabeth about her counselling course, A, in the hope it would go away, and B, because the Elizabeth I married was a solicitor, a member of the legal profession. To think of her joining the 'caring professions' gave me no pleasure. There are Inns of Court. There are no Inns of Caring.

understood him. Now Elizabeth, on both their behalves, wanted me to understand. Tony had never sought wealth. Wealth had sought him — as Elizabeth's partner — and moved him in next door, rent-free. He was thankful for Guy and Sophie's generosity, which he wished to reciprocate. But he never could. Gratitude turned to envy and resentment — why were Guy and Sophie greener and more charitable and more 'world' than he was?

Tony couldn't help himself. He drove off to Reading, to deliver the cello to the woman who ran the African charity. But then he called her to say he wouldn't be coming. He called her from an Audi that belonged to me, an Audi he could never afford. I, his partner's richer husband, compounded his envy.

He drove past Reading to Oxford, where the wife of his old college friend Matthew ran a musical instruments shop. He sold her the cello and bought himself two suits, a coat and several pairs of shoes. When Elizabeth commented on his new wardrobe, he explained that his great-aunt had died and left him a couple of thousand pounds. He did not spend all the money on himself. For Elizabeth, he bought a beautiful Indian silk scarf; for Isobel, the *Complete Works of Shakespeare*; for Max, an England soccer strip.

Thus did Elizabeth justify Tony's behaviour, where no justification existed. His behaviour showed contempt for law and morality. And it insulted Elizabeth's intelligence. Great-aunt? Who, outside the pages of Wodehouse, has a hitherto-unmentioned great-aunt who remembers one in her will?

Elizabeth herself acknowledged that her explanation explained nothing. 'I thought I knew him,' she said. 'You're all unknowable, aren't you?'

It took me a moment to understand. 'You all' were 'men'. I was a man, as Tony was. I was being invited to speak for us, as if we were fellow members of the Union of Unknowable Men. This was too much.

'I don't think you can compare me with Tony,' I said, with admirable evenness.

'I spose not. No. He's more of a risk-taker.'

Why did she say it so wistfully? Tony had run off with my wife and fraudulently sold our daughter's cello. These were the risks he'd taken. Now, somehow, I was the lesser man for failing to take such risks. What was Elizabeth asking of me?

'Freya's right. You've never learned to express yourself sexually and emotionally.'

There. Now my sister had arrived in the marital bed. Who would be next?

'I think you should have therapy. Then you'd learn who you are and how to do something about it.'

The circle was complete. We were once more on that sofa, before Elizabeth left, when she told me I needed to 'grow' and 'change'. Once more, my soul was under threat. My soul, like the face of the singer Michael Jackson, could be improved with alteration.

'Why don't we start with marriage guidance counselling? That's been around a long time.'

This was skilful, this appeal to my conservative instincts. Aldeburgh ladies, with pearls, had been to marriage guidance counselling, with Aldeburgh men. They had, perhaps, been counsellors themselves. *Is everything all right in the bedroom department?* That was the kind of 1950s question they'd asked. In the fifties, of course, women were content with a department. Nowadays, they want an entire floor.

I didn't answer Elizabeth's question. Instead, I volunteered to 'do the family shop' while she and the children prepared for their Christmas visit to her parents. Do you see? She talked of love, I of shopping; just as, when Freya told my father to love, I told him to go to the cinema.

'OK,' she said. She was pleased. I could tell. She even turned out the light.

I waited in silence, to make sure the last word had been said. There is often a word after the last word. It is usually spoken by the wife.

'I can't go back,' said Elizabeth.

'You *can* go back. And you have. And I admire you for it.'

★ ★ ★

Elizabeth gave me a short list. I was then instructed to go round the house and see what else we needed. This I duly did, opening and closing kitchen and bathroom cupboards with aplomb.

I got to Sainsbury's at eleven o'clock. No longer did I have to pretend I was shopping for my family. That was precisely what I was doing. I was not, though, quite what I seemed.

It was 23rd December, Christmas Eve Eve. Anger was rampant. Aisles, which were after all no more than *space*, were under ferocious attack. Working-class women with too many children exploded like mines. What was I doing in this retail Somme? Was I varying the terms of our marriage contract? Was I henceforth responsible for *Family Shop, Doing the?* No. This was a stopgap measure, pending the closing of the Tony matter and the resumption of normal service. It was imperative, therefore, that I did this shop sufficiently well to convince Elizabeth I'd done my best, but sufficiently badly to ensure she'd never ask me to do it again.

I did the shop and returned home. I unpacked and waited for Elizabeth's verdict.

'You forgot some vital things,' she said.

'Maybe so,' I replied. 'But I remembered some too.'

'Yeah,' she said, grudgingly, then returned to look for the present she had bought for Max to give her parents.

'What did I forget then?' I asked, careful not to sound too interested.

'You'll find out, I'm sure,' she said. 'Well done on getting the rest.'

I'd done well. And, thankfully, I'd done badly too. I congratulated myself on my success.

★   ★   ★

Elizabeth and the children were intending to set off for her parents' house at ten the next morning. They were delayed by an hour-long phone call from Ticky Pilkington.

As she left, Elizabeth asked me why I'd invested twenty thousand pounds in Mike Bell's film. Would she have known if Ticky hadn't told her? Or was this another thing I intended to keep to myself?

'You'll get nothing back. You know that, don't you? You could buy *ten* cellos with that.'

Once more, she was putting me on a moral par with Tony. Exploiting arithmetic, she was implying, absurdly, that what I'd done was ten times as bad.

'A, I took the money from — '

'Don't 'A' me, please. At least Tony got some money out of selling the cello.'

'You can't justify a crime by the proceeds,' I replied, softly, measuring each word.

I have to say — for who else will say it, if I don't? — that this was me at my best.

'No,' said Elizabeth. 'I suppose not.'

She looked, for a moment, like the girl I'd met after *Ridgeon* v. *Kelly* (1989) — a woman, younger than me, who admired my intellect.

'We'll call you from my parents,' she said.

★ ★ ★

An hour later, from the toilet seat of the bathroom en suite of our bedroom, I reached for the toilet paper. There was nothing but a tubular cardboard husk.

Toilet Rolls, New, Purchasing of.

★ ★ ★

Two minutes later, I'd successfully shuffled my way out of the bathroom, out of the bedroom, to the top of the stairs and downstairs to the landing, then downstairs to the ground floor, all the while maintaining the posture of a man on the toilet. It is an 'L' shape with an 'I' descending. In profile, appropriately, I looked like a giant stair.

I reached the downstairs toilet without incident. I opened the door. There was no toilet paper in the downstairs toilet. I advanced to the kitchen cupboard, traditionally the repository of *Toilet Rolls, New*. The kitchen cupboard was under the sink. I clasped the sink with both hands and sank to my knees. Did I pray for toilet rolls? No. I did not pray then and I do not pray now.

I opened the kitchen cupboard. It was bereft of rolls. I shut the kitchen cupboard. Then, I confess, I put my hands on the floor in front of me. I put myself in the posture of a dog. This posture brought me comfort. Of course it did. It made me feel I was no longer a desperate man but an ordinary dog. I thought of Buster, who had died just a fortnight before. I became the ghost of Buster.[1]

I palmed and kneed my way out of the kitchen and down the corridor, towards the front door. As the crow flies, as the dog walks, it was a distance of fifty feet. And yet the journey was

---

[1] Such is the strength of my feeling for dogs. I would ask you to recall this scene when we reach the events of 29.9.03. Oh yes, the hour of the crime's approaching.

epic, in the time it took and the momentous thoughts it induced.

I had found out, as Elizabeth knew I would, what vital thing I'd failed to buy when I *Family Shop, Did the*. Why had she not told me before she left? In her unbalanced state, she wanted to teach me a lesson. She must have told Max and Isobel to take tissues with them when they went to the toilet, from tissue boxes which she'd doubtless taken to her parents. I was convinced she'd thought of everything. It was her thinking that hurt.

I crawled to the telephone table in the hall. Next to the telephone was a plant, which I removed with great care and placed on the floor. What was the nature of this plant? I couldn't say. Elizabeth had bought it. I sniffed that plant. I buried my nose in it, just like Buster.

I then denuded it of several leaves, using them to bring to my hind quarters what comfort and dryness I could.

I knew I couldn't stay in the family house. My dignity had been stolen.[1]

---

[1] In the course of this confession, I have come to identify more and more with footnotes. I have realised that over the course of my life — 1956 to 2006, the time of writing — I've evolved into something approaching a human footnote. I am diminutive, as footnotes are. I am obliged, as footnotes are, to protest my importance. 'Look at me!' they shout from the bottom of the page. Christmas Eve 2002, under the telephone table. That's where it started, my footnoteness, my footnoteworthiness, my footnotoriety.

In the New Year, I told Elizabeth I'd made arrangements to move to a rented flat. I'd be leaving in mid-January. She went quiet. Then she thanked me. In the fortnight that followed, she was courteous and attentive. She laid out clean white shirts for me. She cooked delicious meals. On the final Sunday, she exercised her conjugal right, saying we should do it one last time. We did it and I understood it to be an expression of her gratitude.

Normal service had, however belatedly, been resumed. It could therefore be resumed again. I would return when Elizabeth had forgotten about Tony, who still rang her. I took one of his calls myself. I even pretended not to recognise his voice. I made him tell me who he was and I said: 'Tony. Right. Hold on, Tony. I'll get her. Elizabeth! It's Tony! She's just coming, Tony.' I tortured him with his own name.

When Tony was forgotten, I'd come back and everything would be as it was.

18

Andros
(2003)

When I told the children I was moving out, they already knew. They always 'already knew'. They acted as if my departure were, if not predictable, typical. They'd moved to Hereford; they'd moved back; and now, typically, I was moving. Disturbingly, they now regarded change as the norm. Where was the status quo, the norm that is the norm that is the norm? I reminded Max and Isobel that the three of us would always have Aldeburgh. Aldeburgh wasn't going to disappear, I said. It wasn't going to fall into the sea! With this remark, I tried to introduce jocularity, but Max just said he knew that already.

Touchingly, my children gave me flat-warming presents. Isobel gave me a silver napkin ring. Max gave me a packet of sea salt and vinegar crisps, the size of a nosebag. I ate them in one sitting, on my first night in my new flat, regretting afterwards that I didn't yet own a bin.

The napkin ring, by contrast, was something I'd keep for the rest of my life. It was a present one could have given to a father leaving for Canada, never to return. That was why I preferred the sea salt and vinegar crisps.

Thirteen years earlier, before we moved to our family house in Highgate, Elizabeth and I lived in my bachelor flat — Flat B, 19 Canonbury Terrace, London N1. Therefore, thirteen years later, when I moved out of Highgate, I decided to move back to Canonbury. My logic was impeccable: that which had happened before was likely to happen again. In a fortnight, a month, a year — however long it took for Elizabeth to be ready — I would once more move from bachelor Canonbury to family Highgate, in accordance with precedent.

Sadly, in January 2003, Flat B, 19 Canonbury Terrace was not available to rent or buy. I had to content myself with a rental flat nine doors down. Most days, however, I walked past 19 Canonbury Terrace. On many occasions, I saw Dr Pearson, the Cambridge graduate. She still lived in the ground-floor flat. Her exterior paintwork was now blue. Her hair was grey. But it was unquestionably the woman with whom I'd had my 1983 altercation, resulting in our not speaking to each other and refusing, mutually, to replace the worn-out light bulb in the hall.

The first time I saw her, after many years of not, our eyes met and went their separate ways. We recognised each other and tacitly agreed we would not say a word, as we had not said a word when we previously saw each other, and would not say a word when we saw each other again.

The precedent was honoured, with a clarity and a certainty that were devoutly reassuring.

History was honoured. We remembered what had happened and abided by it. Compare that with Ticky in the Co-op: *I should have held onto you, shouldn't I?* That is a distortion of history. There was never the slightest chance of Ticky Moxon-Smith 'holding onto' me. We couldn't wait to let go of each other.

★ ★ ★

As with all letters, I looked at the signature first. The letter was sent care of my chambers. It arrived in February 2003.

> *Dear Robert,*
>
> *I'm so glad to have the chance to get in touch with you again after all these years. Congratulations on your elevation to the ranks of QC. I always knew you'd be a success in your chosen profession. Alan Temperley tells me that you live in a beautiful house in Highgate with your wife and son and daughter who's a gifted cellist. He told me he spent a wonderful evening in your garden last summer with guests including Lord and Lady Rodwell. You all dined on the lawn and then after dinner your daughter played Bach. It sounds magical. I have a gifted daughter and I know how rewarding those moments are.*
>
> *I'm writing to you and a few hand-chosen people to*

Why did I carry on reading? I was persuaded by her restraint. There was a certain idiocy in the writing style — 'hand-chosen' indeed, as if people were pomegranates on a fruiterer's stall! Nevertheless, the tone was respectful, celebratory even, which was far from what I expected when I saw the signature. I'd braced myself for *I gave you a taxi blowjob you wouldn't anser the door now I will cut off your gentals and bake them in a pie do you like pie*

But there were no vicious references to the past. I was now a QC. That was the best thing about me, as Judy Page understood. She knew what kind of man I was and judged me by the company I kept. Lord Rodwell was now a law lord. Alan Temperley was Lord Chancellor, one of the few to be chosen from Parliament rather than the Lords.

Andros is the northernmost of the Cyclades Islands. Prosperous, fertile and beautiful, it is the second-home island of choice for the elite of Athens society.

Judy Page lived in Andros with her daughter Alana. She was the Marketing Director of MR Travel, an Andros villa-rental company *founded by Martha Ray, a native New Yorker with over twenty-five years' experience in high-end travel and leisure. Judy Page looked forward to welcoming you and your family to a spacious, beautiful and peaceful villa under the most ancient skies in the world.*

I booked a four-bedroomed villa — the smallest they had — in the knowledge that Greek skies were no more ancient than England's. I hoped to take the children but, in my haste, booked a fortnight that overlapped with Max's cricket tour of South Africa.

'Two weeks without bridge!' exclaimed my father, when I invited him. I never thought he'd say a word against the great game.

I thought it would be inappropriate to write back to Judy Page. The letter was essentially an advertisement. One doesn't respond to such a letter, any more than one shouts at a poster on the side of a bus.

* * *

Big Ben was premiered in March 2003. The premiere was in aid of an East End homeless charity called ROOF. The first two rows of the cinema were occupied by homeless people. Defined by their unfortunate status, they stood out like theatre critics at the first night of a play. Their presence did indeed seem like a backhanded critical plaudit: *you've got to like a film that's shown indoors!*

Nevertheless, Mike Bell had produced a film, a finished film, not a notion or a concept or a draft or a great idea. I was proud of him. I willed the film to be good.

Big Ben begins with a shot of a riverside building near London Bridge, on the south side of the Thames. Then we cut to the eponymous Ben standing at his living-room window. Like all Mr Bigs, he's in philosophical mode.

'That's where the real fucking criminals are!'

He stabs a forefinger at the Houses of Parliament, opposite his window.

This is a lie, a geographical lie. No building which stands near London Bridge has a window opposite the Houses of Parliament. The building would have to be two miles wide. Ben is Mr Big. He's not Mr Wide. Why should we believe anything that follows? What is a picture, be it a motion picture or a Constable painting of the Dedham Vale, but an aggregation of truthful details? Here was Bell, painting a picture for us, daubing the sunset in the wrong place.

Then there is the question of the main character's name. Bell had resented my sarcastic coinage of 'Arthur Lampover' as the name for a man who knocks over lamps. But here we were, in a Leicester Square cinema, watching a film in which the main character is a London gangster called 'Big Ben'. Really? Since when is 'Ben' a convincing name for a London gangster? Since the Kray Twins, Ben and Ben? No. The name is a wretched contrivance, a spurious reference to a London landmark of which audiences in Tokyo and Iowa will have heard, if such audiences ever exist. Bell might as well have called him fucking Nelson Scolumn. Forgive me. One cannot write about the film without swearing. In the next scene, set in a fashionable restaurant, Ben says to Headcase, his henchman: 'Pass me the f***ing salt and the f***ing pepper, you c**t!' The very condiments are swearworthy, *on an individual basis*.

After two scenes, those of us with homes to go to wished to go home.[1]

★ ★ ★

The post-premiere party at Jimmy's followed what is known in Bell's uncaring profession as an 'arc'. In the first act, false jollity reigned. Then, with the time and alcohol that heal all wounds, the film was forgotten and the jollity was real. Then, with more time, more alcohol and the departure of most of the guests, the film was remembered again, cueing a final act containing no jollity at all.

Bell, at this point, took out of his wallet — why did Bell need a wallet? — a photo of Hilary Drew. He told me he carried it 'for luck', though it hadn't yet brought him any. She was, apparently, the finest American actress of her generation. She was 'a cross between Julia Lewis

---

[1] Camilla Johnstone, the film critic of the *Sunday Telegraph*, described it as the worst in the 'dismal genre' of 'self-regarding British gangster films that prize suits above characterisation and plot'. I felt pity for Bell. Here was two years' work dismissed in a paragraph. I must, though, declare an interest. I knew Camilla Johnstone at Oxford. She was a first-class debater and a product of St Paul's Girls' School, my daughter's school. How many journalists these days can even *spell* 'St Paul's Girls' School'? What price 'St Pauls' Girl's School' — the school with one pupil?

(?) and Christina Ritchie (?)'.

Bell had wanted Hilary Drew for the part of Jake's girlfriend. Bell was 'well in' with Hilary Drew. Genevieve, a friend of his friend Luke, worked at Hilary's management company. He'd sent her, via Genevieve, the script of *Big Ben*. But she'd never even read it. One day, he said (to the photo), he'd meet her. He seemed to think that, had she read it, she'd have agreed to be in the film.

I advised him, if and when he met her, not to reveal he'd been carrying that photo. She'd think him at worst a stalker and at best an adolescent. He said I needn't worry. He wouldn't be carrying that photo. He changed the photo at regular intervals.

I attempted to leave. Bell restrained me. He told me I had no need to leave. 'Admit it. You've got nothing to go home for. Chris told me. I'm sorry.'

'Chris', I deduced, must be a reference to Pilkington. I looked around the room. Pilkington was seated on his own, under the photo of the young Jimmy with the young Michael Caine.

This was remarkable. I had never seen Pilkington on his own, except when he was driving a sports car. Even then, he'd given the impression of having an invisible blonde by his side. A crowd of intimidated boys, a posse of teenage drinking companions, a table of diners, a floor of traders, a waitress, a pair of sons, a wife running about — Pilkington's energy and swagger demanded the attention of others. Now he sat there, ignoring everyone.

Bell manoeuvred me towards him. Pilkington looked up.

'Did you hear? The Ticky threw me out. She changed the locks. We're in the same boat, mate.'

'Face it, we're all in the swamp together,' said Bell.

These swamps and boats, these maudlin clichés, were too much to bear.

'I think not,' I told them both. 'I left of my own accord. And I'll return when Elizabeth's ready.'

Then I cursed myself. I'd exposed my private life. Now it was public.

'She'll never be ready, mate,' said Pilkington. 'Markets and women. The two things you can't control. Believe me, I've tried. Why have I got so much anger?'

This was an abject non sequitur. Not merely was it unconnected to what he'd just said; it was unconnected to his entire previous life. It was embarrassing and had to be stopped.

'Will you be up in Aldeburgh in July?' I asked. He was always up in Aldeburgh in July. His answer, surely, would make everything normal again.

'I don't know. She'll be up there with the children, staying at my parents. I don't know. You?'

'As it happens, I've booked a villa in Greece.'

'With the children?'

'No. They'll be in Aldeburgh with their mother. Max can play with Harry and Tom.'

'Yes. They'll like that. Who you going to Greece with?'

'My father. While we're away, Elizabeth and the children can have the run of his house.'

'That'll be nice for them.'

'Yes. Though Max is off on a cricket tour for the first week I'm away.'

'Will you be there for the Pilkington Putter?'

'What date is it?'

'Twenty-fourth.'

'Good. We'll be back by then. We actually get back that morning.'

'What time?'

'God, this is so fucking boring!' said Bell.

'Sorry,' said Pilkington, with his new-found humility, the humility that caused him to sit on his own, pondering the origins of his anger.

'No. *I'm* sorry,' said Bell. 'That was wrong of me. Very wrong.' He seemed determined to out-humble Pilkington. 'Carry on. You carry on.'

Jimmy approached and told us, mercifully, that it was time to leave. Bell thanked him for the use of his club. Jimmy thanked Bell for the invitation to the premiere. What, asked Bell, did Jimmy think of the film?

'To be honest, I thought it was a load of shit,' said Jimmy.

'Yeah. You're right,' said Bell. He turned to me and shook his head: 'It's all shit, isn't it?'

I found this somewhat tactless, given that I'd invested twenty thousand pounds. But it wasn't the tactlessness that upset me. I resented what I can only call the swamp camaraderie. According to Bell, it was *all* shit. To what did *all* refer, if not everything? Bell and I were in the mire together, he as producer, I as investor, we and Pilkington

352

as men without wives, together in an East End drinking club, in the small hours, as spiritually homeless as those front two rows were literally so.

No. This was not Bell's position in my life. I helped him. I was superior to him. I was not his swamp equal.

★ ★ ★

The following Monday, he rang to ask if I'd seen the *Sunday Telegraph* review. Did I remember Camilla Johnstone from Oxford? He'd always hated her. How could she be so disloyal? I pointed out that there was no reason to be loyal to a person who'd always hated you. He was, at least, his old self, full of irrational vigour.

He thanked me for coming to the screening and the party. Now I was a single man, we should see more of each other.

'Listen, I hate the idea of you going to Greece on your own.'

I told him I was going with my father.

'OK. I hate the idea of you going on your own with your father. Is there room for me? Why don't I come with you?'

★ ★ ★

At nine o'clock on the Saturday morning of the Whitsun bank holiday, I arrived at the family house to take the children up to Aldeburgh. Elizabeth made me a cup of coffee. She herself drank a drink made from dandelions, a

353

decaffeinated, decoffeenated coffee.

She claimed to be looking forward to a long weekend on her own, as she had to write her application form for the Psychodynamic Counselling Course at the Highgate Counselling Centre. This did not sound like sufficient activity to occupy a long weekend. I suspected the imminent arrival of a man.

'And how's Tony?' I asked. I always inserted that 'and' to make it sound more casual. Elizabeth said she didn't know, then asked me: 'And how's Mike Bell?'

Wishing to avoid the subject of my investment, I replied: 'He's fine. My father's delighted he's coming.'

'To what?'

'Greece.'

Elizabeth paused.

'I didn't know you'd asked him to Greece.'

'He volunteered.'

'He volunteered,' she repeated, with contempt.

Elizabeth, I could tell, was discontented, hence her lashing out at Bell. I was convinced she had no boyfriend. Either that, or he was unsatisfactory.

As we drove up to Aldeburgh, I asked the children: 'How's your mother's boyfriend?'

I could have been referring to Tony. Equally, I could have been referring to his successor. Either way, my wording told them that I knew their mother had a boyfriend — which of course I didn't — and was only too happy to discuss his welfare with them. Isobel said nothing, guarding her mother's privacy. But Max said: 'She doesn't want any boyfriends any more.'

'I see,' I replied; and left it at that. But Max thought I'd changed into one of those fathers to whom you could say anything. So he asked, as we turned off the M25: 'Do gay men get stuck?'

* * *

For his 'last dog' — his words not mine — my eighty-five-year-old father chose a basset hound. He plumped for a basset on account of its aristocratic demeanour and gift for companionship with old men and their grandchildren. He named it Edward.

He told his Aldeburgh chums that Edward needed more than an hour's exercise a day, adding: 'But so do I!' The remark was relayed to me a few times by my father and a few more times by Geoffrey Moxon-Smith.[1]

In fact, my father, who'd had a hip replacement, struggled with the amount of exercise required by Edward. In this respect, Max was a godsend. As soon as we got to Aldeburgh, Max and Edward set off on their own, followed at a distance by my father, who was free to turn back whenever it suited. Max

---

[1] Geoffrey Moxon-Smith was now a widower too, Amanda Moxon-Smith having died in January. Aldeburgh was a duller place for the loss of its leading gossip. As Ticky remarked at the funeral, she did not feel right relaying the news of her mother's death. It was the kind of news normally conveyed by her mother.

and Edward would certainly get an hour of exercise; my father would get as much or as little as he liked. Everyone was happy.

While they were out, I took the opportunity for a drawing-room chat with Isobel. I congratulated her on her excellent results, so far, at St Paul's. I told her how pleased I was to know that she and Max would be in High Ridge while my father and I were in Greece. One day, I told her, High Ridge might be her home. I wanted her to know that I'd inherit the house and would subsequently bequeath it to her, as I was sure she'd uphold its traditions.

Isobel looked alarmed. Did this mean she couldn't change the sofa? It was true that the brown chesterfield sofa had been there since I was a boy, handing round the Christmas Eve Eve crisps to Bert Gage, who knew it wasn't his place to sit on it.

'Isn't it against the law?' she asked. 'Aren't there regulations about what sofas should be made of?'

I was delighted. My daughter was looking at that sofa through the prism of the law.

'You're absolutely right,' I said. 'When your grandfather dies, I'll replace it with one that conforms to regulations.'

She asked if she could go and listen to her new CD. I suggested we listen to it together. Isobel explained that it was only possible to listen to the CD on headphones. I agreed to this, not fully understanding the implications, and found myself listening to Gorillaz on tiny musical earplugs, while Isobel watched.

I knew my daughter would never listen to

second-rate music. I could tell there was musical intelligence involved and remarked that it was 'not without merit'. Isobel told me I didn't have to shout.

I took the earphones off.

My father returned, shortly followed by Max and Edward. He was in a most benevolent mood, having purchased a new sun hat for the trip to Greece from O. & C. Butcher, Aldeburgh's leading outfitter. He asked whether Isobel might care to listen to Bach with him. She agreed. My father selected a long-player by Tortelier. Skittishly, he wore his new sun hat for the recital.

Like many basset hounds, Edward had a great affinity with stringed instruments. The cello spoke to him, especially in its lower register; he responded with *sympatico* howls.

'I'll never be as good as him,' said Isobel, referring to Tortelier.

'You can try,' I said.

★ ★ ★

As the car ferry approached Gavrion, the port of Andros, I saw Judy Page waiting for us on the dock. Twenty years hadn't altered her outline, as seen from the passenger deck. Tanned and taut, wearing sunglasses, she could have passed for an outdoor version of the woman I met at the 1983 British Record Industry Awards.

'God, which one's the daughter?' asked Bell. Alana, her teenage daughter, stood next to Judy Page. She was chubby and pale and looked reluctant to be in her mother's company. (How lucky I was to have a daughter not characterised by reluctance!)

When we got out of our hired car to greet Judy Page, I could tell she'd not been accurately briefed as to the composition of our group. She was expecting a husband and wife and two children.

Having kissed me on both cheeks, she turned to my father and said: 'Hello, Michael, nice to see you again.'

I was greatly impressed. How, after all this time, had she remembered my father's Christian name?

'Do you remember me?'

'Of course, my dear,' said my father. 'You look just as you did when we last met.'

'If only!' said Judy Page, denying what she knew to be true.

'Hi, I'm Mike,' said Mike Bell, annoyingly, since I, as the group's host, was about to introduce him.

Judy Page said: 'Hi. This is my daughter Alana.' Alana nodded at Bell's right foot.

'Is there anything you need before I lead the way to your villa?'

Mike Bell said: 'Yeah, when do the boats go to Mykonos?'

'Oh dear,' said Judy Page, 'are you bored with Andros already?' I was pleased. I could see that she'd have no trouble dealing with Bell.

'No, no,' said Mike Bell, 'I love ports. They're really cinematic. Beginnings and endings. Lovers meet, lovers part.'

'You're not in the film business, are you?' asked Judy Page.

'Yeah.'

'Alana says I can read men's minds. Don't you?' Alana made a minimal movement of her head.

'May we have a photo for our files?' asked Judy Page. 'Go on, Alana.' Obediently, Alana took a camera from the bag at her feet. She angled herself so the sun was behind her. My father, Bell and I squinted at her. Then, surprisingly, Judy Page joined us, having magicked a large parasol from nowhere. The parasol kept the sun out of our eyes. She had done what was needed.

★　★　★

Our villa, near the village of Fellos, was most satisfactory, high up in the hills and isolated, though within reach of the beach and the village's sole taverna. One could not term it 'easy' reach, since the drive was arduous, so steep that Mike Bell wondered if it were possible for a car to do a reverse somersault. Thankfully, I — who don't see film scenes in my head — was the one doing the driving.

Judy Page was most solicitous, phoning the villa once a day to see if there was anything we needed, which there was not. She asked, always, to speak to my father, deferring to him as the senior member of the group.

'She means 'oldest and most falling apart',' he said, but I could tell he was delighted by this acknowledgement of his status as our knight and retired judge.

By the third morning of our stay, we'd arrived at a routine. I would get up before the others and drive down to Gavrion to purchase our minimal requirements, given that our main meal of the day was taken at the taverna. I would then arrive back at the villa just as my father and Mike Bell were getting up, to the strains of Oasis. I would then ask Mike Bell to turn the music down for the sake of my father, and he would reply that my father was perfectly capable of asking for the music to be turned down, if he so wished. My father would then say it did not matter to him, as he was increasingly deaf, at which point Mike Bell would turn the music up.

When Oasis had finished shedding their load, I would suggest an excursion to either or both of the two most interesting places on the island, according to my guidebook: the Archaeological Museum at Hora (also known as Andros Town) with its finds from the geometric settlement at Zakora; and the cylindrical Hellenistic tower at Aghios Petros, almost twenty metres high, 'one of the best preserved towers in the Cyclades'.

Bell would then raise a fatuous objection such as 'What does the tower do?' to which I would say: 'It towers.' I would then look to my father, who had brought me up to respect and follow guidebooks. Be it Sicily, Madrid or Newcastle, my father would arrive in a place and not be diverted by signs or crowds or sensual appetites. His appetites were intellectual. A guidebook, for my father, was a menu, with hors d'oeuvres

(*Walk up the four hundred and twenty-six steps and enjoy the panoramic views*); main courses (*Michelangelo's David*); and things he simply didn't eat (*Sicily's finest ice rink*). The *Archaeological Museum at Hora* was clearly a main course. Why then did he reply, three mornings running, that he didn't feel the need to go anywhere today?

Mike Bell sided with my father, converting my father's negative into a 'positive need' to go nowhere. Bell's mornings and afternoons were spent drinking, listening to music, getting in and out of the pool (where he lay like an upturned crab), half reading scripts, half reading magazines and playing what he called 'air guitar'. So restless was Bell that, by the second afternoon, he moved on to 'air drums'. Surprisingly, none of this irritated my father, who appeared to regard Mike Bell as a three-dimensional television he was happy to watch all day. In return, Bell was solicitous as to his welfare, constantly moving chairs and parasols so that my father was kept in the shade.

After the sun went down, we repaired to the taverna, where Costa the proprietor was always absurdly surprised and pleased to see us. Mike Bell ordered the food and wine, which he drank while the three of us ate, and then, when the bill arrived, he got up from the table to walk to a spot where his mobile signal was better. He then called the Los Angeles management offices of Hilary Drew, after which he returned to the table and said, in a sullen fashion, nothing.

When we returned to the villa, however, he

said a great many things. He could not rid himself of the notion that night in Andros was day in Los Angeles. Films were being developed, written, produced and screened, were 'stiffing' and 'opening well', while he and I sat there and 'talked shite at the moon'. I took umbrage at this, on both nights, claiming I'd said nothing that could be construed as 'shite'. This didn't appease him. Why was he the only one prepared to feel properly sorry for himself? Weren't we all lonely men with nothing to live for? I asked him to keep his voice down, as my father might be listening.

'Course he's listening. He's ten foot away. You're listening, aren't you, Michael?'

'I am, thank you,' said my father.

'So what have you got to live for?' asked Bell.

'Don't answer him,' I said to my father.

'Let the man speak,' said Bell.

My father's stomach rumbled. Then, to my distress (and, indeed, his own), he repeated that the purpose of life, according to his daughter, was to learn how to love.

He sounded defeated, as if she'd convinced him his life had been a failure. He slumped in his chair. A gap developed between his shirt and his concave chest. I took immediate action.

'You and Mother were married for fifty-two years.' This was a change of subject, since he and my mother did not deal in love. Nevertheless, it was far more years than Freya had clocked up with Murray.

'Jesus!' said Bell. 'Fifty-two years. Judge gives himself life sentence.' My father shook his head. 'Well. Goodnight.'

362

'Goodnight, Father. Sleep tight.'

'Goodnight, Michael,' said Bell, adding, with a kind of public-house sincerity: 'You're a good man.'

When my Father had shuffled off, Bell said: 'So, come on then. What went wrong with you and Elizabeth? Did she find out what you were like? That's what always goes wrong with me. I start out intending to be someone better than I am. I start out trying to be like the woman. Cos they're usually better. Then — '

'Elizabeth and I are still married. That's all I want to say. And I'd ask you not to make any more provocative remarks.'

'Why did you invite me, then?'

I was too gracious to point out that I hadn't. Sulkily, he picked up my guidebook. Discovering it was illegible in the dark, he tossed it into the pool. To give him his due, he then retrieved it and hung it on our X-shaped clothes-drying stand. By the morning, when I got up to drive to Gavrion, it had attained a nice dry crinkle.

★   ★   ★

An hour later, alone in Gavrion, I ordered a Greek coffee. I sensed the waitress's respect. Here was an Englishman willing to immerse himself in local customs.

I wrote a postcard to Elizabeth, putting it in an envelope so the children wouldn't see it. I told her my father and I were having a splendid time, which I knew she'd want to hear, since she felt affection for him. I didn't mention Mike

363

Bell. Instead, I mentioned Judy Page. I told Elizabeth that the villa company was co-run by an old girlfriend, Judy, whom it was very nice to see again. The phrase 'very nice' was uncharacteristically bland. It was designed to suggest I was concealing something.

My intention, of course, was to make Elizabeth jealous. When I met Elizabeth, she had a secret boyfriend, Guy. Later, she had another one, Tony. Was I not entitled to a secret girlfriend? There was no point, however, in keeping her secret. I should use her to my advantage.

Let me be clear. I had no intention of reviving my affair with Judy Page. I wanted the benefit of an affair, without the affair itself. She need never even know she was my secret girlfriend. I'd keep the secret from her.

* * *

I heard no Oasis as, half an hour later, I made my vertiginous ascent to our villa. Judy Page's car was parked on our track.

I opened the gate to the villa's courtyard, which contained the swimming pool and the villa's four bedrooms, facing the pool in a row, like a line of cubicles. Judy Page performed an ocular striptease, lifting up her sunglasses so they perched on her head. Then she smiled at me. For the first time in twenty years, I saw her eyes. As the sun, over time, makes a currant of a grape, so the skin around her eyes had wrinkled. But the eyes had lost none of their potency. They

364

directed me to the vacant seat beyond my father and Mike Bell. I walked over to it as discreetly as I could, so as not to disturb the musician.

Alana was halfway through Purcell's 'Trumpet Air'. I knew immediately she was not a natural musician, though her mother had called her 'gifted' in her letter. She looked vacant, neither lost in her music nor found. She played with energy and competence, certainly, but did not give the sense that she knew why she was playing.

Judy Page poured my father a glass of retsina. He beamed. He was wearing his floppy white sun hat, as opposed to the panama he donned for our infrequent outings. Judy Page had evidently told Alana that my father was the guest of honour, since Alana directed the bell of her trumpet in his direction.

Mike Bell, meanwhile, reacted very physically to the music, more for the mother's benefit than the daughter's. He made movements with his hands that may have been 'air drums' or even a knee-high form of 'air conducting'. When Alana finished, he and my father applauded with great enthusiasm. I applauded with half their enthusiasm, which I thought appropriate as I'd missed half the performance.

We then learned that Alana had won a place at the Athens Conservatory of Music, that Alana was bilingual (though monosyllabic in both), that Judy Page had lived all over the Cyclades for the previous twelve years and found there a freedom she'd never found in England. With this, Judy Page stood up and, prior to leaving, asked whether the pool cleaner had visited yet. My father informed her that he had. Mike Bell suggested Judy Page stay and have a swim. She demurred, saying she had calls to make and hadn't brought her costume. Provoked, Mike Bell invited her to come back later, for dinner. He looked from my father to me and, not detecting a chef, suggested we bring back a takeaway from Costa's.

Judy Page volunteered to cook. I, however, felt pity for Alana and suggested we call the whole thing off.

'I'm sure Alana doesn't want to spend the evening with a bunch of old people.'

'Of course she doesn't,' said Mike Bell. Then he turned to Alana: 'Don't come. You'll hate it. Stay at home. Practise.'

His remarks broke all the laws of politeness. Yet I must acknowledge, in his defence, that for the first time in our presence, Alana smiled.

My father said: 'It's a shame my granddaughter isn't here. She's an excellent cellist, isn't she, Robert? She and Alana could play a duet.'

'Theoretically,' I said. 'But it's quite impossible. There's nothing written for trumpet and cello. Chalk and cheese.'

My father nodded, as did Judy Page. Like Elizabeth, like all the women in my life, she deferred to my superior knowledge. I was, actually, unsure of my facts. But sometimes one can win an argument without them. It's a matter of confidence.

*   *   *

Judy Page cooked lamb chops, Greek salad and rice. Mike Bell kept the wine flowing. I laid the table, fetched, carried, cleared and attended to our various candles, some designed to repel mosquitoes, some to create 'atmosphere'. I also provided the taramasalata and hummus without which no Greek meal can begin, thought I hadn't yet seen a Greek eat either. Then again, I'd barely seen a Greek.

Judy Page began the evening by asking my father if he knew Alan Temperley. He did, of course. She then made it clear she knew Alan Temperley better than he did — better than I did, for that matter. She'd helped Alan during what she called 'the pivotal moments'. Should he stand for Parliament? Should he be prepared to contest an unwinnable seat, just to gain his political spurs? Was he right to let it be known he was interested in the post of Lord Chancellor? *I was there*, she kept saying. Was she? She'd lived in Greece for twelve years. Surely, she was here.

What did my father make of her? Did he remember that my mother and he had fought her off? That my mother called her 'common', to which he said she took 'great pride in her appearance'? I, for one, had no intention of asking him.

Mike Bell, meanwhile, kept tapping the retsina bottle with his knife. She ignored him, in favour of discussing with my father the loneliness of the life of a judge, as compared with the life of a politician. She ignored me too. The difference was, unlike Bell, I was happy to be ignored.

Bell excused himself and went off to make his nightly call to Los Angeles.

By midnight, my father was nodding off. He'd greatly enjoyed his evening. When he stood up, we thought he was going to bed. Indeed he was. But first he made a detour to the chair on which he'd hung his sports jacket. As Bell had remarked, it was the only sports jacket on the island. From it, he withdrew some money. He was tired, it was dark and he had drunk alcohol. I am not convinced this most meticulous of men knew what denomination of note he offered, shakily, to Judy Page. Ten euros? Twenty? Fifty? She refused, prettily, knowing he'd insist, which he did with the words: 'She who cooks shouldn't have to pay.' *She who cooks shouldn't have to pay.* The proposition is, at least, arguable. But my father gave it the wisdom of a Latin tag. Then he bade us all goodnight.

Once my father had gone, conversation speeded up. Judy Page asked Bell what his next film would be. He said he had a number of scripts he wanted to give to Hilary Drew and was talking to her people on a daily basis. Jason, her manager, was due at his villa on Mykonos any day. Hilary would be there sometime next week. He was going to pop over and see them.

'Ooh,' said Judy Page, sounding keen to accompany him.

I was not expecting an invitation. My role, I knew, would be to drive Bell to the ferry at Gavrion. From there, I thought wistfully, I could drive on and visit the Archaeological Museum at Hora.

'I really like Hilary Drew,' said Judy Page. 'She's subtle and she has a good body.' This was an ingenious compliment, since she somehow suggested the description applied equally to herself.

I asked if anyone would like coffee. Bell and Judy Page shook their heads.

'Right then,' I said. Judy Page then addressed a rare remark to me, thanking me for bringing everyone together. I, in return, thanked her. Then, finding myself without portfolio, I volunteered to clear away the plates.

'Goodnight,' said Bell.

This didn't follow, didn't follow at all. I'd made no reference to going to bed. When a waiter volunteers to remove your plates, you do not say 'Goodnight'.

Nevertheless, I cleared the plates and went to bed.

*　*　*

When I woke up, at the usual time, my father, in the bedroom to my left, was snoring. I put my shorts on, then my sandals, then one of the four short-sleeved shirts I wore in cheerful rotation. I stood up and headed for the door, the slats of which were filtering the sunlight.

Then I heard the door to my right open. Three seconds later, I heard a splash. I knew at once it was not Bell's splash. It was too small, too neat, too *taut*. It was followed by a bigger splash.

'Shhh!' said Judy Page. 'You'll wake Sir Michael up.'

Their union did not annoy or upset me. I regarded it as inevitable. But they were naked. I knew. They *sounded* naked. This had consequences. It meant I was a prisoner in my own bedroom. I couldn't drive to Gavrion for bottled water, cheese and yesterday's *Daily Telegraph*. My routine was destroyed.

'Sir Mikey sleeps like a log,' said Bell. 'And Robert's gone off to Gavrion.'

He could have checked. He could have opened the gate and looked for our car. But he couldn't be bothered.

As they splashed, I waited for Judy Page to say something about me, now I was presumed gone. I hoped against hope it would not be insulting or resentful. In the event, she said nothing. This was a relief but, I confess, it was also a disappointment. Was I wrong to expect some passing compliment? *It was nice he provided all that taramasalata. The hummus was great too.* That would have been enough. I could then have said, to Elizabeth: *She really liked my hummus.* To which Elizabeth could have replied: *What's that supposed to mean?*

'So come on then,' said Bell.

'Come on what?'

'I don't know anything about you. Who's the father of your daughter? Is it Alan?'

'It could have been. He's never publicly denied it. I've always known I'd end up with a really important man.'

This was a most curious answer. Temperley had never publicly denied he could have been the father of the daughter who bore the feminine

370

version of his name. It was not a yes.

'Anyway,' she continued, 'he's in England. I couldn't take England any more.'

'England's finished,' said Bell. In my cell, I repressed a snort. 'I don't reckon I'll make my next film there.'

'I couldn't agree more,' said Judy Page, as if determined not to make her next film there either.

This was pretentious rot. Yet I cannot deny they sounded heart-felt. There was a bond between them: England had let them down.

'The English are so small-minded,' she said. 'They're jealous of you if you try to make something of your life. And the English are lousy lovers. With exceptions.'

This was brilliant, loathsome but brilliant. One knew that she'd said this to every English lover she'd ever had. Every man jack of them had been an exception to the rule. (Except, of course, me.)

'What happened with you and this Tina?'

'It's complicated. I'm not living with her any more.'

'Where are you living then?'

'A house in Chelsea.'

'Ooh. How much did you pay for that?'

Bell was quiet. This was a man who'd never paid anything for anything. How would he answer? He gave a mumbled answer, as if the mumbling would somehow make the answer less true.

'It's not mine. It belongs to a friend of mine, Luke. I'm just staying there while he's in LA.'

By contrast, Judy Page's words were clear: 'So you don't own a house.'

A car braked, a car door slammed. Then a woman spoke, not bothering to conceal her very American anger.

'Hi. Alana said you'd be here. You're meant to be in Gavrion. Half an hour ago. You're meeting two clients off the boat.'

'This is Mr Bell,' said Judy Page, in the affronted tones of a lady incommoded by bad manners.

'Mr Bell, hi, excuse me, I'm Martha, how are you today? Was her pussy to your satisfaction?'

'I'll leave you,' said Bell, and with a slurp of water he got out of the pool and wet-footed it speedily back to his bedroom. Now he was imprisoned in the cell next to mine.

In his absence, Martha got louder, as if he'd gone out of earshot. 'You can have all the rich man's cock you want! But you don't do it on my time! Ever! Do you understand me?'

Only I heard as Bell said, sadly: 'My cock's not rich.'

'I find your jealousy pathetic,' said Judy Page to Martha.

'I don't give a fuck what you find! That's it, finish! You don't work for me any more.'

A few seconds later, the car door opened and slammed. Martha yelled: 'Psycho *bitch*!' Then she drove off.

At this point, I expected Bell to come out of his bedroom. I was even less likely, after all that, to come out of mine. Instead, the door of my father's room opened.

What did he see? He saw Judy Page in the pool, looking distraught. Or did she look distraught? I was a witness in audio only.

'Are you all right? I heard an altercation.'

'It's difficult. When you're living in another culture. People don't understand you.'

'I'm sure.'

'How are *you*, Sir Michael? I hope that awful woman didn't wake you.'

'No, no. I was waking up anyway. If you'd like to get out, I'll turn around.'

'Thank you.'

Did I hear my father turn around, so Judy Page could get out of the pool without exposing him to her nudity? I believe I did. From this, one could assume that, ashamed of her nudity, she covered herself when she saw him come out of his bedroom. Why would he volunteer to turn around, if she'd already shamelessly revealed her nudity? On the other hand, it could be that the shame was his. It was he who didn't want to carry on looking at what she was perfectly happy for him to see.

On the one hand, on the other. This is the legal mentality. These are the scales of justice.

★ ★ ★

Fifteen minutes later, with Judy Page gone, Mike Bell and I emerged from our rooms, he with a highly unconvincing yawn. My father told us what had happened:

'She came here for a swim. And then her employer turned up and abused her.'

373

'Really?' asked Bell. 'I must have slept through it. Too much retsina.'

'She fetched her clothes from your room,' said my father. He did not say it in an accusatory manner. He was simply recording a fact.

'Good,' said Bell.

Keen to get away, Bell suggested he and I go for a drive, advising my father to stay behind, to keep out of the morning sun.

* * *

'Did you hear the way she said, 'So you don't own a house'?'

Not wishing to discuss it, I replied: 'I have to concentrate on driving.'

'You didn't hear the mirror, did you? In the night.'

I concentrated.

'She took the mirror off the wall and held it over my face. If it wasn't for my nostrils, I'd be dead.'

'I have no idea what you're talking about.'

'She looked at herself while she sat on top of me. Do I have to spell out everything?'

There was more of this, much more, till I stopped the car and got out. Bell followed me.

'Where's the taverna?' he asked. I ignored him. I cracked open my desiccated guidebook and told him to look up. *The tower at Aghios Petros was built in the Hellenistic period.* I didn't stop reading, out loud, till I'd reached the last word: *antiquity.* I had waited many days for this. I would not be denied.

Bell gazed at the twenty-metre-tall tower, with its *base diameter of 9.4 metres*. It only depressed him further.

'Where's the rest of it?' he asked. It was true that we were seeing the jagged rump of what had once been a taller edifice.

'Jesus, Bobman, my life is shit. Hilary Drew's not coming to Mykonos.'

'Oh dear.'

'She's gone into rehab.' Returning to the tower, he said: 'Why don't they tear it down and start again? That's what we should do. Start a-fucking-gain.'

Here it was again, that swamp camaraderie I had not remotely solicited. He'd now chanced upon a new metaphor. We were towers whose walls had to come tumbling down, so we could rebuild ourselves, brick by brick. This nonsense had to be stoutly resisted.

'I'm happy as the tower I am, thank you. Elizabeth's broken up with her boyfriend and he hasn't been replaced.' I left the rest to his imagination. But he devoted no time to imagining it. Instead he said: 'Listen, Luke wants to rent out the house in Chelsea. It's been great living next door to you, we haven't done that since college. Why don't I have the spare room in your flat?'

My Canonbury flat had three bedrooms: one for me, one for Isobel, one for Max, though they'd never spent a night there.

Why, then, should Bell not have one of their rooms? I advanced my reasons, for the simple pleasure of hearing him try to gainsay them.

375

'My son's room only has a bunk bed.'

'That's fine. I'll put a mattress on the floor.'

'Do you own a mattress?'

'Course I own a mattress. I just don't own a floor.'

'I have every confidence I'll move out of the flat and back in with my family.'

'That's great. I'm happy for you,' said Bell. 'Then I can have your room.'

Ten days later, Bell moved out of Luke's Chelsea flat and installed himself in Max's bedroom. Touchingly, he covered the walls in Liverpool posters, as a way of ingratiating himself with his godson, should Max ever want 'his' room.

I thought it would be cruel and unnecessary to repeat what I'd told Bell many times before, which was that Max supported Manchester United.

⋆ ⋆ ⋆

I'll say little of our last ten days in Andros, which were just as the first four days, save for the absence of Judy Page, from whom we never heard again, to Bell's and my relief. The self-pity and bitterness didn't leave him, though. He started referring to himself as 'the man who doesn't own a house'.

Meanwhile, my father sat and read and beamed and kept his old head protected from the sun. It was in Andros that he started making remarks. By this, I do not mean that he insulted those present. He did not lose the grace and inhibition by which good manners are defined. His remarks were disconnected from the company he was keeping. Once, when I offered him an olive at Costa's, he said: 'I should have invited him to the wedding, don't you think?' I did not ask him to explain himself. But Bell did.

'Who's he, Sir Mikey? Why should he have been at your wedding? Let's get it all out in the open. We're all bonkers here.' My father shook his head. I don't think he remembered what he'd just said. His remarks were thoughts, inadvertently expressed then forgotten.

On our last night, as we were packing, Bell called me into his bedroom.

'I found this under my bed.' He produced a soft, shiny, Y-shaped black object of indeterminate purpose. Seeing my bemusement, he said: 'It's a thong.'

It pained me to see him holding this thing, this thong, which was so scant, so nugatory, it was almost no thing, no thong. Yet in his bedroom it loomed large and black. A primitive man might have thought it an evil spirit.

★　★　★

On our return, I drove my father home to High Ridge. To Edward, the first member of the household to greet him, he said with childish gusto: 'The nice lady will walk you up and down!' What 'nice lady' was as clear to the dog as to me. Possibly, it was a nice lady he regretted not inviting to his wedding.

Then Elizabeth approached and my father

gave her an uncharacteristic hug, which delighted me. It was a father-in-law's hug. It acknowledged and took pleasure in the fact of her marriage to his son. In the afterglow of the hug, I advanced my face in Elizabeth's direction but was obliged to withdraw it in chicken-like fashion when no kiss was proffered.

Max had gone crabbing in Walberswick with various pals. Isobel was at her tennis course in Thorpeness. While my father napped, I found myself alone with Elizabeth. This was rare. Elizabeth was about to take the children to Tarifa for a week's holiday with Tom and Harry Pilkington and their mother, Ticky; after which, following a parental handover, they would have a second week's holiday with Tom and Harry Pilkington and their father, Pilkington.

We discussed how she and the children (and the dog) had enjoyed their time in Aldeburgh. Nothing remarkable had happened, which was as it should be. She asked how my holiday was.

'Fine,' I said. 'Very nice.'

Thanking me for my postcard, she said: 'It must have been nice to see this woman Judy.'

'She's there and I'm here,' I said, adapting Judy Page's line about Alan Temperley. It was perfect for my purposes: bland, unarguable and yet suggestive. How would Elizabeth react?

In the event, she overreacted.

'Listen, Robert, this is your only life.' I did not like the enormity of this, nor her use of my first name. We were the only ones in the room. There was no confusion as to whom she was addressing.

378

'Wouldn't you be happier living with a man? I don't mean sexually. Why don't you set up house with Mike Bell? At least you'd have some companionship.'

'It's only temporary.'

'What?'

'He's moving into my flat.'

'He's moving into your flat?'

We had had this kind of exchange before. It was only a few weeks since she'd said, *I didn't know you'd asked him to Greece*, to which I replied, *He volunteered*, to which she replied, *He volunteered?*

Of course, this was my influence again. She'd acquired from me the barristerial technique of incredulous repetition.

19

The Queen
(2003)

Geoffrey Moxon-Smith, Philip and Valerie Hamilton-Wood, Ping Mottram, Pidge Holt, Richard and Dorothy Risdon, Alan and Jean Thoday — my father had his troops to look after him. After Andros, I phoned him most mornings but I didn't see him for weeks. He always claimed he was 'very busy', of which I was glad.

Then, in early September, I had an agitated call from Geoffrey. Had I seen my father lately? I told him I hadn't. Was my father ill?

'No. He's happy. He's very happy. In my judgement, he's *too* happy.'

Geoffrey would not say more than this. He did not think it his 'place'. Let us not forget that Geoffrey was a solicitor. My father was a client as well as a friend. A solicitor doesn't breach the confidences of his client. The call was in the nature of a hint.

I thanked him and phoned my father straight away. How was he? Uncannily, he replied that he was very happy. He'd just written to Freya to tell her so.

'Why are you happy?' I asked.

'Hmm?'

'I want to come up this weekend and see you.'

There was a long pause. I could hear him gumming his spittle.

'I'm going to a concert on Saturday. At Snape. *The Messiah*.'

'That sounds delightful. I'll come.'

'No, no. I'm busy on Saturday. I'm going to a concert at Snape.'

'Right then. I shall drive up on Sunday morning.'

'Yes. Yes. I'll see you then.'

It was Wednesday night. I'll always regret that I didn't get in my car, there and then.

* * *

On the Saturday night, I went to bed early. When the phone rang, at one in the morning, I assumed the call was for Mike Bell. Then, when I saw Max's bedroom door was open and Bell's sleeping bag unoccupied, I assumed the call was *from* Mike Bell. He was probably on the pavement, with a minicab driver sitting on his chest, pending payment of the fare.

'Mr Robert Purcell?' It was a female police officer, calling from Leiston, near Aldeburgh. At approximately ten fifteen on Saturday night, my father had had a car crash on the way from Snape to Aldeburgh. He'd overtaken and found himself in the path of an oncoming vehicle. Both drivers swerved and came off the road. The other driver came to a halt in a field, sustaining only whiplash injuries and shock. My father was not so fortunate. His car hit a garden wall.

She asked me to go to Ipswich Hospital. I

asked my father's condition. She repeated her request. Police officers and medical orderlies, I knew, are reluctant, in a phone call, to inform a relative of a death. They prefer to do it in person, so that any suicidal impulse on the part of the relative can be countered by their presence.

I did not feel suicidal. I felt like my father's son. I even spoke like him, in his measured way, giving every word due weight.

'I appreciate,' I said to this young woman, 'that you cannot tell me his exact condition over the phone. But would I be right in thinking that my father is no longer alive?'

I believe she wanted to say 'Yes' but didn't know if I would take it to mean *Yes, you're right to think your father's no longer alive* or *Yes, he's alive*.

This officer, like the youth in that burger emporium in the Holloway Road, was following verbal guidelines. She didn't want to depart from them. After all, it was possible that our conversation was being monitored for training purposes. But I had no training purposes. I was already trained. I'd been trained by our finest institutions: Winchester, Oxford and the Bar. I rephrased my question, putting it in the form of an instruction which she could not disobey.

'Young lady, I will say this once and once only. Please listen to me carefully. If my father's dead, say 'The Queen'.'

She thought about this for a long time. She understood that I was protecting her from using forbidden words. No *your*, no *father*, no *is*, no *dead*.

'The Queen, sir.'

I could hear in that 'sir' her acknowledgement that I'd handled a difficult situation with aplomb. It was her voice, not mine, that was quivering. I was calm, from the satisfaction of a job well done.

★   ★   ★

At four thirty in the morning, having visited my dead father at the hospital, I turned off the A12 to drive down the road that leads from Snape to Aldeburgh, the road off which he'd been killed. I'd driven down this road many thousands of times, as had he. Young people and owners of fast cars drove down it too fast. Of course they did. They were young and/or they were fast. The elderly, famously, did not. Old Aldeburgh drivers were notorious for their walking pace. A yacht club wag once remarked that the town needed speed-minimum not speed-limit signs.

My father overtook a vehicle, at speed, blindly. Why? My father was a man of the law.

★   ★   ★

I woke up alone in High Ridge, which I'd never done in my life. Yet I had the feeling I was not alone. My father was out there, somewhere. I got up, dressed and walked around the house, looking for my father. This appeared to be mystical, religiose and barmy. But I'm none of those things. Everything I do makes sense. Therefore, my search for my dead father made sense. It was just that I didn't yet know what the sense was.

I was right. I was right, I was right. My instinct — that he was 'out there' — made sense. It was just that I'd got the wrong 'he'. It was not my father who was out there but Edward. Where was the dog?

I searched without success in the pantry and the drawing room and the wellington-boot cupboard and the corridor and the hall and the downstairs lavatory and the mumby, then walked outside to investigate the greenhouse, the front and back gardens and the garden shed. Had the dog been in the car with my father? Surely, they tell a son of the death of his father's dog. Why, though, would my father have driven Edward to a concert hall, and left him in the car park, albeit he was a known lover of classical music, who howled at strings? I sweated. Where was the dog?

When, therefore, an hour later, I opened the front door and saw Edward, I felt only gratitude to the person who'd brought him safely back home.

'Were you worried? I've been looking after him. I'm so sorry. Your father was a wonderful man,' said Judy Page.

I wanted to hug her. But I didn't, for you cannot hug a person who is holding a dog on a lead.

* * *

'Excuse me,' I said, a few seconds later. The three of us were now in the kitchen. Next to the

384

drum of Nescafé, the phone was ringing.

'Of course,' said Judy Page, bending to pick up Edward's bowl and fill it with water. For privacy's sake, I took the mobile handset into the drawing room.

It was Elizabeth. Geoffrey had rung her with the news. I told her what I knew, which, in its painful detail but absence of context, was both too much and not enough. She'd already spoken to the Hamilton-Woods and the Thodays and Ferocity Pilkington. She said she'd come down to Aldeburgh to help with the funeral, but it was difficult, with the children at school. I said that I understood perfectly.

Concerned for my welfare, she asked if I was alone.

'No,' I said. 'There's somebody with me.' How could I explain the presence of Judy Page, in Aldeburgh, on my father's doorstep, with his dog? I could not explain it. No. But I could exploit it. It made sense to exploit it.

'Judy Page is here. My old girlfriend. She's over from Greece.'

'Oh. Right,' said Elizabeth. She was taken aback. There was no question of that.

'Just a second,' I said. I turned my head away from the mouthpiece and said, loud enough for Elizabeth to hear, but not so loud I'd be heard in the kitchen: 'I'll be with you in a moment, darling.'

I was not an actor. But I had observed at close quarters an actor at work. Alf Stone, in the back room of Jimmy's, had the courage of his convictions. He'd convinced himself he was

385

'Bernard Brown' and was fearless in convincing others. I was 'Judy Page's Boyfriend'. Fearlessly, I said into the mouthpiece: 'I have to go now. I'll call you later.'

'He was a wonderful man. I'll miss him.'

'Yes,' I said, with the impatience of Judy Page's Boyfriend, keen to get back to Judy Page.

★　★　★

Why, in the name of Aldeburgh, was she there? That was what I intended to ask as I headed for the kitchen, before being diverted by a knock at the door, the second of many that morning. By eleven, there was not an unoccupied chair in the kitchen. Geoffrey was followed by Ping Mottram, then Pidge Holt, with flowers. Then came the Risdons and the Thodays, lowering the level in the Nescafé drum by a further half-inch.

As I ladled the seventh spoonful into the seventh cup, my hand shook and the granules fell to the floor.

'Delayed shock,' said Ping, just as Isobel had when I wept on the towpath.

'You sit down. Let me take over,' said Pidge. By this point, Judy Page had already got out the dustpan and brush. She knew where the dustpan and brush were kept.[1] Was she, as she swept, wearing a thong? Did her black dress, which

---

[1] What's more, the dustpan and brush were new. They were plastic and looked almost weight-less. What had happened to the trusty metal dustpan, with which you could knock a man out?

resembled a nightie, connote mourning? I was not, as was assumed, too bereaved to make coffee. I was too unsettled by Judy Page's still-unexplained presence.

I had hoped, when Geoffrey arrived, that by introducing him to her I'd get my explanation. Out of politeness, he'd ask where she lived and how long she'd been in Aldeburgh. What, he'd enquire eventually (though in less forensic terms), was her relationship with the deceased? Instead, as did all my guests that morning, he greeted her as a familiar. Nobody questioned her presence, though Pidge Holt looked askance, in that way women do, when confronted by a woman of a similar age who's thinner. Most women, I should record, are thinner than Pidge. That morning, she was dressed for sailing, her already stout girth padded and quilted. If Judy Page's dress could have passed for a nightie, Pidge's could have passed for bedding.

I was impatient to get to the explanation. But first I had to plough through cliché.

'It's so extraordinary,' said Dorothy Risdon. 'We were playing bridge with him only yesterday morning.'

'Yes. It's unbelievable,' said Richard Risdon, to synchronised nodding.

This was rubbish. It was not in the least unbelievable that a man would play bridge on the day he died, when he played bridge on most of the days he lived.

'You can't choose how you go,' said Pidge. And once more the heads made their sage movements. Why Pidge thought this would comfort me, I cannot say. It was not even true.

'You've obviously never heard of suicide,' I said. Pidge looked stunned. Dorothy and Richard Risdon were quick to defend my father.

'I'm sure it wasn't suicide, Robert.'

'On the contrary,' said Richard. (What is the 'contrary' of suicide?)

'No, no,' I said. 'I know it wasn't suicide. I was just making the point that suicides choose how they go.'

'Very true,' said Richard Risdon, reintroducing harmony; and soon the heads were on the move again.

'Would anyone like some cake?' asked Judy Page. 'I bought him his favourite ginger cake from the Co-op.'

'No thank you,' said Pidge, sharply, as if the cake were the cause of death.

★ ★ ★

These were the facts, as vouchsafed by the Risdons, the Thodays and Geoffrey, who'd accompanied my father to the concert.

Geoffrey had offered to drive him but my father said he'd rather go in his own car, a Volvo of unimpeachable safeness. At the end of the concert, the Risdons, the Thodays, Geoffrey and my father assembled in the foyer to debate the merits of the performance with the other old folk, then walk to the car park together. They all agreed, as they knew they would, that the concert had been marvellous. At this point, my father told Geoffrey he was in a rush to get home. This explained the overtaking.

'It's my fault,' said Judy Page, alarmingly. Why would she say that, unless she knew it was true but wanted the company to deny it? It was surely a double-bluff. 'I said I'd pop in before he went to bed, to make him a nightcap.' She made 'nightcap' sound far more intricate than a drink. She made it sound as if she were going to knit him a cap to wear in the night, like a woman in a painting called *The Nightcap Maker*, by Vermeer.

'What time did you say you'd pop in?' asked Alan Thoday.

'Half past ten,' she replied.

'Well. The concert finished at ten. It's only a ten-minute drive. You can't blame yourself,' said Alan Thoday, with all the authority of a former High Commissioner to Kenya.

'I waited here till eleven, then I thought, I better take Edward back to my cottage. I didn't want to leave him here on his own. I left a note for Michael and everything.'

So. Judy Page made my father nightcaps, had a key to High Ridge, lived in a cottage. How had this happened?

'Your father was so kind to me,' said Judy Page, causing me to sit up straighter in my chair. 'I was so miserable working for that woman in Greece. I'd never have come to Aldeburgh without him.'

'I'm glad you did,' said Richard Risdon.

'And so's Willy,' said Dorothy Risdon.

'And Moppy,' said Valerie. Suddenly, everyone was cheerful.

389

'Did Alana get her place at school?' asked Geoffrey.

'She can go there next term. But the music's poor. We're applying to the Royal College.'

Now, and over the next few minutes, I got my explanation. Willy and Moppy were, of course, dogs. Judy Page was a dog-walker, with threefold credentials: two legs and my father's recommendation. In the two months since she'd arrived in Aldeburgh, renting a small damp cottage near the marshes, she'd become indispensable. Dogs were just the beginning. She'd cooked for Ping Mottram. She'd collected the Risdons' grandson from Heathrow airport. She was teaching the Thodays conversational Greek. She was also in charge of the redecoration of their master bedroom. She'd probably taught the Thodays the Greek for 'beige'.

In all this, there was some relief. I'd imagined that my father was the sole reason for her presence in the town. But all these good citizens had welcomed her into their homes, with the exception of Pidge. Pidge, wary and scornful, wanted to seem hostile to Judy Page; instead, her disgruntlement made her seem like a fat, rejected lesbian suitor.

Then it was over. Judy Page was no longer the centre of attention. I was. My feelings were remembered or, rather, presumed, as Alan Thoday stood up and said: 'Robert doesn't want us to stay too long.'

Within minutes, the kitchen had emptied, save for Geoffrey and me, though not before Judy Page had embraced me, for the first time in more than twenty years. It was purely a 'bereavement' embrace. Nevertheless, an embrace it was. I imagined we were at the funeral, with Elizabeth watching us.

Judy Page said: 'We're going to be very good friends.'

★   ★   ★

I was due to appear the following month in the House of Lords. It would be my first appearance in front of the Law Lords. I was leading counsel in the Revenue and Customs Commissioners' appeal against the Court of Appeal judgment that the commissioners should be responsible for payment of a receiver's remuneration. I would argue that the receiver was entitled to be indemnified in respect of his costs out of the receivership assets.

Geoffrey was sure I had a great deal of work to do, which was true, and volunteered to make the funeral arrangements on my behalf. We compromised. I'd spend the following day in Suffolk, registering the death and visiting my father in the mortuary. Then I'd return to London and Geoffrey would take over. He assured me that my returning to chambers was 'what your father would have wanted'. It was the first cliché to which I was happy to subscribe.

He asked if he might solicit the help of Judy Page. She was, he said, 'highly capable'. I knew this to be true. Equally, I knew it to be true that my father had died from driving too fast to her nightcap. This was not a statutory offence, though. There was no Causing Death by Offering a Nightcap. No, she'd not killed my father, no more than Lord Rodwell had killed his first two wives, nor Freya had killed Murray, nor Judy Page had murdered Theo the Cypriot from the mini-market, as he shivered on that balcony, with incipient pneumonia and sexual excitement, while she nakedly hoovered my flat.

I acceded to Geoffrey's request. I wanted Judy Page to be, or appear to be, involved in my life. That would help me reclaim my wife. She had also, Geoffrey told me, offered to look after Edward, with the help of Alana. For that I was grateful.

★ ★ ★

I drove back to London. In my flat, I told Mike Bell my father had been killed in a crash. He burst into tears. I put my hand on his shoulder.

'That's all we've got left now, isn't it?' I wasn't sure what he meant. Should I ask?

'We're all going to die, aren't we?'

We're all going to die, aren't we? might be moving and profound, if said, for example, by a five-year-old girl who'd just been told she had a terminal disease. Spoken by a forty-seven-year-old man, who still hadn't turned down the sound on his DVD of *Pulp Fiction*, it was mere self-indulgence.

His tears stopped. He said, calmly: 'I'm going to die without making a decent film.'

What had that got to do with my father?

'If you don't mind, I won't come to the

funeral. I'm low enough as it is.' I nodded.

'In that case,' I said, 'could you put the rubbish out on Friday morning?'

'It's done,' said Bell, going into action immediately, finding pen and paper and writing RUBBISH OUT FRIDAY MORNING, then putting the note next to the kettle where he'd be sure to see it. But by the time I departed for Aldeburgh on Thursday morning, the note was no longer there. I suspect Bell had put it in the rubbish.

★ ★ ★

At a Little Chef on the A12 at Colchester, I ordered a breakfast of unimpeachable Englishness, imagining myself already in the kitchen of High Ridge. Fried egg, beans, mushrooms, tomatoes, two swimming sausages: I wanted everything that had the power to stain. Then I rang my daughter. I hadn't talked to her at any length since my father had died.

She agreed to play the Second Minuet of Bach's Cello Suite Number One which, on account of the Lemon Man, she'd been unable to play at my mother's funeral. I was delighted.

'When your parents die, does that mean you haven't got any parents?' It was a question that displayed her formidable intelligence. How can a person ever be said to have 'no parents'? Equally, how can the state of parenthood survive the body of the parent?

★ ★ ★

On this parentless question, Freya was in no doubt, embracing me in the kitchen of High Ridge with the exclamation: 'We're orphans now!'

Judy Page, who'd just emptied Freya's ashtray, embraced me too. This can only have been for Freya's benefit, since she'd embraced me four days earlier; in the interim, nothing had happened that would necessitate a further embrace.

'I better go, you've got a lot to talk about,' said Judy Page.

'No, no,' said Freya. 'I want to hear more about Greece.'

'I've got to get the glasses from the off-licence,' she said.

'We'll see you in a bit, then. Really good to meet you.'

'Really good to meet you too. He always wanted me to meet you,' said Judy Page, picking her car keys off the table. I had not been with her more than a few seconds, yet already I was colouring with anger, offended by her proprietorial *he*. As for the *always*, that was positively deluded. She knew nothing of what my father *always* wanted.

I stood at the window to watch her car disappear, wanting, before I talked about her, to make sure she was fully gone.

'She's taken the Escort!' I was as angry with myself as I was with her. How had I failed, thus far, to notice the Escort no longer living in the drive?

'Daddy gave her that car,' said Freya.

'No, he didn't.'

'Yes, he did.'

'No, he didn't.'

'Are we going to argue like six-year-olds?'

'If you're six, I'm eight. I'm telling you, he didn't give it to her because it wasn't his to give. That car was given to Max by Mike Bell.'

'Given to Max?'

'Please don't repeat what I say!'

'I think Judy needs that car more than Max, don't you?'

On the table were two battalions of photographs, seemingly advancing towards each other. One was Judy Page's, one Freya's. From Judy Page's pile, my sister gave me a photo of my father, Judy Page and Edward, on the river wall, with the Martello Tower and the yacht club in the background. Judy Page held Edward's lead in one hand and my father's arm in the other.

'Look how happy she made him,' said Freya. 'Now read what he wrote to me a month before he died.' She put a letter in my other hand, bombarding me.

Dear Freya,

I hope you and your children are well and happy. I am very happy. I have met a woman called Judy. She looks after me well.

'Are you sure this is his handwriting?'

'What are you talking about?'

'It has all the makings of a forgery.' I thought, of course, of my own forged letter from 'Max' to Lady Rodwell. This was similarly skilful. One could only admire the way Judy Page had written *you and your children*, as if, at eighty-four, my father had forgotten his grandchildren's names. And what of the short sentences, bespeaking the shortness of breath and staccato energy of an elderly man?

'Don't talk nonsense. He adored her. He had fifty years of Mum, who was a cold fish, and then he found this gorgeous thing who needed his help and he loved her. He was rushing home to see her when he crashed. I think that's beautiful.'

'You're mad. You know nothing about this woman. She's a gold-digger.'

'You're just jealous cos you're incapable of love.'

'For God's sake, woman, how can a car crash be 'beautiful'!'

'The door was open,' said Geoffrey, nervously. Of course it was. Aldeburgh back doors were always open. 'Is Judy around? We're meeting the caterers.'

'Excellent,' I said, 'you've come at the right time. We were talking about love.'

He looked more nervous.

'Did my father change his will in the last few weeks?'

Geoffrey looked scared. He was right to be. He was a humble family solicitor, I a QC.

'I couldn't possibly disclose the terms of the will until all the executors have been informed.'

'Judy's a gold-digger. Isn't she?' He didn't answer. 'Just say 'The Queen' if he changed his will in her favour.'

'For Christ's sake!' said Freya.

Geoffrey shook his head. I'd upset him. I did not mind upsetting Freya, which I'd always regarded as an important part of my life's work. But Geoffrey was a decent, honourable fellow.

Judy Page entered the kitchen. Could someone help her unload the glasses from the boot? Geoffrey ambled off, gratefully, like an elderly dog. Freya followed. I stayed behind.

I watched Judy unlock the boot of the Escort. I watched her concern for Geoffrey, as he lifted a crate of glasses. I could see she might have brought my father some happiness and he, with his distinction and fine manner, would have elevated her.

Geoffrey arrived back in the kitchen first. He went to put his crate on the sideboard.

'Would you like some coffee?' I asked.

'The Queen,' said Geoffrey.

20

29th September
(2003)

Since the sofa declaration, eighteen months earlier — *How can you be so dense, Robert?* — Elizabeth's face had been changeable. In our Contented Years, her expression had been consistently cheery and purposeful. Then came the Lemon Man and, with him, a complicated face. She was in love (with him), she was angry (with me), she was determined (to make Hereford 'work'), she was relieved (when she and the children came home), she was angry (with the Lemon Man *and* me, two unknowable men out of billions). Recently, she'd looked withdrawn. Of course. She'd withdrawn from men.

At the funeral on 29th September, Elizabeth was in the front row, with me and the children and Freya and Judy Page, who was surprised but delighted when I asked her to sit next to me. She thought this was on account of her significance to my father. I could hardly say she was there to provoke my wife.

Only once, in those last eighteen months, had Elizabeth looked so radiant. At my mother's funeral, fourth in the line of Chief Mourners after my father, Freya and me, Elizabeth had worn an expression that refreshed all who passed. Was today's expression, then, simply the one she wore for her in-laws' funerals? No. There was more to it than that.

I glanced over my shoulder. Ticky Pilkington, oozing unhappiness, was sitting with her sons Tom and Harry. Her estranged husband Pilkington was alone, on the other side of the aisle. Elizabeth had just been on holiday with Ticky and Pilkington, separately. Doubtless, she had heard them, night after night, berating each other *in absentia*. That must have made Elizabeth think fondly of what we had had: the ability to rub along together. We had rubbed along together for twelve years. Spurred by hearing my 'intimacy' with Judy Page — *I'll be with you in a moment, darling* — Elizabeth arrived at the church determined to outshine this woman. Elizabeth wanted me back. I would grant her her wish. I knew exactly what I'd say to her, when the moment was right: *Let the dramas be over.*

Judy Page had served her purpose. I didn't speak another word to her, in the church or at the funeral drinks. I broke up with her, right there, in the front row of that church. I felt elated. I'd never ended an imaginary affair before.

★　★　★

'Sir Michael's granddaughter will now play the Minuet from Bach's Cello Suite Number One. Isabella?'

Isobel tried not to look upset as she stood up and approached her instrument.

'Isobel!' I boomed. Max grinned.

'I'm so sorry. Isobel,' said the vicar, putting himself right, when his job was supposedly to put us right.

I felt proud. I was at the head of my family, doing what the head of a family does: protect his flock. Elizabeth raised her eyebrows at me.

When Isobel finished playing, I applauded, then Max applauded, then, behind me, his best friend Harry Pilkington applauded. Soon the entire congregation was applauding.

The vicar was uncertain. Was applause appropriate at a funeral? He raised a hand. If he'd angled it in the manner of a traffic policeman, he could have silenced us. But the man was a follower, not a leader. He followed Jesus. Now, he followed me and Max and Harry Pilkington. He did a curious one-hand-clapping movement. Then he clapped. The vicar clapped and, on account of his microphone, his clap was the loudest in the church.

★ ★ ★

As we filed out of the church, I told Elizabeth that the woman next to her in the pew, with the legs, was Judy Page, the woman from Greece, who meant nothing to me.

'Didn't she look after your father? That's what Freya said.'

I agreed, glad to have sorted it out.

400

The line of Chief Mourners outside the church consisted of Freya and me. I couldn't ask Elizabeth. I couldn't anticipate our final reunion, imminent as I believed it to be.

Of my encounters at the head of that short line, three were significant. First came a lengthy encounter with Lord and Lady Rodwell. This was not just socially but professionally significant. Michael Rodwell made a point of saying that he'd be seeing me soon 'in another place', a reference to my appearing before him and his fellow Law Lords in *Marshall v. Revenue and Customs Commissioners and Another (No. 2)*. Then his wife Sheila complimented me on my daughter's musical gifts, just as she had on that midsummer night, two and a quarter years earlier. There was a wonderful sense, in all this, of normal service finally being resumed.

The Rodwells were followed by a stranger. He was a short, thick-set man of no obvious education, with a rough London accent. He told me he was happy to meet me. My father meant a lot to him. His name was Maurice Perlstein. I said I'd known that name for my entire life.

'I won't take up your time,' said Maurice. He proferred pen and paper and asked me to give him my address.

Maurice the greengrocer was extending the courtesy that Jack the coalman and Nancy and Jim, the newsagents, extended to my father on those Christmas Eve Eves. When talking to my father, their main concern was to reassure him they'd soon stop.

'I won't bother you now,' said Maurice. 'I'll drop you a line.'

'Won't you come to the house for a drink?' I asked, knowing he'd refuse.

'No. I won't bother you now,' repeated Maurice. With that, he made way for the last of the mourners, Pilkington.

Pilkington, clearly, had the opposite instinct from Maurice Perlstein. He'd hung around in the church, waiting to be last in line, just so he could talk to me as long as he wanted. Elizabeth was standing fifty yards away, talking to various Risdons and Hamilton-Woods. As Pilkington embraced me, I saw her looking. I remembered how proud she'd been of me when I'd wept on the towpath of the River Wye. So I prolonged my grief-embrace with Pilkington, preventing him from releasing me, nestling my face deeper into his massive right shoulder. There was this to be said for embracing Pilkington: one couldn't see his face.

When I did look at his face, it was like looking at the Lemon Man's face outside Great Witley Church. What had this face, this whole head, gained or lost? With Pilkington, there was a gain. Pilkington had gained niceness.

'I want you to be all right,' he said, giving me the business card of a psychotherapist called Ian Ayton, whom he'd been seeing four times a week. Ayton was a 'genius' who'd helped Pilkington in an amazing number of ways. I should overcome any prejudice I had against psychotherapy. I said I had none. My prejudice was against people with business cards.

I was hoping this might annoy Pilkington. But he was unannoyable. I have always considered niceness — unlike grace — to be more of a façade than a quality. His niceness, however, was running deep. Deep! That was not a word I had ever associated with Pilkington.

'How do you find the time to see him four times a week?' I asked, hoping to deflect him from talking about the ways he'd been helped and the amazingness of their number.

'I've retired,' said Pilkington. 'I've made enough money. Life is not about money. Your father's life wasn't about money, was it?'

When he said *Life is not about*, I knew I had to get away, before he told me what it *was* about.

'Will you excuse me? We have to go to Ipswich for the cremation.'

'Of course,' said Pilkington, backing off. Then he added, with hyperbolic niceness: 'I totally understand.'

There was no need for that. Basic, bog-standard understanding would have sufficed.

⋆ ⋆ ⋆

It was half past seven, on the evening of my father's funeral. The drinks at High Ridge had commenced at six, as they had on the day of my mother's funeral. My parental funerals guaranteed me several hours in Elizabeth's presence. At eight o'clock, when the drinks ended, I'd have run out of such funerals.

I looked across at Elizabeth. She was on her own. *Carpe diem*. I made my way over.

'Let the dramas be over.'

'What do you mean?'

I hadn't thought it would be necessary to explain what I meant: the Lemon Man, her leaving, my mother's death, the cello theft, her return, the toilet paper, my leaving, my father's death. *Let the dramas be over* was akin to the ticket request one rehearses, in French, to pronounce clearly to the booking clerk at Gare du Nord. One doesn't rehearse further explanations, qualifications, alternative versions. One's words should, by rights, elicit the tickets.

'Let my father's death bring us together.'

Elizabeth looked embarrassed. She didn't want anyone to hear.

'I don't want to hurt you. Not today. Can you not just accept our marriage is over? Please. For your own sake.'

Such was the force of this that I made no reply. She said it with a clarity I can only describe as radiant.

★   ★   ★

Where does one go to accept one's marriage is over? I sought refuge in the den. That was where one always went in High Ridge, as a child, to escape the company of adults. What difference, now I was an adult myself?

I left the drawing room and walked down the corridor. Pilkington was sprawled on the stairs, looking at photos.

'Hi!' he said. 'Just looking at the photos from the holiday.'

'Will you excuse me?'

'Of course,' he replied, without moving. 'Are you OK? You're not OK, are you? Is there anything you'd like to talk to me about? I'd understand if — '

'Stop understanding!'

Without a word, he got to his feet and let me pass. I walked as slowly as I could, alarmed by my own vehemence. I resolved to spend a period of quiet in the den, then return to the mourners. I was, after all, their host.

I had not been in the den more than twenty seconds when there were two soft knocks at the door. I should have known, from the softness, it was Pilkington again, totally understanding Pilkington.

Pilkington, too, had his statement prepared, his Gare du Nord pronouncement. It was based on a misunderstanding of my anger on the stairs, which he thought was caused by knowledge I did not, in fact, possess.

Why did I know what he meant, even before he said it, even before the preamble, which in this case was no more than *Um*, delivered with all the humility a large rich man could muster? I knew what he meant because Pilkington was so knowable.

'Um, I hope Elizabeth told you how serious I am. This isn't some holiday romance. I just want you to know she's precious to me and I'm going to take care of her. And your children. They're our children now. All of us. Elizabeth. You. Me.

'I know this is painful for you,' he continued, his bulk blocking my path to the door. 'I know you don't like me. *I* don't like me! Well. Not exactly. I *didn't* like me. I didn't know how to love myself, so I couldn't love anyone else. That's what's so great about Ian Ayton. He gives you the tools. You know?'

What hope was there for me — for anyone — when bullies talked about love?

'I'm sorry it had to come out today. That's not what we wanted. We'll tell the kids when the time is right. It's great Max and Harry are best mates. That's really positive.'

'Will you excuse me?' I said, as I'd said to him on the stairs. But, this time, I wasn't trying to get past him. My intention was to stay exactly where I was and get him to leave. It took him a while to work this out.

'Course. Yes. I totally . . . just call me. Any time. We'll talk. We'll go out and have a beer.' To his credit, he qualified this ghastly invitation. 'I mean, we don't have to have a beer.'

'Actually, I've changed my mind,' I said, which alarmed him, as I knew it would. 'Would you mind staying here?'

Pilkington shook his head.

'Thank you,' I said.

I left and shut the door behind me. To leave him trapped inside that den was a small but exquisite victory, for Pilkington had no idea how long he was meant to stay there. What is more painful than an indeterminate sentence? Had he asked me, I would have told him, as teachers once told children, that he'd have to stay there till he'd finished thinking about what he'd done. When does one finish thinking about what one's done?

★　★　★

I couldn't face the mourners, not now. I'd get the urn from Freya and scatter the ashes on the beach. She could explain this to anyone who asked where I was. They'd understand. But they wouldn't, of course. How could they know that, in scattering those ashes, I was accepting that my father was dead and my wife was radiant because she and Pilkington were in love.

I stood at the doorway of the drawing room. Freya — Earth Mother, Earth Widow, Earth Orphan — was telling Geoffrey that her parents' demise was a beginning not an end; the start of a journey of discovery that would last her the rest of her life. Who were they, her mother and father? What were they? Geoffrey nodded, then pointed out I was waiting to speak to her.

Freya told me Judy was worried I was harbouring a fantasy about her. Why had I been so strange with her, wanting her to sit next to me, then ignoring her? By way of reply, I asked Freya for the urn. She said she was planning to scatter the ashes at Kaiteriteri Beach, on the South Island. I asked why my father would have wanted his ashes scattered in New Zealand, when he'd never been there in his life.

'Exactly. He can go there now.'

As a compromise, I asked her to pour half of

my father's ashes into a container. She could do as she wished with the other half. Freya left then returned with half the ashes in an old Nescafé drum, telling me to scatter them, with her blessing, but not to look at them before I did so, as that brought bad luck. I humoured her and left the house.

Outside, Elizabeth and the children were heading for their car. I hid the drum behind a dustbin and caught up with them.

'Where were you?' asked Max. 'We couldn't find you!'

'Did you have a nice time?'

He looked at me with suspicion. He didn't know he was supposed to have had a nice time.

'I'll pick you up from school in a fortnight's time and we'll come here again.'

This confused him further. 'Can we still come here now Grandpa's dead?'

'Of course,' said Isobel. 'High Ridge belongs to our family. It's an heirloom.' Elizabeth kissed me on both cheeks. 'Goodbye. See you in a couple of weeks.'

'Pilkington told me,' I said, so the children wouldn't hear.

'Oh. That wasn't what . . . I'm really sorry. Do you think you could call him Chris? For the sake of the kids?'

'Of course. I wish you and him every happiness.'

Elizabeth thanked me, even though I'd called him 'him'.

★   ★   ★

408

By the time I reached the seashore, I'd understood why Elizabeth was with Pilkington.

Her first boyfriend had been Giles, Pilkington's youngest brother. She was therefore predisposed to find Pilkingtons attractive. Secondly, she was destined to be with high-achieving males. Guy was one, as was I, as was Pilkington. But, crucially, Pilkington satisfied Elizabeth's craving for a Lemon Man too. Pilkington was looking for a new way of being. He was convinced there was more to life than money and — luckily — had the money to find out what that might be. He was a hybrid between an alpha male and a spiritual seeker.

My father would have been proud, I thought, as I levered off the top of the Nescafé drum. I'd found the logic to their union and could therefore accept it. I'd made sense of it.

I scattered his ashes on the shore, near the tideline, to give myself a few more seconds with them, till the sea took them away. I reached down and felt for them. I found a pinch and rubbed it between my thumb, forefinger and middle finger. The texture was granular. I brought the pinch towards my mouth and flicked out my tongue.

On the shore of the North Sea, I'd scattered my father's coffee. Very well. Let Nature add water, as my father would have done.[1]

---

[1] Freya later told me she'd withheld my share because the balance of my mind was disturbed. I'd asked for 'half my father'. How absurd. Here was a smoker who could not differentiate

When I arrived back at High Ridge, the guests had gone, along with the caterers. I sat on the chesterfield sofa, staring at the fireplace. I thought about making a fire but found myself becalmed. I simply wanted to sit still, surrounded by my heirloom.

'Hello,' said Judy Page, entering the room. 'I didn't know you were here. Freya's gone off to look after Ticky. She's upset, I don't know why, poor thing. Maybe it's cos she's overweight. Everyone thought it went very well.'

What was she doing in High Ridge, when the invitation was for six to eight and it was five-and-twenty to nine?

'I've put the caterers' invoice on the kitchen table.'

'Thank you.'

How did she make these minor services sound so crucial? If she hadn't been there, would they have buried their invoice in the garden?

'Can I get you a drink? Michael showed me where your mother kept the drinks.'

'Yes. A small brandy. Thank you.'

I'd done it again. I'd thanked her again.

She gave me my drink but did not take one herself. I found this offensive. It was the host's prerogative to pour the drinks of the house for others but not himself.

She stood with her back to the fireplace. Then, like a bird spreading its wings, she raised her elbows and rested them on the mantelpiece,

---

between the contents of an ashtray and the contents of a packet of cigarettes.

leaning back at an angle of twenty degrees. It was done with a confidence that made one think: oh yes, this woman has practised.

'Do you like this rug? I took Michael to Norwich and we bought it together. It's from Uzbekistan. It cost less than six hundred pounds, you know. That's a fantastic price for a rug this big.'

I hadn't seen this rug before. It had been concealed by mourners' feet. But this is a poor excuse. I had had many chances, between the death and the funeral, to notice a nine-foot by six-foot rug in the drawing room.

'Do you like it?'

'No.'

'I'm sorry. What don't you like about it?'

'It's new.'

'That's what he liked about it. It cheered him up.'

'Did it? Or did you just tell him it cheered him up?'

Judy Page could not accept that our conversation was about rugs. It had to be about her, my feelings for her, her feelings about my feelings for her.

'I'm sorry I can't reciprocate your feelings.' She said 'reciprocate' as if she'd looked it up in the dictionary and had been waiting for a chance to use it.

'You and I bought a rug together. Do you remember?' I wouldn't admit I remembered, nor that I had the rug still. I'd declared war on Judy Page and wouldn't be appeased with nostalgia.

'May I ask what you're doing here?'

'You're not helping, you know. We've all got to live together.'

'There is absolutely no reason why we've all got to live together. I suggest we live as far apart as possible. I'd like the Escort back, please.'

'Your father gave me the Escort.'

I explained to her that he couldn't give that which wasn't his. I left the room to fetch the car registration documents from my father's study, only to realise they were in my flat. I returned. I told her I'd send her a copy of the documents, if she didn't believe the car was mine. Annoyingly, she believed me, without a struggle. I wanted her to struggle.

While I'd been out of the room, she'd transferred to the sofa. She was sitting with her feet tucked under her, facing the fireplace as if it were a huge camera lens. She'd got herself a drink too, a green drink. Was it crème de menthe? It was typical of my mother's drink purchases, bought 'in case people wanted it'. We all knew 'people' meant my mother.

'You can have the car. Do you want the dog too?'

'Yes,' I said, aggrieved by the way she lumped in the dog with the car. I was intending to entrust Edward to Geoffrey, not wanting to force him to live in a London flat.

'You have to clean his ears,' she said, 'with some stuff from the chemist. They'll tell you what it is. Just mention my name.'

'I will not mention your name at the chemist! I've been going to that chemist since I was four! I will mention my own name, thank you!' Then I said with a quiet authority: 'I'd like you to leave.'

'Certainly,' said Judy Page, getting to her feet. 'You enjoy it while you can.'

'What does that mean?'

'It means he was a great man and he loved me. That's why he left me his house.'

'He did not leave you his house.'

'Ask Geoffrey if you don't believe me. He changed his will a week ago and he left me the house.'

'If he did that, I shall contest it. He was clearly of unsound mind.'

'Really? Ask the Thodays. He played bridge with them on the day he died. Ask them if he knew his clubs from his diamonds. Ask them if he could count his tricks.'

Judy Page had cunning, energy, timing and shamelessness. She had the bookless intelligence of an animal. She had all the low virtues of the thong-wearer.

'The Thodays witnessed it. They witnessed the codicil.' Codicil! She pronounced it perfectly.

There was nothing to be done except accept the truth, another terrible truth, another Pilkington-is-with-Elizabeth truth.

'I'll get you your car and your dog,' she said, making a businesslike exit.'

* * *

Five minutes later, when I heard the car pull up in the drive, I shored myself against further intrusion by drawing the curtains and putting on an LP of Britten's *Sea Interludes*, very loud. I

413

was sure Judy Page would hate this music. She would claim to like it, to the Aldeburgh people into whose path she'd snaked, but in her cottage, alone with her greed, she'd hum along to Sir Elton.

I heard the knock on the door, then the second knock, then the bell, then the bell again. I waited and waited for the engine to start, so I'd know she'd gone back to her cottage. I turned down the volume, in order not to miss it. But this was illogical. Why would an engine start? She wouldn't return the car then drive it away. Then came several knocks on the window. Then peace.

★   ★   ★

Mike Bell rang a few minutes later. I'd given him the number in case anyone needed me. In fact, nobody needed me. He was ringing to say he was leaving my flat in a few hours to fly to Los Angeles. His friend Luke had got seed money [sic] to develop a script about the American adventures of Bell's hero, John Peel, the disc jockey, who was 'resident Beatles expert' on a radio station in Dallas in 1964. He knew, already, that the project was better than all his previous projects. Peel was real. What could be more authentic than a real person? Bell's confidence was at an 'all-time high'.

I didn't, for once, bring him down. Disaster would do that, in its own time, with no help from me. Disaster was Bell's forte and calling. It was what he was put on this earth to survive. Sitting in High Ridge, on our ancient brown sofa, with my feet on the new Uzbekistani rug, I had never felt so close to Bell. I, too, was a man of disaster. I had introduced Judy Page to this house. Had I not married Elizabeth as a consequence? Do not misread me. Elizabeth is and was a person of the highest qualities, or I wouldn't have chosen her as my wife and the mother of my children. But let us not pretend. One of her greatest qualities was her non-Judy Pageness.

Yes, Mike Bell was right. I was in the swamp with him, after decades of looking down at him while I glided overhead. It was not that our parallel lines had converged. I had sunk to his level.

Bell knew nothing of what had transpired. That was a liberation and a relief. There was no danger of his 'understanding' me, since there was nothing for him to understand, till I selected it, edited it and conveyed it down the phone.

I told him Judy Page had moved to Aldeburgh, to be near my father. Bell was excited. He was excited by the *story*, even though what I was telling him was not a story. In his excitement, he filled in holes, making the narrative neater. While we were visiting that Aghios Petros tower, she'd gone back to our villa, in the (satisfied) hope of finding my father on his own. That was when she'd hatched her plan to move to Aldeburgh.

When I told him my father had left her the house, Bell was no longer excited. Now this was not my story, but his own. He was angry.

'See? She had to have a man with a house. Don't let her get it. Promise me.'

'There's nothing I can do. His will is a legally valid instrument.'

'Fuck the lawyer shit, Robcat. Burn it down!'

'Do you think so?'[1]

'Leave the bitch a bonfire. Listen, sorry, I have to go. There's a call on my mobile. Hi, Luke, just a second, I'm on another call. Listen, some bills came. But they weren't Final Demands.'

'Don't go,' I said.

'I'll talk to you later. Bye.'

★ ★ ★

It is important to understand that I am responsible for what happened next. I, of sound, bridge-playing mind, did what I did in the knowledge that a great wrong had been done to me and my family. I had waited my life to inherit High Ridge. I'd promised to leave it to my daughter. High Ridge was my life and my afterlife. What right did she have to them?

Wrap me in your arms, be sorry for my loss, totally understand me, give me the tools to change myself into someone better: there was none of that. I could have seen myself as a victim, with a right to pharmaceutical, psychological and pastoral care. But I did not. I saw myself as a master, a man in control of events.

---

[1] Consider the absurdity of this exchange. *'Fuck the lawyer shit, Robcat. Burn it down!' 'Do you think so?'* That is your guarantee of veracity. I could not, as they say, have made it up; and I didn't.

There were precedents. I'd burnt the taxi trousers. I'd burnt the letter Elizabeth and I wrote to the High Mistress of St Paul's, saying Isobel wouldn't be taking up her place. And, yes, we'd burnt my father.

I went to my mother's drinks cabinet. I removed all the bottles. Some were sticky and dusty. On a quarter-full bottle of cherry brandy was a price — one pound, nineteen shillings and sixpence — which pre-dated the United Kingdom's conversion to decimal currency on 15th February 1971.

I poured the cherry brandy, as I poured all the bottles, on Judy Page's new rug. It lay there and stank.

There was a multipack of matchboxes on the table by the fireplace. That multipack, I suspected, was bought by Judy Page for my father.

As I held a lighted match over her rug, I was reminded of another precedent, of a more ambivalent kind. 'Bernard Brown' had spoken of holding his match over that 'mangled purple thing'. What does it do, to compare yourself with an actor playing a character? It makes you question whether you exist. It was a question I answered easily. Yes. I existed, all right. To prove it, I dropped the match. The rug caught fire.

This was the action of a man committing arson. But it was not the action of — I cannot underline this enough — an arsonist. Arsonists are criminals. I am not a criminal. I committed a crime, certainly, but that did not make me a criminal. I didn't commit arson, as a crminal would have done, to defraud an insurance company or cause criminal damage or simply to sit in a nearby tree and laugh at the flames.

Mine was not a destructive act, as a criminal's would have been. I didn't want to destroy High Ridge. On the contrary, I wanted to save it. I wanted to stop it getting into the wrong hands.

Having ignited the rug, I was unsure if that were sufficient to burn down the whole house. Do you see? An arsonist would have known. A professional criminal would have worked it out. I was, in the best English tradition, an amateur.

The fire spread from the rug to the chesterfield sofa. My daughter was right. Of course she was. She'd inherited the authority of her father. The sofa, not conforming to current safety regulations, burst into flames.

I walked out of the drawing room towards the front door, stopping to take my coat from a hook in the hall, stooping to pick up the Escort car keys that Judy had put through the letter box. I took a last look at the mumby. Then I walked out of High Ridge, for the last time.

These were not the actions of a guilty man. He'd have run. I moved at the stately pace of a man who knows he has done the right thing.

Outside, I shivered. It was a cold autumnal night. Or was it? It may simply have seemed cold, on account of my recently having been proximate to an engulfing fire. I looked behind me. The fire was going well. Through a crack in the curtains, it looked as though the room had been redecorated in a colour called 'Fire'.

I approached the Escort. To irritate me, she'd parked it on the street, as opposed to leaving it on the drive, where it had lived for years. I struggled to get the key in the door. Then I heard a voice.

'Your house is on fire,' said Peter Something-Something, on his way (I am sure) from the pub to his cottage. Which pub? The Cross Keys? The White Hart? The Mill? The Victoria? The Railway Tavern?

His voice was unnecessarily loud, given that he was only a few feet from me. It may have been that, in his mid-sixties, Peter Something-Something was getting deaf. More likely, as a consequence of living on his own, he didn't use his voice that often. Therefore, he pitched it too loud when he did.

'I'm afraid I haven't drunk enough. Or I'd put it out myself.'

I smiled politely, not understanding.[1] He looked at me. I can only say I felt his spirit pass into my body. If that sounds mystical, so be it.

From across the road, Alan Thoday shouted: 'What's happened?'

'I've set fire to the house,' I said. 'Can you ring the fire brigade?'

'Wilco!' Moving as fast as his old legs could carry him, he sprint-shuffled back to his house, the Sandlings, on the doorstep of which his loyal wife Jean was standing. It did not occur to Sir Alan Thoday, retired High Commissioner to

---

[1] I realised (several hours later) that he was referring to the impossibility of his quelling the fire with urine. A criminal, with his vulgar streak, would have understood this immediately.

Kenya, that I, a QC and the son of his late friend Mr Justice Purcell, had burnt down the house deliberately.

Peter S-S, by contrast, knew. He could see into me.

'Why did you do it? Were you bloody pissed off?'

'Not every crime's committed by a criminal,' I said.

★ ★ ★

I drove off in the Escort, which smelt appalling. Why did I not take my sweet-smelling Audi? I believed it was right to take the Escort. High Ridge was destined for Isobel. The Escort was destined for Max. I had a primeval concern for my children's things.

I parked outside the police station. Before I got out of the car, I decided I'd collect up all its rubbish, intending to deposit it in the station bin, which would doubtless have been supplied by a private company that had won the contract to supply all UK police stations with bins. The company would have a warm and friendly *we're not in it for the money* name, along the lines of Green Guy. Binlove.

I picked up two empty crisp packets, probably bought by Alana.[1] I picked up a small aerosol

---

[1] Were they empty when she bought them? The question's not as foolish as it sounds. Alana was the kind of girl — a chubby, bilingual, taciturn, 'gifted' trumpeter — who might well have been

420

can. It had an illustration of a dog's head, in profile, with a highlighted ear. This was Edward's aural medication. I put the can in my pocket.

Finally, there was a black pair of tights, of the same family as the thong. It seemed that, wherever she went, Judy Page left a black mark.

I got out of the car without approaching the tights.

★ ★ ★

I confessed my crime to the duty officer. I told her who I was and what I had done. I gave her my own address and the address of High Ridge.

The duty officer was bemused. She couldn't cope with a citizen walking into the station to confess to a crime. She wary, wary of the truth, of which, in her professional life, she had seen so little.

'You burnt down this house, then you drove here to report it.' Why now, of all times, this incredulous repetition? The technique is designed to expose falsehood, not ridicule truth. This was a moment — forgive me, Elizabeth — typical of the times in which we live. Were Jack the Ripper alive today, he couldn't go into a police station and say: 'I am Jack the Ripper.' That is the action of a fantasist, wasting police time. No, Jack the Ripper's the little old black chap in handcuffs shouting 'You've got the wrong man!' Denial, not

---

bullied by teenage thugs into buying their empty crisp packets. I felt sorry for Alana. She was a victim of her mother.

admission, is your proof of guilt.

'Would you care to expand?' asked the duty officer.

Elation. Yes, I felt elation. I felt a surge of pride. I had done what was right. And then I'd confessed it, in accordance with the values instilled in me by my father.

'My dear,' I said — and here I smiled — 'all short men would care to expand!'

* * *

At 11 p.m., I was interviewed, under caution, by the CID officer. I was accompanied by my solicitor, Geoffrey. It was extremely sporting of him to come to the station at so late an hour.

I was then charged with arson contrary to Sections 1(1) and 1(3) of the Criminal Damage Act 1971. The charge was that, without lawful excuse, I damaged or destroyed by fire a dwelling house belonging to Sir Michael Purcell (deceased), intending to destroy or damage such property or being reckless as to whether such property would be destroyed or damaged. I was required to appear at Ipswich Magistrates' Court on the following Monday morning.

I thanked the CID officer for a job well done and extended my hand.

'That won't help you, sir,' he said.

'I don't wish to be helped. I simply want to shake the hand of an officer who's done his duty.'

'I'm not allowed to shake hands,' he said. But I didn't believe him. He was simply lacking in social skills and grace.

Geoffrey was kind enough to offer me a bed in his house, as my bed and house were destroyed.

★ ★ ★

As we sat down in Geoffrey's living room, he brought out a bottle of malt whisky he reserved for 'special occasions'.

'It's certainly that,' I said, my dry humour perfectly intact.

'Why did you do it?' asked Geoffrey. I explained.

'No, no,' he said, looking very old and very, very sad. 'No, no. You've got it wrong. He didn't leave her his house.'

'You're confused, Geoffrey. He changed his will. The Thodays witnessed the codicil.'

'Don't tell me I'm wrong! My wife spent forty-four years telling me I was wrong!'

This silenced me. I didn't wish him to think of me as his wife.

'Yes. He changed his will. He left her five thousand. To buy a car. You burnt down a house. For no reason.'

'She told me he'd left her the house. That was she told me. That was the intelligence I had. I had no reason to disbelieve it.'

'He wanted to leave her the house. I persuaded him not to.'

'You persuaded him not to?' I replied, resorting, I fear to incredulous repetition of my own.

Geoffrey was vexed. Very vexed. He told me my father was an eighty-four-year-old man who thought he was in love, which was madness. Judy

Page didn't love my father. That's why Geoffrey had dissuaded him from leaving her the house. He'd advised my father to leave her some money, then come back in a year's time if he still wanted to leave her his house.

I greatly admired this. Geoffrey was the last of the family solicitors, the man who counsels caution, the man who values privacy, the man who places property above love.

Then he did something which caused me to revise my opinion. It caused me, in fact, to leave his house, declining the bed after all.

Geoffrey went to his mantelpiece and came back with a framed photo of Judy Page and Geoffrey and his border terrier, Malcolm, on the river wall, with the Martello Tower and the yacht club in the background.

'You see? Judy likes *me*.'

★   ★   ★

At 1.14 a.m., I abandoned the Escort at High Ridge, got in my Audi and turned on the ignition. I remained stationary, with the motor idling.

A man of integrity does what he believes to be right at the time he does it. When I burnt down High Ridge, I had a good reason. I had an honest and genuine and reasonable belief that my father had left the house to Judy Page. I was right to do what I did, at the time I did it.

Surveying the remnant from the driver's seat, with the fire brigade long gone, I marvelled at the refusal of High Ridge to die. Most of the ground floor remained, minus windows. It was a proud ruin. High Ridge was made of stern stuff.

On either side, the Farquharsons' and the Holts' houses were completely untouched.

I'd burnt down a detached house, causing no damage to my neighbours' properties. I'd left the house promptly, making sure the fire brigade was informed. Then I'd driven directly to the nearest police station, in order to confess.

We have all heard the phrase 'a perfect crime'. Perfect according to whom? The criminal. The criminal who sets out to evade detection and wickedly succeeds. I had sought and embraced detection. I had taken due care of my neighbours. I had behaved in a conscientious and law-abiding fashion. Here was a perfect crime worthy of the name.

★ ★ ★

I telephoned Geoffrey at seven in the morning and asked him to relate the events of the night to no one. I told him to say I'd driven back to London, after the funeral drinks. This was, in its weasel way, the truth. Let the cause of the fire remain unknown.

On Saturday and Sunday, alone in my flat, I failed to answer the phone on twenty-nine occasions. My sister, who'd spent the night with Ticky, left six or seven messages. In the last, she directed me to a website for people who lose their homes in fires, a trauma apparently known as 'fire bereavement'.

Mercifully, she then flew back to New

425

Zealand, where, true to her word, she began her journey of discovery. It led her to a series for National Radio, with the folksy title *In Search of Mum And Dad*. Three Septembers later, she invited me to go into a studio in London, to be interviewed by her from Auckland on the subject of 'being a son'. I declined. I knew this was, by any other name, a phone-in.

★   ★   ★

On Monday morning, I took the train from London to the magistrates' court in Ipswich. I indicated a plea of guilty and was committed to the Crown Court for sentence. Geoffrey and I decided to brief Kieran Harris to represent me.

On the street outside the court, I heard a shout of 'Mr Purcell?'. I turned my head in the direction of the voice, as anyone would. But now I was no longer anyone. The owner of the voice was a young woman whose companion was wielding a camera. I turned my head away. I dispatched Geoffrey to find out who they were.

I walked down the street, towards Geoffrey's car. (He was giving me a lift back to Ipswich station.) I walked at great pace, looking neither left nor right.

'They're from Anglia Television. You're going to be on the news,' he told me, breathlessly, when he finally caught up.

'They'll get it all wrong,' I said.

'You've walked past my car,' replied Geoffrey.

I bade him farewell and walked, the long way, to the station. I had no intention of facing that camera again. I knew all about the local news. I'd watched it many times in High Ridge, with my parents. There'd be an item about seagulls denying residents sleep. An old woman and her husband, she disgusted, he taciturn, would complain about the closure of a public lavatory. Then the woman presenter would say: *A forty-seven-year-old man pleaded guilty today to the*. No. It must be I who gave the news, not that woman with her local face and her sing-song facts, devoid of context and gravitas.

When I got back to London, I picked up the phone. I did not put it down till late that night.

★ ★ ★

My first call was to Terry, my clerk in Crown Yard Chambers. I could not now appear in *Marshall v. Revenue and Customs Commissioners and Another (No. 2)* before Lord Rodwell. My destiny had changed. Of that there was no doubt. The appointment to the bench letter, the knighthood letter: these would remain eternally unwritten. Nevertheless, *I* had not changed.

'I can't appear in *Marshall*, Terry. I burnt down my father's house.' Like Alan Thoday, Terry presumed an accident, a trauma, a pretext for compassionate leave. I was not, he said, to worry.

In my second call, in my forty-second call, I used a form of words that was without ambiguity: 'I burnt down my father's house to stop it falling into the wrong hands.' That was all I said. I took no supplementary questions. I wished to be understood, not 'totally' understood.

At 6 p.m., by which time Isobel was back from school, I called the family house. Elizabeth answered. She offered to put me on something called 'speakerphone', so I could address Isobel and her at once. It was, I thought, a kind offer. (There would have to be a subsequent call to Max, since he was at boarding school.)

I knew, of course, that she'd already heard. Women have always already heard. They regard the sharing of information as power, whereas, as the son of a judge, I have always regarded the withholding of information as power. A judge, after all, withholds his judgment or verdict till the end.

I didn't, therefore, give Elizabeth and Isobel my standard form of words. I simply said I took full responsibility for my actions; and I'd done what I'd done because I'd believed my father had left the house to that woman.

'Will you go to prison?' asked Isobel.

'It's possible. Will you visit me? Like I visited you? In Hereford?'

'Yes,' said Isobel.

'Of course she will,' said Elizabeth. 'We all will.'

'That's right,' said Pilkington.

★　★　★

I waited two minutes, while Max was fetched from the school dining hall.

'Hello?'

I explained what had happened. Max was upset.

'Zack will say you're nuts.' Zack, I deduced, was a boy in his class.

'You can tell Zack I'm perfectly sane.'

'Burning stuff's nuts!'

'No. It's a crime. It's wrong. But sometimes a crime can be committed for the right reasons. You must never do it. Do you understand? In my circumstances, it was right to do it. But you'll never find yourself in those circumstances.'

I could hear him not listening. I was boring my son.

'Thanks for getting me out of dinner,' he said. 'It's fish.'

★ ★ ★

Maurice Perlstein's letter arrived the next day, with a request that I forward it to my sister.

Maurice Perlstein was my father's younger brother. My father was *b 3rd July 1919*, as stated in *Who's Who*. But he was not *s of late Robert Arthur Purcell and Margaret Susan (née Hindmarsh)*. My father was *s of late Simon Perlstein and Ruth (née Ginsberg)*.

My father was a Jew. He was not a descendant of Henry Purcell, the greatest of all English composers before Benjamin Britten. Nor, on his mother's side, was he related to Prince Alfred, son of Queen Victoria and Prince Albert of Saxe-Coburg, hence the slightly Germanic cast of his eyebrows. My father's eyebrows looked Germanic because his parents were German immigrants, who settled in the East End of

London in the early twentieth century. My father, Michael Perlstein, was a very clever boy, far cleverer than his younger brother Maurice, who described himself as 'good with his hands' where my father was 'good with his brains'. Their parents were poor and worked in a clothing factory. But their father's brother, Sidney Perlstein, was a furrier who'd 'done well' and bought a house in Pimlico. Uncle Sidney helped his brother and sister-in-law with money for his nephew Michael's education. Michael won a scholarship to Winchester in 1931, an extraordinary achievement; thence a scholarship to Christ Church, Oxford, in 1937. By the time he arrived at his alma mater, my father had changed his name to Purcell. For fear of anti-Semitism? Or anti-German sentiment? Or was it nothing to do with fear? Was it a positive espousal of the English values with which he'd been inculcated at Winchester?

My father lied to *Who's Who*. To whom else did he lie? By the time he met my mother (in 1947), his parents were dead, killed in the Blitz when a bomb dropped on their street in Stepney. His Uncle Sidney was dead, too, of a heart attack. In 1947, my father was living with his Aunt Margaret in Pimlico, the Wodehousian aunt of family legend. Her name was Margaret Bailey. She was an English rose, from a Gentile Surrey garden. Sidney had, in Maurice's phrase, 'married out'.

I believe my father told my mother exactly what he told my sister and me: that his parents were killed in the war and that he lived, after their death, with his aunt in Pimlico. He didn't lie. He was a man of the utmost probity. How else could he have risen to the rank of circuit judge, at the age of forty-four?

Consider what he told us about Maurice. He said Maurice was a Jewish greengrocer who lived in Whitechapel. True. He said he'd known Maurice since childhood. True. He said his father had forced him to go to a boxing club, where Maurice hadn't hurt him as much as he could. True. Maurice was fourteen, my father seventeen. The handy brother could have humiliated his brainy older sibling. But Maurice respected his brother and Maurice was kind.

No, my father didn't lie, except about the names of his parents. He never said he wasn't Jewish. That would have been a lie. He omitted. He omitted to say the Jewish Maurice was his brother. He omitted to say he, therefore, was himself a Jew.

Was it possible he sustained this omission, through fifty-two years of marriage? Yes. My parents were married in an age when privacy was considered a right and a value, not a flaw.

I wrote back to Maurice, thanking him for his letter. I promised to visit him in the Whitechapel house where he still lived, in retirement.

I omitted to say I'd burnt down his brother's house.

★ ★ ★

What did I feel when I discovered my father was Jewish? I felt fine. The Jews had made an

431

immeasurable contribution to the law, medicine, science, literature and the arts. (I shall omit psychoanalysis.) It was not as if I'd discovered my father was a New Zealander.

Though a Jew himself, was he an anti-Semite? 'Your father thought he was better than me,' wrote Maurice. Indeed. But that wasn't because Maurice was a Jew. That was because he was a working-class Jew without higher education. As a child, my father was a working-class Jew without higher education. But he progressed, in a way Maurice didn't. May not a man feel superior to his childhood self?

This brings us to the question of 'passing off'. Was he a Jew playing a non-Jew? Was he a kind of *Michael Perlstein I Am Not*? If so, did that make me *Robert Perlstein I Am Not*? No. My father was born Michael Perlstein and became Michael Purcell. I was born Robert Purcell and remain Robert Purcell. My father was a Jew who became non-Jewish. I have never been a Jew. Judaism, as I'm sure you know, passes through the maternal line.

I felt unchanged after Maurice's letter. Yes, I was a half-Jew. But a complete Englishman.

Sadly, however, the Perlstein revelation changed everything for Freya and Elizabeth. Here was the therapeutic *Eureka!*. The riddle was solved. The story was ended. The book was slammed shut with a triumphant *aha!*.

I was, as they now saw it, the Great Omitter, born with an omitting gene. I omitted to tell them I intended to burn down the house. (Of course. They would have tried to dissuade me.) I

432

omitted to tell Elizabeth I'd bought her a carpet. Somehow, in Elizabeth's mind, I denied that carpet because I couldn't control it, any more than my father could control his own birth. My father was a secret Jew. I was a secret carpet-buyer. Do you see?

No. Neither do I.

★   ★   ★

At no small expense, I'd hired a firm to clear the rubble at High Ridge. I thought it my social duty.

Five days after the fire, they found the charred corpse of Edward the basset hound in what had once been the kitchen. They called the police, as I would have done.

How had the dog got in the house? I had no idea he was there. Of course I didn't.

Judy Page must have delivered Edward when she delivered the car. She must have opened the back door and left him in the kitchen. The back doors of Aldeburgh were always open. It was a place of trust, a community without crime.

★   ★   ★

On account of my relationship with Kieran Harris, we decided there was no need for Geoffrey to attend the pre-trial conference. Geoffrey's work was done. The terms of my father's will were now public. He'd left his house to me and his shares and money, in various differing parcels, to his daughter, his grandchildren and Judy Page.

433

Kieran's chambers were at 17 King's Bench Walk, where I'd spent the early part of my career. 17 KBW was the fount of many of my triumphs, from *Diamond Bay Records* v. *Planet Q Records* (1983) to *Ridgeon* v. *Kelly* (1989).

It was curious to go back there as a client. Bill the clerk, whom I hadn't seen for years, shook my hand warmly. How else do you shake an arsonist's hand?[1]

'Still a bastard for a chocolate digestive, sir?'

'I am, thank you, Bill,' I said. I felt weak, as if my stomach were being scoured.

This was the last time a clerk in chambers would ever bring me a biscuit.

'How are you, you daft bugger!' said Kieran Harris. 'Come into the torture chamber.'

I followed him into his rooms.

'Sorry about your dad, fine man, mine's still going, ninety-two, the old grey feller. Determined to die after I do. I can't *afford* to die. Did you know I got divorced again? Sit down, sit down. Great dinner in your garden. Thank you. When was that? Two summers ago now? Your daughter played the big fiddle. Marvellous. Right. Let's go.'

---

[1] This is deliberate schoolboy humour, of the kind that Max was forced to endure. Q: How do you know if Purcell's dad has been in your house? A: It's burnt down. That was a joke by his classmate Zack. Frankly, I despaired. Where was the verbal wit or conceptual ingenuity? They would not have let that joke through the gates of St Paul's Girls' School.

Kieran Harris had known me nearly twenty-five years, yet he'd taken the trouble to give me all his finest blather and blarney. He was exercising his curious gift: Kieran made criminals feel at ease. In my case, of course, there was no need. I was at ease already.

Kieran said it was 'a fabulous start' that I'd pleaded guilty.

'Nothing beats a plea,' he said, though he knew I knew that already. A judge was always grateful when a man 'put his paws up'. With the plea in place, our business was straightforward. What would Kieran say in mitigation?

'Begin at the beginning,' said Kieran.

★   ★   ★

I need not relate what I said to Kieran. With thoroughness, persistence and belligerent charm, he wheedled out of me, in shortened form, the contents of this book. He was only doing his forensic duty. He was not a shrink trying to make me understand myself while offering me 'interesting' teas that don't lend themselves to milk. His mission was to persuade the judge to give me a noncustodial or minimal sentence.

As a consequence of our mutual professional admiration, Kieran exposed his working methods, much as a doctor might when doctoring a doctor. We started at the end, with the bad points.

The fire was a deliberate and premeditated act, not an accident nor a reckless act of the drunk-man-smoking-and-falling-asleep kind. Secondly, there was the dog. Of course, I didn't know the dog was there. But, then again, I didn't check the house for doglessness, like a 'Boy Scout arsonist' (his phrase) would have done.

These bad points, Kieran claimed, were outnumbered by the good. *Is there not a case for saying?* This was his constant refrain.

'Is there not a case for saying that your father's death was the most terrible blow you've ever had in your life? One that shook you to the very core of your being? One that made you so stricken with grief that you could not control the outpouring of your sorrow?' Well. It was certainly not the kind of thing *I'd* say. But, ye-es, there was a case for saying it.

'Is there not a case for saying that this bully boy kissing your dog was the most disgusting thing you ever saw in your life?'

'Well. That was some time ago.'

'Yes, yes. But?'

Kieran was concerned with the interconnectedness of all things. To lose my wife to the man who bullied me as a child was one thing; to lose my wife to the man who bullied me *and* snogged my dog was worse. Like Russian dolls, each offence done to me on the day of my father's funeral sat inside a bigger offence, till there was a Russian doll the size of a man, the man being I, the man who burnt down the house.

At this point, I can do no better than record the fruits of his afternoon's work. In fairness, I must acknowledge it was a first draft, subject to revision. This is what Kieran read to me, at quarter to five, three hours after my chocolate digestive:

Your Honour, Robert Purcell is a man of distinction, without previous stain on his character. He was educated at Winchester and Christ Church, Oxford, where he achieved, like his father before him — the late lamented Mr Justice Michael Purcell — a double first in law. He was called to the Bar in 1979. For many years he was a valued member of 17 King's Bench Walk, before joining Crown Yard Tax Chambers in 1993. He frequently accompanied the set's silks to the European Court of Justice and the House of Lords. The professional directory Legal 500 described him as 'extremely technically able' and 'possessed of a brain the size of a football'. Your Honour is well aware what a compliment that is![1] With Martin MacDonald QC, he has edited four editions of Emerson's UK Taxation & Trusts. In 2001, he was commissioned to work on the volumes of Halsbury's Laws of England relating to Taxation and Trusts. Then, last year, Mr Purcell took silk himself. As Robert Purcell, QC, a barrister with twenty-four years of service to the law behind him, he was due this very month to make his first

---

[1] I was to appear before Mr Justice Ableman. Kieran knew that his brother Derek was a director of Charlton Athletic Football Club.

appearance in the House of Lords. Tragically, he cannot.

So far, so good, apart from that absurd use of 'tragically'. I wanted to stop him to point this out. But I couldn't. He had the wind in his Irish sails.

I don't use that word lightly, Your Honour. What happened to Mr Purcell, on the day of his father's funeral, was a tragedy with which he'll have to live for the rest of his life.

It's my intention, with Your permission, to describe the events leading up to the crime, the first crime my client has ever committed and, I assure you, the last.

My client was grief-stricken by the death of his father, whom he rightly believed to be a great man. My client had devoted every hour of his working life to emulating his father, to making himself worthy of his father's praise. To have his father taken from him in a car crash was the most terrible blow he'd ever had in his life.

Oh dear. This was Lemon Man 'sorry about your loss' guff. My father was not taken from me. My father was killed, not stolen. I made a note. He sailed on.

Then came another blow. My client believed he was the son of Michael Purcell, an only child descended from Henry

Purcell. But outside the church, he met for the first time his father's brother. His father was not who he said he was. He was Michael Perlstein, the Jewish son of factory workers. He wasn't the English gentleman my client had known all his life. It was as if his father had been taken from him twice.

'I really must stop you. I didn't meet my father's brother outside the church. I didn't know he was my father's brother till later.'

'For God's sakes! You met a man. He was your father's brother. You met your father's brother.'

'That's not — '

Let us now turn to his marriage. My client had been living apart from his wife for eight months. But he still cared deeply for Elizabeth and the children: Isobel, aged twelve, a gifted cellist, and Max, aged ten, a champion sportsman. I've got some photos of them here, Your Honour, if you'd like to have a look. Ahh.[1]

The funeral brought my client and his wife together. After the funeral, he suggested to her that they put aside their differences. They'd enjoyed twelve contented years of marriage, till she left to pursue another relationship, which had then gone wrong. Everything seemed set fair for a reunion. Then she devastated my client

---

[1] Kieran did not actually say this. But he made one think he had.

by telling him the marriage was over. That was bad enough, Your Honour. But worse was to come.

A man who'd bullied my client as a boy then took him aside. He told my client he'd fallen in love with my client's wife. And my client's wife had fallen in love with him. Once again, Your Honour, a terrible event was compounded by something worse. My client's father is killed — then my client discovers he never knew his father at all. My client's wife tells him their marriage is over — then he discovers she's leaving him for his oldest enemy.

Your Honour, that's not the end of the story. I only wish it were.

Let us now turn to the house at the centre of this case. High Ridge, built at the turn of the twentieth century, was a magnificent double-fronted house in Aldeburgh, that most charming Suffolk town. My client had spent the happiest days of his life in Aldeburgh, bicycling along its promenade, playing cricket and tennis with his well-behaved friends or simply walking his dog. He has always loved dogs. It's his greatest regret that he didn't know there was a dog in High Ridge at the time of his crime.

For all his adult life, my client had understood he'd inherit High Ridge from his parents. Indeed, he'd told his only daughter that she'd inherit the house from him when he died. High Ridge was not just a house, Your Honour. To Robert Purcell, it was a glorious way of life, a seaside world without casinos and fast food and hooligans, where people respected each other and had a deep sense of community. It was England at its best, Your Honour.

At the end of his life, Sir Michael Purcell formed a relationship with an attractive woman, some thirty years his junior. My client knew nothing of this relationship until after his father died. He discovered the woman had moved from Greece to Aldeburgh to be near his father. She walked his dog. She cooked for him. She kept him company. And what did she expect in return? On the night of the funeral, my client found out exactly what she expected.

She boasted to my client that his father had left her High Ridge. My client had been waiting a lifetime to inherit that house. And now he found his father had left it to a woman he'd known for a matter of weeks, when he was old and widowed and lonely and vulnerable.

My client did not believe her. But she had persuasive evidence. Sir Michael had visited his solicitor before he died, telling her he was going to change his will.

Your Honour, let me now reveal to you that this woman had once been my client's lover. Let me reveal to you that, twenty years earlier, my client had rejected her. Your Honour, hell hath no fury like a woman scorned. What cruel pleasure it must have given her to tell my client that his father had fallen in love with her and left her his house.

In the event, Your Honour, my client's father had not left the woman his house. That is irrelevant. The court is only concerned with what my client honestly and genuinely and reasonably believed to be true, on the night of his crime. And he honestly and genuinely and reasonably believed his father had left her the house.

At approximately 9 p.m. on 29th September 2003, my client found himself alone in High Ridge, having insisted this woman leave, so he could grieve alone. Grieve for the loss of his father, his wife and the house that was meant to be his.

The phone rang. It was my client's closest friend, since Oxford days, when they'd had neighbouring rooms in Christ Church, a college Your Honour, as an Oriel man, knows well. This friend had been best man at my client's wedding. He is godfather to my client's son. Since my client had been living apart from his wife, the friend had been sharing his bachelor flat. They had recently been on holiday together. In this most traumatic time, his friend had been a constant source of joy and comfort. And now the friend was ringing to say he was moving to America. To the loss of his father, his wife and High Ridge, he now had to add the loss of his best friend, a man he cared about deeply.

My client blurted out the terrible

catalogue of that day's events. His best friend, furious on his behalf, told him to 'burn it down!'. Your Honour, you or I would have understood that this was a casual remark, like the colloquial 'I could kill him!' or 'I could murder a beer'. It was not a remark any sane person would take seriously. But my client was not sane, Your Honour. The balance of his mind was disturbed. The balance of his mind was so —

I stood up.

'No! You've misunderstood. The balance of my mind was perfect. I did what any reasonable man would have done.'

'Sit down, Robert. Please. Calm yourself. Have another biscuit.'

'I do not need a biscuit!'

'Come on now. Be sensible. A reasonable man doesn't burn down a house.'

'Yes he does. *I* burnt down a house.'

'Listen to me. We all want what's best for you. The judge will order a psychi — '

'No. You listen to *me*. We don't need any psychiatric reports.'

Kieran grabbed a biscuit. Half of it snapped and fell out of his mouth, landing on the floor. He didn't pick it up, for fear of looking weak. But he looked weak already.

'Robert. I'm trying to keep you out of prison. Do you understand? You went doolally, man. You set fire to your daddy's house. You're an arsonist. Do you know what that means? You're either a teenager or you're nuts. That's the law. If you just admit your mind was disturbed, there's a chance he won't lock you up.'

'I admit no such thing.'

Kieran shook his head. He looked even weaker.

'Jesus, you're the same arrogant pup you were when I met you.'

'Thank you. Was I mad then? No. So I'm not mad now.'

'Do you want to go prison, Robert? Answer me that!'

★   ★   ★

Kieran's plea in mitigation was an insult to both of us: Mr Justice Ableman and me. No judge should be obliged to listen to such a thing; and no man of dignity and integrity should have it said on his behalf. Kieran had boiled my life down to a soap opera, a melodrama, a hand-wringing aria. *His friend had been a constant source of joy and comfort.* He had reduced and traduced me. He had turned me into a bisexual lunatic, when I was simply a man out of his time, the last Englishman to have a happy childhood, the last to want strangers to be strange, the last to believe a contract of marriage was a contract, the last to feel a male affection that transcended sexuality, as in the friendship of cricketers or rowers or infantrymen in the Great War.

I dispensed with the services of Kieran Harris and decided to represent myself.

Did I want to go to prison? Yes. I'd committed

a crime. I'd done, for the right reason, a wrong thing. I deserved to go to prison. I was the last Englishman who wanted to go to prison. Where else could I go, after all? Not Aldeburgh, not the Bar, not the family house. I'd go to prison. They'd call me 'The Prof'.

★ ★ ★

I didn't want the children in court. Max was too young. Isobel had told her mother I made her feel lonely, as she no longer knew who I was. I hoped, in time, she'd understand.

I did, however, want Elizabeth there. I'd met her at *Ridgeon* v. *Kelly* (1989). It was only right she was present for *R* v. *Purcell* (2003). I needn't have worried. She wanted to be there. The fire, along with the Perlstein revelation, had changed her perception of me. I was at the same time more exotic and more familiar. I was familiar because she was now a counsellor and I had turned into a case, a case for counselling. (It was as if a telephonist's husband had turned into a telephone.) I was exotic because of the strangeness of my 'passionate outburst', a phrase, I fear, she'd learned from Freya. It was no use protesting that the fire was not an outburst but an outcome, a logical outcome.

In the public gallery, along with Elizabeth, were the Thodays, the Risdons, Ping Mottram, Pidge Holt and Geoffrey. Was I pleased to see them? Yes and no. There were already invisible bars between us, not bars as in prison but zoo. Nevertheless, these were Aldeburgh old folk.

They had to fill their day. I was glad to have given them a reason to go to Ipswich, on a mid-December morning. After court, they'd go into town to shop. Let them enjoy their seats in the gallery; later, they'd be on their feet.

She came in late and sat apart from the others. There is, of course, only one 'she'. She was dressed in — what was she dressed in? I had no interest or knowledge. She was dressed in black, in a kind of Crown-court couture. Doubtless she'd bought it with the gold she'd dug from my father. She wore sunglasses. She exuded a kind of glamorous grief, which I shall call *glief*. In *glief*, one draws attention to oneself, through expensive clothes and sunglasses, while appearing, with one's dark clothes and concealed eyes, to repel it.

★ ★ ★

Mr Justice Ableman established my guilty plea, then acknowledged I was representing myself. He asked if I would care to say anything before he passed sentence.

'Thank you, Your Honour.' My stance was proud. My voice was clear and authoritative. Mr Justice Ableman would already have suspected, from those opening four words alone, that mine was a head on which, for years, a wig had happily sat.

I began, as Kieran Harris had, with a history of my glittering education and highly successful career. Then I went my own way:

'At this point, Your Honour, you'd expect me

446

to give excuses for my burning down a house in Aldeburgh, on the night of the 29th of September, 2003. You'd expect me to try to wring your withers with a hard-luck story, full of self-justification and pain. Your Honour, let your withers remain unwrung. I did what I believed to be right, for honourable and decent reasons, which I shall keep to myself. I wish to be judged on my actions, not my motivations. I shall not plead for my character. I shall not enter a plea in mitigation.

'Your Honour, I'd ask you to imagine that my crime was committed not by me but by an Irishman, whom I shall call 'Kieran'. Imagine, if you'd be so kind, that I stand here before you representing Kieran. What plea in mitigation would I enter, on Kieran's behalf? I'd begin by saying *he's sorry he did it*. I'd go on to say *it wasn't his fault*. Whose fault was it, then? It was his upbringing, of course. Kieran's parents fashioned him. Kieran's parents are as responsible for his crime as Kieran, as responsible as if they themselves jointly lit that match. But, Your Honour, why stop there? Who made Kieran's parents the people they were? Why, Kieran's parents' parents. And who, perforce, made Kieran's parents' parents? The answer, of course, is that fateful octet: Kieran's parents' parents' parents.

'And now, with the great wind of history in my sails, I'd go on to say: *Your Honour, in 1846, Kieran's ancestors were forced to flee an Ireland gripped by famine. They sailed across the Irish Sea, in search of a potato. Lonely and*

447

frightened, chipless and mashless, they suffered a trauma from which their children, their children's children and, yes, their children's children's children could never, ever recover. Hopelessness and its eternal hand-maiden, alcohol, were handed down from Kieran to Kieran to Kieran to Kieran, causing all Kierans to act in ways they had no power to control. Your Honour, it's a long way from Tipperary to that house in Aldeburgh. And yet, in a very real sense, it's no distance at all.

'Your Honour, I am responsible for my actions. Let us leave it at that.

'My only regret is that I did not know there was a dog in the house. Had I known, I would have asked the dog to leave, politely. Then, and only then, would I have burnt down the house.

'The Court of Appeal in *R* v. *Banks* (1975) said it was unwise to sentence in a case of arson without ordering a psychiatric report. Your Honour, there is unwisdom and there is unwisdom. I stand here knowing I've done wrong, albeit for the right reason. I've done wrong and therefore I deserve to go to prison. I see no purpose, in these circumstances, in ordering a psychiatric report. A man who's brave enough to say, in open court, 'I've done wrong, send me to prison,' should surely be granted his wish.

'Like you, Your Honour, I am a man of the law. Let me be judged by the law. Let me be punished by the law. I recommend a sentence of two years' imprisonment.'

I sat down. Pidge Holt clapped. In twenty-five

years at the Bar, I had never heard anyone clap in open court.

Mr Justice Ableman raised a hand to quell her.

'Mr Purcell, you are a man who has dedicated your life to the legal profession. It is nothing short of a tragedy that a person of your distinguished provenance has destroyed years of scholarship and attainment with one egregious act.

'I am mindful of the fact that this is a first offence. I am also mindful that, after committing the offence, you drove immediately to the nearest police station to report it.

'I am also mindful that a dog was burnt to death on account of your criminal activities.

'As to the statement you have just made, I could not see the relevance of much of it. Furthermore, I would remind you that is I, not you, who's trying this case. I do not appreciate your recommending to me the sentence I should impose. It is most unwise of you to speak to a judge in the manner of a judge.'

I looked at Elizabeth. She had married a man whom we both believed would one day be a judge. It was not to be, and yet it had been. I'd acted, in my own trial, in the manner of a judge. The judge himself had acknowledged it. That, as far as I am concerned, is the culmination of my story.

★ ★ ★

Mr Justice Ableman sentenced me to three years in prison, without ordering a psychiatric report.

He should have given me two years, as I requested. But he was driven by professional jealousy to give a sentence of his own.

★ ★ ★

A category D is a prisoner who can reasonably be trusted to serve his sentence in open conditions. I was sentenced to three years in Hollesley Bay, a Suffolk prison about half an hour's drive from Aldeburgh.

The case was reported in the *East Anglian Daily Times*. Of course it was. A bird up a tree is reported in the *East Anglian Daily Times*. But then the report was spotted by the *Daily Telegraph*.

How refreshing, said the *Telegraph* leader article, *to find a defendant who, having committed a crime, reports it, pleads guilty and wishes to be punished for what he's done, without recourse to a psychiatric report. Perhaps Mr Purcell recalled the exhortation of former Prime Minister Sir John Major to 'understand less and condemn more'. But Sir John would not have imagined in his wildest dreams that a criminal would apply this notion to himself. Mr Purcell issued an invitation to the judge to condemn him, not understand him. We salute him for his bravery and high moral standards. If only they'd been high enough to stop him committing his crime.*

It was clear, after four days in Hollesley, that I was the only prisoner who ordered the *Telegraph*, since no other inmate referred to

450

the article. In Aldeburgh, however — where the *Telegraph* covered the waterfront as if delivered by seagulls — the Thodays, Risdons and Hamilton-Woods reached for their scissors, cutting out the article and sending it to me en masse.

Then I got a letter from one Henry Keith-Jones of Magdalene College, Cambridge, telling me he was President of the newly formed Robert Purcell Society. Its purpose was to 'further the aims of the true Conservative Party' and dine four times a term. Would I honour them with a letter of support and grace them with my presence upon my release?

No. As a man, I was above celebrity. And as a judge, a quasi-judge, I was above politics.

That was that, I thought. Now I could serve my sentence in the obscurity I craved.

★   ★   ★

It was my cell mate, Jez — prisoners' names! — who first pointed it out. He didn't point it out to me, though. He pointed it out to everyone on the wing, who formed a disorderly queue in the canteen to point it out to me.

On the Sunday before Christmas, she was pages 7 and 8 of the *News of the World*, a paper whose very name was a travesty. Where was it, then, the World? I could find only a parallel universe, in which I was 'the son she loved' and my father 'the father she loved'. There she was, with my father and Edward, out walking. There she was, in the rubble of High Ridge, with the charred Edward, the dog she loved. And there she was again, in her sunglasses, outside Ipswich Crown Court, *glieving* over the deaths of the judge and the dog and 'the beautiful house he burnt down — for nothing!'

The judge, the dog, the beautiful house, the son's mistress, the father's last love, the Greek island villa, the sex with the best friend, the son's revenge: everything was there. There was even a Cabinet minister, Alan Temperley, with whom she'd had a 'torrid seven-year affair'. What did Temperley have to do with the judge and the dog and the beautiful house and the son? Nothing. He was mere spice, he was titivation; he was the apple in the mouth of the roasted pig.

'We should call you 'Dog-Burner',' said Mal, a toast-munching Glaswegian.

'That's right,' I said. I'd taken the precaution, throughout my life, of agreeing with everything Glaswegians said. I saw no reason to change that policy now I was in prison.

I don't know if he talked his father out of leaving me the house. She placed the thought in the reader's mind, even as she denied knowing if it were true. *I'm sad I met Michael too late in his life for us to have a sexual relationship.* She suggested my father's spirit was willing; as for her, she was sad, but sex wasn't everything. Truly, the woman was a thong-barrister.

I used to hoover for him naked, Mal read — and believed. It was useless to tell him, 'No, I was there. She hoovered for herself!' I was there, which meant she hoovered for me. What

452

red-blooded Glaswegian lifer would think otherwise?

'Great arse,' said Mal, of the photo of Judy Page hoovering my flat. Except, of course, the photo — taken from behind — was no such thing. Only I could have taken such a photo and I certainly did not. Was this woman even Judy Page? I no more recalled her 'arse' than I did when I'd last tried to recall it, on that glorious summer night in our garden. But I knew that this woman's hair was thicker than Judy Page's.

The paper could argue it had to use an impostor; one couldn't ask a fifty-year-old woman to represent her younger nude self. Yet nowhere in the article was the body credited to anyone other than Judy Page. Furthermore, the nude woman in the photo was quite clearly using a Dyson. Dyson didn't even start manufacturing vacuum cleaners till 1993 — a full decade after the naked hoovering look place.

To the gathering crowd in the prison canteen, none of this mattered. They saw the buttocks, they saw me; they put two and one together.

'Fuck 'Dog-Burner',' said Mal. 'We'll call you 'Lucky Dwarf'.' He laughed. Jez laughed. And I, of course, laughed too.

Her article brought me the respect of men I feared. 'Lucky Dwarf' was not my hoped-for 'The Prof'. But it soon gave way to the perfectly acceptable 'Lucky'. Should I thank her for that?

I shall speak no further of prison, from which I was released in July 2005, after serving half of my sentence. I shall only say this: after that article was published, I received over four hundred letters from dog lovers. I did not reply to any of them. I rose above such abuse, as a gentleman should. These were not dog lovers but people haters, low in intelligence and ignorant of the truth. I wouldn't entrust a dog to any of them.

At most of the crucial moments in my life, a dog has been present. I have always cared for dogs. I shall leave you with documentary proof of that. I am a civilised man.

Dog Index
(2006)

Bumper (Yorkshire terrier), 56
Buster (Airedale terrier), 201, 310, 311, 329, 340, 341
canine, 14, 207, 331
Cleo (Dalmatian), 90
death, dog, 201
dog, a, 16, 287, 329, 340, 384, 440, 448, 449, 454
dog, boy and, 15
dog, dead, 118
dog, elderly, Geoffrey ambled off, gratefully, like an, 397
dog, he felt nothing for that, 15
dog, his, 440
dog, his father's, 384
dog, last, 355
dog, my, 16, 71, 247, 436
dog, Nescafe and, 270
dog, ordinary, 340
dog, our, 14
dog, sausage, 206
dog, the, 14, 15, 88, 98, 118, 247, 287, 288, 340, 377, 378, 384, 412, 433, 436, 448, 452
dog, your, 17
dog basket, 20

Postscript by Mike Bell
(2011)

The manuscript of *A Short Gentleman* was sent to me in Los Angeles in the summer of 2006. I was living in the house — actually, the garage — of my friend and collaborator Luke Maidment. I hadn't seen Robert or spoken to him since our phone conversation the night before I flew to the States, leaving a forwarding address on his kitchen table.

I didn't know how fateful that night had been. I knew nothing about his crime or prison sentence, which never made the Stateside news.

For a long time, I didn't even read the manuscript, not wanting to dwell on the past. When I did, it had a profound effect on me. It's a strange and unsettling experience to read about yourself in a book. You see yourself as others see you. In a way, you discover who you are, as opposed to who you think you are.

I first appear in Robert's story as a fellow student, knocking on his door to ask for his help with my law essay. In my last appearance, nearly twenty-five years later, I'm ranting at him down the phone to 'leave the bitch a bonfire'. At that point, I'm staying in his flat.

From first to last, I'm someone who exploits

Robert's good nature. I see him because I want something. Help with my essay. A free meal. Investment in a film. The phone number of his rich banker friend, Pilkington. A place to stay.

Sometimes, I appear to be generous but it's only want in disguise. I give my godson Max a car because I can't afford to run it and want Robert to pay the tax and insurance. I offer to accompany Robert on holiday when truthfully I want to be near Mykonos, in case Hilary Drew turns up.

To read all this in print was shaming. It was clear from the book that Robert cared for me, more than I cared for him. I never thought about his needs. As far as I was concerned, he didn't have any. I was the one with needs.

Why was our relationship like this? Robert's right to say that, as a young guy arriving at Oxford from a south London working-class background, I was very insecure, though I covered it in a show of confidence. Oxford was full of people with more money and grander backgrounds than me. Robert was one. He was a man who knew who he was. He had the confidence to be himself.

My exploitation of Robert came from a deep-seated compulsion to take from him that which I didn't own for myself — self-knowledge. It was part of a pattern of compulsive behaviour that continued until I changed my life in late 2006. That change was due, in no small measure, to Robert. I thank him for that.

If you go through the book, as I did, checking on my appearances, you'll see that I almost always appear with a drink. When I knock on his door in Oxford, I'm carrying a bottle of wine. And when I rant at him to burn down that house, I've drunk one. (Not that he knew it.) I was compelled to drink and exploit people. That's what I learned from *A Short Gentleman*. I decided to do something about it.

On a cold night in December 2006, I walked into a church hall on Wilshire Boulevard at Plymouth. The relief was overwhelming. At last, I found myself with people like me. The most important thing I learned that night was that we all have the capacity to renew ourselves. But first we have to be honest. We have to tell ourselves and the world who we are. Only then can we change.

To me, that's the theme of Robert's book. In the middle of our lives, we have crises which can be portals to the creation of new selves, if we own up to those crises and find within ourselves the strength to act.

That night, I owned up. I said, 'I am an alcoholic.' From then on, I attended AA meetings at least once a week. I formed a supportive bond with a woman who went to those same meetings. But I respected her privacy too much to invade it in the outside world. Then one night, in March 2007, when we were leaving the building, she asked if I'd like to go get a coffee.

That woman was Hilary Drew, one of the most beautiful, talented and insightful people I've ever met. Relationships between alcoholics are fraught with danger. But we persevered. Six months later, we were living together in Hilary's house in Malibu. Four years later, we're still together.

For a while, Hilary's alcohol issues blighted her career. In 2007, clean and sober, she was ready to get back to work. That year she made three movies. One was a sequel and the other two were 'threequels' — industry-speak for a sequel to a sequel. She ran down corridors. She threw bad guys through plate-glass windows. She shot them before learning their names. Hilary, like so many actresses in our town, felt frustrated by the quality of the parts she was offered.

Then she read *A Short Gentleman*. She found some of the British references obscure. But the story fascinated her. She was immediately drawn to the central character, whose struggle to overcome impossible odds she found 'inspirational'.

The central character, as she saw it, was Judy Page. Hilary identified with Judy. Judy's father was a builder, Hilary's was a housepainter. They both started with little. Judy's mother dated Michael Caine. Hilary's had bit parts on TV series like *Columbo*, before giving up acting to have her kids. As Hilary saw it, both she and Judy were trying to live out their mother's (failed) dreams. They were passionate and sexual women, hungry for life, with a powerful sense of their own destiny.

By mid-2008, Luke and I had written the first draft of a screenplay called *Woman of Fire*. We decided early on to transpose the story to America. We constructed our arc from a few key dramatic events — Judy's meeting with the rich son of an East Coast legal dynasty, her rejection by the son and his parents, then, twenty years on, her reunion with the son and his widowed father, followed by her love affair with the father and the son's burning down of the father's house. In our screenplay, the crime is motivated by the son's belief that he's the victim of an act of revenge by his ex-lover. Judy's motivation is more complex. Hilary, who read each page as we wrote it, insisted we should never be sure if Judy was in love with the old man or not. She was a woman who'd had a hard life. Was she capable of love? Was love something she could afford?

Hilary took *Woman of Fire* to independent producer Mo Bergman, who'd always taken a paternal interest in her career. Mo was excited. He saw echoes of the 'women's pictures' he loved from the thirties and forties, when audiences flocked to see Joan Crawford and Bette Davis making their way in a man's world. He also loved the frank and unsentimental sexuality. He found our script 'authentic'. When he heard it was based on a real woman's life, he asked if we had the rights to her story. In our headlong rush to get the story down, we hadn't thought about that.

I tracked Judy down. She was back in Andros, running a café, while her daughter Alana was at music college in England, living with her grandparents. Judy was thrilled. She had no hesitation in selling us the rights.

In early 2009, Judy came to stay with Hilary and me in Malibu. Mo immediately saw how

461

invaluable she was to the project. Hilary had the luxury of observing first-hand the woman she was to portray. And Judy, whom Mo nicknamed 'The Survivor', would be a great boon to the marketing of the film.

Judy soon adapted to life in Malibu. She took tennis lessons. She read the trades. She hired a car and drove it to the gym every morning. Judy stayed with us throughout the making of the film, which came together with remarkable speed. With Mo and me co-producing and Luke directing, we were turning over by the fall of 2009. The budget was minimal. Actors worked for scale. To save on locations, we used Mo's own house to shoot the swimming-pool scene.

We all knew the film would stand or fall by Hilary's potrayal of Judy in her twenties and Judy in her forties. It was a virtuoso performance. Here's what Camilla Johnstone wrote in *Vanity Fair* after *Woman of Fire* won the Audience Award in the Dramatic category at the 2010 Sundance Film Festival:

> Sex as power, sex as pleasure, sex as narcissism, sex as destiny. Has there ever been a film in which the sex scenes were less gratuitous or better acted? In Hollywood, female desire is often a sign of villainy, like smoking. Here, it's a sign of life, a life as complex and ambivalent as the one we live when we walk out of the cinema.

Woman of Fire performed remarkably at the US box office, paying for itself in the opening

462

week. It was one of those low-budget indy movies that kind of sneaks under the wire. This was thanks in no small part to the 'Mirror Scene' in which Judy makes love to her own reflection. Even before the movie opened, That Scene found its way onto the Internet, where it received over one million hits. I thought it would find its way onto the Web, so I took the precaution of putting it there myself.

Hilary and Judy went on a nationwide promotional tour in the fall of 2010. As Mo predicted, Judy's presence beside Hilary on talk-show sofas made our movie an even more marketable proposition. Just as Hilary had studied Judy prior to playing her, Judy studied Hilary, learning how to present herself to the cameras. She was a natural. Within weeks, she'd gotten a contract to write her autobiography.

In spring 2011, Hilary was maid of honour at Judy's wedding to Mo. Mo, who doesn't believe in holidays, suggested he and Judy spend their honeymoon on his tennis court. Mo won by two sets to one, an impressive achievement for a guy of seventy-three.

Prior to the UK release of *Fire*, I sent a DVD to Robert. Respecting his privacy, I didn't ask him to make any contribution to the promotion of our movie. I explained its genesis in Judy's life as opposed to his book, nevertheless enclosing a cheque for ten thousand dollars to acknowledge his inspiration. I suggested that if *A Short Gentleman* hadn't already been published, it would make sound marketing sense to brand it as The Book That Inspired *Woman Of Fire*.

But my letter was not just a business letter. The eighth of the Twelve Steps tells you to make a list of all the persons you harmed through your alcoholic addiction — and to try to make amends to them all. I itemised all the occasions on which I'd done Robert harm and apologised for each and every one.

I concluded with the heartfelt wish that Robert write back and tell me how he was. I hoped he was enjoying the second half of his life.

I reproduce his reply unedited. It is brutally honest, which is no less than I expected and no more than I deserve.

Dear Bell,

Thank you for your letter, with enclosures. I was very glad to hear from you again. Where to begin?

First, let me congratulate you on your film. It is certainly a great advance on *Big Ben*. What a shame I invested in that one and not this, though your cheque for ten thousand dollars goes some way — about a quarter — to healing that particular pain. I jest. Your girlfriend is, as you once assured me, a remarkable actress. She makes 'Judy' a complex and fascinating character for whom, extraordinarily, I found myself rooting. She's a monster, though. Of that there's no doubt. It astonishes me that Judy Page should revel in her association with 'Judy'. Astonishes me, but doesn't surprise me.

You make great play of the film's authenticity, always a favourite Bell word. Equally, you

464

depart from the facts when it suits. My character is now an American called Ralph. I imagine, though you do not say so, that your lawyers advised you to make 'Ralph' different from me — sufficiently different that I wouldn't sue, yet not so different that you couldn't claim, for whatever publicity it was worth, that my book 'inspired your film'.

My dear chap, I'd never have sued. Not just because I'm delighted that you've finally made something of your life, but because I wouldn't have won. Libel laws exist to protect reputations. How do you damage the reputation of a dog-burning ex-con?

And yes: should my book ever be published — and, I concede, your film's success makes that more likely — I'll insist they mention your film somewhere, preferably on the back. Thank you, at least, for not putting me on 'talk-show sofas' with the actor playing Ralph. I see he goes by the splendid name of Philip Seymour Hoffman. Please congratulate him on capturing my patrician bearing. Could he not have made himself shorter for the role?

Let us now turn to your twenty-two pages of *mea culpas*. I appreciate your apologising to me for such offences as telling me to leave my own stag party, one of the many 'acts of cruelty' you attribute to your former drunken self, whom you call 'Bad Mike'.

Forgive me, Good Mike, but I cannot tell the difference between you and Bad. After all, it's eight years since I've heard from you. And then, when you finally get in touch, it's not as if you don't want something. You want me to get my book published, for your own publicity purposes.

Sorry, but I cannot see you've gone through a crisis that's a portal to a new self. Such bibbly-bobbly Stateside psycho-babble strikes me as typical of Bad Mike, with his chameleon nature. Good Mike, Bad Mike, Indifferent Mike — all of you have gone native. You write that Judy Page — Judy Bergman? — has 'gotten a contract' to write her autobiography. 'Gotten'? You're a graduate of Christ Church, Oxford, man. Speak English!

'Ah yes,' you will say, 'but there's proof I've changed. I'm an alcoholic now.'

Do not mistake me. I respect your commitment to Alcoholics Anonymous, with one reservation. I don't believe you're an alcoholic. You liked a drink. Always did. I'd go no further than that. Bizarrely, now you don't drink, you claim to be an alcoholic. Is a man who doesn't work a workaholic? It's a nonsense.

If you're not an alcoholic, though, why did you go to that meeting on Wilshire Boulevard at Plymouth? I think we both know the answer. Are you telling me that of all the AA meetings in all Los Angeles, you happened to walk into Hilary Drew's?

Now let us turn to my own well-being, about which you were kind enough to ask.

I still live in that Canonbury flat. My wife visits me, from time to time, to talk about our children. You'll note I refer to Elizabeth as my wife. This is fact. We're still married. She didn't want to get married again. I take this as a compliment.

On a recent visit, I had the pleasure of meeting Charlotte, her five-year-old daughter, an energetic child like her father. I gave her a present: *Small Fry Freya*. She spent far more time on the drawings than the text. She's definitely not as advanced as Isobel was at her age. What is my relationship to her? I'm not her father but I'm her mother's husband. I'm her motherhusband. So be it.

Isobel, I'm delighted to tell you, achieved first-class honours in part one of her psychology degree at University College, London. This is remarkable, given the turmoil of her adolescence, over which I shall draw a veil, being the last drawer of veils in England. In the most recent *Times* survey, UCL ranked third among university psychology courses, behind only Oxford and Cambridge, which, let's face it, are provincial backwaters compared with our capital city. I'm not disappointed she's not a cello-playing law student.

As for Max, Pilkington has proved a most assiduous houseman. Max didn't want to go to university, wishing to get into profit not debt. Pilkington helped him find a job at a bank, though he himself hasn't set foot in one since his phone-throwing days. He works for charities. He studies Buddhism. He sails and paints.

What do I do, though? I don't, for obvious reasons, pursue a legal career. I avoid the environs of the law courts and all Marks & Spencer Food Halls, which seem to attract in huge numbers the barristers who were once my colleagues. (I avoid Aldeburgh, too, for fear people will pretend not to see me or, worse, hold their dogs to their chests.)

Sometimes, there is sport to be had from my leprous status. Alan Temperley, spotting me on a Knightsbridge pavement, turned to stare in the nearest window. Fearing I'd seen him, he then took refuge inside. I took up a position outside the shop, to prevent his emerging without bumping into me. It's a tribute to his political skills that when he finally came out, fifteen minutes later, he acted both surprised and pleased to see me. The shop sold women's underwear. He had purchased several bras, since a politician who loiters in your underwear shop's a pervert, while a politician who invests heavily in your bras is a man who wins your vote.

I work six days a week at the Cancer Care charity shop on the Essex Road. This is not an attempt to 'give something back' since I took nothing other than what was mine, left to me in my father's will, plus a basset hound, for the deprivation of whose life I served my sentence. I work there because it's local and I passed the interview, declaring my ex-convict status before I was asked. (Arson, not an offence of dishonesty, didn't rule me out.) The ladies in the shop were surprised, since I don't resemble an ex-con. I simply look eccentric. The balder I get, the longer I grow my surviving hair. My daughter says I look as if I've been electrocuted, which is exactly what I thought when I first saw the hair of the late Peter Something-Something.

After six years, the ladies — I have always been the only man — still don't know what to say about my crime, which is as it should be, since my criminal 'career' lasted less than an hour, while my legal career lasted twenty-four years. Once, when I took possession of a doll's house, Shona advised me to give it to her quick, before I burnt it down. Nobody laughed. Shona was not giving voice to a shared sentiment.

I apply the same rigour to the job as I did to my work at the Bar. Over the years, the stock hasn't changed: *Pingu* videos, dead women's blouses, *Monopoly* with the top hat missing, shoes bought in the delusion they'd grow comfortable with use. One day, those who run the charity will come to understand I am right. I am right that 'charity shop' is too restrictive. We should be charitable agents. We should be agents for chattels too large and expensive to fit into a shop. Everywhere, there are rich people with charitable impulses. Why should we not be agents for selling their cars, boats and houses?

I wrote to Guy on this very subject. As an American Englishman, you may be unaware that Guy's opened two hundred Green Guy supermarkets in the last five years, nor that ten per cent of the price of every item you buy goes to the Green Guy Charity Foundation.

(Let me put that another way: ninety per cent of the price of every item you buy doesn't go to the Green Guy Charity Foundation — of which, incidentally, 'Chris' Pilkington's a trustee.)

I wrote to Guy three times, urging him to open a charity estate agent and a charity car showroom. On each occasion, I received the same reply from the same Suzy, saying how much 'all the guys at Green Guy' valued my suggestion, which, evidently, was nil.

I write frequently to organisations. Writing to organisations is the duty of all older people who know they're right. In this activity, I'm assisted by my neighbour Dr Pearson. A few years ago, Dr Pearson was in front of me at the checkout queue in Sainsbury's, the nappy Sainsbury's. By the time I was aware of her, I'd placed all my items on the conveyor belt, which doubtless has a name like 'purchalator'. She claimed a bunch of my bananas as her own. It was obvious to me that she did this on purpose. But a banana is a banana and a bunch is a bunch. I was forced into conversation.

Dr Pearson, who was born a month after me, gained a double first in natural sciences at Cambridge, after which she studied medicine. She's a consultant paediatric neurologist at the Royal London Hospital. Her colleagues regard her as the foremost diagnostician in their department.

A long time ago, when she lived in the flat below me, Dr Pearson wanted to find a man,

470

aggrieved that the men who found her were always married, or art college lecturers, or male doctors, often on drugs, looking to relieve the burdens of the job with sexual exercise.

I was a candidate, believe it or not. She saw me with Judy Page and had the instinct to save me. Nowadays, Dr Pearson has no such instincts. Her heart has hardened. She wants to acquire knowledge and impart it and then go to bed on her own and listen to the World Service.

We're companions. We go to the Wigmore Hall. We go on holiday. We get through Christmas. She describes me as arrogant, bad-tempered and obstinate; but she describes herself as the same. Our bodies and toothbrushes are never conjoined.

If you want a union with another soul, you can't always be right. But I have known I'm always right since I was eight years old. I haven't changed, any more than you have, Bell. Or Pilkington. The essence of Buddhism is to not want. Does Pilkington not want? Does he not want when he partners Elizabeth in the Laser class at the Aldeburgh Regatta? Of course not. He not not wants with a vengeance.

Finally, we come to Maurice Perlstein. Last December, his local, the Black Cow, won the Whitechapel Pub Quiz Championship. He attributed this, rightly, to the recruitment of Dr Pearson and myself.

The key question, the tie-breaker, was: Who

...the FA Cup in 1978? That, as you know,
a football question.

My father brought me up to be a cricket
man. He told me, as a boy, that football
crowds were 'ill-mannered', never applauding
the opposing team's goals, whereas cricket-
watchers always clapped a boundary, even if it
brought the winning runs for the side they did
not support.

Uncle Maurice knew I wasn't a football
man. So he gave me the Football Association
Yearbooks that belonged to his late friend, Alf.
(He lived with Alf for thirty years, though not
once has he shouted: 'I'm gay!') He gave me
the Yearbooks so I could learn them. He
trusted me to memorise their contents, though
the contents didn't interest me.

Who won the FA Cup in 1978?

'Ipswich Town!'

'Yes!' said the quizmaster.

All our team got to their feet: Dr Pearson,
Maurice, Lesley, Pat, Big Sharon. They
cheered and stamped their feet. Big Sharon
wet my head with beer, the poor man's
champagne.

'I told you the Prof would do it!' said
Maurice. I'd never felt so happy in my life.

A few days later, Dr Pearson and I went to
his house for Christmas lunch. Dr P banished
Maurice and me to the living room, saying she
couldn't bear to have people in her kitchen
while she was cooking. It was not her kitchen,
though. It was Maurice's.

In the living room, Maurice and I donned